HEADCRUSHER

Born in 1975, Alexander Garros and Aleksei Evdokimov both work as journalists in Riga, Latvia. Friends since school, they decided to write a novel together. The result was *Headcrusher*, which went on to win the prestigious Russian Literary National Bestseller Prize in 2003.

Garros-Evdokimov

HEADCRUSHER

VINTAGE BOOKS
London

Published by Vintage 2006

2 4 6 8 10 9 7 5 3

First published in Russian by
Limbus Press, St Petersburg 2003

First published in Great Britain in 2005 by
Chatto & Windus

Vintage
Random House, 20 Vauxhall Bridge Road,
London SW1V 2SA

www.randomhouse.co.uk

Addresses for companies within
The Random House Group Limited can be found at:
www.randomhouse.co.uk/offices.htm

The Random House Group Limited Reg. No. 954009

A CIP catalogue record for this book
is available from the British Library

ISBN 9780099474722

Printed and bound in Great Britain by Clays Ltd, St Ives plc

Authors' Note

All lexical and syntactical liberties taken in the present text, including variants in the writing of words from various areas of professional, national, criminal and youth slang, should be blamed on the authors. Or rather, on that turbulent linguistic reality which they have taken as their model, and which has not yet settled into the standardised definitions found in dictionaries and text books.

The majority of the characters in this novel have real prototypes. The majority of the settings in which the events of the novel take place are real. The fragments of business texts quoted in the novel or composed by the central character on his hard drive are not figments of the authors' imagination, they are all taken from life.

If your boss comes down on you, remember: it takes forty-two muscles to frown and only four to straighten your middle finger!

URBAN FOLKLORE

1

A New Year's Greeting to the Management of REX Bank

Right then, you lot, everyone down.

Press-ups.

1–2, 1–2, 1–2.

What's with the panting, Citron? Too paunchy, you old git? Never mind, a hundred sit-ups in the snow should help shed the pounds. We don't mess about round here.

Now, WALKING ON YOUR HANDS.

Oh dear, looks like Pylny's snuffed it. Finally the old fart's croaked for real. What a bummer. Never got to work him over properly. Quit on us, the lousy slob. Got off easy. Oh, he's breathing is he? Fantastic! Put his balls in that vice. Let's bring him round a bit. What's he yelling for? Well yeah, I know it hurts! Stick something in his gob. That's better. We've had enough fucking whinging from him.

What is it Four-Eyes? Broke your specs, did they? You poor bastard! Now, you chip off the old bourgeois block, used to sleeping, screwing and stuffing your belly . . . You won't be screwing any more! You won't have anything left to screw with! But why would you want to anyway, when you've only got three . . . no, make that two and a half minutes left to live? And that's assuming I'm feeling KIND! Because otherwise it'll take you TWO WEEKS to die. Yeah, and why not? That's a fucking great idea. Right, chuck him in the basement . . .

Tired, you wankers? Lost any weight yet, Citron?

Don't you go anywhere because this party's just fucking getting started!

Right, give him a **PASTING. Waste him!**

Look at that, still alive. Breathing.

Right then, stand him upright. Well yeah, I know you can't pissing well tell which end's his legs and which end's his head, because the fat bastard is absolutely spherical. Let's find his head.

Waste him! That's it! The bit he's yelling with – that's his head.

FINISH him! Excellent, excellent! That's him done.

HAPPY HOLIDAY, DEAR BOSSES! HAPPY NEW YEAR!

And, by the way, where's the champagne?

For about five seconds I gazed at the result of an hour's professional effort with the same feeling of satisfaction that follows a fleeting and uncomplicated casual sexual encounter. Then I quickly exited from the file and automatically glanced over my shoulder.

In the course of a year, this conditional reflex had become firmly established.

Nimbly manoeuvring the cursor, I tore through the tangled hierarchies and their miscellaneous suffixes of **dat**s, **bmp**s, **sys**es, **exe**s, **prv**s, **tmp**s, **log**s and **pif**s. Prodding ENTER, I emerged from the gullies of the WORDART administrative directory, moved the cursor left and up, clicked and surfaced from the directory TEMPT. Another upwards twitch, and I slipped out of HKGRAPH. Tumbled out of SYSTEM. Slid out of COPYCAT. Dodged out of WORDOUT. And finally broke out of LAYOUTT into the top level of the 2GHz Pentium PC's hard drive.

A ten-metre-square press room, divided into a dozen transparent, functional cells by a simple labyrinth of glass and plastic. Background noise. The patient murmuring of ink-jet printers. The gentle, efficient farting of processors. The obsessive gasping of photocopiers. The perplexed sobbing of faxes. The insistent jangling of phones. The rapid rattling of keyboards. Work in progress. Employees on the job. Business purposefully assuming visible form in words, arithmetical ideographs and sometimes – very rarely – hieroglyphs. Swarms of operational data scurrying through the local network. Official letters being assembled out of prefabricated blocks. The powerful mechanical organism of a big bank functioning efficiently.

Payments being made. Interest accruing. Money talking. Business meeting money.

Throughout the whole of the civilised world, this particular way of organising office space is regarded as the most progressive and efficient. On the one hand, your vulnerable, fragile privacy is considerately respected, in total compliance with the universal code of political correctness. Look, you have your own private, inviolable compartment. 1.5 square metres of personal space. But on the other hand, you always remain in full and open view of everybody else. The ideal of totalitarian democracy, rendered flesh by the genius of bureaucratic design: each and every employee subject to a constant cross-monitoring that is not autocratic and malign, but universal, reciprocal and mutually advantageous. Having as its goal to prevent you (imperfect and prone to malfunction as you are) from slipping out of synch with the perfectly-tuned metabolism of REX International Commercial Bank.

'Vadim, where's the budget document for quarterly advertising?' asked the bright young PR talent Olezhek, leaning round from the next cell and agitatedly twitching the thin little moustache above his whimsical upper lip.

A glance at the moustache, the lip, the cream-coloured waistcoat and the sunset tones of the highly tasteful silk tie, convinced me yet again that the rumours concerning the young talent's inclinations were absolutely true.

'Vadim!' A faint note of hysteria had appeared in his voice, 'I want the document! I've got an efficiency of 59.6 here, and I distinctly remember it was 63.2!'

'Try looking under x,' I told him, after a pause. Then I turned away towards Murzilla.

This massive work of art was a bronze Tyrannosaurus Rex with an aggressively spiked crown, designed in a style of palaeontological realism by the sculptor Gochei Huskizadze, and the only entity in the office that I could look at without a feeling of loathing. Perhaps even with a certain degree of goodwill. He was all teeth and malice. More than once, groping around in the back pocket of my subconscious, I'd come across the thought that some day Murzilla's six kilogrammes of bronze would cease their passive personi-fication of power and prosperity, come to life and devour every last one of the bank's damned employees. Me too, probably.

The door to the press room whispered a gentle warning as it opened to reveal in its aperture the nonchalant figure, evenly tinted by authentic tropical tan, elegantly attired by Hugo Boss, ergonomically harmonised by thrice-weekly workouts in the expensive gym of the World Class Sports Club: my boss, the head of the bank's press service, Andrei Vladlenovich Voronin.

Four-Eyes.

He scanned the premises with lazy irony through the smoked glass of his futuristically designed and strato-spherically priced Yamamoto spectacles. Paused. Looked through his sites. Took aim. At me. Launched himself elegantly across the labyrinth.

I turned back to my keyboard, jerked the cursor across the screen, prodded enter and landed splat in the putrid little swamp of *congrats.doc*. Focusing intently, I ran my fingers over a couple of keys and my eyes over the few lines.

On the cold, frightening threshold of the new millen-nium one feels more keenly than ever the need for the warm, strong, dependable shoulder of a Family. You and I, dear colleagues, have been exceptionally fortunate. Because REX is a Family, and every Family, especially if it's written with a capital letter, has its own . . .

Four-Eyes was already standing behind my shoulder. I didn't turn round straight away. Instead I shook my head gravely, massaging the bridge of my nose in a gesture of noble

4

fatigue, slumped against the oval back support of my chair . . . and only at that moment appeared to notice the boss.

'Andrei Vladlenovich!' I half-rose from my seat with the pious respect of the honest toiler. 'I was just . . .'

Four-Eyes stared into the monitor with a derisive smirk that showed off the tips of his ultra-white incisors.

'And every Family,' he declaimed with feeling, precisely highlighting the capital letter with the climax of his intonation, 'has its own freak.'

He sniggered. Slapped the honest toiler patronisingly on the shoulder. He was two years younger than me.

'Attaboy, Vadik! Go for it. When Citron reads that, he'll just lap it up. A fucking Family . . .' he sniggered again, this time in a different tone. For Four-Eyes, this really was his family.

He swung round, grazing me invisibly with the ethereal wing of his environmentally friendly Kenzo perfume, and disappeared into his own office. A separate office. But – separated from the rest of the press room by the same kind of glass and plastic wall . . . But – a wall fretted by the fine horizontal ribbing of blinds . . . Democracy maintained. But seniority too.

Feeling almost flattered, I returned my gaze to the screen and my hands to the keyboard in brisk inspiration; shuffled my fingers in the vigorous gesture of a surgeon or a pianist. Stimulated by its standard one-shot hit of dutiful enthusiasm, my brain strained to formulate the missing ending of the unfinished phrase. Has . . . its own . . . But the praiseworthy impulse never reached my fingers. Before it could produce the intended result, the effect of the shot of undiluted conformity flipped over into loathsome, tacky withdrawal. The way they say a fix of heroin only lasts veteran junkies a couple of seconds. I gazed with increasing apathy at the three and a half sentences of the New Year's greeting to our great chiefs and beloved leaders – commissioned by Four-Eyes from me as a former notable shark of the pen – understanding the meaning of what was written there less and less. The forefinger of the hand that had wilted on to the keyboard drove the cursor backwards and forwards along the four lines of text. Then I roused myself and, with renewed resolve, pressed **alt x**.

Picking up speed, I tore into LAYOUTT, squirmed into WORDOUT, slid into COPYCAT, tumbled into SYSTEM, and crashed into HKGRAPH. I moved the cursor right and down, prodded ENTER, and dived into the thickets of the WORDART administrative directory.

Wrinkling up my forehead, I created the file *prayer.txt*.

Oh God! They've really fucking got to me!

All these shitty fellow-employees, all these jumped-up bosses. If I had my way, they'd be taking turns reading their own positive test results for cancer of everything! All these WANKERS, QUEERS, COCKSUCKERS! They've really fucking got to me. Lord, please take them away. Take them Yourself or let Your colleagues have them – I don't give a toss. And if You don't take them Yourself, then I'll take care of it. Just one more day of this life, two at the most and that's it. What won't I do to them. Charlie Manson will die of envy.

Do You get the drift, oh Lord?

They say that hope dies last. That's bollocks. Let me tell you, there was a time when people entertained great hopes of me. Those hopes died a long time ago, and it wasn't exactly painless. But I'm still alive and kicking.

Twelve years ago I graduated from the first arts lycée in the country (or union republic as it was then), an incubator for youthful talent that was hastily contrived in the reanimated fashion of the 1960s. The teachers there were capable of spotting a future Pushkin in a trilobite. And they certainly had no trouble spotting one in me. The ability to erect easily and rapidly, on any pretext and starting from nothing, a highly intellectual and entirely specious structure of false assumptions, strained interpretations, standard clichés presented from a non-standard angle, complete with amazingly apt quotations from Borges, Brodsky, Beckett and Baudrillard, all concocted on the spot as I went along – this atoned for absolutely everything else: the loutishness, the bugger-it attitude, the refusal as a matter of principle to do homework assignments and the regular failure to turn up for two thirds of classes.

This ability continued to be highly thought of for a further four years in the local faculty of journalism. And even for the first two years of the next six, which I spent as a columnist – the in-house, gold-plated pen-pusher of the Riga daily newspaper *SM* (the sado-masochistic abbreviation was the compressed remnant of the obsolete Russian word combination '*Sovietskaya molodyozh*' – '*Soviet Youth*'). For a certain period of time I even felt that I was privileged – that must be the way people who work in all sorts of minor elite subgroups position themselves in the context of life.

I didn't have to comb the city in search of fugitive, well camouflaged pretexts for reporting. I didn't have to humiliate myself fishing for dreary interviews. I didn't have to rework kilogrammes of texts from the Intermedia information agency: *Di Caprio screws the whole island! Lada Dens has never tasted sperm! Lesbian rocker artificially inseminated from pop idol junky!* I was transferred around and used with apprehensive respect, like an expensive and delicate piece of apparatus – quite literally expensive, since I was rather well paid for my ability to analyse, formulate and articulate quickly, comprehensibly and not entirely trivially. For being able, essentially, to express my own Private Opinion intelligibly.

At first I accepted my new role with the old, familiar feeling of being an inadvertent impostor that went back to my lycée days. A feeling of unpremeditated, but not exactly unconscious, chicanery. I knew that vigorous exegesis simply oozed out of me as easily as Colgate Total out of a new tube. All I had to do was chop the said substance up into bite-size chunks, lay it out in columns with the standard ten-point-type, top it off with trenchant, aphoristic headlines and dump it on the baking-tray of the page. Fashionable politics and trendy economics, chic culture and cult social chic were spliced together in this progressive salami like the red and white stripes in the aforesaid Colgate. There was one lesson I had mastered thoroughly when I was still in school: just as there are no more than nine degrees of kinship separating any two people, it is possible to connect absolutely anything you want with anything else you like, and the absence of any real knowledge of any of the areas that are linked together is no hindrance at all, in fact it's a positive bonus. My pen's agility was born of irresponsibility. But I very rapidly stopped feeling embarrassed about that and even began enjoying myself. My chicanery was not exposed. On the contrary, it brought me direct and tangible dividends, and I soon began to regard them as well deserved. I realised that I was clever.

And that was when everything began to change.

Imperceptibly but implacably the newspaper's premises contracted and the wages shrank. The Head Men were following each other with the speed of machine-gun bullets, due to the same economic processes which, in more lucrative and less cultured walks of life, had assumed the crude form of the contract and the hit. The latest Head Man dropped into my columnist's corner office for a drop of the strong stuff less and less often. Then the consumption of strong stuff in the work place was strictly forbidden. Then the ephemeral Head

Men were replaced by the Head of the Head Men, the personal representative of the owners of the controlling block of shares.

The Head Head had the voice of a church choir master, the appearance of a middle-level Sicilian Camorra boss, the dimensions of a compact, well-nourished Montgolfier balloon and a habit of smoking phallic cigars with the romantic name of 'Romeo and Juliet'. Nowadays, if the echoes of rumours are to be believed, the Head of Heads is working as a popular toastmaster in the town of Saratov. But, back then, the invasion of the newspaper's minor star system by such a massive and forbidding heavenly body was enough to disrupt it completely. Yes indeed, you know nothing at all about life, said the heavenly body, flashing the gold car-tyre on its index finger at me. Now I'm going to do the talking and you're going to listen. And do what you're told. Point one: do you think we do creative writing here? Like fuck. We 'service people', get it?

The Head Head probably didn't know that, in the language that won the Cold War, the expression 'service people' had a slightly different significance. Or maybe he did. The more time that passes, the more I incline to the second opinion.

From the moment the transition to the oral-genital paradigm was officially adopted, the process of my own financial degradation began to accelerate, first at a constant rate, and then exponentially. At first, out of sheer fatalistic stubbornness, I tried not to notice it. Until they stopped noticing me.

Until I completely disappeared from sight.

From Soviet journalism's massive communal apartment in the twenty-storey House of the Press, the editorial offices of the Latvian periodicals were scattered across the city by the centrifugal force of rapidly rising rents. *SM* was flung a distance of four kilometres, across the river to a separate new building in the city's business supercentre. One move is as good for business as two fires or three floods, and the conveyor-belt of the newspaper's life was halted for a full nine days, at the end of which I showed up at my new place of work, the door marked with the sacred Buddhist number 512. At first the massive brand-new door wouldn't budge. Then it did.

Behind the door were several young men I didn't know in sports jackets and gold-rimmed spectacles circulating very rapidly and purposefully along complex intersecting routes that were clearly not random. They were talking on mobile phones, eating gigantic 'submarine' sandwiches, battering the keys of laptops, dictating to the secretary, sending and receiving faxes, gulping coffee – all at the same time, as far as I could tell. I gazed at them for about five seconds, mentally assembling the primitive phrase, 'Sorry, I think I got the wrong door'. But one of the young men beat me to it. Making a minor correction to his precisely calculated route, he deviated in the direction of the door and, with an economical gesture, closed it right in my face. Without even looking at me.

'Sorry, I think I got the wrong door,' I apologised gallantly to the dark-brown reinforced panel of planed timber. Stood there for a while. Then set off to clarify the situation.

The Head Head, Lev Lvovich, was sitting in the middle of his new office (two and a half times the floor space and volume of his last one) in a synthetic leather armchair of the brand designed to adapt itself to the body of any occupant. I could see that, despite its vigorously promoted elastic conformability to all shapes and sizes, the armchair was having a hard time adapting to the shape and size of the shareholders' personal representative. I registered a brief twinge of pity for the article of furniture. The Head Head was thoughtfully studying something small that glinted glassily. Moving closer, I saw a flask full of yellowish saline solution. Floating in it was half a scrotum, neatly dissected with perfect precision by something very sharp. I shuddered and took a closer look. It turned out to be a naturalistic plastic imitation. And on the flask I spotted a plain laboratory-style label with the laconic inscription 'Faberge's Ball'.

The Head Head raised his head to look at me. In blank incomprehension. I waited for his 'us and them' recognition system to throw up a positive result, but his expression didn't change.

'Lev Lvovich,' I mumbled, 'down there . . . the office, somehow . . .'

The Head Head blinked and carefully set the scrotum down on the edge of his incompletely assembled, high-pedigree office desk.

'What's your problem?' he enquired aggressively.

'Well, it's the office,' I said simply. 'Where is mine now?'

'What do you need an office for?' asked the Head Head.

'To work,' I said, amazed.

'Work,' he repeated thoughtfully, almost dreamily. Then, with the sudden, unexpected agility of a sumo wrestler he stood up and walked over to the wide, bright window. 'So what can you do?' He half-turned away from the window and aimed the digit with the ring at me.

'I'm a columnist,' I said, totally nonplussed. 'Well . . . A commentator. An analyst.'

'What's that then? The cleverest dick on the block?'

I couldn't think of anything to say to that.

Personal representative Lev Lvovich waited. But in vain. Then he nodded to himself in satisfaction and summoned me to him with an infinitesimal twitch of the same ring-bearing finger. I automatically moved closer.

'Take a look, clever dick,' the Head Head said amicably, jabbing his versatile finger at a virginal window with the transparent protective hymen still intact on its frame.

What I saw going on below triggered a momentary attack of déjà vu. It was the same thing I'd seen just a minute earlier in office 512. That same intense, rapid displacement (totally incomprehensible to the outside observer but clearly meaningful from the inside) of manpower units dolled up in expensive sports-jacket uniforms and shiny imported auto-motive technology.

'THEY,' Lev Lvovich growled didactically, grasping me by the lapel with impetuous tenacity, 'ARE WORKING. Earning money. Paying money. Some of it to us. But for them to pay you as well, you have to prove that they need to. They couldn't give a shit that you're such a clever dick. They don't know you. And they don't have to. So you . . .' – he turned me through a hundred and eighty degrees and released his grip – 'go. Go on, go on. Go to them. And think what you've got to offer them. If you think of anything, then you can come back.'

I went. And I thought. And I didn't go back.

The distilled early-autumn sunlight lent my surroundings the patina of a glossy, expensive advert. In the context of the authentically Hanseatic location of the Old Town, things acquired a convincing aura of superiority. Romanesque buttresses, cardboard Coca-Cola cups, neatly trimmed shrubs, saveloys, blondes, cars, beer bottles, cats, Swedish tourists, shop windows, spicy ketchup and fat pigeons became more stylish and attractive, acquired invisible but decipherable price tags. They were for sale and I wanted to buy. Unfortunately, I was insolvent.

With a practised furtive movement, I tipped some vodka into my glass of beer. It was already my second glass.

The demarcation line between the active and the passive, the assets and the liabilities, ran ten metres to the north-east of my right shoe, along the bright new sandy-red paving slabs that covered the road around the medieval heart and capitalist core of Riga.

Stepping out on to the right bank from the fancy off-the-road sports models that moored at the pavement at regular intervals, the *active sapienses* arranged themselves under the awnings and umbrellas of the Old Town's cafés. Boisterously they swigged fine Kilkenny Irish beer in MacShane's Pub. Inquisitively they dissected crustate molluscs sprinkled with lemon juice in the little fish restaurant The Two Salmon. Energetically they munched on oven-baked sausages oozing fat in the local ethnic inn The Lido. Thoughtfully they savoured ultra-slim triangular petals of pepperoni and mozzarella in the Blue Bird Pizzeria. Sensually they sipped layered or stirred B-52s, Margaritas and White Zombies in The Column cocktail bar.

The *passive sapienses* democratically chomped their international crapburgers with inexpensive native beer at the plastic tables in the left-bank fast food joint with a name that I'd never paid any attention to.

The *active sapienses* consumed life, the *passive* ones were consumed by it, and it was no easier to change your existential orientation than your sexual one . . . The fact that both kinds would come to the same bad end bothered no one.

I'd been squatting in my trench observing life on the right bank for more than an hour, still unable to rid myself of the feeling of paranoia that had been haunting me since my visit to office 512. On my way out of the newspaper office following the Head Head's valediction, I'd noticed below the sacred Buddhist number 512 a small nameplate that I hadn't spotted the first time: 'DEPARTMENT OF MARKET-OLOGY and target group feedback'.

Feedback . . . I rummaged in my jacket pocket and cautiously extracted an entire stratum of cultural debris – a stack of scraps of paper with crookedly written telephone numbers, bus tickets, business cards. I found what I wanted.

Andrei Vladlenovich Voronin. Head of PR, REX International Commercial Bank. Flashy card with a special embossed effect, the colour of eggshell. A three-pointed golden crown.

Andrei Vladlenovich was a *hyper-active sapiens*. Young, self-confident, impressive, playboyish, jovial. We'd met in an upmarket eatery at the four-star Radisson SAS hotel, at a conference for the Russian-language press. REX was the conference's sole sponsor. Andrei Vladlenovich had shaken me firmly by the hand, looked me meaningfully in the eye and suggested out of the blue: Why don't you come and work in our press service?

I set the card down in front of me on the scratched white tabletop.

At the time, six months earlier, I hadn't even bothered to think seriously about his proposal. The very phrase 'PR department' was enough to set a popular columnist yawning.

A slim brunette in a slinky lilac dress walked across to a table at The Column from the open door of a ground-hugging, jet-propelled silver automobile. Walked with real class. Sat down. Crossed her legs. Sod it. The slovenly punk in the red jacket who had opened the car door extorted a brief squeal from the alarm system and walked after her. Not a day over nineteen. So when did you earn the money for a car and a woman like that?

No matter how hard I tried to fathom the mysterious mechanism of the stunningly, scandalously sudden wealth of the most various and unexpected of my fellow-citizens in this supposedly poor country with no deposits of particularly valuable minerals, or industry, or secret technologies, I couldn't figure it out. The money seemed to appear from nowhere, in obscene and incomprehensible amounts (a Mercedes 500, an Audi A6, a BMW mark 7, the idiot's silver sports car, another Merc – a 230 Compressor – another BMW . . .). It was all such a crude contradiction of the basic laws of physics – the conservation of matter, for instance – and from the point of view of positivistic science there was no sensible explanation for it. These people bulging with dosh at every seam possessed no special qualities or gifts, no particular intellect or even animal cunning. I had seriously begun to believe they had simply discovered, through some piece of sheer good luck, the long lost end of the rainbow.

I took a mouthful of my fortified beer. I looked at the right-bank population and thought: they're no more talented, interesting, energetic or better in any way than me. They just know the secret. They're members of the Order of Templars, the Rosicrucians, the Masonic Lodge. Knights of the Rainbow's End. Surely an enterprising young man like myself can guess their secret signs and greetings, discover their secret passwords and meeting places, commune with the sacred mystery?

I don't want to be like them. I don't like them. But if they want everybody to play by their rules, then I can play that game too. And I'll beat them. Because I'm clever.

I saluted Andrei Vladlenovich's card with my empty

glass and stood up, enveloped in a warm cocoon of mellow, triumphant certainty. I set out to play by their rules.

One block before the six-storey Jugendstil residence of REX bank, I bought some strawberry-flavoured Orbit – to kill the smell of drink.

During the next two years and three months I wrote several dozen large, and a couple of hundred small pieces of advertising copy, plus press releases, reports, statements and slogans, all adding up to a total volume of about five hundred kilobytes of information. I mastered the basic tricks of black, white and grey PR. I learned how to recognise and make use of a multitude of sub-varieties of the lie (lies can be spoken or written, preventive or defensive, unpremeditated or malicious, with aggravating circumstances when especially distorted). I bought a Philips music centre, fifty-odd CDs, an Aiwa toaster, a blue suit, three pairs of jeans and an avant-garde coffee-table with a glass top framed in an automobile wing. I consumed about a hundred litres of strong alcoholic beverages. I screwed a chance acquaintance from a night club, had my way with the youngest member of staff from the accounts department on the third floor, and entered into what is known in Russian by the depressing term 'a relationship' with a lay-out artist from a design bureau that had developed a series of evocative logos for our advertising campaign. I also blew away, blasted, blitzed, bombed, dismembered, drowned, froze, shrank, splatted and beat to death with my bare hands several tens of thousands of venomous, warty, slimy, shaggy, horned, fanged, multi-legged and multi-jointed monsters from various levels of 3D-reality.

Exponents of Vedic medicine have a special concept to describe the state of consciousness that is most harmful to the health of spirit and body. It's called the 'sleep' state. That's when your life acquires a stable inertia and entirely loses its acceleration. Every day you run mindlessly through a necessary and sufficient set of cloned, repeated, identical actions. And you have no feelings about the situation.

I was in no danger of getting sacked, but I had no prospects of promotion. My pay was neither increasing nor shrinking. I wasn't going to starve to death, but I had no hope of hitting the jackpot. Other people had long since stopped classifying me as highly promising and an investment for the future – and I had long ago stopped letting it bother me. I was healthy and intending to live for a long time yet. Forty years, perhaps. I knew for certain that, in those forty years, nothing would change.

. . . I was eleven years old. My parents and I were spending the summer with my granddad in the country. It was peaceful, sunny and boring. Every day, after a breakfast of chopped herbs in sour milk, I walked out of my granddad's two-storey wooden house, along the empty, baking-hot street and into the little shop two crossroads further down. By that time I already knew the phrase 'village shop', but it was much later before I realised that this big, dark room, crammed to its high ceiling (shelves, shelves and more shelves towering the full height of two walls) was a genuine village shop. It had an insane, unimaginably vast range of goods, and a thick, dense aroma composed of the scents of dusty fabric, dusty paper, dusty oilcloth, tea, spices, rubber, sweets, cigarettes and God knows what else. Hanging on the only wall without any shelves was a faded poster of a shaggy-haired Diego Maradona heading the ball. Beside it was a Japanese calendar with incomprehensible hieroglyphs and girls with heavenly smiles in minimalist swimming suits, objects of my puerile erotic fantasies. But on one of the shelves, behind the fat crumpled shop-woman in her perpetual shawl, there was an equally fat white guinea pig living in a three-litre jar. The guinea pig always stood on its hind legs, baring its big yellow incisors, with the pink and extraordinarily human little palms of its forelegs pressed against the glass. It twitched its nose, also pink, but with a black patch. The guinea pig pretended that it wanted to break out of the jar and escape. But everybody, including the guinea pig, knew for a fact that it didn't really want to. The shop-woman fed him apples and sometimes nuts. One day I came across two locals in the shop, wearing tall fisherman's waders that came up above their knees, and windcheaters the colour of wet sailcloth. The locals were examining floats and fishing line.

'Eh, wish I had a Japanese one,' said one of them. 'A nice red one.'

'Well fuck you,' said the other.

They said nothing for a while. The saleswoman paid no attention to them.

'Hey, look, Semyonich,' the first one said suddenly, jabbing a yellow finger in the direction of the guinea pig. 'A prick in a jar!'

'Shush,' said the shop-woman. 'Not in front of the child.'

I know exactly who I am. I'm the prick in the jar.

2

'At dawn's first light,' – a vaguely familiar, brutal lyric declaimed with ominous emphasis – 'the combat unit sets out . . .'

Combat unit . . . total combat, mortal wombat, battle masters, strictly plastered, serried ranks, flowery banks, of rhododendrons, soldierdendrons, a soldierdendron is this kind of evergreen bush, all-year-round-camouflaged shrub, with very beautiful flowers, smoky-orange, bright-scorching-napalm-orange, one thousand degrees Celsius, blooming flowers, April showers, stupid pricks, fuck the dicks, fucking flowers, blooming, in winter, win-ter, for Christ-mas, for Christ's sake . . .

'Soldier,' sang the voice, 'Soldier, I have faith in your sou-oul!'

Shut your mouth, you bloody freak, Vadim answered, but somehow he couldn't hear himself, as if the volume had been turned right down. He strained hard, levering his eyelids apart, only to have his vision invaded by the well-nourished, army-recruit features of pop star Rastorguev beaming from the TV screen. In desperation Vadim hunted around on the blankets for the remote control. It wasn't there. He'd deliberately put it out of reach yesterday. To make sure he couldn't just mechanically press the red button and collapse back into sleep the way he often did.

'And now – the news!' The pop star was crowded off the screen by footage of a fragile girl with unreal eyes and a radical hairstyle. To the accompaniment of a carefully modulated voice-over that drowned out the off-screen crackle of applause, the girl accepted a hefty gold idol from the hands of a plasticine Jim Carrey. 'The Hollywood star Smilla Pavovich yesterday signed an unprecedented contract. Until recently Pavovich was just one more run-of-the-mill starlet of Ukrainian-Yugoslavian extraction, but last March she was awarded the most prestigious prize in world cinema. Yesterday she was heading for superstardom as she . . .'

The television had been set in alarm mode for nine. It was just plain perverted, getting up so early on a day off. Especially on Christmas day. In fact, it wasn't even perversion, it was out-and-out rape. He'd been well and truly buggered by that bespectacled bastard. May you croak from insomnia, Four-Eyes.

'. . . a fee of four million dollars for shooting the new mega-budget blockbuster from director Roland Emmerich!'

Vadim had been finding it harder and harder to wake up recently. And the washed-out feeling he had every morning didn't depend on how long he'd slept or whether he'd been drinking the evening before.

'. . . the film version of the super-popular computer combat game, *Headcrusher* . . .'

Mein Gott, thought Vadim. Now those Hollywood cretins want to turn Headcrusher into a crappy blockbuster!

The phrase 'headcrusher' had first lodged itself in Vadim's advertising-and-finance-resistant brain one year and nine months earlier, when he'd used the bonus earned for his first major assignment – developing the text for the colour booklet 'The REX Brokerage Investment Account' – to buy himself a two-week trip to Prague by bus. He'd definitely been impressed by the scowling gothic architecture blackened by the smoke of centuries, but he'd been even more impressed by Prague's museum of medieval torture. 'The Headcrusher' was the name of a massive but simple vice for the efficient crushing of heretical heads. It had occurred to Vadim that it could have been the name of a gang of punk tearaways. Or a cyberpunk novel . . . That was the only real reason he'd developed an interest in virtual combat – he'd got hooked on the name.

'. . . In screen tests Smilla Pavovich gave a more convincing performance than all her rivals in the role of the game's sexy and outrageous heroine, the female warrior of a post-apocalypse future, Sara Taff. Her partner Smiley will be played by Tom Cruise, who has postponed the filming of *Mission Impossible III* in order to do this project. And her main enemy, the super-villain Doctor Zero, will be played by John Malkovich. Shooting will start immediately after the New Year, just as soon as Hollywood's bright new Kiev-born hopeful completes her promotional tour of Northern and Eastern Europe. The budget for the movie is in the order of one hundred and thirty million dollars!'

Vadim groaned. The game was pretty much his favourite toy. His outlay on progress through its ever-new, ever-bloodier levels represented a significant portion of his bachelor budget expense account. He couldn't play at work. His office computer might be a Pentium, but it couldn't handle the tortuous convolutions of the head-crushing, arm-smashing, leg-pulping, sharp-shooting, all-singing, all-dancing graphics. The tightwad office supply managers at the super-rich bank had quite reasonably decided that, since the employees of the press department worked with text, their computers didn't need to be any more intelligent than a basic typewriter. So he frequented instead the insalubrious basement bar-cum-games arcade of a certain Vitek.

'. . . The Pop Stars and Financiers' Children's Appeal is continuing. Contributions received in support of orphanages and children's homes have reached more than two . . .'

Vadim finally disentangled himself from the covers and managed to grab the control. He hastily pulled on his usual aging, coarse, woolly sweater. And those lousy wankers sent him regular bills for heating. Pretty stiff ones they were, too . . .

In the bathroom he extended cautious fingers under the tap as slowly, reluctantly, the liquid ice from the freezing pipes mutated into warm water. Vadim raised his eyes to look at his mirror-world doppelgänger. He rubbed his face with his hand. The doppelgänger repeated the gesture after a brief pause.

'Think positive!' Vadim commanded, peeved by his surrogate's non-committal expression.

There was a story behind this exhortation. In the ninth class at school, Vadim's friend Max Lotarev had gone to the States for six months on a school exchange. He had come back a little bit more stupid, with seriously pumped-up muscles. Of all his stories about the Oklahoma life-style, the one that had stuck most firmly in Vadim's memory was about P.E.. About how the jogging-crazy Yankees had required their guest, who was not accustomed to serious exertion, to join them in a fifteen-kilometre run. After only fifteen minutes Max already felt like he'd been put through a combined mincer, juicer and automatic lemon-slicer. He would have given up had it not been for the neat, clean-cut young men with red 'Coach's Assistant' armbands on their biceps, posted at regular hundred-metre intervals around the stadium. They gave each clapped-out jogger a joyful, beaming smile and declared with the soulful regularity of an automatic lemon-slicer: 'Think positive! Think positive!'

'Smile, you ugly bastard!' Vadim encouraged his doppelgänger in the voice of the Last Boy Scout.

The ugly bastard smiled. Vadim didn't believe it. The

ugly bastard was faking it for sure. Every morning the doppelgänger looked less and less like Vadim. And Vadim liked him less and less. He was definitely leading an antisocial and unhealthy kind of life. Going without sleep, sleeping anywhere at all, with anyone who happened to be around, drinking too much low-quality alcohol, taking no physical exercise and overindulging in cholesterol- and sugar-rich foods. What was more, he was inclined to hysteria, had a distinctly uncooperative attitude to his boss, was experimenting with mind-expanding and life-contracting substances, and seemed intent on croaking ingloriously in the nearest back-alley some time in the not too distant future. In fact it was absolutely impossible to understand why a healthy, young, positive-thinking, energetic and creative employee of a reputable, authoritative international bank had put up with such a filthy scumbag in his mirror for so long, why he hadn't just sacked the ugly fucker without severance pay . . .

As if he had read this intention in the keen gaze of Vadim's eyes and taken fright, the doppelgänger swiftly disappeared from view behind a veil of steam. The water had warmed up. Vadim could get under the shower.

It was only now, seated blissfully on the rough enamelled floor of nirvana, that Vadim began to thaw out. Warm rivulets trickled down over his head, creating white noise inside it. Vadim was dissolving.

He had almost dissolved completely when a disagreeable, sarcastic voice – no doubt the vengeful doppelgänger's – spoke into his right ear: 'That's it, Vadim, old mate, time's up. Time for you to clamber out into the hostile, poorly heated environment of your cheap rented flat. Time to towel yourself dry. Get dressed. Toast yourself two slices of bread in your cheap toaster that's such of heap of shit that it will burn them on both sides. Time to put a lump of low-fat butter on your over-toasted, dietetic bread, which in its raw state has the taste and consistency of low-grade plastic foam and is totally inedible. The butter will turn transparent, like warmed-up candle-wax, and its taste and consistency will be no better. You'll wash all this down with a cup of bitter instant coffee well past its sell-by date, into which will have disappeared three tablets of sugar-substitute. And after that . . . After that, things will get even worse. After that, you'll pull on your Chinese duck-down jacket with its ultra-clandestine water-repellent coating. So clandestine, in fact, that very soon you'll be soaked through. It's probably sleeting outside, isn't it? With pus-coloured slurry underfoot. Not even "slurry" but "slurpy", from the verb "to slurp". Slurp-slurp. Slurp-slurp. Up over your ankles. What kind of Christmas would we have in Latvia without slurping through wet sleet? And why is all this happening? Because, Vadim, my old mate, you're not really a young, healthy, positive-thinking, energetic and creative, promising company employee. You're a petty cog, the lowest link in a long chain of cogs. And because Daddy Citron leaned on Son-in-Law Four-Eyes, and Four-Eyes leaned on you, since he is too lazy and can't be buggered to get out of bed and go slurping (not even on the spiked winter tyres of the sunflower-yellow Pontiac that Daddy gave him as a wedding present. Therefore you're going slurping, you wanker. Meek as a lamb. Because you've got no one to lean on. Of course, you'd like to lean on me, but not being fucking Alice, you can't get through the looking glass, can you? You're the one who's going slurping. All alone. In person. To deliver a little envelope in perfect condition with all due respect to Citron's whore. Because she's an expensive whore and you're a cheap one. And with that, adieu.'

After the doppelgänger had bid goodbye and stopped

yapping, Vadim discovered that he was standing on a rubber mat, scowling and curling up his toes, frenziedly rasping at his skin with a coarse waffle-weave towel. He'd seen Citron's whore three or four times before. She looked exactly the way the mistress of the president of a massive, bloated banking house was supposed to look. He had found it quite impossible even to think of her as a woman. This was an exclusive product, separated off from the rest of the perishable world by an ultra-thin but absolutely impermeable financial membrane.

Yet, what puzzled Vadim was that, when he looked at Citron himself, he saw no trace of this protective membrane, even though, as he had had several opportunities to observe, it was demonstrably present around other people of Citron's circle, in fact it was as thick as good bullet-proof glass. But Citron just didn't have it, despite the fact he looked exactly the way the president of a massive, bloated banking house was supposed to look: the caricatured bourgeois sent packing by the implacable proletarian boot in one of those early Soviet propaganda posters. Short, squat, overweight and balding, with a fat-chopped, bulldog-like face and beady little eyes. But if you actually looked into those startlingly prehensile, sober, hard little eyes, you soon began to realise that Citron was not short, but compact, not overweight, but solid, not a caricature bourgeois, but an absolutely genuine, 24-carat capitalist shark, a combat unit at least the equal of the battle-ship *Tirpitz*. Once or twice a week, without making any preliminary declaration of war, Citron made a rapid crossing of the press room's territorial waters on an unpredictable zigzag course, trailing an escort of myrmidons and minions in his wake. Yet every time any employee of the bank, even the most obscure and insignificant, happened to be in Citron's path, he or she was instantly and unerringly identified by name, honoured with a polite personal 'hello' and a firm handshake, and sometimes a precise, practical question. Citron listened to the replies attentively and wasn't too high and mighty to act on what he heard. However, if the talk indicated a clash of interests of any kind, at any level, he clamped down with the speed of Concorde and the ruthlessness of a steamroller.

They said that, every day, he *ate* his way (specifically ate his way, not drank) through fifteen hundred bucks in restaurant bills . . .

Vadim's post box was empty. Almost. A single, solitary, rather hefty pamphlet that looked like advertising lay at the bottom. Vadim was on the point of redirecting it to one of his neighbours without even looking at it, when something caught his eye. 'The REX Brokerage Investment Account' he read on the cover. Well, would you believe it! Vadim chuckled and casually stuck the booklet in his pocket.

Despite the malicious prognostications of the disgusting reptile in the mirror, it was snow that was falling outside, not sleet. Absolutely genuine, White-Christmassy snow. Broad, fluffy, shaggy flakes. So thick it deadened sound and plastered itself over his eyes. Every thirty metres, sexless janitors in brightly coloured nylon jackets scraped at the pavement with flat wooden shovels. The snow, Vadim decided as he raised and lowered his space-helmet hood, was not snow at all. An aggressive non-humanoid form of life from another planet was parachuting down in a mass assault force, an army of invasion. And the thin, uneven line of volunteer janitors was humanity's last, faint hope. Although the battle was uneven, the janitors were resisting to the death. But even if they do hold out, thought Vadim, following the ice-free line of an underground hot-water main as he dashed across a narrow white road in front of a sluggish lorry, even if they can last out the winter, and the next one, and the next, this country will

26

still end up getting tribalised by NATO's peace-keeping, bar-creeping forces. Just a couple of kilometres from here, in Ust-Dvinsk, there'll be an American navy base. And here, in Bolderaya, we'll be taken over by brothels and honky-tonks. A ghetto. Slavonic harlem. By day the natives will extract crisp, green liberal values from the identically optimalised black and white marines, all as beefy and calorific as Big Macs, in exchange for herbal, resinous, powdered and granulated primordial ecstasy. And by night they'll exchange colourful abuse and deadly blows with them in the alleyways and the taverns. And the native women will let the marines have it at democratic hourly rates and die from synthetic narcotics, AIDS and alcohol; or (more rarely), having managed to accumulate a bit of money, strike out for the interior of the continent; or (rarest of all) inspire the envy and hatred of their female colleagues by suddenly marrying a senior marine sergeant, a basketballing black dude with a rastaman tattoo on his prick, and depart for a different continent altogether, to fucking Oklahoma or Kansas. The triumph of a highly developed imperial civilisation, thought Vadim, as he slipped and slithered along, but better them than the crystalline aliens . . .

Diving in through the door of the bus just before it clanged hospitably shut, he was greeted with a friendly elbow under the ribs.

From Bolderaya to the centre was over ten kilometres, half an hour in a frozen Icarus bus with its heater amputated by the drivers and sold off on the side. His brothers-and-sisters-in-the-bus all shared a single, identical facial expression: standard defensive camouflage.

Vadim fished out of his pocket the booklet that had once provided him with five days in Prague and rustled mechanically through the thick pages dense with bombast.

27

'Ticket?' asked the monstrous conductress in a greasy waistcoat, flicking the safety-catch of her third chin and preparing to shoot.

Vadim shuddered and held out twenty centimes.

. . . Maximalising the opportunities offered by the market demands tactics of rational caution and informed responsibility. The flexible adjustment of service to the individual requirements of each Client. 'Client' written with a capital letter. *The portfolio manager pays particular attention to reducing risks and constantly strives to improve the level of return on Your portfolio.* 'Your' was spelt with a capital letter too. So then why was 'portfolio' spelt with a small letter? *An experienced broker reacts more quickly to the constantly changing situation, buying and selling at the most appropriate moment . . .*

A seriously battered and well-worn citizen in tattered nylon packaging, his unambiguously working-class features stamped with the universal 'proletarian morning' logo, downed half a litre of Pilsner and attempted to position the empty bottle between the folds of the bus's rotten rubber concertina.

. . . He possesses detailed knowledge of the market's participants, and this allows him, while ensuring maximum coverage of the gamut of prices linked to supply and demand, to minimise the risk of a transaction not being completed due to the fault of the counter-agent . . .

Two morose-looking teenage girls with amateurishly daubed-on make-up and badly dyed hair worked their jaws up and down on their bubblegum with depressingly mechanical regularity, while thin strands of Russian trash pop leaked out from under the cheap plastic of their earphones.

. . . In order to achieve this, every new account is given a unique number . . .

Slate-like smears of frost on the dirty-brown glass.

. . . REX honours and will continue to honour the same

*unshakeable, fundamental principles of business ethics in dealings
with all categories of the bank's clients . . .*

The grey, choking fumes of cheap fuel.

*. . . and will forward reports on the state of the assets in Your
account, listing all transactions made, replying promptly to all
questions that arise concerning the accounting system in relation to
which Your account . . . putting in nine trillion dollars through its
subsidiaries Solomon Brothers bringing in 'Morgan Stanley' to select
the correct strategy and objectives portfolio of securities taking pride in
this collaboration avoiding hidden reefs and spotting the part of the
iceberg hidden under the surface of the water the authorised financial
controller of payment implementation . . .*

With a concerted physical effort, Vadim tore his eyes
away from the hypnotic, ritual drone of the text that was
suppressing his will and dissolving the convolutions of his
brain. God almighty. Did he really write that?

*. . . The BIA is serviced by the best brokers, many of whom
learned their trade in Wall Street's school of hard knocks . . .*

Vadim saw a clear image of glass doors at opposite ends
of a long office corridor, opening to admit an endless stream
of young brokers in blindingly white shirts and ties from
Valentino who lined up in two phalanxes and advanced
towards each other when the signal was given. Their smoothly
ironed faces were contorted in berserk grimaces of violent
insanity. Hands with polished fingernails raised aloft briefcases,
baseball bats, notebook PCs, vicious screwdrivers, electronic
organisers, bicycle chains. Wall Street's school of hard knocks.

Vadim was now leafing through the booklet that he
himself had written more purposefully. And the longer he
leafed through it, the less he understood anything in the text or
the pictures. He felt like an Egyptologist, some latter-day
Champollion, examining a bas-relief recently discovered in the
desert sands that was densely inscribed with incomprehensible

hieroglyphs, unfamiliar pictograms and mysterious images. They expressed some lost meaning, a coherent story-line, but every attempt to restore it, translate it, relate it to some other reality that had already been at least minimally researched, was an abject and utter failure.

The cover. A monumental Palladian portico. Magnificent Ionic columns. Three doors twice the height of a man, the central one standing open, and from inside it – an otherworldly glow. Chiselled across the front of the pediment: STOCK MARKET. A temple? Had to be. A broad flight of steps. On the left the truncated snout of a Chevrolet. Advancing from the car and up the steps, a dignified, grey-haired gentleman – straight back, the bearing of a general, a first consul, a tyrant. In his hands a bulging buffalo-skin briefcase. A sacrifice? Evidently. Descending sedately towards him with his arms held open in joyous greeting, a younger gentleman who nonetheless appeared full of solemnity and an awareness of the sublimity of his mission. A priest?

As Vadim sat there on his slashed seat, an engrossing mystery from the life and death of the titans, gods and heroes unfolded before his very eyes. Complete with grandiose cosmogony and appalling eschatology. The first two pages of the booklet bore a title in large letters: THE INVESTOR. Shown in close-up against a background of semi-transparent squares and circles (the circle, Vadim recalled, was heaven, the square was the earth, together they formed a mandala), two hands extended out of snow-white shirt-cuffs to fuse together in a super-firm handshake. A symbol of the active union of opposed principles, out of which the whole of existence had arisen. Surrounding them: a thick Parker Stylo pen (a phallic image and metaphor of creation); a clock-face (symbol of time beginning its course and all things made new); and finally, removing any lingering trace of doubt, the handwritten phrase 'A NEW ACCOUNT – A NEW START'. Benevolently observing all of this, a hook-nosed, eagle-faced man – fucking eureka! God, the supreme deity of the pantheon. Zeus, Odin, Woden, Ahura Mazda, Amon-Ra-Sonter.

The next double page. On the left: CLIENT SERVICE, represented in perfect conformity with the ancient traditions of sacred temple prostitution by a full-breasted goddess of love with a moonstone adorning her tall neck. On the right: PERSONAL PORTFOLIO MANAGER – a young man with an icy gaze and cold-forged Aryan features, complete with a full set of big-business martial attributes, from the shining armour of his ideal suit to his double-edged, everlasting pen. The god of war. Mars. And right there beside him another enlightening handwritten slogan – a quotation, Vadim recalled, from some Japanese or other: BUSINESS IS WAR.

Next: BROKERS and ANALYSTS. *Rapid and precise execution of instructions, direct access to the market.* A lithe and limber, curly-headed youth with a mobile phone at his right ear and the receiver of an ordinary telephone at his left. On the table, a laptop connected to the Internet, some wires and aerials. Hermes. The herald. The supplier of information. The god of communications.

And finally: A BRILLIANT TEAM OF PROFES-SIONALS. Everybody at once: the goddess of love, the stern warrior Mars, the telephonised wearer of winged sandals and, up above them, all-knowing, all-powerful, fearsome, appalling to unbelievers but unfailingly benevolent to Clients – Zeus. The full Pantheon.

A high-voltage lightning-bolt of terrible realisation flashed through Vadim's regularly swaying head. All of them – citizen Four-Eyes down to Vadim himself – without even knowing it, they were the servants of anonymous deities standing behind the scenes. Offering up prayers and accepting sacrifices, believing that what they were doing was promotion, PR, consulting and advertising. He remembered the way he'd composed this booklet, guzzling a glass of brandy to dispel the fog of stupefaction and put himself in combat mode before confronting his First Big Assignment. He remembered the moment when he had suddenly been visited by inspiration and taken flight, hammering the entire concept of the REX BROKERAGE INVESTMENT ACCOUNT into the keyboard in only two hours.

No doubt about it. He had been controlled by some purposeful alien will. He had been a medium, an intermediary. But, as his memory threw up the dark, malevolent word 'possession', the bus docked at its terminus with a squeal of relief and Vadim was lifted to his feet and swept outside.

The snow had stopped. The sun, after its late arrival, was hastily putting the finishing touches to the Christmas decorations. Vadim spat superstitiously to his left as he fed the terrible booklet to the first litter bin he came across. It's a load of nonsense, he thought. I must have read something of the sort recently. And never believe the fantastic fabrications of fashionable fiction.

'Who is it?'

'Hello, Lada . . . It's Vadim, Apletaev, from the press . . . From Citron.'

The intercom crackled in electrical disapproval for a while, saying nothing.

'Ah,' it said at last. In a tone of what sounded to Vadim like either annoyance or weary disgust. 'Jussasec.' Another brief pause and then something that took a moment to understand: 'Fourth. Twenty-seven.'

The intercom snorted and went dead again. Vadim waited for a moment, wondering what to do. Pushed the door. Locked. From the opposite side of the unnaturally clean courtyard a retro-lady in maroon cashmere with a bizarre microbiological specimen on a suede lead was watching him suspiciously. Vadim waved his extended middle finger to both of them. Immediately he heard a clunk from inside the door.

The building was old but, like the entire district of apartment buildings it belonged to, it had been subjected to cosmetic external repair and profound internal intervention, massive euro-bypass surgery. It now contained elite apartments for those whose pockets did not as yet extend to cottages in the dunes at Jurmala, but for whom the damp dormitory districts were definitely not appropriate. Creaking melodically, the old-fashioned lift with its internal facing of quality timber stolidly transported its socially alien contents to the fourth floor. Flat twenty-seven.

As Clint Eastwood used to say, there are only two types of people in the world: some stand there with a noose round their neck, others have a revolver in their hand. Although not in disagreement with this, Vadim had, through bitter experience, come to see that there were other criteria by which to categorise the human race.

Some people were forever struggling and scheming, buying expensive things, making desperate efforts to lose excess weight and to sculpt their profile in the gym, having fat suctioned out and silicone pumped in by plastic surgeons, skilfully employing make-up for purposes of emphasis and camouflage, attempting by means of regular self tuition to lend the expression of their face and their posture the requisite aura of unfaltering assurance – and even then it was only with incredible difficulty that they achieved the desired result (if they achieved it at all, of course): to reformat their imperfect flesh as MARKETABLE GOODS; to condition their external integument so successfully that it would convince everyone around them that these were goods they could buy, needed to buy, must buy. Other people could smoke, drink continuously and neglect their diet, consuming starchy, sweet and spicy foods in Rabelaisian quantities, wear absolutely anything and regard morning exercise as the devil's own invention – and still, whatever state they were in or outfit they wore, they looked like pricey articles from the Neckerman catalogue shot by professional photographers. And any blemish or imperfection in or on them appeared like some especially subtle device exploited by designers, stylists and make-up artists to hike up the already spiralling price of the goods.

When Vadim had a really bad head, children and domestic animals always gave him a wide berth, while the cops, on the contrary, showed an unhealthy interest.

The young woman Lada, the official, full-time, up-market lay of the president of the major international bank REX, looked even better than something out of Neckerman, she looked like the cover of *Vogue* or *Cosmopolitan*, even with a murderous mother of a hangover (which was perfectly obvious to Vadim, as a connoisseur of the genre). Vadim suddenly realised at last the true nature of the membrane that divided Lada's person from the rest of the universe. It wasn't the thin, easily torn cellophane in which respectable super-markets package exotic fruits such as January strawberries. It was that dense polythene into which every copy of a glossy, prestigious magazine is hermetically sealed at birth.

Without favouring him with a single glance, the Cover Girl admitted Vadim into a front hall the size of gym and then, without uttering a word, staggered away on legs the requisite length into the depths of the flat's oriental décor and

34

disappeared round a corner. Vadim thought for a moment, gave an independent shrug and separated his right sole from the floor to take a step. Then he carefully lowered it back again. The melting snow was dribbling off his shoe in a stream of black sludge. The elegantly simple floor was made of unpainted boards, oiled so that they glimmered like amber. Vadim himself would have been hard put to define what lay behind the instinct not to move: good manners, an inferiority complex or aesthetic sensibility.

He heard a muffled mumbling of obscenities from round the corner. Something fell. Vadim hesitated for just a little longer, then thought to hell with it and set off towards the sound, leaving an offensive trail of greasy blotches on the delicate amber surface.

Lada was bent forward at the waist, her top half buried in the wall, presenting him with the requisitely rounded form of her backside, precisely delineated by the black ink of her silk kimono. Vadim blinked. It was the bar: up-market, hand-sculpted bottles, with intimate lighting glinting on their facets and slipping across their curves then drowning in the ruddy velvet of cognac and the straw-tinged tweed of whiskey.

The bottles jangled as they were raked aside.

'What's up?' said Vadim.

She turned round too fast to wipe the expression of acute nausea off her charming face.

'Bastard hell,' the Cover Girl said to Vadim. 'Nothing but lousy spirits.'

Then, once again losing the slightest trace of interest in this inopportune messenger from the outer realms, she walked round him, grazing him with the requisite fragility of her little shoulder, and disappeared into the kitchen. Vadim followed her, his fury mounting.

Lada was swaying in front of the gaping maw of a

refrigerator of epic proportions, tugging at her plump lower lip. The expression of nauseated disgust on her Cover Girl features had been replaced by deadly despair. Then, suddenly, a flash of hope flared in her eyes and, with a rapid, birdlike movement, she grabbed a dark-brown bottle off a shelf. The hope faded away in her face like the bright, tiny flame of a cigarette lighter. The bottle clattered against the tiled floor in emphatic disappointment and began to roll in a graceful arc towards Vadim's feet. 'Spicy Soy Sauce'. The Cover Girl followed the spicy sauce's journey with a blank gaze. The gaze stumbled against his shoes. Then it scrambled upwards.

'Oops,' said Lada, making a vain attempt to bring the gaze into focus. 'Listen . . . You . . . haven't got any beer, have you?'

It was as much as Vadim could do to shake his head.

'Buggeration,' said Lada, concisely summing up the situation. She tousled her already tangled thick mane of hair, the hair of a species as rare as the magical unicorn, the so-called 'natural blonde'. 'You . . . eh . . . go get some beer, eh?'

This was discourtesy at the critical level of intensity that edges it over an imperceptible boundary into the realm of noble absurdity.

Submitting to this imperious, Kafkaesque edict, Vadim walked meekly out through the hall, across the landing and down the stairs. He was already out in the courtyard, between the North American sedan and the South Korean coupe, before the imbecility of the situation hit him. He gave the middle-class tyre of the coupe a hefty, heartfelt kick, jumped back at the hysterical screech of the alarm and stomped off doggedly towards the bus stop.

There was the semi-transparent crate of a grocery kiosk standing less than two metres away from the little tin flag with the list of bus numbers. Vadim looked at it contemptuously.

36

He went in.

'What's the cheapest beer you've got?'

The sales-girl squinted indifferently at the price tickets. 'Pilsner.'

Vadim remembered the proletariate in the bus. He sniggered vengefully to himself and rapped out: 'One.'

But his spontaneous act of sabotage was an abject failure. Lada snatched the bottle out of his hand, disregarding the lowly label, and shot a rapid glance round the kitchen, evidently searching for a bottle opener. She pulled out a drawer and rummaged in it. Not finding anything, she lodged the bottle-cap against the edge of the table's mirror-bright surface and pressed her pampered little palm hard down on it with surprisingly productive precision. The bottle-cap tinkled briefly, settling under the sink. Impatiently blowing off the beige foam, the Cover Girl set the mouth of the bottle to her lips and polished off a third of it in a single swig.

She wiped her mouth and snorted in relief. Her face recovered a semblance of intelligence.

'Fantastic,' she declared, transferring her newly rational gaze to Vadim. 'What was it you said you came about?'

3

Ants.

The forest-dwelling *Formica rufa*, the red-breasted, wood-boring *Camponotus herculianus*, leaf-cutters of the species *Atta cephalotes* . . .

Red and black.

Advancing under the skin in arterial columns, from the pads of her fingers and toes, into the veinous whirlpool, along the echoing, tubiform tunnels of the metatarsal and metacarpal bones, through the transport hubs of the wrists and ankles, elbows and knees, across the rugged terrain of muscle, until they reach her shoulders and hips, and assemble en masse to dash towards their point of intersection, their meeting-place at the solar plexus. There is an explosion. Shock waves blast outwards like a radar beam, illuminating the interior outlines of her torso, the continental contours of her internal organs – kidneys, liver, stomach, pancreas, spleen, bladder, small and large intestines, womb, vagina, heart . . . There is a momentary pause and then, for the first time, the heart hammers against the ribcage, the diaphragm plunges down and the framework of ribs expands admitting air into the lungs and parting their cellophane walls with a brand-new crackling sound. Blood swirls into the brachiocephalic trunk; with a turbine rumble it shoots up the carotid arteries, flooding into the deactivated brain, engorging it, until the brain flutters, heating up like a wolfram filament as it stirs into life and she opens her eyes.

They are met by a boundless arctic plain extending into infinite distance.

She shoots upright.

Her backside is freezing. She glances down. Clammy marble. A slab.

She turns her head to the right, to the left. Twilight. A homogenous suspension of semi-darkness. And, all around her, receding in uniform rows, identical rectangles dissolving into the gloom.

Underneath her the same thing.

She touches herself. She isn't there. The rubbery surface of her body yields insensibly under her glassy fingers. Her hand feels out the soft hollow under her throat. Slides over the triangles of her collar-bones. Fondles a compact, round breast. Cautiously plucks at a sharp nipple. Edges down over the cold, rock-hard segments of the abdomen. Reaches the navel.

Growing out of the navel is a cool metallic chain.

Her fingers run rapidly along the little links until they come to a hefty, turnip-shaped pocket watch.

Click.

The lid pops open.

The chords of 'Rule Britannia' skeeter across the marble in staccato rhythm and slither off on to the hard floor.

Five dials, their tiny phosphorescent eyes glaring malevolently.

The hand on the biggest dial is stuck at the top. Three others point to the bottom of their respective dials. Only on the very smallest dial is the hand pedantically ticking away.

100%

0

0

0

0.10 0.11 0.12

She clicks the watch shut and jumps down.

The floor's rough indentations bite into her feet. Suddenly, acting of its own accord, her rubber body uncoils its stiff limbs and recasts them in praying-mantis combat stance: feet positioned at right angles, legs set in a springy frame, the supporting right leg leading with the knee forward, hands held half a metre apart with the palms clenched as if clasping a long, heavy, invisible cylinder, ready to thrust it forward at any danger.

0.15 0.16 0.17

With an enormous effort of will she softens herself, as if she is a little plasticine figure rendered stiff and stubborn by the cold. Looks around again. Homogenous space ruled off into equal, identical rectangles. No difference between forwards and backwards, right and left, north and south. It makes no difference where she goes. So she follows the closest straight line and doesn't worry about it.

The rectangles decant space drop by drop, in unison with the dial-hand's decanting of time.

0.21 0.22 0.23

She walks on, and when the flat, gun-sight grid of surrounding non-reality has accumulated a critical mass of bare, slapping footsteps, it begins layering off into distinct dimensions and distending into detail.

Lying on rectangular marble tables are bodies, fragments of bodies, fragments of fragments.

She glides past them evenly and economically, observing intently.

Dolls. Dead dolls. Some complete. Some in pieces.

Hundreds of oval wooden heads painted with emphatically meticulous human faces and adorned with fibrous wigs. Thousands of plywood limbs with openings cut into them revealing thick, twisted springs inside. Hinged joints.

Metal keys protrude from the torsos.

Crude, non-operational likenesses of people, people, people, people . . . a big dog. A huge, black, lacquered dog. In places – she moves her face closer and adjusts the definition of her vision – the lacquer has flaked off. Through an elaborate opening carved in the dog's side she can see oily-metal entrails, a ceramic likeness of a heart, chipped round the edge. She glides on. Figures of people again. Two, four, six, ei . . . A whitish cockroach the size of a man. Turned over on to its back, its six legs thrust out in a gesture of distress, another carved key stuck into its segmented belly.

0.57 0.58 0.59

A sound behind her.

Suddenly she is flung upwards, spun round in the air, stretched out into a tense hieroglyph and then stuck to the ceiling, twelve feet up. Her right foot is pressed against the chubby backside of a carved cupid, the toes of her left foot are thrust into an insignificant indentation in the ceiling, her left hand clutches the damp, boa-constrictor body of a cold pipe, overgrown with weird, prickly sponge like the bottom of a ship. Her right hand is contracted into a small fist.

0.60 0.61 0.62

A rat.

The grey body rustles between the tables, its whiskers brushing the floor, its tail applying a final polish.

She gathers in the struts of her limbs, lands soundlessly right behind the rat and grabs it. The creature emits a chatter of protest. She swings it round. Through a small glass window in its back she can see the busy, spider-like motion of tiny cogwheels. A microchip.

ACQUIRE? NO.

She tosses the rat aside and moves on.

At 1.32 she sees the door. At 1.43 she reaches it. The door is locked.

A sharp blow with the base of her palm just above the brass lock smashes it open. She creeps inside. A short black corridor. Another two doors. A strip of light under the one on the left. A faint draught blows from beneath it. She draws it into her nostrils. A smell of dust and man. A living man: sour old-man's sweat . . . tobacco . . . alcohol . . . gin . . . She pulls herself upright. A man . . . unknown . . . dangerous. Go right.

The door on the right opens easily on well-oiled hinges. Behind it a room eighteen feet by twelve, its darkness diluted by furtive lighting. She looks for the sources of light: a jar inside a glass-fronted cabinet; a flask on a table; on another table, a two-foot long model of a tea-clipper. In the jar a glowing fungoid growth, something like a tea fungus, a thick, fringed pancake swaying in dull, murky liquid. In the flask a stirring of little lights. Fireflies! An incessantly churning, living mass – welling up out of itself, like the cap of foam on a pot of Turkish coffee, suddenly freezing, then collapsing back. At the moment of freezing, she glimpses briefly the contorted skeleton of a small mammal.

She shivers.

Glimmering along the clipper's rigging are the trembling, pinpoint lights of St. Elmo's Fire.

At regular intervals the deathly glow of the room is lit up by a synchronised, convulsive flash of spectrally pure colours: the fungus emits lightning flashes of bright lemon-yellow; the fireflies explode into intense lilac; the ship's masts broadcast a lush green. Each time, the colour combination changes.

The flashes disclose the details of her surroundings: tiled walls, glass-fronted cabinets, an operating table in the middle (with the flask standing on it), in the corner an elephantine writing desk with drawers set into ponderous, carved columns (with the clipper standing on it), a leather armchair peering out disdainfully from behind the desk. On the walls: anatomical posters with cross-sections of bodies. On one tiled wall hangs the grandiloquent patterning of a shaggy Afghan rug, and gashing its hallucinatory decorative surface – the nickel-plated steel of respectfully suspended surgical instruments: lancets, scalpels, forceps, clamps, gouges.

Saws. Files. Forceps. Syringes.

Only one door. No others. A dead end.

Shrugging off her fascinated stupefaction, she sets off aimlessly round the operating theatre (dissection room?). Freezes in front of the carpet. Takes down a lancet, big and dangerous. Tests the cutting edge with her finger. Razor-sharp.

Submitting to a sudden impulse, she runs the blade across her palm.

The super-fine thread of claret pauses before reluctantly oozing out – a long, taut drop that instantly runs down towards her elbow in an expanding trickle. The pocket watch jangles in alarm, the hand on the big dial shifting from 100 to 98. Slowly she licks away the blood (it leaves a taste of iron in her mouth).

ACQUIRE? YES.

She conceals the lancet in her fist, the blade pointing towards herself.

98%

01

0

0

2.32

She slips out into the corridor.

In through the door opposite.

Whirling furiously like a dancing tornado, the knife held at the ready close to her face, she cuts straight across the spacious hall with its bright yellow lighting. On one half-bent leg, with the other drawn up to her chest, the lancet-sting vibrating in her hand, she freezes into the corner, taking in the entire ninety-degree sector of visible space.

There he is, the man. Alone. At a dark wooden counter. Or rather, on the counter. His sleeping head with its receding hairline cradled in the crook of his arm. Snoring gently. Grey sideburns lying on the threadbare cloth of his sleeve. Behind him a row of hangers. A cloakroom. On the hangers . . . She glances, can't make anything out, darts her glance back to the cloakroom attendant – sleeping, not pretending – darts it away again . . . On the hangers . . . clothes. A lot of clothes. A dark mackintosh. A sable coat trimmed with ermine. An elegant jacket, blue velvet with gold braiding, and beside it a hat with a feather, a scarlet cross-belt, a tarnished sword. A spacesuit, the tinted screen of the pressurised helmet lowered, tagged with the code number NC235-H and a little flag – stars and stripes – on the left side of the chest. A suit of armour complete with perforated visor, sharp bird-chested cuirass. A diving suit, and beside it an orange aqualung, black mouthpiece, flippers, mask. An empty human envelope, semi-transparent, streaks of bluish veins, shaved skull and thick growth in the crotch, blurred facial features, unzipped from the throat to the fork of the legs.

ACQUIRE? YES.

Keeping the cloakroom attendant in her field of vision (he gives a long, sobbing sigh and scratches at his sideburns without waking), she takes eleven steps and lifts the mackintosh off its hanger. Puts it on. Buttons it up and takes another three steps over to the sleeping man.

ELIMINATE? NO.

The door leading outside is in the far corner.

She goes out, raising the collar.

Outside there is fog – heavy, choking, damp, like wet cotton wool. Sounds sink into it, losing their way and tumbling out on to the cobblestones of the road in the wrong places. She looks around: visibility is fifteen or sixteen feet. Steam rises out of the grilles of the drains and blends into the fog. Gas lights glow along the avenue, each one surrounded by an oily, appliqué halo. As she sets off, hugging the clammy brick wall, a cab comes hurtling out of the fog (she presses back against the bricks) and rumbles past. The steam-powered Cyclops pulling it clanks its hooves and pumps its pistons. The cabby has the face of an indifferent owl.

Sitting by the wall is a legless beggar. Bristling sideburns. A hat – wide-brimmed, crumpled – lying in front of him, copper coins glinting on its bottom.

ACQUIRE? YES.

Without stopping, she bends down, picks up the hat, turns it over on to her head. Coins shower down on to her shoulders. Without looking, she plucks two of them out of the air and walks on to the crossroads.

Big Ben skewers the low, damp sky, looming up over her head through the gaps in the fog. A transparent water tower. She can see coloured liquid circulating through the thick, meandering pipes: bright lemon-yellow, intense lilac, lush green. Up at the top, in the box with a dial facing each corner of the world, is the four-chambered bulk of a gigantic heart, driving the liquid round as it pulses. The single hand of the clock notes each of its contractions by moving forward one division.

She clicked open the turnip-shaped pocket watch and checks.

4.46   4.47

'Sensation!'

An urchin in a checked cloth cap darts out of the thick folds of fog.

'Sinister secret of the suburbs! Jack the Ripper's latest victim! Another prostitute savagely slaughtered last night!'

She holds out one of the two coins to the boy – a small, rough nickel with a portrait of Queen Victoria. Then she unfolds the damp, distended pages of *The Times*, which decline to rustle.

'HEAD CUT OFF!'

The large print leaps out at her. Beside it a photograph of a severed head.

Her head.

She leafs through the other pages.

'HEAD SHIP OF HER MAJESTY'S FLEET LEAVES SCAPA-FLOW.' An admiral in a peaked cap smoking a bent Peterson. The admiral is her.

'CITY HEAD APPEALS TO LONDONERS' CONSCIENCE.' Up on a platform, the mayor wearing tails, one arm extended. Her again. And again. And again. And again.

ACQUIRE? NO.

She crumples up *The Times*, half-expecting the water to stream out between her fingers as if she were squeezing a sponge, and tosses it away. As she crosses the square, unseen mutant pseudo-pigeons rasp their mandibles together, applauding with leathery wings as they flutter up from under her feet. There is the glint of a ruby-red eye. Then, mingling with the applause of the wings, a clicking sound. A blind man. White cane. Grubby sideburns. Round, rose-tinted glasses.

ACQUIRE? YES.

She snatches the glasses as she glides past, clutching them

between her finger and thumb. The blind man tuts despairingly, clutching wildly at the fog with hands clad in fingerless woollen mittens. She moves on. She likes the glasses. Through them the world changes instantly and completely.

She discovers the fortune-telling machine on the corner of Paddington Street and Baker Street (as she reads the street name signs, she shuns the cold fog by huddling up inside the mackintosh, but still it feels as if some lout is trying to stick his chilly hands underneath it). She drops the second coin, a silvery dime, into the machine and pulls the lever's ebonite handle towards her. Somewhere in Babbage's karmic computational mechanism something wheezes and grunts; bluish-grey exhaust fumes belch out of its various nozzles in fits and starts, there is a heart-stopping clang and the little wheels in the countless windows begin whirling. Past her eyes flicker the various sign systems of mankind: Latin, Cyrillic, Hebrew; hieroglyphs, cuneiform, pictograms, kana syllabic script, Arabic curlicues. She shifts from one bare, frozen, dirty foot to the other as she waits for the verdict of Fate. One after another the letters click and come to a halt in their little windows.

'WHEN THE HEAD IS OFF, WHY MOURN THE HAIR?' She carries on stamping her feet for a little longer.

5.52 5.53

She presses the 'return' key. Hammers her fist against the machine's casing. The mechanism starts puffing again, belching out a puff of smoke and twirling its little wheels hysterically.

'TWO HEADS ARE BETTER THAN ONE.'

She curses and trudges on.

After the third or fourth corner (someone tries to mug her along the way, she kicks out without looking and the riff-raff in a moth-eaten bowler hat bounces off and disappears in the mist), her eyes encounter the bright blaze of a picture house. An array of light-bulbs one and a half storeys high offer the bored citizens of London two films: PROFESSOR DOWELL'S HEAD and BRING ME THE HEAD OF ALFREDO GARCIA.

Three more corners later (she is turning them now without thinking about it, leaving her silent internal course-recorder to note each change of heading), there is a policeman wearing high lace-up boots standing with his feet apart, his hands clasped behind his back and his chin jutting out. A Smith and Wesson weighs down the pigskin holster on his belt.

When he notices her, he beckons with one finger.

She walks over, clutching the lancet in her pocket.

The bobby leans down. He is at least six feet tall and smells of brewer's yeast.

'The heart,' he hisses in a suggestive whisper, 'should never rule the head.' He thinks for a moment and adds, 'Ma'am'.

ACQUIRE? YES.

ELIMINATE? YES.

With a polite movement she slits the policeman's throat from ear to ear and steps back to avoid the falling body (eyes goggling, hands still clasped behind the back, blood surging impetuously from the gash). Plucking the dead man's revolver from its holster, she sticks the weapon in her pocket, wipes the lancet on the defunct bobby's uniform, and walks away quickly, the hem of her mackintosh trailing along the pavement.

98%

02

07

03

10.12 10.13

Around the next corner a whiff of chemical putrefaction announces the wide expanse of the Thames.

She cuts along the embankment. Virtually stagnant, the river glistens through the gaps in the cast-iron railings. Here and there six-inch-long flying leeches covered with short, thick bristles leap high out of the water, fluttering their rainbow-coloured wings. London Bridge, almost eaten away by fog, seems about to collapse on her head. Occasional steam-powered locomobiles turn off the road on to it.

In the middle of the river, a leviathan looms up out of the fog: the Royal Navy's latest aircraft-carrying submarine dreadnought, 'Son of Thunder'. Only two of its eight decks project above the water, the gleaming, armour-plated skin goose-pimpled with rivets. Against the forged iron of its stern, the thick bitumen of the Thames slowly crumples. Tall funnels smoke thinly.

Suddenly a siren howls. Floodlights begin sweeping their beams to and fro and out of the bowels of the ship rises a flit-wing fighter with the imperial crown on its flank. Its wings start flapping. Thick brown smoke billows into the air.

A block further on, the words blink at her: THE HEADLESS HORSEMAN.

Pushing open the low doors, she goes into the saloon – a public house in the North American style fashionable with the inhabitants of the metropolis. Behind the bar an octopus-like barman in a waistcoat twitches his ginger sideburns. She sits down on a tall, extremely heavy stool and places her hat at her elbow. The shelves are groaning with gin, whiskey and rum. Leaning across the bar, the barman inspects her bare feet. She wiggles her frozen toes amicably and he gives her a knowing wink.

'Always keep your feet warm,' he declaims didactically, 'and your head cool.'

Without bothering to ask, he takes a thick-walled glass and pours out three fingers of his strongest rum – 146 degrees proof, classy wax seal.

'On the house,' he says with another wink.

She takes a sip. It tastes good, hot and very heady. She wipes the corners of her eyes with the joint of her middle finger. Inside the mackintosh, the pocket watch jangles. Click. The hand of the dial is back up to 100. She puts it away and finishes the rum in a single gulp. The scorching heat shoots up into her eyes, setting the world shimmering like a mirage.

'I want the key,' she says, hearing her own voice for the first time.

The barman puts on a puzzled face, knitting his ginger eyebrows in amazement.

'I want the key,' she repeats, clenching her fists. Something bursts, scattering in a firework display of glinting stars. The barman spreads his arms in protest. She glances down. The glass. She forgot.

She is wrapping her palm round the large butt of the revolver in her pocket when tuneless sleighbells tinkle inside the barman's waistcoat. With a gesture of apology he extracts two ivory cups connected together by an electric cord. Mr Bell's latest invention: a wireless telephone apparatus. He puts one cup to his ear and listens, all the while watching her intently. Then he puts the apparatus away and nods.

'Follow me.'

She obeys and finds herself shut in the toilet.

She strokes the edge of the porcelain sink. Takes off her glasses and puts them in her pocket with the revolver. Washes her hands. Then, after glancing round, sticks first one dirty foot and then the other under the powerful jet. There is a huge mirror hanging on the wall in an ornate bronze frame. She looks herself up and down. Short hair sticking out in every direction like ash-grey feathers. Crazy eyes. Chin with a dimple. Neck. Mackintosh. She reaches out a hand and prods her reflection in the chest. The mirror swings away with a gentle squeak, revealing the iron steps of a spiral staircase leading down. A long way down.

The space behind the dusty plush curtain is saturated with a heady, sweetish odour. There are half-naked people lying on old mattresses, soft, fluffy little clouds hovering above their heads.

A chubby Chinaman in a dirty robe minces up to her and jabbers in an incomprehensible fashion whilst tugging on his ponytail. She waits for him to finish.

'I want the key.'

The Chinaman begins jabbering again. She grabs his Adam's apple between her thumb and forefinger.

'I. Want. The. Key.'

The Chink begins nodding desperately. A nodding Chinese doll. When she releases her grip, he scurries away through the curtained doorway and returns seconds later with a hookah that looks like a large, complicated hourglass, and a small boxwood casket. She waves her hand and the obsequious Oriental is gone.

Sitting down on the floor with her legs crossed, she grips the hookah between her teeth and opens the casket.

Lying inside in tight, embryonic curls are little, wrinkled, dried lizards . . . no, little Chinese dragons. With whiskers just like shrimps. She scoops up a handful, tips them into the bowl of the hookah and sets light to them.

The white, translucent flame flares up and spreads outwards in avid concentric rings.

Smoke is born.

She draws it into herself through the seething water. One drag. Another.

There is a strange new sizzling in her head. A hissing. Suddenly it is raining myriads of weightless fish scales. The white, translucent flame in the bowl contracts to a point, then blasts outward in all directions. Swamping the entire basement. She feels the terrible, moist heat with her entire body. Her mackintosh is instantly soaking wet, inside and out. She stands up, unable to feel herself and tears open the sopping wet cocoon, scattering buttons across the floor. She is streaming with sweat. She runs her hands over her hips and her palms skid.

The fabric of reality is warping in the unbearable heat, contracting, shrivelling, cracking, splitting, falling apart. Shattering into shreds and tatters. Falling at her feet. Her feet are burning painfully. She staggers – and then she sees.

There is no basement. There are no mattresses. There are no drugged bodies. There is no Chinaman. There is no plush door-curtain, or hookah, or iron spiral staircase.

There is only a crude, clumsy, slipshod stage set. Cardboard. Dribbles of glue. Papier-mâché. The opium den has been daubed on the backdrop by a drunken hack. The people lying on the stage aren't people. Only wind-up dolls. Oval wooden heads painted with emphatically meticulous human faces. Fibrous wigs. Plywood limbs with openings cut into them. Hinged joints.

Stacked haphazardly are other backdrops depicting a saloon bar, London Bridge, Big Ben, streets and corridors. Through cracks she can see other toy-like, table-top-size models. The eight-deck dreadnought 'Son of Thunder'. A locomobile. A cab. Babbage's fortune calculator. An embroidered rag-doll policeman.

Suddenly, two dolls rise jerkily to their feet from the wooden floorboards and advance towards her, strutting like chickens. She grins and blurs into a somersault, hurling herself towards them.

Chips of wood go flying. The dolls are smashed and scattered. A severed wooden head bounces across the floorboards.

Hearing a rustling behind her, she swings round.

Perched on a lopsided gantry is a doll in a leather waistcoat. Coarse ginger fibres dangling from its cheeks. A large bottle of rum in one hand.

She flings herself at it.

The doll squeezes the bottle and the glass is suddenly soft, like rubber. A flexi-jet of lush green spurts towards her and wraps her in its viscous, prehensile tongue. She falls. The final green ring closes around her throat.

The doll hobbles across to where she lies. Rummaging through the tatters of her it draws out the Smith and Wesson and takes aim at her forehead. She closes her eyes tight.

'A bad head gives the legs no rest,' squeaks the doll.

And shoots.

Leaning down over the naked body sprawling in the green puddle, the doll uproots the pocket watch with blunt, splintery fingers and opens the lid.

The triumphant chords of 'Rule Britannia' ring out.

LIFE	0%
WEAPONS	0
CHARGES	0
BONUSES	0
TIME	15.06

'Well,' Vitek chortled behind his back. 'Bought it again, have you, kamikaze kid?'

'Pretty much.'

Capitulating, Vadim moved back from the low radiation monitor that was flooded on the inside with blood and squeezed his eyes shut.

'Some tricky bloody level . . .'

DO YOU WISH TO LAUNCH THE LAST SAVED VERSION?

'No.'

'That's simple shit,' giggled Vitek. 'I've got a lot further than that. There's this real mindbender, fixing this tower together with screws . . .'

DO YOU WISH TO EXIT?

'Yes.'

'Give me a drink.'

'For your own wake?' snorted Vitek. 'Go for it, zombie. It's on the house.' He mimicked the game with a mocking grin.

Vadim pictured Vitek nonchalantly taking down the brown bottle of Riga Balsam from the top shelf and crushing it in his powerful palm, sending a narrow black rapier-blade springing out of its neck to pin him to the wood-veneer of the wall like one of Nabokov's scaly-winged victims.

HEADCRUSHER III DEMO VERSION
Mission 4. THE AGE OF INNOCENCE
Level 1. JACK THE RIPPER
Difficulty level 3: I'LL KILL ALL THE OTHERS
Time: 15 MINUTES 6 SECONDS

Vadim tossed back three shot glasses to the eternal rest of Sara Taft and was surprised to feel a hideous cramp in his calf muscles as he exited from the warm semi-darkness of Vitek's basement into the 5 p.m. gloom. His face was stung by an aerodynamic stream of loathsome wet snow. What would our Christmas be like without driving sleet?

He'd agreed to meet Rita in the Eldorado hotel at half past five. Maybe he should give her a bell . . . 'I'm sick . . . a virus . . . at home in bed.' She'd see through him. Okay: 'I'm busy. Urgent work. A delegation of fraternal Santa Clauses from Morgan Stanley, meet them at the airport, lunch the bankers, munching wankers . . .' No. He turned a corner and the snow continued mysteriously to lash straight into his face.

From the Christmas window displays of the city's main street, serried ranks of matey red Santa Clauses in assorted sizes extended pressing invitations and offered glittering seasonal reductions. And, at their very head, where the street's perspective lines converged, the gigantic figure of the central, dominant Santa Claus. The boss and commander of all the Clauses – an inflatable, five-metre-tall Santa with electrified eyes, baring his gleaming and no doubt extremely sharp teeth, each the size of a Soviet spade, at the very same spot occupied a dozen years earlier by the cast-iron Lenin, and standing in the very same right-hand-outflung, big-chief pose.

Vadim shivered and realised that his jacket was soaked. He needed some hot punch. Hot, sweet plonk. Squeeze the juice out of half a lemon. Sprinkle in some sharp crushed cloves. A pinch of cinnamon. Honey. And add something strong, nice and strong. Sit at home, watching the blank window, seeing nothing. Switch on the television, switch off the sound. And sit there. Sipping away. On . . . his . . . own.

The streets were filled with slightly hyper people combing the city centre in a life-affirming quest, getting sucked into the gleaming vortices of the shops and the cosy little drains of the cafés, each one lugging along something edible or giveable, or else hunting for it, slamming car doors, packing things. Thinking positive. The wheels of the exhilarating holiday-season industry turning as normal.

Slurp-slurp. Vadim turned another corner. A leviathan standing smack in the middle of the pavement loomed up out of the falling snow. The latest off-the-road dreadnought Jeepster. Gleaming chrome-plated skin, goose-pimpled with glinting droplets. The condensed-milk current of humanity crumpling against its tubular frame. The exhaust pipe smoking thinly. And – squeezed out through the micron-wide cracks of the hermetically sealed body under the pressure of extreme decibels – thin, sharp jets of gangster-rap. Crossing the street at an angle, Vadim arrived at the row of flower kiosks along the edge of Wermansky Park.

Behind their dirt-and-snow-spattered windows, glass cubes and parallelepipeds held tropical swirls of varicoloured blooms. Candle-flames lurked in the thick of the jungle, combusting the damp air into nutritious carbon dioxide. After a moment's hesitation, Vadim bought a metre-long banality, the spiny sword of a pink Dutch rose. The tightly folded bud with the unnaturally lush colour had absolutely no scent at all. The saleswoman drew the sword out of the tin-plate scabbard of a vase and wrapped it in newspaper. The woman had the face of an indifferent owl.

Arsehole, said Vadim to the slimy blue shrimp of a Mazda speeding on its way after splashing him with liquid mud.

Looming up over his head through the gaps in the snow, skewering the low, damp sky, was the national symbol, encased in scaffolding. The monument to the Freedom that had been given. But now, instead of the green woman sitting on a grey stone phallus and holding three stars in her hands (not five – an ordinary and average Freedom, not the vintage variety), there was a tall, wooden Aztec pyramid, draped in advertising awnings. And blazoned right across the word FREEDOM in massive letters: RIMI!! EXCLUSIVE!! RIGHT HERE AND NOW!! 25% OFF!!! And higher up:

the CHRISTMAS BIGBURGER, wearing a scarlet and white Santa-Claus hat made of ketchup and mayonnaise under the universalist emblem of McDonald's. Down below, replacing the guard of honour discharged from duty by the repair work, a policeman strode backwards and forwards, then paused, his feet planted wide apart in their high lace-up boots, his hands clasped behind his back and his chin jutting out. A standard-issue truncheon in a holster of imitation leather providing an unimpressive final touch to the impressive law-keeping backside.

Slurp-slurp.

Before entering the Eldorado, Vadim paused, glancing around absentmindedly. The stunted skyscraper of the Hotel Latvia was like a live broadcast from the storming of Grozny. With its facing panels removed, its reinforced concrete innards spilling out, the stripped box that looked as if it had taken several direct hits from tank cannon. The hotel was undergoing repairs too, thoroughgoing ones. After reconstruction, this high-status, third generation illegitimate offspring of the dalliance between Soviet modernism and le Corbusier was due to be reborn as presentable, four-star, euro-standard, euro-real-estate that would no longer gaze down in barbaric menace at the neatly ironed euro-pensioners unpacking themselves from their euro-buses at its foot.

What a genuinely dynamic, creative, vital mini-power we do live in after all, thought Vadim. Always something being built, repaired, finished, retouched, painted, varnished, upgraded. However, if you took a close look, then it was always – with the exception, of course, of the national phallus – hotels, or taverns, or underground carparks, or casinos, or computer-game arcades, or supermarkets that were benefiting from this make-over. Facilities for servicing the public. He chuckled. Services high and low. All specifically designed to trap money in these hotels, inns, casinos, carparks, filling stations and supermarkets. The fastest-growing sector of business? Gaming machines. Where all those bucks came from, who was spending them and on what, remained as unclear as ever.

We don't produce anything and we don't export to anybody else. All we do is service each other, the tourists from the west, the cash flow. A country of service. Serviceland. In this conveyor-belt Gruppenservice, servicing and being serviced, exchanging – not item for item, or goods for money, or money for power – but service for service, you yourself are varnished, plastered, retouched, upgraded: rapidly and imperceptibly averaged into presentable euro-standard euro-real-estate. Into a bright, shiny state of permanent unreality.

Vadim was fleetingly reflected in the glass door of the Eldorado. He reached out his hand and prodded himself in the chest. Then he floated up to the second floor on a convection current of confectionery odours. Two tables from the door of the café, he spotted a competently styled, light-chestnut bob. Sitting in quarter-profile, with one leg crossed over the other, but not forgetting to hold her back straight, Rita was leafing through the brightly coloured pages of a plump and popular weekly publication. Meanwhile, with great precision, her right hand was using a tiny, gleaming spoon to detach tiny, identical petals of sponge from a piece of layer cake the shape of a flat-iron. The three layers were different colours. Bright lemon-yellow, intense lilac, lush green. Into the top was stuck a dry biscuit heart.

Vadim hesitated again for a moment and watched the snow through the windows.

As sharp and stinging as a boxer's fists outside, from inside the white flakes appeared unhurried, burrowing through the air with the stubborn perseverance of moles.

Coaxingly caressed, gently smacked and cautiously squeezed, his prick moved into position – like a kung fu fighter holding his stance before the beginning of another duel. Rita's lips immediately closed on it in a firm, competent embrace.

There was something calmly assured and possessive about the way she took him. With his back buried deep in the soft mattress of the Lithuanian bed, Vadim swayed his hips forward to meet the slippery, measured thrusting of the tongue, the sharp, painful pricking of the teeth. The head of his penis was glowing like a forty-watt light bulb. Mechanically he drew a straight braid of light-chestnut hair from behind Rita's ear and coiled it round his fingers, observing the gradual erasure of a patch of 'delirious plum' lipstick that, by some miracle, had not yet been rubbed off her upper lip (there was nothing delirious about it, it was just lilac with a sparkle). Eraser-prick, Vadim thought and almost giggled, but instead began stimulating every thrust of his cock with a gasped vowel. O. A. E. O-o-o. U. O. O. O. He released the braid of hair, fumbled briefly at Rita's dangling breasts and stroked one of her airily bouncing buttocks.

'. . . It is the custom at this joyous festival of Christmas to be positive,' declared the boorish voice of Acting Prime Minister Stelle, continuing the annual goodwill message to the country from the television behind Vadim's shoulder. 'But I am not inclined to deceive the country with a note of unjustifiable optimism! I am not Santa Claus, I am the leader of a crisis government! And therefore, my fellow-citizens, you must forgive me if even today I tell my people unpleasant but wholesome truths!'

At the phrase 'my people', Rita released the slobbery prick from her mouth – plump, red, bigheaded – threw herself backwards in quizzical entreaty and spread her slim legs. Vadim obligingly slid down and slithered in between them, with his left elbow skidding across the black, silky Lycra sheet (after a couple of dozen washings, the gift from an old girl-friend may have lost some of its negroid sex-appeal, but it still dutifully served the function of erotic allusion). Thrusting his face into the smell and taste that provoked such a mixture of excitation and irritation in him, he fastened his lips on the dark, shiny, out-turned lobules. Yes, yes, said Rita. Vadim paused for a moment to overcome the irritation and used his index finger to assist the insertion of his surgically stiffened tongue.

'. . . Complaining is pointless!' the acting premier said behind Vadim's back, hammering home his point. 'Many . . . very many people are still inclined to follow their old Soviet habit and blame us, the government, if they are poor or unsuccessful; or they blame big capital and the financiers! The only answer I can give to them is one of our trouble-some eastern neighbours' sayings: don't blame the mirror for the pockmarks on your own face. You yourselves, you yourselves . . .'

Why you rotten bastard, thought Vadim, toiling away honestly at the bitter, yeasty interior with monotonous, lapping movements . . . forwards and back . . . up and down . . . left and right . . . He was somewhat disconcerted to discover that his own spring had slackened off a bit. Well, what do you know.

He wasn't firing on all cylinders, his sexual engine required a fuel injection boost. Vadim applied a mental effort that was, alas, becoming habitual. His male chauvinist brain began throwing up alternatives.

A homogenised silicone blonde with a Playboy rabbit's profile stamped on her shaved pubis. A curly-haired mulatto woman with her legs open, her thick lips set in a cynical smile and her eyes in a whorish stare. A poster one and a half metres long, extracted from the thick block of the Scandinavian porno magazine *Privat*: six or seven different-coloured bodies – at first glance you couldn't tell how many – woven into one mind-boggling knot, the hyperbolically huge pricks of male professionals thrusting into the one-size-fits-all openings of female professionals at action-hero angles. Interesting, thought Vadim, still forcing his tongue through its excruciating gymnastic paces: in the 1950s long-distance lorry-drivers used to hang cartoon pin-up girls in lacy panties in the cabins of their behemoths, now they stick up naked girls of the month; perhaps in another ten years they'll turn to hard-core . . .

'. . . If you happen to have earned a hundred lats, don't spend them on drink, buy something, for instance a saw . . .'

Rita mooed politely, he mewed ritually in reply and clamped his lips on her clitoris almost violently. Having used the extremist banquet from the Swedish poster – an extravaganza of pink and brown flesh bordering on catastrophic, bloody carnage – as a mental springboard, he rummaged further in the stockrooms of his memory, reviewing the latest acquisitions. Smilla Pavovich. The frail, fragile Hollywood starlet-superstar. That was the one.

Vadim roughly grabbed hold of the Yugoslavian-Ukrainian starlet's tousled, spectrally coloured locks and dragged her into the active focus of his fantasy. Gazing intently into the unreal eyes, he began firmly, relentlessly slamming, thrusting, pounding, forcing her down into the soft dough of the bed . . . His prick, engorged once again, pressed hard against the sheet, his lips curled in a sneer. Oh, I want you, said Rita, almost in fright. Aha. Vadim jerked away and pushed himself up, hastily sealed his fifteen and a half centimetres into the thin latex of a Singapore condom, fell back down, thrust, slipped in. They were off.

It was easy. He began moving around inside her, cantilevered on his outstretched arms, scrutinising the rim of violet mascara on Rita's closed eyelids.

'. . . Instead of abusing the government, why not try being a bit less lazy and at least cleaning your teeth every day! If you're a failure, a loser, as our western friends say, if you are, to put it bluntly, a waste of space – then you've only yourself to blame! Your happiness and prosperity are your own problem and nobody else's, and you have to deal with it!'

Mr Sandis Stelle was the leader of the National Conservative Party, an industrial magnate, one of the richest men in the country, a constant subject of despatches from the criminal and financial fronts and the object of regular investigations by state prosecutors that failed miserably with equal regularity. He had begun his career selling tulips at the Sokolniki market in Moscow.

'We're not going to do it for you. If your old parents can't feed themselves on their pension. If your children have no food and no money to get them to school. Then it's your fault! And what sort of man does that make you?'

Moving in time with his own jerking to and fro, Rita's angular shoulder alternately obscured and revealed the acting prime minister's wild-boar-like face. It resembled a hairy, meaty fist. Vadim propped himself up on his left elbow, gripped the bony promontory of Rita's hip with his right hand and pulled her back towards him, assisting her hot wetness into a loose, shallow fit over his flagging prick. The end was nigh at last.

With every successive beat of the accelerating rhythm some key tightened the spring in his crotch one more turn. Again, again. Again.

The spring threatened to snap. With an effort of will Vadim slowed the key a little.

Now . . . Rita gave a brief moan and shuddered to a standstill. The starting signal. Do it. He released the key and immediately it span through several more turns. Zing – the spring snapped. The repulsive talking head slid out of his field of vision like the ground below a swing, and into the upwardly mobile lay-out artist of a fashionable design bureau, the junior office-worker of the press service of a leading bank came. Or rather, into the disposable, hygienic package of a South Asian condom. He waited a moment, then withdrew with a soft plop, like a cork out of a bottle.

' . . . That doesn't bother us,' concluded the acting premier, peering over Rita's impeccably styled and still unruffled bob, straight at the bridge of Vadim's nose. His eyes glared out from under his eyebrows like the frenzied Red Army man in the famous poster *Have You Volunteered*. 'And nobody, do you hear, nobody is going to help you!'

Rita sat up. Hastily averting his eyes, Vadim gave a quick smile, lobbing the need to say something over into her court. But she answered him with an identically appropriate, precisely judged smile. Stood up. Slipped her feet into his slippers. Went out. Vadim watched her go gratefully. Thirty seconds later he heard the shower running. Vadim rummaged in Rita's handbag and took a cigarette from the pack of Barclay Lights.

The TV camera crept slowly along the ranks of the most important faces in the country – the same expression of sanctimonious propriety frozen on all the indistinguishable, large-format features; sweat drying in the cold air, tightening the skin; candle-flames flickering above hands piously clasped together. The Barclay Light had a soapy taste. The bass notes of the organ shuffled ponderously from one leaden, governmental foot to the other.

Vadim stubbed out the half-smoked cigarette against the convection heater, stood up and squeamishly tugged off the shrunken rubber with his finger and thumb. Then he trudged through into the kitchen and dropped the condom (which had immediately puckered up and looked like the cast-off skin of a pygmy snake) into the rubbish bin. In the hallway the door of the toilet clicked. After a moment's thought, Vadim poured himself some cheap Cahors, shaking the last drops out of the bottle. It made almost a full glass.

When he went back into the room, Rita was sitting half-dressed on the edge of the bed, gazing into a little round mirror as she completed her war-paint with rapid brushstrokes.

'Where are you going?' Vadim asked in surprise and took a sip.

'I didn't want to upset you before, darling,' she said, smacking her lips together like a fish to tamp down the 'delirious plum'. Still not looking at Vadim, she froze for a moment to assess the results of her work and then snapped the mirror shut, satisfied. 'But I've been invited to Uldis's place today. You know, I told you about him, our deputy director for development?' She finally favoured him with a glance. Vadim took another sip without offering her any. 'He's having a party at the dacha, the bosses will be there. It's important.' Remembering to check that her nail polish was intact, she fluttered her fingers in front of her face.

'Ah.'

Rita fished a petite little mobile out of her handbag and

ran her fingers over the green, glowing buttons.

'Hello? Svetik? Are you on your way? Okay. I'll be downstairs.'

Vadim sat in an armchair, covered himself with a rug and carried on drinking his Cahors in small sips, watching as she quickly adjusted her dress, slipped on her shoes, tidied her hair, flung on her coat, gave him a hasty kiss (engulfing him in the fragrance of an unfamiliar perfume), tossed him a smile, said 'Ciao, darling, call me tomorrow, okay?' and slammed the front door behind her. He thought belatedly that he ought to be feeling offended, disappointed, perhaps even angry. But he didn't feel anything of the kind. On the contrary, what he felt was something like relief.

On the TV an excited, jangling holiday peal of church bells, sleigh-bells and jingle-bells rang out. Vadim glanced at the black square of the window then ran his eyes over the walls in search of entertainment. Assessing the level of liquid in his glass – one mouthful – he threw off the rug and, just as he was, naked and shivering, dragged himself across to the little copper frame hanging on a nail beside the door.

He reread the old text with a wry smile.

Typed in bold sixteen-point Palatino, it was a beautiful print-out of his first creation in the secret WORDART directory. It had been one year old yesterday and had as its origin a perfectly innocuous requisition form put together by Four-Eyes during the pre-Christmas spate of stocktaking and ordering. It went like this:

From the Press Room to the REX Bank office supplies department:

We request the following more or less essential items.

Absolutely essential items:

1. 4 (four) wastepaper bins (meaning buckets. We're going to kick them).
2. 5 (five) display stands. And 1 (one) vodka still to hide behind them.
3. 2 (two) chairs for visitors. And 1 (one) sharp stake, also for visitors.
4. 1 (one) additional Pentium computer as stipulated in the plan. (The safe will have to be removed to make room for the necessary desk to put it on. Please have it brought back full of American dollars, pounds sterling, deutschmarks, French and Swiss francs, Swedish and Danish crowns, securities, gold and silver ingots, precious and semi-precious stones and antiques.)
5. 1 (one) crate of Regalia vodka to celebrate the new computer's arrival. And then a crate of the same beverage every day to inspire the employees with greater enthusiasm.
6. 3 (three) grams of hashish, so there'll be something to go with the vodka. Every day, of course. This is for Apletaev personally.
7. 10 (ten) grams of smack. Every Friday, to improve the mood before the weekend. This is for Apletaev too (the poor guy can't just keep doing hash, there has to be some variety).
8. 1 (one) tab (LSD) on important public holidays. You can guess who it's for yourselves.

Not such absolutely essential items:
1. 1 (one) little table, like a coffee-table (if that's possible. And if it isn't, I still want one).
2. 1 (one) music centre (radio/cassette/ideally plus a CD).

3. 1 (one) Fly grenade-launcher – for office requirements.

Head of the REX Bank press service:
Andrei Vladlenovich Voronin.

Vadim raised his final mouthful of communion-quality wine to eye-level, saluted the print-out with his glass, clinked the Cahors against the copper frame and drained it in one.

5

'Without your pass,' said security guard Gimniuk, gazing into Vadim's eyes with a supremely benevolent and exquisitely courteous smile, 'I can't do that.'

'Listen,' said Vadim, struggling hard to remain within the accepted limits of propriety, 'you know perfectly well who I am. Because you see me every day, don't you? Ten times a day.'

'Not every day,' security guard Gimniuk objected with dignity. 'My shift is every other day.'

'Well . . .'

'Your pass, please.'

'I already explained,' said Vadim, beaming in affectionate loathing. 'I. Forgot. It. I. Was. Hurrying.'

'Then, unfortunately, I can't let you through.'

'What the fuck!' Vadim finally exploded. He felt a sense of relief and liberation combined with a simultaneous awareness of undeniable defeat. 'Bugger it, you know perfectly well. I! Work! Here! I don't want to steal the photocopiers or download porn from the Internet. I'm going to work!'

Security guard Gimniuk's extravagantly patient and supremely polite expression didn't falter; his intently gazing eyes merely glistened a little more moistly.

'I don't know why you're going in, SIR. Every employee of the bank has to carry his pass with him.

'Okay,' sighed Vadim, burned out, 'all right, then. I'll go straight back home. And when my boss asks me to explain why I wasn't at work I'll simply tell him the honest truth – that Mr Gimniuk wouldn't let me past the checkpoint . . .'

'I'm sorry, but that's nothing to do with me,' said Gimniuk, slowly savouring every word. 'I've got my own boss, and precise instructions. Not to let anyone without a pass into the bank. ANYONE. And if anything happens, I'll be in trouble.'

'God Al-mighty!' Vadim guffawed hysterically. 'What can possibly happen?'

'I don't know.' Gimniuk remained unrelentingly serious. 'Something.'

'But that's crazy.'

'Your pass, please.'

Just imagine, my friend, – the words surfaced in Vadim's memory – *I can do that for four hours on end without even getting tired!* How long before you get bored with this, you jumped-up jerk of a janitor? He searched for an answer in the blank eyes and impenetrable mask of sanctimonious officialdom of the spotty punk from the back desk of the classroom, who was always kept down a class and used to spend his time relieving his younger, less hulking classmates of their pocket money.

Scenes like today's were a regular, if not frequent, occurrence at the security checkpoint of REX Bank. Passes, passports, ID cards, credit cards and the driving licence that he didn't have: out of innate thick-headedness, Vadim constantly forgot them all. Unfortunately the bank's security structures were impressive in their range, incorporating an extensive variety of species. These included both internal and external security men in both plain clothes and uniforms specially designed by the avant-garde pacifist designer Birmanis, who for a substantial fee had temporarily become a conservative militarist. Also circulating in the REX Bank bloodstream, constantly mutating and expanding, growing ever more precise and more complex, was a highly intricate system of instructions, rules, regulations, restrictions and authorisations, black and white lists with appropriate amendments and relevant exceptions. As a consequence, every now and then the forgetful press service employee Apletaev would be stopped and, depending on the particular personal inclination and specific good-heartedness of one or another guard, either be let off condescendingly with the good-natured admonishment 'Bring it next time!' or subjected to a long and tedious interrogation: Why? What for? Where? Who gave permission? Till when?

And among the rich natural fauna of the REX Bank's security system there were also one-off specimens like Sergei Gimniuk.

Gimniuk was the same age as Vadim; it even turned out that he'd gone to school in the next district. But, while the future press service employee had been busy honing his demagogic skills, smoking grass and heroically courting the predominant female majority of the student body at the Riga University Faculty of Journalism, the future internal security worker had been FLYING on the HANDWALK and taking ELKS and JARS at the central base of the Northern Fleet of what was then still the Soviet Navy in the town of Severomorsk in the Murmansk region. 'Do you know what a CARP is?' security guard Gimniuk had asked Vadim one day in the smoking room, his eyes glowing brightly after ingesting half a litre of vodka on the occasion of the general office banquet to celebrate REX's seventh anniversary. 'A CARP in the navy is the same as a STINK in the army. A common sailor in his first year of service, get my drift? Take me, for instance: I'm a warrant officer, while you . . .' with a friendly gesture Gimniuk almost thrust his cigarette into

Vadim's face, 'you're not even a STINK! You're just a smell!'
Gimniuk had related the details of YEARMANSHIP, that is,
of the navy's version of the army's GRANDPAHOOD
('yearman' = 'grandpa', i.e. a serviceman of more than one
year's standing) to many people, eagerly and at great length.
He took perverse delight in describing the way he had
ground down recruits when he was a yearman, and the way
they had ground him down when he was a carp. So it was that
Vadim had acquired a lot of very detailed and useful
knowledge about the Northern Fleet's modus vivendi and
operandi. He had learned, for example, that a carp's basic
occupation was not sailing at all, not even on a BOX (a
warship), but FLYING. There were various ways of flying:
scrubbing out the latrine with a toothbrush, or shovelling
up the snow that was sprinkled incessantly from the polar
sky for three quarters of the year (carrying out your own
fatigue duties and your yearman's); DYING ON THE
HANDWALK for hours at a time – that is, walking on your
hands on the parallel bars (how long a carp spends dying is
determined by the particular preferences of his yearman);
receiving into palms crossed in front of the forehead the
generous thrust of a yearman's fist (that's an ELK); or
welcoming a heavy navy stool (a JAR) across the backside
whilst down on all fours.

Having served his time and got his fill of flying and
yearmanning, Warrant Officer Gimniuk, with his brutal,
cherished North Sea memories lovingly preserved in the
demob album of his soul, had got himself fixed up as a
doorkeeper and guard at REX. Through the patronage, of
course, of one of Citron's innumerable deputies, assistants
and special consultants, whose nephew he just happened to
be. And now he proudly trod the vestibules and corridors of
the bank with his compromise stride (the arithmetical mean

between the ceremonial pace of a Kremlin cadet and the swaggering roll of a New Russian bandit). Gimniuk never wore anything but Birmani's designer uniform, despising civvies loudly and publicly. He unvaryingly held his long arms, which reached almost down to his knee-joints, slightly away from his body – the implication obviously being that the bulging, highly trained biceps, triceps and quadriceps, sliding over each other like plates on a suit of armour, made it awkward for him to press his arms against his sides. At the same time, the copiously sweating palm of his right hand continually stroked (with the incessant, nervy passion of a virtuoso wanker) the handle of the black swagger-stick or truncheon that was always dangling at his massive right hip.

'Screwed up again, Vadim?' a spitefully patronising voice asked behind Vadim's back. Four-Eyes was striding cheerfully towards him from the entrance doors, brushing the droplets of water off the orange leather of his Paul Smith coat with an embossed document file. 'Forgot your fake ID again, you Chechen terrorist?'

Nonchalantly, Andrei Vladlenovich Voronin tossed a ready-made gesture of semi-salutation in the general direction of the instantly rigid security guard (the way you might toss your fur coat into the arms of a doorman) and waved the file at Vadim: come on, let's go. Vadim walked past Gimniuk, who had managed in some miraculous manner to merge with his post and become a useful but unobtrusive element of the décor.

'I'll be needing you,' Four-Eyes threw out as he walked on and began whistling the old Soviet favourite 'I do not need the Turkish shore'. Vadim kept pace with him. The doors of the lift closed behind them. Vadim peered furtively sideways, examining Four-Eyes' exquisite tan, and recalled how, on his return (from Tahiti, no less) to a Riga soaking in the grey watery suspension of November, Anrei Vladlenovich had democratically shared his impressions of Polynesia with the enraptured men of the press room. 'Your Van Gogh and the rest of them knew what they were doing all right,' he had said with a majestic gesture. 'That's for sure. The women there are really something else, I tell you . . .'

'Tahiti, Tahiti,' Vadim had chuckled to himself, quoting another old song, 'we haven't been to Tahiti, the food's okay round here!' But Four-Eyes' personalised soundtrack for a combined 'Adventure Library' volume and tourist firm advertising brochure had really been the final straw.

It has come to pass, gentlemen. This lousy fuck has completely lost the plot. Can you hack it? Can you bloody well fathom it? It's absolutely fucking incredible! This rotten, brass-necked, little scumbag bursting at the seams with bucks EARNED BY OUR LABOUR and contemptuously stolen from us by this miserable coward, has the nerve to tell me – would you bloody well credit it? – TO WRITE SOME COPY! Eh? What is the world coming to? If every brazen four-eyed fucker is just going to walk up to you and then – just get a load of this, you dumb cluck! – TELL YOU TO WRITE SOME COPY, then . . . it's the end. The absolute end. A-po-ca-lypse time. Right now. And incidentally, I'm planning to bugger off out of here and drink some vodka. Even if it means I have to dismember, castrate and poke in the pretty, pretentious specs and protruding peepers of ten – no twenty! – lousy fucks like you, Four-Eyes!

FUCK YOU, VILE BOURGEOIS COMPRADORES! DEATH TO THE OPPRESSORS!

And in conclusion, a march. Sing!

Forward, bold legionnaires, to battle we must go,

> Crushing forts with fists of iron, our eyes ablaze with
>   flame,
> With boots of iron trampling down the craven foe
>   (that's you, Four-Eyes)!
> Swords gleaming with the fresh blood shed in our
>   cause's name!

Exactly what copy it was that the employee of the press service had been told to write by the brass-necked scumbag bursting at the seams with bucks earned by our labour and stolen from us in such a cowardly fashion, Vadim didn't have a clue any longer. But he enjoyed rereading his files. In the course of a year the WORDART directory had become swollen with these alien texts: there were probably more of those parasites in there now than honest veteran program files. And even when he had nothing new to contribute to the art of the word, Vadim took pleasure – naturally, as long as there was no one else around – in skimming through his countless inflammatory missives to various demons from the bank's multi-level mythological narrative. It goes without saying that the predominant addressee was Four-Eyes. But every now and then rather larger managerial beasts put in an appearance. For example:

So, how can we sum up the day?
  Why so silent, Pylny? Have you got NOTHING to say? That's bad. Of course, I'd already guessed, but it's a pity all the same. You see, Pylny, A REAL MAN ALWAYS HAS SOMETHING TO SAY! Even if he is so decrepit you can smack the dust out of him with a carpet-beater.
  Ergo: you are Pylny. Not even a man at all. And certainly not any kind of likely lad.
  And by the way, citizens Four-Eyes and Citron, I wouldn't advise

you to start feeling too smug about things. I'm going to put you two up on a white horse. With the royal seal of approval. Kapish, you useless jerks? Right then. Our ten-minute moral education session's over. A-bout turn . . . Quick march! To the handwalk.

The white horse had galloped in from the folklore of the Skoptsy, the Old Believer self-castrator sect. Putting someone up on the horse meant, in the florid language of the old ascetic radicals, 'to deprive of the twins of the member', or simply castrate. The royal seal meant cutting off the member itself as well.

From somewhere behind Murzilla's toothy grin Vadim heard the creak of the gleaming leather trousers that encased the plump young legs of PR talent Olezhek like the skin of a saveloy. With a rapid sequence of touches learned off by heart like musical scales, Vadim catapulted himself out of the incriminating directory and began sifting morosely through the discarded fallen leaves of the regular market summaries and quotations.

Essentially, thought Vadim as he merged, copied, moved and printed files that he didn't need, the PC, the personal computer, is a projection of the human mind as described by the obsessive Freud. On the one had there are the countless X-, T-, W-, and Z-drives, associated with various sectors and planes of the external world, presenting and proposing acceptable versions of yourself to all kinds of potential contacts; on the other hand, the password-protected, shock-proof C, no unauthorised access allowed. The hard drive. And then, deep in the inmost recesses of the hard drive: some WORDART directory, a digitised Freudian id, a binary subconscious, the cesspool and sump of complexes, phobias, philias, manias, suppressed desires. Creep into the hard drive of any computer and you're bound to find the same kind of repository of personal diaries, bad poems, prose that will never be published, letters that will never be posted . . .

'Vadim, is this free?'

It was the junior employee of the discount department on the third floor, the cause – or pretext? – of Vadim's triple orgasm six months previously. Without waiting for an answer, she seated herself determinedly at the cafeteria table where he was imbibing a much needed coffee, and set to work with her knife, fork and jaws in deft desecration of the smug corpse of a well-done steak.

'How are things? Where have you been? What did you do for Christmas? How were the holidays? What are you doing for New Year? Staying here? Or going somewhere? I'm off to Tunisia. Why so glum? Been drinking? How d'you like the weather? Foul, isn't it? Listen, where do they sell joke fireworks? Someone told me there's a shop in the Old Town. What d'you make of that address by Stelle? Did you watch the message? What an incredible guy, eh?'

'He's a wanker,' Vadim just managed to interject. The junior employee faltered for an instant, gave him a quick glance of total incomprehension and carried on in the same vein and in the same rhythm. Marvelling at his own lack of fastidiousness in matters sexual, Vadim despairingly stuck his face into his almost empty cup of espresso and disconnected his external response system.

Outside the cafeteria he made a pit stop in front of the mirror in an attempt to arrange his excuse for a haircut, only to be confronted (in reflection) by the unholy trinity from drive C: plump, round Citron; long, skinny Pylny; and, between them, the robust, optimal Four-Eyes – a kind of transitional evolutionary link between the two. The triumvirate turned in behind a plush curtain that separated off a small room with a fireplace from the hoi polloi in the cafeteria.

'. . . then at least keep your head down,' Vadim heard Citron's irritated voice say, 'and no horseplay with the women, all right, my friend?'

'Not so loud,' Pylny hushed his boss in a gritty voice. Pylny was walking behind the others and Vadim glanced at him as the three passed through the plush curtain. Pylny returned his glance – more prolonged and seasoned with lingering, professional hostility. Then he firmly drew the curtain.

Mikhail Anatolievich Pylny was ageless, like the mummy he resembled. He had his origins in the Fifth Department (the section that dealt with dissidents) of the Committee of State Security (KGB). The committee had ceased to exist. But Pylny, apparently through the diligent efforts of his brother-in-law, Edward Valerievich Citron, had continued with his previous existence, even remaining in charge of security matters, as he had been before. Not state security matters, though. Private security. Information security. A department of REX bore this name, and Pylny was its head. The nature of Pylny's present employment was extremely unclear but it undoubtedly involved fiscal engineering. It was that, and his caustically corrosive personality, that had earned him pride of place in the WORDART directory.

When he got home that evening, Vadim dropped the day's catch from the post box into the circle of light imprinted on the couch by the standard-lamp. The rent bill, an advertising newspaper. A rough cardboard rectangle. An advertisement. Again. In bold letters, the word ACCOUNT leapt out at him. Again? This time, though, it was not an

INVESTMENT ACCOUNT, but a pension account. In an easy-to-follow sequence of drawings, the rectangle of cardboard suggested that he should open one today, in order to guarantee himself a happy and secure old age tomorrow.

Farsighted Youth (in the office-gentleman's costume of shirt-tie-glasses-parting and the business-lady's outfit of blouse-suit-bob) was seated at the indispensable computer, thriftily dropping a coin into a euphorically crimson piggy-bank. The pig proceeded to expand with the speed of a diagram in an animal husbandry textbook. The ultimate mega-piggy was then enjoyed by secure, unisex Old Age decked out in shorts-panama-waistcoat-rucksack-idiot-camera. Vadim observed the living embodiments of this cartoon-strip depiction of the twilight years every day from the windows of the press room. Ever since de-Sovietised Riga had acquired a listing as one of the must-do places for visiting, viewing and capturing on Kodak film by western tourists, the place had been full of them.

In the previous century, tourism took place before joining the state service, acquiring a family, turning respectable and putting down roots. Even the shabbiest offshoots of the aristocracy used to make the rounds of Europe, warbling 'Gaudeamus, igitur!' in the likes of gloomy Göttingen, gambolling wildly in the likes of gay Paris and wallowing in leisurely epicurean delights under the olive trees of Greece. In the process accumulating, like a subcutaneous deposit of vitamins, a store of sensual and intellectual impressions to last for the whole of life ahead – before the nerve-endings were worn out, while vital responses were still fresh and emotions still intense.

But nowadays, the dominant sequence was precisely the reverse: you devoted the best, most active and productive years of your life to making a career, earning yourself haemorrhoids by squatting in a square box of an office, goggling short-sightedly at a monitor and assiduously nurturing your future pension income. So that years later, having attained the cherished position of senior manager and acquired the thoroughly homogenised consistency of an impotent old fart, you could launch happily into retirement and take your place on the planes-and-boats-and-trains of the well-worn tourist routes. You were free. Your life was your own. The world was your oyster. No pleasures were barred to you. Except that you were no longer capable of doing anything or wanting anything, and you really didn't need all of this. You were emasculated, squeezed dry. Used up. All your vital juices had been expended on the attainment of alienated, abstract goals. What did a successful career mean, after all? A babe with D-cup boobs and legs up to her armpits? A Rabelaisian lunch? A tankerful of Veuve Clicquot? Like fuck.

A gold-plated tin medal. A 'Successful Life' badge of honour. But the real significance of your run – 'think positive!' – was only known to the guy who pinned that badge on you. The guy who had used up your vital biological energy in the furtherance of his own non-biological interests.

Vadim was reminded once again of his favourite film *The Matrix*, in which humanity is enslaved by cybernetic intelligence and transformed into a plantation of living batteries, ripening in rows of hermetic containers and disposed of when exhausted. It had always seemed to him that this was not the fantastic anti-utopia of the critics' reviews, but perfectly straightforward realism.

English had a good word that was hard to translate into Russian: 'wired'. It meant something like 'plugged in'. Connected to the grid.

Maybe it was some kind of organic, subconscious

resistance, a rejection of the idea of being 'wired', that prevented Vadim, for instance, from acquiring a mobile phone. Maybe subconsciously he perceived this convenient, portable and entirely affordable means of communication as a marker, a precise radio beacon, like the ones ornithologists use when they ring birds. Now, my boy, they will always know where you are – so whenever they want, they can claim you, activate you, use you . . .

Vadim spilled some tea on to the kitchen table and put the pension account card under his steaming mug. He smiled faintly at the gentle menthol-light tickle of yet another attack of pleasant paranoia. His memory promptly reminded him that the previous attack had been triggered by the REX BROKERAGE INVESTMENT ACCOUNT booklet, a gift to him from the same post box. But maybe, thought Vadim, taking a gulp of hot tea, there was some meaning to all this? Maybe the sequencing of all these supposed advertising texts and slogans and their contents was not accidental at all? Maybe someone out there – or even *over* there – was using them to communicate with him via the oracle of the post box? Trying to tell him something? Warn him about something? Or prompt him to do something?

But what could it be?

6

Too many. Too many parents, drivers, ice-creams, sounds, beggars, meat pasties, children, lovers, pick-pockets, trolley-buses, teenagers, toys, cops, passers-by, kiosks, lumpen-proles, metal, passengers, cables, taxi-drivers, passers-through, flood-lights, petrol fumes, clowns, cigarette butts, music, dirt, winos, fast-food stalls, plastic, petty gangsters, cars, advertisements, whores. This section of the station square was occupied by a stray Dutch funfair. Devices resembling domestic kitchen and laundry appliances gorged on steroids and pumped up to a thousand times their real size covered the ground. Centrifuges for separating the soul from the body, mixers for whipping brains into a smooth homogenous mousse, shakers for agitating the mind. The air was filled with sparks – welding-rod bursts of crimson, purple, egg-yolk yellow, venomous orange – joining with electronically amplified orgasmic screams, shrieks, howls, wailing, gnashing of teeth, and the jostling elbows of rap, pop and hip-hop. Choking all input channels simultaneously: sensory overload from the visual to the olfactory, battering, flattening, swamping, flooding, cocooning in sensation.

Vadim was particularly taken by a ride that looked like a gigantic catapult: between two tall steel masts a sphere was slung on rubber cables. Constructed out of metal tubes, it contained a pair of chairs like those you find at the dentist's. Unwitting visitors were grabbed, seated in the sphere, fastened in with leather belts and shot high up into the air, from where they came hurtling back down, only to be sent soaring upwards again. And so on, for ever.

With the deft aplomb of hardened pros, Boschean monsters – toothy rat-pigs, human heads that had sprouted feet, fish with legs, pterodactyls in boots – whirled sinners round on carousels, rushed them down roller-coasters, inverted them on swings, and raced them along in little goggle-eyed cars.

Vadim tossed his beer bottle into a bin, stumbled by chance on a tent with a rifle range, blasted away ten times with an air rifle at the affably raised hands of the targets, won a marzipan toad as a prize, foisted it on a disdainful little kid, bought a red-hot meat pasty and departed, tipping his last small coppers into the cap of a beggar encamped on the steps leading down into the underpass.

Tacking his way through the meteor stream of oncoming foot traffic, his teeth glued together by the hot cement of dough, minced meat and onion, he squeezed past the serried ranks of smash hits and bestsellers outside the underpass's various commercial outlets. It was all there – from *Poses of the Kama Sutra* to *All on Your Own*, from *Special Services of the World* to *Kremlin Wives – 12*, from *American Psycho* to *The Distinguishing Features of Russian National Literature*, from Balabanov's new film about hunting vampires on the Great Barrier Reef to Greenway's new film about Siamese twins who pull tights over their heads and storm the Louvre, from Lavazza to Nescafé, from Snickers to Schweppes. At the final kiosk Vadim picked up a can of Guinness, leaving a fifty centime counter in exchange.

Two days after Christmas, another four to go till New Year. An empty pause – a gap between the precise points of the two holidays. There would be almost no one working at the office. By four o'clock they were all out the door with semi-legal but perfectly respectable excuses. Four-Eyes had scooted off to a club in his sunflower-yellow Pontiac, having bellyached for days about what a complicated life he had, the poor guy: two parties in the same evening, how could he fit them in and then anyway he had to take the driver, or else what was he going to do? Not drink at the first one? The funny bit was that the bellyaching had been for real.

But even lazy, work-shy Vadim found himself thinking that this slack period between holidays was not much fun. He had absolutely no idea what to do after that 4 p.m. borderline was crossed. He had been about to make for the computers in Vitek's scruffy little basement, but thought about it for a moment and dropped the idea. He couldn't go every day. The Rita idea popped up, feeling obligated, but knowing in advance that it wasn't really wanted.

For a while he sat aimlessly over a tall mug of cranberry grog, the house speciality, in the Master's Inn (the waiter there, a charismatic personality and master of his trade, had once knocked him stone cold dead with an apt quotation from La Rochefoucauld that Vadim hadn't heard before). Then he cruised around the centre of town, like a billiard ball launched at random off the cushion. He didn't feel like going home. Suddenly he got the crazy idea of going back to the office. And then suddenly it didn't seem so very crazy. On the contrary, it even had a certain perverted charm about it. The place was empty. No one there. And his pass was warm in his pocket.

Vadim had heard they'd set up a video camera on the roof of one of the buildings that bordered the main square. So now this cult urban site (a regular point of assignation with a constant flow of people waiting under the clocktower named after the Laima sweet factory) was transmitted on-line in real time via the Internet. You could set up a date, and then cosy up in the warmth of your own home with a cup of tea to watch on your computer the dumb girl hanging about in the frost, shuffling her feet, freezing, too daft to naff off to the nearest café. There was someone sitting comfortably in front of his monitor now, sipping tea and gloating as he observed Vadim cross the square and disappear into the Old City.

On the filthy wing of the immense, once-white Cadillac lording it over the parking lot at the Hotel de Rôme, someone had traced out in the dirt: 'Nobody washes tanks!' As Vadim drew level with the Irish bar, he gazed up at the suspiciously accurate stencilling on the façades of the Old City, which passed off its tiled pinnacles plagiarised from Hans Christian Andersen as a subtle historical allusion in typical post-modernist fraudster style. On the corner of the little square a girl in a poncho playing a violin was like a beautiful photographic negative: dark, swarthy face and bleached hair. She was holding the bow almost motionless, like a wood turner holding his file, and the sparks of wild Celtic dance music seemed to fly out from under it of their own accord.

'Excuse me, do you mind if I have a word with you?' An irksome youth with the smile of a travelling salesman moved between Vadim and the pavement in front of him in a well practised, perfectly executed manoeuvre.

'Yes, I do mind,' Vadim growled, attempting to outflank this commercial traveller, but the youth space-warped and materialised again dead ahead.

'But surely you'd like to know about your future?' he rapped out quickly, still holding on tight to his smile. 'To get some answers to the most important questions of existence and solve your problems? We offer you universal . . .'

Vadim irritably took the little piece of paper from the importunate hand – THE CHURCH OF UNIFIED ENERGIES, which had as its logo a cross inscribed in a mandala on a star of David – and crumpled it up, despatched it into the gaping violin-case at the feet of the photo-negative girl. The future . . . Future indefinite. The New Year, its conventional boundary, that dividing line that changed lives, only four days away. Four strange days when everybody, no matter how sober-minded they were, strained to understand the karmic balance of the past and cast a spell over their immediate future – and actually almost believed in those toasts about next year being different from this one.

Glancing rapidly round to make sure there were no cops, Vadim set down his empty can of Guinness on the road. On his left he could see into the glowing, bluish interior of Nostalgia, a café popular with the well-to-do youth of Riga. Behind the tall, thick glass that made up the entire front wall of the establishment, and among cascades of greenery, well-to-do youth was present in abundance – glancing out with cool curiosity at those glancing in from the outside. The same way exotic, bright-coloured tropical fishes exchange glances with visitors to an aquarium, whilst hanging indifferently in the electrically tinted water between shell-lined grottoes, artificial sunken ships and artistic heaps of coral. But then again, maybe the people on the inside were the acquarium-goers, and the people in the street the fish . . .

Vadim had passed this glass wall a thousand times on his way to and from work. He knew well enough that there was nothing stopping him from going inside. That he quite often had more than enough money to take a seat at one of the Nostalgic little tables. That his biological age and social status positively obligated him to spend some time at one of them every now and again. But he also knew, with no less certainty, that he would never go in and sit there. To do that, he would have to swap his lungs for gills – or the other way round.

The provenance of this gut-intuition that there were

immutable zoological differences running at a level deeper than that of the species, despite abundant external similarities, was unclear even to Vadim himself. They dressed the same, looked the same and even behaved almost the same as he did. Listened to almost the same bands. Watched almost the same films. But somehow he was entirely unable to understand where they'd sprung from and what for. How they lived. What they lived on, goddammit. It seemed safe to assume that these mass-produced individuals, risen up from the pages of various *Playboy*s, *Homme*s, *Men's Health*s and *M-Vogue*s, who frequented various Nostalgias, Black Cats and Pepsi Forums, and provided the filling for all those Opels and Audis, the hangers for all those designer suits, were, to a number, little daddy's boys and girls. The offspring of various greater or lesser Citroëns. Children of big business gradually drinking, eating, travelling, shopping and fucking their way through the disposable elements of the fortunes that their parents had ripped out of the flesh of reality during the period of primitive spoliation. However, that still didn't account for their sheer countless numbers. Nor did it help Vadim to empathise with them. In fact, it inspired in Vadim an acute contempt for the entire test-tube-produced lot of them. It was possible to have respect for their predatory papas, at least the kind of respect that is rooted in the instinct of self-preservation – or, to put it more bluntly, fear. (The way you respect a nine-metre-long crocodile with a jaw pressure of 200 kilograms per square centimetre – stupid, scaly, repulsive, but very big and very, very dangerous.) But these Nostalgic homunculi didn't have the omnivorous vitality of their begetters. They didn't have anything. Apart from dosh. Other people's dosh.

Sometimes Vadim had the idea that they weren't really related to the alligators of finance and crime at all.

Instead, they were a miracle of genetic engineering and nanotechnology, a Wunderwaffe, the Soviet weapon of revenge, nurtured in the murky depths that lurked behind the post-office-box addresses of super-secret, spectral Scientific Research Institutes, assembled on the high-tech production lines of defence-industry factories. Chameleon bio-robots, monsters of mimicry, unbelievably receptive to the prompt-ings of mass culture, adapting ideally to the dominant behavioural stereotypes. Produced in huge quantities for deployment in the terrain governed by that potential enemy, NATO. There, having mingled with the local bourgeois population, at H-hour on D-day, they were to initiate their secret military programme, and then . . . They had been all ready, lying in the army munitions depots of the Western Forces Group, all set to infiltrate. But then, due to circum-stances beyond the control of their developers and the military command, the USSR had suddenly ceased to exist, and the period of primitive spoliation and all the subsequent spoliations had begun. The developers had been packed off on unlimited unpaid leave, the military command had gone into battle for convertible greenbacks, the Western Forces Group had been disbanded – and everyone had forgotten all about the Wunderwaffe. For a few years they had lain in a polystyrene coma on the dusty shelves of the privatised, but still unexplored depots. And then one day something had happened. Probably a short-circuit in some wire. And the bio-robots had synchronically switched themselves on, unpacked themselves and looked around. Infiltrated. Mingled. Adapted. Merged. And now, with no specific operational mission, they continued to patrol the expanded enemy territory. With their larval combat programme still lying dormant within.

For the time being.

From his desk, Vadim had a good view of the samurai in the open white kimono, kneeling in front of a bamboo mat. His expression was intent and stern. His left cheek was tattooed with a pictogram that looked like an elephant's head. 'Ka-ze'. It meant 'wind' and it consisted of the signs for 'roof' and 'strong'. In one hand the samurai was holding a short sword wrapped in fabric that was also white; in the other he was holding a pair of chopsticks, entirely inappropriate for the ritual of hara-kiri. Standing on the bamboo mat in front of the samurai was a large porcelain plate. And written above him, in a script designed to resemble brush-stroke calligraphy, were the words: A FESTIVAL OF THE STOMACH. And below that in really small letters: The Banzai Japanese Restaurant and Entertainment Complex.

The superior restaurant with the superiority complex was one of the most expensive in town and had a reputation as a mobsters' joint. Mobsters – the most reputable and high-status of them, that is – liked to straighten out their tortuous mobsters' problems over a cup of sake and a plate of sushi in the restaurant's private rooms, separated from the hoi polloi by sliding screens. So the associations of 'roof' and 'strong' (in the sense of protection) were both quite appropriate here. However, the advertiser's subtle stroke of associative flattery had gone unappreciated by the restaurant's owners, with the result that the Banzai was now advertised by an ox-eyed geisha with her kimono slipping off one shoulder, and the one and only remaining copy of the samurai ad had been dragged up to the press room by Four-Eyes, where he had stuck it up on the plastic sliding screen of his own private compartment in a moment of humour. Or perhaps menace. Citron and the owners of the Banzai Japanese Restaurant and Entertainment Complex had agendas of their own that Vadim knew nothing about.

But, whatever they were, the whole Family was involved. Or at least the Cover Girl. Vadim had glimpsed Lada's invitation to the Banzai when he delivered the glossy piece of cardboard to her apartment. He had even seen the date and time: the invite was lying on the kitchen table, where the overhung Lada tossed it, having given it a brief glance: 29 December, 20.00. Vadim had been maliciously delighted at this proof that the rich and fat were so totally lacking in imagination: if the fashion's going to be oriental, then let's do the whole shoot in Eastern style – from our favourite eating-house to our mistress's flat. Aw, come on, Citron-san.

Still not turning on the lights, he went over to the window. Down below, abandoned until the New Year festivities were over, lay the rubble of what had once been the old wing of the bank. They had demolished it to make way for a new building that would connect his building with REX's main residence via a mirror-glass gallery. The foundations had already sprouted the metre-long shoots of eternally rusty reinforcement rods. In the main building not a single window was lit up. The bureaucratic folk in the Ministry of Prosperity were more diligent – at the back of the detached building opposite a whole floor glowed bright yellow. The streetlamp on the corner pointed out, in parentheses, that it had started snowing again.

The remains of Vadim's third beer of the evening descended into a ceramic mug fashioned to look as if it had been squashed, and equipped with the Polish inscription 'Nikdo neni dokonaly'. The meaning of the phrase was not entirely clear: it could have been 'You've really done me in' or 'You'll never do me in'. In either case the mug was a loser, it just wasn't clear whether it had already given up or was still struggling. Vadim aimed the empty beer bottle at the wastepaper bin, but stopped himself just in time. According to the extremely strict office rules, the mere appearance of alcohol at a person's work station was punishable by severe fines, and even an empty bottle could serve as adequate evidence for indictment. Especially since he'd signed at the security desk for taking a key outside working hours. The bottle slowed, reversed and was despatched into his jacket pocket.

Vadim lapped at the hissing foam with his lips as it settled and then set off across the covroline floor, avoiding stepping on the pale, streetlamp-lit spots, shadows in reverse. The sleeping computers, photocopiers, faxes and printers lay like stones in a Zen garden. Someone's vainglorious chair had rolled out into the centre of the room.

This was a new press room – deserted and silent. In the usual, day-time room, in the translucent, see-through shrine to the unified energies of banking PR, you could only be the social version of yourself. In this one, you could be anything you liked. You could do something wrong. Reprehensible. For instance (Vadim took a sip) have a beer. Or (Vadim sat on desk) sit on the desk. Or wave your middle finger (Vadim waved his middle finger) at the office door of Mr Four-Eyes, the boss. Or even . . . Vadim jumped down, pulled out the drawer of someone's – Olezhek's – desk and rummaged in it at random. He discovered a pack of slim, unmanly More cigarettes in the far corner. And a simple little Cricket lighter one partition further on. Take that, Vadim thought, savouring a delicious drag. Then, stung instantaneously and simultaneously by two thoughts – the alarm might react to the smoke and the security man might smell it on his evening round – he furiously stubbed the cigarette out against the arm of the chair. All right then.

We'll let that go. But then . . .

He switched on his PC. Waited for it to finish whirring, chirping and mewing. And with an affected insolence, not even bothering to glance round, made his way to the files he had so cunningly secreted in the depths of the hard drive. Feet up on the desk, he began lazily leafing through his work, nodding euphorically at the obscene words in black on the light-blue background through the light haze of almost a litre and a half of beer.

'. . . And anyone who makes life hard for us must realise that he is overfilling the cup of proletarian patience. And sooner or later he will be a) collared b) clobbered good c) fucked silly d) hung out to dry. This is axiomatic. This is the absolute truth. This is a constant, the alpha, omega and dick knows what else as well. But if dick knows anything, then he won't say so. He's not very talkative. Fuck talk. He prefers not to bugger about, but act (he's a dick, not a cunt, after all, isn't he?). Amen.'

Soon his bladder began making it clear that almost a litre and a half was no joke. Vadim reluctantly took his feet down off the desk and set out for the loo. Or, as security guard Gimniuk invariably called it, the heads. In the corridor he waved to Vitalik from the computer department, who was cautiously winding a fluffy scarf round his neck.

After taking a leak, Vadim mimed a pair of major left hooks to the chin in the loo mirror. Polished off the fight with a crushing uppercut. Continued with the countdown – as his own referee – on the way back to the dark press room.

He'd already taken a few steps towards his desk, when he noticed the shadow of a head cast on to the partition screen by a glowing monitor.

His monitor. Vadim mechanically took another step and the seated man swung round on the rotating chair.

'Our answer to Four-Eyes.

Aha, you bastard, shit-scared now, are you? Shaking now, are they, those filthy, sweaty little hands of yours, stained with blood sucked from the veins of honest toilers – that is, from us? Trembling now, is it, that foul, repulsive, shrill little bourgeois voice? Pissing yourself, are you, you vermin? And so you should be. ON THE BAYONET, that's where you belong! ON THE STAKE! IN THE CONCRETE! THE CONCRETE! THE CONCRETE! That's where you ought to be! In the guts of an opencast mine! Get the idea, you fucker? One of those mines where the proletarians you've plundered die for the sake of a few coins, you bastard! Well, you petty lackey of the big sharks of capital? Well, you fat-bellied, bloated bourgeois left-over, you lousy light-fingered queer, you swindling shyster with neither shame nor conscience? Not only do you eat bourgeois shit, you want to give an honest Russian working lad like me the taste for it too!! You PUTRID SCUMBAG!!!

Your fucking time's up, Four-Eyes. You're for rapid, brutal, merciless buggering by the iron prick of the proletariat.

The end.'

'No, Vadik,' said Four-Eyes with a smile of boundless sincerity, 'it's YOUR fucking time that's up.'

But buggering hell, you're at the club . . . The crushing uppercut finally connected with Vadim's chin, triggering a muffled rumbling in his ears, a momentary disorientation . . . What the fuck?

'You think I'll just sack you, you wanker, don't you?' Four-Eyes continued sympathetically and shook his head as a hint at the truth. 'Oh no. No fucking way. I'm going to pulverise you, dear Vadim. Smear you across the floor. Mix you with shit.' With every phrase his smile grew wider and brighter. 'You, Vadimushka, will never work again, not in this city, not in this country, not in the entire bastard world!'

He banged his hand hard down on the desk.

'Not any-where, get it? They won't take you on to clean out the shithouse, Vadichka. Not even to lick it clean.'

Four-Eyes was obviously half-cut. At the stage of slightly superfluous gestures and over-emphatic intonation.

'What were you thinking, you shithead?' Four-Eyes lounged back in the chair, dangling the pointed toe of his shoe. 'That no one would ever find out? That no one would ever find anything?' His tie glittered from under his Paul Smith coat. Ink-blue scarabs running across a field of gold. For some reason Vadim's gaze locked on to them. 'Pil-lock! What-a-pil-lock! You stupid little ponce!' Four-Eyes suddenly jerked forward and twirled his fingers in Vadim's face as if he was unscrewing a light bulb. 'You're nothing but a fucking louse! A mingy little crab!'

For a moment Vadim was lost in a clammy, viscous mental haze. The only thoughts he had, circling furiously round his head with a sickening buzz, were: 'What's going to happen? What's he going to do? Am I in deep shit now? Just how deep is it?' And just at the moment when the little whirring wheels all clicked and stopped together and spelled out 'Deep! Very deep! Very, very deep! Way over your head!', somewhere inside him he felt a nagging little itch. The sticky feeling instantly evaporated and a palpitating sensation of agonising anticipation began rising rapidly from the pit of his stomach.

'You're just envious, you useless plonker. There's absolutely fuck all you're any good at. Fuck all! What would you have done without me? I was the one who took you on here. You were eating off my table. Then you go and shit on it. On the sly. Because you didn't dare say anything to me, you arse-licking toady. You were too afraid. Pissing yourself. Just sat here in your stinking little burrow, jerking off into your fist. Zapping away. You useless fucking tosser. You snivelling little whelp . . .'

It felt like just before an orgasm. Every word Four-Eyes spoke, each one more avidly triumphant than the one before, twisted a spring somewhere inside Vadim one turn tighter.

' . . . Limp rag. Waste of space. Shagging doormat . . .'

More, more. More.

'. . . Sordid piece of trash. Slimy little runt . . .'

The spring snapped. Something came apart. Without actually feeling anything, Vadim reached out his hand, grabbed hold of the reptilian neck of the bronze Murzilla, lifted the artificial dinosaur with a considerable but insensible effort – and swung the round weight-lifter's disc of its base sideways into Andrei Vladlenovich's temple.

7

Which way was he standing? Like that? Facing me? No. Sideways on. Like that . . . Wait. Which side? This one? No. The right side. Like that?

Vadim twisted Murzilla round on his little pedestal, trying to recreate the angle at which the dinosaur was so impressively foreshortened. It was important. More important than anything else.

Andrei Vladlenovich lay sprawled in front of Vadim's desk, his face thrust sulkily against the floor. Vadim could only see the back of his head. The pointed toes of his shoes, sticking out at awkard angles, looked especially stupid.

What could be wrong with him? Had he blacked out? Vadim knew that he had to go closer, bend down and feel his pulse: on the wrist, or the carotid artery . . . but he couldn't do it. He lifted one foot and took a step backwards. Edged away towards the light switch. Flipped it.

The sudden salvo of dozens of cold, white, incandescent trumpets was as deafening as a siren. Vadim instantly turned the lights off. He couldn't see anything at all: flickering duckweed . . . He paused for a moment and turned them on again.

When he got back to his desk he froze: the monitor, the keyboard, the polished brown desktop, the bustling printouts bursting with rows of figures were all brightly embellished with cheerful red stripes. Like the strokes of a Russian literature teacher's pen, two vigorous parallel lines running across the screen had angrily struck out the indecent phrase 'PUTRID SCUMBAG!!' From under Vladlenovich's head, a thick, lacquer-bright Antarctica had cautiously crept out on to the dirty floor, as if it were the lower edge of a map of the world.

Vadim squatted down and touched the leather shoulder hesitantly, as if he were preparing to say: that's enough clowning about, get up. He tried to turn his recumbent boss over. No way (for the second time the thought ran through his mind in racing neon letters that Four-Eyes was simply playing the fool). Vadim braced himself. Finally he managed to tumble the improbably heavy, strangely flabby body over on to its back.

The head bobbled tipsily and gazed up at him with a blank, drunken stare. Once smeared, the tidy little puddle of blood proved catastrophically abundant. The same way as an almost empty cup of coffee, overturned, somehow manages to swamp your table with brown liquid, liberally splatter the adjacent tables and disastrously stain the people sitting next to you in the chic, comme-il-faut coffeehouse. The entire left side of Andrei Vladlenovich's face, his cheek and his chin, were coloured a glossy, wet claret red. Vadim didn't look closely at his boss's temple: he knew without looking that the broad, gruesome depression in it reached back to the ear, and the model haircut was hopelessly dishevelled and besmirched.

There was something else fundamentally wrong, but it took Vadim some time to realise what it was: Four-Eyes wasn't wearing his glasses. They had settled comfortably on the floor beside him, with their matt metallic arms sticking into the air. Vadim automatically picked them up.

Slowly, as if he expected to encounter icy rigidity or glutinous semi-decay, Vadim reached out his hand and touched his boss's throat. It was warm and soft; he could feel the little wedge of the Adam's apple. He searched for a stirring of the blood. Squeezed. Felt the prickly points of invisible shaved hairs. Didn't feel any pulse. He went on squeezing, pressing his hand into the skin that wouldn't respond. Under its folds he could feel the larynx, the emptiness around it, the thickenings at the side of the neck, but nothing more. With his hand pressing into Four-Eyes's throat, he waited a long, long time for even the most insignificant, intermittent signal – maybe an hour. Or three. The longer he waited, the more clearly he saw.

The head of the press service of REX International Commercial Bank, Andrei Vladlenovich Voronin, aka Four-Eyes, was as dead as a doornail.

Vadim's next spontaneous, instinctive reaction was an overpowering urge to turn tail and run right now. He already had his hand on the door-handle of the press room when he recalled very, very clearly the sight of his own writing in the columns of the register at the security desk. His name, the number of the press room, and the exact time when the key had been taken. A signature under a full and frank confession.

Vadim froze. Slowly he reached his hand down to the lock, from which the key still protruded, and locked himself in. The body. Body of evidence. He couldn't leave the body here.

He went back to his computer. The blood-spattered monitor was still radiating patiently. Vadim prodded a switch and cut it off – leaving a derisively clear red print from his index finger on the plastic rectangle with the oval indentation and the inscription 'power'.

His right hand, the one he'd used to feel for the pulse, was covered in blood too.

Vadim found himself teetering on the edge of final and total loss of control. A howling, swirling, supercharged tornado: the base of its lithe, swirling column in his scrotum, the wide funnel between his ears. His head span . . . Fear.

TERROR. Not a single coherent thought, only a clamorous, strident roar.

The blood. The blood had to be cleaned up (take the corpse out). What could he clean it up with? The floor was carpeted, it had soaked in, no way you could wash it off, only with a special vacuum cleaner, incredibly expensive vacuum cleaners, special fittings they advertised on the box for cleaning carpets, no good! The body, where could he put it? Where could you take it? It was heavy and awkward as bloody hell. Covered in gore. And where could he put it? In the loo? Someone must have seen Four-Eyes: at the security post, on the staircase (Vitalik! Vitalik from the IT department!). They could even have seen him going into the press room . . .

On this pre-holiday evening the empty building suddenly turned out to be absolutely packed solid with people. There were security guards, office clerks working late and cleaning ladies teeming everywhere, swarming over everything. The bank was awash with them – vigilant, specially coached to keep an eye on colleagues eager to dispose of the mutilated bodies of villainously butchered bosses . . . Where could he put him? Stick him in some dark corner: 'I don't know anything about it, he just slipped, fell, banged his head . . . He was drunk. He was raving, losing it.' They'd ransack the entire building, turn everything inside out. They'd find traces of blood (the carpet!). Who was in the press room yesterday evening? Apletaev, see, he signed in.

Pointless. It's all pointless. You're shafted, Vadimushka. He was overwhelmed by a feeling of absolute numbness, lethargy, exhaustion. He wanted to curl up in a corner and whimper: do what you like with me, yes, I'm the guilty one, I killed him, I bopped him on the noggin with this big lizard . . . They'd give him five to eight at least, even for unpremeditated. The prison camp zone, the convicts, ritual humiliation, registration as a stooge. The rusty blades of the penitentiary meat-grinder.

'Out of the building,' the voices all prompted him with indifferent insistence. You must get the body out of the building. As far away as possible, so no one will think Four-Eyes was killed in the bank. Best of all, so far away they'll never even find him. Take it away, drown it, bury it.

What if someone wanted to come into the press room now? Somehow got the bright idea he had to, just like that? Four-Eyes had got the idea from somewhere. The door was locked, the light was on. Security had a second key . . . Fucking garbage, he had to think calmly! There were cameras everywhere. This was a bank: financial secrets, confidential accounts . . . How could he take him away? In Four-Eyes's Pontiac? ('. . . I'll have to take the driver, or else what am I supposed to do? Not drink at the first one?') The driver? Was he waiting? Cool it! Search him. If the car key was on him, he drove himself.

Vadim frenziedly wiped his fingers on a fax from the State Revenue Department and was just going to throw it into the bin . . . Blood! – Where? – Fuck! He stuffed it in his pocket. His hands were shaking as if he had a raging hangover. Trying to avoid getting smeared with red gouache, he began frisking the body. The boss looked on contemptuously, didn't even notice him. The left coat pocket was empty, it had a slippery lining. The right coat-flap was bent under him. To get into the other pocket Vadim had to turn the body back over. Four-Eyes stuck his face into his own blood like a drunk sticking his face into his own vomit (all this hassle with the defunct Vladlenovich kept reminding Vadim of his squeamish ministrations to a friend who had drunk himself legless). There they were! Keys. Car keys.

But how was he going to lug the body out to the car? Along the corridors, past the internal cameras, past the security post, out through the main door, past the external cameras . . . Through the window, you idiot! The building site was down there. No cameras. Drive the Pontiac on to the site, stick the body in, drive it away, get rid of it.

Aha. Fourth floor. Eighty kilos. Ka-boom! Splatters in all directions. And they'd spot him heaving Four-Eyes over the windowsill: from the Ministry opposite and the main REX residence on the left.

He suddenly realised he was in full view. In a brightly lit room with the blinds open. He bounded over to the window, tangled his fingers in a feverish knot, untangled them, closed the hideous-pink boudoir blinds. There were a couple of lights still on in the Ministry, but they were over on the left side.

Where was the car? In the bank's car park? How could he explain that he had suddenly decided to take a ride in his boss's Pontiac? Think, asshole, think. The cameras . . . He didn't remember there being many cameras in this wing of the bank, which housed the press department and similar secondary support services that didn't handle financial operations directly. There were some on the stairs. At the main entrance, inside and outside. Along the perimeter. The building site. Yes. The building site was probably the only place not under constant observation after all. Of course, there were cameras at the corner of the two bank buildings. But right under the wall there ought to be a blind spot. Had to be. Naturally, Vadim had never really paid any attention to the way the security system was set up. Okay, let's suppose they really wouldn't be able to pick him up down there. But how could he carry the body down?

In pieces . . . Ha bloody ha. With bells on. Vadim

imagined himself, streaked with gore from head to foot, sawing through his boss's leg with a paperknife. He giggled hysterically. It would take all night. For one leg. What a gas for his colleagues in the morning, finding Apletaev sitting in the middle of an office awash with blood, holding the boss's foot in his hands. Foot in hand. 'Your feet are in our hands' – an advertising slogan for a shoe shop . . . Think!

He couldn't get his bloody brain to think. Down the back stairs . . . to the back entrance. Bound to be locked. And have a camera. What other ways were there out of the building? Windows, door? The old door into the old wing? Out through the main vestibule, the guards, the camera . . . What else. Eh? Stop. There was another door . . . Where? Through the kitchen? Vadim screwed his eyes up tight, trying to recall the floor plan. Right. Straight out on to the life-saving building site. What had they done to it? Boarded it up? Walled it up? Probably boarded it up. Then we'll unboard it . . . Maybe that would do the trick. Maybe. And maybe he'd run into someone in the corridor while he was dragging the corpse out . . . And maybe there was some concealed camera he'd never noticed round here after all. Or out on the building site. And maybe the back staircase was locked (dead certain to be). And maybe Four-Eyes's motor was in the parking lot, where you couldn't pilfer it without some explanation that made sense, and what the hell kind of explanation could there be that made sense for all this? No matter what, they saw Voronin go into the bank and they didn't see him come out again . . .

A relapse into mind-numbing panic. Acute but brief. No escape from the feeling that all his logical calculations were just loony tunes and even if he did act in a way that he thought was rational, they'd still collar him and bang him up anyway. There was some little thing, some pitiful, stupid but all-important little thing he was guaranteed to slip up on.

Absolutely convinced that there would be a crowd of guards and policemen waiting outside the door with Pylny and Citron, all carrying guns and handcuffs, ready to nab him and put him away, Vadim went out into the corridor. Empty. Absolutely empty. He immediately locked the door behind him and started looking for cameras. There was one at the top of the stairs, pointing its lens straight at his forehead. That was all.

Vadim went down one flight of steps, walked over to the window – and immediately spotted the Pontiac. Lemon-yellow, low to the ground, conspicuous, it was standing out in the cold opposite the main entrance with its crossfire of cameras. Four-Eyes had only intended to drop into the office for a moment . . .

'You can tell them that in the cash office on payday!' said a loud, unfamiliar voice somewhere below him.

Vadim hurtled back up the steps to the corridor, but no one appeared.

Then he set off towards the back staircase. Six steps from the press room. A right-angle turn. Another ten steps to the smoking room. The light wasn't even on in the smoking room. It could stay that way. In the gloom Vadim could barely make out the door to the stairs. But of course. Locked. He tugged at it senselessly. It was a rickety sort of door, not really serious. Which made sense, in case there was a fire, so as not to waste too much time on it. And what if you had to take a dead body out? Vadim took aim and slammed his foot against the door under the handle. The sudden boom echoed through the bank and he cringed. Ah, bugger it. The whole floor was empty. But the door wasn't going to swing open for him just like that. He obviously wasn't very convincing as Chuck Norris.

He lashed out again. And again, much harder. He felt the pain shoot up into his knee. But he thought he heard something crack in the lock. Vadim took a step back and hit the door with his shoulder. With his whole body. Harder! That hurt! Harder! It felt like he'd pulverised a couple of bones somewhere, but the door had parted from the frame with a sickening crunch. Behind it there was the same darkness. He closed the door carefully: everything the same as it had been . . .

He ran back to the press room, trying to outpace the stuttering stopwatch that was positively choking on fatal probabilities. Right then. Think. Body. Head. Blood. He had to wrap the head in something. Something leak-proof. Plastic. A plastic bag. What could be simpler or more common than a plastic bag? Vadim began ransacking desktops, fumbling through drawers. Papers, audiocassettes, magazines, cigarettes, videocassettes – bugger it, why didn't anyone have an ordinary plastic bag? Cretin. The litter bin. Bugger it . . .

He shook the crumpled paper out of the bin closest to hand and pulled out the black, rustling liner.

Thin, too thin. It would tear . . . Another one. And another. He tossed the rubbish back into the bin and shoved it under the desk. He had to turn Four-Eyes over yet again. The foul sludge had turned darker and thicker, like engine oil. Maybe he ought to close Andrei Vladlenovich's eyes? What the hell for, if they were going in the bag anyway? It only took him a few seconds to get hopelessly slimed and smeared. Up to his bollocks, up to his eyes. Somehow Vadim managed to pull a bag over Voronin's head. The left temple yielded hideously under the pressure of his fingers. The bag was much bigger than the head, it flapped about. A second one on top. And a third. They were bound to slip off. Get something to tie them on with.

He was about to yank the cable out of the nearest computer, but stopped just in time. String, string . . . Another bloody brainteaser. Where would you find string in an office? The tie. Four-Eyes's gold silk tie.

Bugger it. He yanked back the plastic bags and stuck his hand under the pointed Oxford collar. His slimy fingers slithered over the squirming silk. It was a tricky knot, a sailor's knot. Bugger it, nothing done the simple way, not even his tie . . . He gave it a tug and Andrei Vladlenovich's head thumped dully against the floor.

Vadim lifted his hands up and blew on them. Now. He breathed in, breathed out.

With his finger and thumb he tugged the tie's tightly furled little flower-bud away from the coffee-coloured neck. Then, clamping his nails on one little petal, as if he were pulling out a splinter with a small pair of pincers, he tugged it loose, worked it free, shook it out. He had it. Vadim jerked the crumpled choker out from under his boss, pulled the crackling plastic bags further down over his head and wrapped the scarab-littered band of gold three times round Four-Eyes's neck. He tied it securely with a knot.

Vadim stood up too fast and staggered: everything around him suffered a sudden displacement, a single-centimetre shift. In his ears was a swift, rushing rivulet of sound. He grabbed another print-out and scraped at his hands. Put it in his pocket. Touched Four-Eyes's foam-rubber wrist, his elbow . . . No. Tried grabbing him from behind, under the arms. Started dragging him. Four-Eyes was like a sack of rocks. Like a bundle of sacks . . . The body flopped all over the place, flinging out its arms and legs. The black plastic spheroid kept nudging Vadim obtusely in the belly. The coat and multiple layers of clothing slid apart awkwardly, like the skin of a mushy banana. Something small popped off — a little mother-of-pearl disc. Vadim let go of Four-Eyes, picked up the button. No. That wasn't going to work. He looked around, exhausted.

A desk. A rotating office chair. On castors. Vadim pushed the light grey, rolling structure over, loaded Four-Eyes on to it and tried to sit him up. Four-Eyes gave a stubborn shake of his plastic bin-liners and immediately slipped over sideways. Vadim caught him, hissing under his breath. Bracing himself he levered the body's belly over the back of the chair. The oval blade of the back rest lodged against Four-Eyes's diaphragm, creaked under the weight and began to topple. Holding the seat down with his knee, Vadim launched Four-Eyes on his final journey, his mitts dangling, the hard toes of his shoes scraping lines in the carpet. When they reached the door, Vadim thrust the pre-requisitely tanned forehead of his superior against the doorpost, cautiously removed his hands from the chair and glanced out. No one there. Clacking its castors over the flat metal strip of the doorway, the chair trundled out into the big, wide world.

It wasn't easy to get the chair to accept the direction imposed on it. It balked and bobbled a bit before succumbing. One, two . . . five, six, turn. The chair strained, tried to wriggle free, the lousy bastard. Fuck you. Ten steps to the smoking room. Now. Now someone would appear round the corner. The chair shuddered against the doorstep to the back stairs, kicked back with its castors, and dumped the body on to the hygienic tiles of the corridor with a thud. Vadim gaped dementedly, uncomprehendingly. . . Then, with a convulsive jerk, he flung Four-Eyes through the door and on to the smooth concrete of the back staircase.

Now, the walk back with the chair in tow. The open press-room door looking like a gaping hole in his own belly.

He flew inside, snapped the key round in the lock. Leaned back. Bang!

Bang! Bang! Bang! Ten square metres of filthy, bedraggled material evidence. Vadim swept the remaining faxes up off his desk in a long, pale paper streamer and carefully wiped down the monitor.

The keyboard. The desktop.

The processor! The rippled bar-code of papillary lines on the 'power' button. He pecked at the button with the corner of a piece of paper and the Pentium obediently sprang to life, started chirring, blinked its screen. Vadim squeamishly switched it off with the unstained knuckle of his little finger.

Right. Now for the most important thing. He went down on his knees and ran a fax over the patch of half-dry gravy. The harsh, rancid smell by-passed his nostrils, adhering directly to his frontal lobes. The fax was instantly transformed into a wad of brown garbage. Where could he put it? In the bin? No. In his pocket? It would never wash off . . . Down the toilet? It would block it. Tear it up? Time. Burn it? Smoke . . .

His nose began itching and stinging unbearably. Vadim stretched out his arm and rubbed his nose furiously against his elbow, avoiding his soiled hand. Hide it! His desk drawer with the lock that had never been locked. Vadim pulled out the drawer, crammed the garbage in, slammed it shut. The stain on the floor was still there; it had just straggled out a bit wider. What else . . .

Vadim grabbed the thin-paged pop-culture magazine *Right On!* from the next desk. The fish-eyed sex symbol of one sixth of the earth's surface, Vladimir Vladimirovich Putin; the portly procuress of post-Soviet light music, Alla Borisovna Pugachova; the golden voice of Russia, Nikolai Baskov: their top-of-the-ratings faces all scoured scrupulously at Four-Eyes's slippery seepage. After Vadim had used up

Filip Kirkorov, Leonid Agutin, Boris Moiseev, Angelica Varoom, Richard Gere and Britney Spears, he realised there was nothing more he could do. He'd got rid of all the gunge, but the forty-centimetre-wide, dark, damp amoeba was still resisting extermination. It didn't evoke any particular associations with blood. But it could still attract attention. It would. It was bound to.

The bloody magazine giblets went the same way as the faxes. Vadim locked the drawer. There was some gunk left on the key. Into his pocket. Already full. Into the drawer then. In goes the empty beer bottle too . . . Lock it. Now, cool it!

Now what to do about his hands . . . the amoeba . . .

First the amoeba. Cover it with something. Murzilla's stand? They'd notice. It was too far away . . . Aha! He was tempted to push, then remembered about his hands, ran round the desk and, panting, kicked the free-standing set of drawers out from under the table. Carefully he adorned the top of the drawers with the deliberately crumpled mug with the Polish motto 'You'll never do me in!' He had to hold it between his forearms to set it in place.

Bloody rubbish, absolute crap! But he couldn't think of anything better . . .

With the collar of his jacket between his teeth he made his way to the door. The key to the room was obviously covered in shit too, but at this point he couldn't care less.

In the loo he spat the salty Chinese waterproofed cloth out on to the tiled floor, turned the red and blue handles round as far as they would go and poured so much liquid soap into his hands that he gave the floor a generous slavering of the semen-like gunk. The blood was a bugger to wash off, as if it had eaten into his hands. Vadim kept on adding more and more soap like a maniac, until the sink was filled to the brim with a light, fluffy, dimpled cushion that looked like the oxygen cocktail they used to give him as a treat in the children's sanatorium. The foam was even oozing out of the hole under the tap, as if the drain refused to take it. Vadim's hands had tinted it a delicate shade of vermilion.

He did manage to scrub them clean, though. And both keys – from the room and the drawer.

But before he could get round to the final victims of middle-level managerial seepage – the chrome taps and white soap-dispenser with the embossed brand-name KATRIN – the door to his left swang open with a resolute whoosh, almost hitting Vadim, and in came a bulky, red-faced gent whose features looked vaguely familiar. The bank's electrician, or plumber, or some ancillary individual like that. Gosha or Zhora or Pasha or Kesha . . .

'What are we up to in here, eh? Slaving away, are we?' Gosha or Kesha inquired with disapproval or indifference and, without waiting for an answer, he heaved up his belly with a gasp, opened his flies and installed himself at a urinal.

'Ahhh . . .'

A single, massive, petrifying spasm cramped Vadim's body and mind. The coloured foam had no intention of subsiding. Any second now the plumber would stop sighing, shake it, button up and want to rinse off his mucky mitts . . . Vadim just stood there, hunched over, mechanically moving his hands about under the stream of water. I'm just washing my hands.

Here he comes.

Pasha stopped sighing. Shook it off. Buttoned up. Farted. Squinted at the jacket sprawling on the floor. Walked straight past the sink and out of the loo.

At the centre of Vadim's palms the sleek, dense, woolliness of concertinaed socks was replaced by the rough, sparse, hairiness of bony ankles. He had to work in short bursts. The coat, the jacket, the shirt and all the rest had spread out backwards, trailing stickily over an ever-increasing number of steps. The raised arms – 'I surrender!' – plucked unmusically at the banisters. Four floors. Eighty-eight steps if the flights were standard-length. 88. Two eights. Two infinities perched on their bums.

Vadim was tugging Four-Eyes along by the feet, constantly glancing round behind him. The black polythene bubble counted off the steps with a rustling squelch. Vadim was afraid even to think about what was inside the bubble. In the fifth form at school he and some mates had filled a condom under the tap and dropped it down the school stairs. The dull, semi-transparent, overblown drop of mercury had cheerfully plumped down as far as the first landing and then hopped sideways with a capricious lurch, taking precise aim and bursting under the feet of the headmistress, Ludmila Petrovna. A Peterhof fountain. That time they'd managed to hop it.

Slither. Clonk. The light soles of Four-Eyes's shoes were like well-worn blocks of parquet flooring. The next landing, with a fire extinguisher in the corner. If he shot at it, it would explode with a thunderous boom, revealing a secret hiding place or another passage. Slither-clonk. Slither-clonk. Vadim didn't realise at first that the stairs had come to an end. The ground floor. Door on the left leading outside. Must have an alarm. And a light. And an external camera. Door on the right leading inside . . . Andrei Vladlenovich's heels clattered against the concrete like a saluting hussar's. Vadim tried the right-hand door. It was no stronger than the one he'd already smashed open.

Only one fucking catch: this one opened INWARDS. Towards him.

He couldn't smash it in.

Break it out. What with? What with?

He had no idea how long he loitered there in the dark, trying to come up with something. But without coming up with anything. Without even hoping for anything. He went further down, into the basement.

The internal door here was locked too, naturally – but the spacious hallway had been used as a dump for all sorts of building-and-repairs clutter that he could barely make out in the faint ricochets of light drifting in from the outside lamps through the slit windows set under the ceiling. A tall cylinder with pressure gauges on a horned trolley – for welding? Planks. Pieces of metal. For a long time Vadim clanked and clattered among the defunct ironmongery, off-cuts of piping, reels of wire. Sooner or later he was bound to find something that would do it. It was later. A short aluminium jemmy, a door-handle, with no lock attached.

Fight like with like. He wedged the sharp end into the crack of the door. Leaned hard with his chest. The lever wasn't long enough. Frowning, Vadim began hammering with his open palm. Bang! Bang! Bang! Paying no attention to the agonising ache that became more unbearable with every blow, to the blood (his own this time), to the clangiferous echo.

A dead loss.

He stopped to lick off the blood – and suddenly heard a jittery, convulsive, unbelievable noise: the obscene, frivolous music of the *cancan* . . . Vadim recoiled from the door and swung his head round, dumbfounded. The phone. The mobile . . . appealing to the reinforced concrete darkness from deep inside the innermost recesses of Four-Eyes.

What should he do? Switch it off? If only he knew how . . . Ah, bugger it, let it ring. The person you are calling is temporarily unavailable. If only.

But someone obviously wanted Andrei Vladlenovich very badly – the phone kept trilling, on and on. Churning out that cabaret melody. A second time. A third. Shut up, will you, you bastard! Any longer and Four-Eyes would probably have no choice but to return to this world, muttering black curses – a good job he couldn't have gone too far yet – and answer . . .

It stopped. About time . . .

Vadim waited for a little while, then carried on breaking out the door.

There was a splintering of wood.

'Yes!'

The little hallway that the breathless Vadim and his even more breathless boss had broken into turned out to be a kind of back lobby to the company café that they both visited on a daily basis. It was pitch black. Four-Eyes snuggled up forlornly among some boxes. Vadim's hands ran over the walls. The right one was stinging like hell and oozing blood. Bugger it anyway. A cupboard. Metal. Not big, hanging on the wall. A doorway . . .

Three doorways discovered. Two doors locked, but one actually standing open. That was absolutely incredible, he couldn't be that lucky. But there it was, see. The kitchen.

The windows may have been barred, but even so the visibility here was beyond all comparison. Tables, cookers, cupboards. If his memory was any good at all, then the way out into the demolished extension used to be at the other end. But either Vadim had remembered it wrong, or the indefatigably keen cooks had shifted everything around: when he finally located the correct corner, it was filled with a huge fridge twice the height of a man and just as wide. Just looking at it, he could see it was unliftable, unmovable, impregnable. A massive great refrigerator. Refrigeratorus rex.

Oo-oops . . .

Vadim pulled open the door. Tinned ham. THREE LITTLE PIGS. The bristling snouts of a tight-order tin-can combat unit leering in crazed delight at the bridge of his nose.

Vadim took down the ham, the paprika in tomato sauce, the young sweet-corn, the pickled cucumbers, the blanched fish, the Bonduel finest-quality garden peas, and put them all down outside the fridge. The repetitive, assembly-line action was anaesthetising.

Took them out. Put them down.

It made him feel better.

It was almost a joke

It was a stupid joke. Not funny.

In this world there's nothing that can't be done. Vadim became convinced of this truth a geological era or two later, after having exhausted his reserves of physical strength many times over, only for them to be mysteriously restored; after having ruptured everything inside himself that could possibly be ruptured and realised a shagging heap of times the total pointlessness of all this constipated grunting and groaning. And after having disinterestedly discovered at a certain point that the lousy fridge had moved more than half a metre away from the wall.

But the next moment Vadim became convinced that there are some things in this world that can't be done after all.

Yes, the door was there all right. Exactly where he'd been expecting it to be . . . But not only had it been bricked up, it had been plastered over as well.

Vadim ran his entranced fingertips over the unbroken surface, as if he suspected that it really did conceal a barrier of puny wood, the gateway to salvation, total innocence, good health, a law-abiding, happy life, professional success, family harmony, respectful children, loving grandchildren, a contented old age and death in his sleep . . . Then he simply sat down at the foot of the wall and stayed there. His reserves might have proved extensive, but they were finite after all.

Somewhere in a neighbouring galaxy Four-Eyes's phone made another couple of dutiful attempts and abandoned them in dejection. Vadim's stupor was limitless and motionless, but far from mindless. Its distinguishing feature being that the various thoughts scattered randomly through the different strata of his consciousness without coordination or hierarchy merely wandered aimlessly and independently at their own level without finding any purchase in Vadim or making any attempt to foist themselves on him. They included, among others, an abstract meditation on the mobile phone jangling away to no one in particular as not really being an ancillary technological device that was no longer required and had therefore forfeited all relevance, but an entirely self-sufficient entity; on its idle trilling as something like the melody that anybody in a good mood might whistle under his breath. Maybe the mobile was simply feeling cheerful too.

But from way down further in the murky, agitated depths, a far more concrete thought rose to the surface – a prehistoric monster with great big teeth like the tyrannosaurus Murzilla's. A thought about the big lizard's round bronze base – about the fact that, in his haste, Vadim had forgotten to wipe it clean . . . And it was followed by a long string of even ghastlier specimens.

In graduated increments synchronised with the advance of searing agony in Vadim's hand, the realisation dawned on him that everything he had done and was planning to do was absolutely moronic. What had he been counting on, as he smashed in doors one after the other? That no one would trace the route he had taken? Could he seriously have believed that it was possible to lug a cumbersome piece of baggage out of a building that wasn't just any old building, but a large, well protected bank? And that no one, including at least two cameras on the perimeter, would pick up on the Pontiac breaking into the building site? The Pontiac that Vadim probably wouldn't be able to drive anyway, given that he didn't have a driving licence. And what chance did he have, even if he wrapped himself in Four-Eyes's orange coat, of making it down the corridor, past the security checkpoint and starting up that playboy roadster in open view? And even if he did make it, what would they make of Apletaev's mysterious disappearance into thin air in the press room?

This was such an absolutely dead end that not even the footsteps, or the squeak of a lock nearby, or the sudden blaze of light, or even the vision of security guard Sergei Gimniuk in his military-style uniform, complete with regulation night-stick, stirred the slightest emotional response in Vadim. Not the very faintest.

8

'Well, you're in real deep shit,' security guard Sergei Gimniuk drawled with stupefaction, but stupefaction evidently alloyed with gratification and exultation. 'You're well and truly shafted, dickhead!'

At that moment the rigorously punctilious and irreproachably proper security guard was strangely unlike his usual, everyday self. If Vadim had still been capable of surprise, down there on the floor, he would probably have been astonished. Sergei Gimniuk's transformation had progressed gradually, beginning with the sight of the broken door leading on to the back stairs, advancing via the horizontal sight of the thoroughly bedraggled Andrei Vladlenovich indignantly averting his plastic bin-liners from all these outrageous goings-on, and continuing via the pigs, fish, peas, peppers, tomatoes and maize that had taken over half the kitchen, and the forgetful bank employee Apletaev collapsed at the foot of the wall, from which the super-refrigerator had been moved out for some reason . . . eventually terminating in the analysis of these sights and the assembly of these facts to arrive at a uniquely correct conclusion. Initially, security guard Gimniuk had become agitated, acting out a chaotic, uncoordinated sequence of displacements from the lobby to the kitchen and back again. Then he had idled ineffectively among the tin cans for a while. Eventually, though, his attention focused on Vadim, he had palpably dilated with resolute righteousness and implacable determination to discharge his professional function to the letter. In fact, he had already begun discharging it by performing the essential preliminary action of grabbing his walkie-talkie . . .

Then suddenly, as if shaking himself out of some trance and refusing to believe any such crazy nonsense, Gimniuk had jerked his chin gently and smiled uncertainly. His pale eyes had shed their dull, tarnished patina and begun glittering like genuine ninety-per-cent-pure silver.

'So,' he whispered, afraid of startling away his woolgathering bird of good fortune, nodding as he spoke in the direction of the lobby, 'you offed him?'

The little aerial on the walkie-talkie scratched at a pimple on the side of the security guard's nose, vacillated briefly and then took aim at the refrigerator.

'Going to put him in there, were you?'

Perhaps it was the sheer absurdity of such an assumption (as if that might compromise his reputation even more seriously than a stiff in plastic packaging) that made Vadim protest, or perhaps the pointlessness of stubbornly keeping his mouth shut was simply too obvious, or perhaps someone somewhere inside him had already begun rehearsing a confession for the inevitable, all-understanding criminal investigator, but about five minutes later Gimniuk had acquired a pretty good handle on the situation. As each of those minutes went by, he had become even more excited, his eyes had glittered even more keenly, he had caressed his democratic equaliser even more vigorously – until finally he had drawled in exultant stupefaction:

'Well you're in real deep shit! You're well and truly shafted, dickhead!'

At that moment Gimniuk resembled a man who has been trying for ages to din into the people around him something that he feels is absolutely self-evident. For years he has merely been brushed aside with condescending derision and completely ignored. But then comes the day when his correctness is suddenly convincingly proved – incontrovertibly demonstrated to everyone. And the sweetest part – the fame, the honours, the recognition – is only just beginning . . . Gimniuk looked around for a place to sit down, acknowledged the edge of a preparation table as a worthy spot and installed himself side-saddle. He looked as though he would have dearly loved to light up a fat Havana cigar, take a sip of ancient vintage brandy and fold his arms across his chest.

'You savvy this is like totally premeditated, you fucker?' he enquired in a tone of regretful condemnation. 'That it's a definite ten-year ticket? Maybe even a fifteen-year stretch?' He listened briefly to what he'd said and confirmed it. 'Definitely the big fifteen. For sure. They'll stick it to you real good. The whole fucking works. And fit you up with aggravating circumstances too. Have you got any bastard clue who Voronin is to the Man? He's married to his frigging daughter. The Man'll lean on his contacts in the fuzz, and you'll go down for the max! But don't start getting all hot and bothered. You'll never do your full stretch in the zone anyway. Because the Man'll call in a couple of favours from the mob and they'll soon have you cut down to size. Know what they'll do to you the very first day? While you're still in the holding cells? They'll *register* you. Screw you silly and shag you stupid. Fuck you up the arse.

'You getting the picture? Do you know what a *paraffin* is? That's when they stick their dick in your gob – that's the way they *lower* you and make you a *cockerel* for the rest of your life. A stinking *stooge* for ever. After that anyone who feels even half-inclined will fuck you. Every day. They'll make you crawl. Man, will they make you crawl . . .'

Lost for words, Gimniuk rolled his eyes.

'I was in the navy. I've seen the way they grind guys down. Your sort of guy.' He jerked his chin in Vadim's direction. 'I know what it's like when they break someone. The way they turn a man into a piece of shit. Absolute shit. Round here you're a real flash fucking git, like you work in a bank, in the fucking press service. Like you're a real clever dick, know all sorts of big words, went to college. Get to fuck all the skirt . . . In the fleet they couldn't give a two-cent toss for all that. They'd ram all your smart-ass colleges straight back down your throat. You'd be the skirt there. Everyone else would fuck you there. They'd turn you into a lump of meat. No messing, straight off, still in training. But that's in the navy. And it's not the navy you're looking at, it's the zone.'

Gimniuk stopped speaking, evidently not thinking it necessary to add anything else to these final words. They said it all; the verdict was not subject to appeal. Bypassing Vadim, his grave, pensive gaze slid obliquely down and away, his left eyebrow rose and fell like the hammer of an auctioneer rapping out 'Sold'. His lips pleated themselves into a public prosecutor's frown. His right hand took up his walkie-talkie again and raised it to the approximate level of his chin.

'Right then, you fucker . . .' When his gaze returned to Vadim it was tinged with fatalistic sadness. 'Like they say, "Bring your stuff to the door . . ."'

But the halting progress of his communications link stopped short of his mouth.

It was as if security guard Gimniuk had suddenly been visited by an inspired insight, suddenly seen the situation in an unexpected and extremely interesting perspective. He scanned the future 'cockerel' from head to foot, weighing him up, and lowered his walkie-talkie (not, of course, in the occasional sense of that verb which Gimniuk himself had used, but in the commonly accepted one).

'Fancy a laugh?'

The security guard leaned forward, resting his elbow on his knee and peering sullenly at Vadim.

'A real laugh? You see, if I really wanted to . . . I could get you off the hook. What are you gawping at? I could, straight up. I was the only one saw Voronin come into the building. Fedya, that's my partner,' (he was the balding, mild-mannered middle-aged guy who had issued the key to Vadim, chuckling sympathetically at the lie about working overtime) 'was in the back room. And now,' – Gimniuk glanced at his watch – 'in about fifteen minutes, maybe, he'll bunk off somewhere for half an hour. For some meet or other he has lined up . . . He asked me not to tell anyone, of course. We're not allowed to skive off from our post like that. But it's evening, holiday-time and all, so who's going to check? And if anything happens I'll just say he went out to the heads or something . . . So if I wanted . . .' Gimniuk gazed fixedly, almost ingratiatingly, into Vadim's face, as he had during their altercations at the security desk, 'if I wanted, I could turn off the alarm and give you the key to the back door. What about the cameras? No fucking sweat. I know,' he said, prodding himself in the chest with the aerial to illustrate the point, 'about the cameras. They only come on when something moves. I know all about how they work. All the cameras record on a single disk. I can get into it no problem. Over in the main building, where they keep all the dough, they've got a system you could never fucking hack into without three access codes. But over here it's a heap of crap. Why would anyone bother protecting a load of jerks like you?

'So I could just wipe out this Voronin of yours. How many cameras would that be?' Gimniuk screwed up his eyes as he totted it up. 'Outside the entrance, that's one, inside in the hall, that's two, on your fucking floor, that's three. And then the back door when you load him in the car . . . A fucking breeze,' he said with a mocking grin, 'you savvy?'

The derisive reply was a frolicsome, shrill, electronic cancan from round the corner. Gimniuk gawped all around in sudden confusion, leapt down off his table, ran out into the lobby and said 'Fuck it!' in a startled voice. But he soon came back into the kitchen and squatted down in front of Vadim.

'D'you fucking understand, that I've got you like that?' Gimniuk waved a pale fist with contrasting pink knuckles under his confidant's nose. 'Anything at all . . . I can do whatever I like with you . . . To you . . . Anything at all. If I tell you, that's it, you can clear off, but first you give me a blow job, you'll give me one! And enjoy it too. You'll smile while you suck, get the picture? Wassup, that's right, isn't it? Eh? To save your own skin? Understand? Yeah, I see you understand all right. You're a clever dick. You went to college.' Gimniuk stood up and set off round the kitchen without looking at Vadim. Gave the Three Little Pigs a kicking. Carried on as if he were talking to himself or just into thin air.

'But why the fuck would I want you to suck me off? I'm a normal guy, not some kind of scummy queer . . .' He slouched around indolently for a little longer, pretending to take an interest in the microwave ovens, juice extractors, dishwashers, fan ovens and shelves of dishes. Then he swung round sharply, strode towards Vadim, bent down, thrust the knob of his truncheon hard up under Vadim's chin so that it hurt and the back of his confidant's head was pressed against the plaster, and began speaking emphatically, hammering home every word, baring his teeth and engulfing Vadim in the tepid smell from his mouth:

'Right then, you wanker. Listen carefully. Now you're

going to get up. Tidy this lot away. Give me the key to your shitty office. Sign the register – and keep it neat and tidy! You'll get the back door key. Then you'll go out, start up his motor and drive it round here. If anyone sees you, it's your fucking problem, not mine. You're going to open the door. Quickly. And collect this jerk. What you do with him after that is for you to sweat over. You'll leave the key in the kitchen, right here. If anyone notices you, I don't give a toss. If you try to finger me – I'll still get off. You nicked the key, I've got everything on disk. And you've got it in for me because I gave you a hard time at the security post, everyone saw it, my uncle's a consultant, they'll believe me . . . If no one notices, you can reckon you're in the clear. But in that case . . .' He pressed the truncheon home even harder and Vadim began to choke. 'In that case you'll do everything I tell you to. Everything, get it? And don't even think of getting uppity. Just you try spilling your guts to anyone . . .'

How do you drive? When you get in, press the clutch pedal. There are three pedals, the clutch is the one on the left. Release the hand brake. You have to release it or the engine will stall. The alarm! The first thing, before anything else, before you open the door, don't forget to switch off the alarm! That's all you need now, to start that thing howling and tip off the entire population of the Old Town. Where was the key-ring? He fumbled in his pocket, running his sweaty fingers over the keys to the Pontiac. There. Okay. Release handbrake, turn key in ignition. Start with first gear – left and up . . .

Vadim peeped out from behind the corner. Still hanging about. Still hanging about, the lousy git. Smoking – that must be his second! Arnold, the advertising manager. Vadim had run into him the moment he stepped outside the doors of the main entrance: he was standing on the steps in his jacket, with his back to Vadim, his hands in his pockets, a cigarette in his mouth. Facing the Pontiac. Maybe eight steps away from it. Or five maybe. Advertising Arnold had turned round. Vadim had given him a wild stare and without even saying hello-goodbye gone darting off at a tangent. A passing motor had braked sharply, beep-beeping obscene abuse. Vadim had crossed the narrow street, moving out of the bank cameras' visual range, walked as far as the corner, turned and stopped with the most leisurely air he could muster. A little later he had stuck the tip of his nose out. There had been five windows lit on the façade. Now it was four. Two covered with blinds. Two left . . . But there was nothing he could do about that.

'. . . You should be thanking your lucky stars, you jerk! Get me? You thank God I swapped shifts with Slavik today,' Gimniuk had hissed through his teeth without turning round as he shambled ahead of Vadim to the security desk, his navy waddle (aka his mobster strut) suddenly intensifying to the lurch of a TV cartoon bear. 'It's my fucking day off today . . . If it was anyone else clocked you, you'd be sweating bricks in the monkey-house by now . . .'

He was leaving! Arnold flicked his cigarette butt into the bin on the wall and pulled the frosted-glass door out towards himself. Vadim tensed, ready to dart out from behind the corner, but the back of the jacket reversed direction to allow an unidentified female silhouette in a long coat out through the back-lit doorway. Christ, how many of them were there in the building at half-past seven in the evening?

'. . . 19.35', Fedya on the security desk had prompted him condescendingly when Vadim realised after glancing twice at his wrist that he had never really understood the meaning of those black divisions round the edge of the dial, or the alignment of the hands. He had caught glimpses of Gimniuk in the room at the back (yes, you wanker, let him fucking see you leaving!) as he was signing the register. Beside the imbecilically crooked '19.35' there was a casually innocent '18.10'. An hour and a half had gone by since he entered the building. Only an hour and a half . . .

Time to move! He waited one, two, three seconds and broke cover. The hardest thing of all was not to break straight into a run. Release handbrake, insert key in ignition, no, first the clutch, depress clutch pedal and with clutch pedal depressed turn key . . . If anyone looked out of the window now, he was a goner. If anyone came out through the doors, he was a goner. He was already under intense scrutiny. A coagulated clot of emptiness. He turned his back towards the entrance of the bank.

Took hold of the car door.

The alarm!

Vadim began feeling for the little button on the fob – the keys slipped through his fingers on to the pavement. He bent down, keeping his back towards the bank. He missed, scraping his fingers along the asphalt under wet, snowy slime. He was a goner for sure now. He caught the keys. Pressed the fob.

Beep!

Vadim pulled the yellow door open so hard he almost tore it off and dived face-first into the low space. With the top of his head pressed against the roof, he slammed the door shut. Okay . . . Okay, okay, he was halfway there already. A third of the way. No one could see him here in the dark, fragrant interior behind the dark–tinted glass. Gimniuk would erase all record of him getting in. So what if the Pontiac had stood there for an hour and a half for no particular reason and then driven away again? Was that strange? It was. But it was no crime. And the main thing was that Apletaev had had nothing at all to do with it. He just needed to get the thing moving right. So it looked convincing.

Handbrake. Clutch. Left pedal out of three. Ignition. First gear – left and forward.

It was then Vadim realised that the fun was only just beginning.

Instead of the anticipated gear-stick that waggled in two dimensions, Voronin's swanky, leather-trimmed set of wheels had a mysterious lever that only moved backwards and forwards along a channel marked with cabbalistic symbols. And there were two pedals. Not a third pedal in sight.

This was so unexpected, so absolutely simple and indisputably final, that for some period of time – fortunately not a very long one, apparently – Vadim lapsed into cataleptic stupor. His processor froze. And it cost him a serious effort to make himself grasp the elementary fact that what he was looking at was an automatic gear-shift. Much simpler. For dames and dummies. Like an idiot camera. Mistake-proof. An idiot-proof system for idiots.

Idiot-proof. That was the problem. Vadim was a total idiot. So the system worked against him – he didn't understand a thing. What were those hieroglyphs beside the lever? The one closest to the dashboard was P. The lever was in that section now. Then came R, 1, 2, D, De in that order. O-kay.

Bugger it. Later. First things first. Handbrake. Just like any other handbrake. That was a good start. Positively wonderful. The important thing was to make a start. Okay. Pedals. Accelerator and brake – logical? In an ordinary motor the sequence was clutch, brake, accelerator, left to right, wasn't it? So the left pedal must be the brake.

Let's try it like that then. Vadim pressed down the left pedal. Managed to insert the key at the third attempt. Turned it clockwise. About as decisively as if he knew there was half a kilo of plastique wired to the ignition.

Ba-ba-ba . . . boom. The treacherous techno-heap shuddered awake, mumbled and muttered in the deep throat of its engine, peered out hazily at the snow with its dipped headlights. As if activated by the same impulse, something clicked into place inside Vadim: P was for Parking, R was for Reverse.

There was an Audi parked about five metres behind him. He had to move the lever into the right section. Now careful – very, very careful: inexperienced drivers always stepped on the pedals too hard! Release the left pedal, press the right one and turn the wheel gently to the right.

He had no doubt that he would crash into something, that this arsehole of an auto would react quite differently from the way he was expecting: for instance, maybe even zoom off in the opposite direction, and canon like a cunt into one of the nearby cars with a clang and a clatter, setting its alarm howling. And Vadim could sense – not on his skin, but on the slimy, quivering surface of his soft entrails – the gaze of the camera, seeing everything, recording everything, in images that no Gimniuk would ever be able to erase.

He didn't need to use the accelerator. He only had to release the brake for the Pontiac to start edging its slim rear end backwards, rea-lly, rea-lly slow-ly, as if it were amazed at itself, bearing right along a wide arc around the deadly Audi, then crossing the narrow street and almost running into an indistinct streamlined object nestling against the opposite kerb. Fuck. Vadim slammed the pedal down to the floor.

Calm down. Cool it. Let it up again. Ea-sy does it, ea-sy does it, left, straighten up, okay, okay, okay. A paltry little sidestreet. Hardly any lights at all. Down to the end, fifty metres maybe, then turn right and there's the bank's service door. Just one problem. Now he had to drive forwards. Where should he put the lever?

Vadim shifted the lever straight to D. Totally off the top of his head. It could just as well have been the position that activated the auto-destruct sequence or broadcast a signal to the police. But the Pontiac began moving forward. It jolted over the kerb. Vadim had misjudged the arc of the tight turn. Emboldened, he nudged at the accelerator. Very gently. Excellent. Fast-track transformation into Schumacher by the accelerated learning method. Brake. The crunching of ribs against the steering wheel. The usual learner driver's trick. Bugg-ger-ing hell.

He turned into a sort of parking bay and stopped in the pool of light outside the service entrance door. If he took his foot off the pedal now, the car would start moving. What should he do? Set it to Parking, dickhead.

There were no windows in the blank end wall of the building. No one would notice anything. But there was a camera. That was Gimniuk's job. He'd better not have forgotten to switch off the alarm . . .

Leaving the left door of the car open and opening the right one as well, Vadim unlocked the service door with Gimniuk's key. There was no protest from the alarm system. He grabbed Four-Eyes under the armpits, like he had before. In Hollywood gangster movies they usually put the bodies in the boot. But Vadim didn't know if the Pontiac even had a boot, or if its owner would fit into it.

Four-Eyes across the seat, twisted sideways with his shoes sticking out of the car. Vadim shoved the body further in, gripping it by the ankles, bending and folding his boss like a sofa-bed, then pressed him down and slammed the door on him. He went back to the kitchen, tossed the key on to the table, closed the broken inside door, then the outside one, then jumped into the driver's seat. Four-Eyes had already installed himself behind the wheel, slumped trustingly, sack-like, against the back of the seat. Vadim shoved him back into his own place and discovered that he was covered in brown crap again. Despite the neck-tie, something had managed to seep out of the plastic bags.

Right, *now* he was halfway there.

Vadim made his way back out into the street by carefully repeating his previous actions, only in reverse. After that, things would get much worse: he had to find his way out of the Old Town, packed with people, cars and police – and on to the embankment? Yes, obviously on to the embankment, and then drive through heavy traffic as far as the Vantov bridge, through the complicated junction on to the bridge, over the river into Zadvinie, on as far as Imanta, and then to the salubrious Kleist forest where, as far he could recall from his childhood escapades, he would find any number of shagging ditches and at least a couple of biggish pits.

Every now and then Four-Eyes tried to sneak his cellophane-wrapped head down on to Vadim's shoulder and Vadim frenziedly jabbed him away with his elbow. Round the very first corner, in the narrow central channel of the street, the Pontiac came nose to nose with a Merc going the other way. The Merc sounded its horn in irritation: pull over! Vadim would have been only too glad to pull over, but that would have required him to process too many considerations and calculations and convert them too rapidly into actions, preferably precise ones . . . His processor froze again. The fat-faced driver visible above the teutonic visor of the Merc's radiator gestured energetically to the left with his open hand to make it clear what he expected the dimwit facing him to do. Realising he was wasting his time, he struck himself no less energetically on the forehead, reversed and pulled into a gap between the cars parked beside the pavement. Vadim unfroze and pressed the accelerator.

He drove past the low Ford taxis, barely scraped past the apathetic traffic cops guarding the orange barrier at the entrance to the conservation zone of the historical centre. Catching his breath and trying not even to come close to the thirty kilometres per hour supposedly permitted here by law, he crept out on to the embankment. And came to a dead stop at the corner. Three cast-iron-black Red-Army riflemen huddled back to back outside the knobbly-topped pencil-case museum that used to be theirs before it became the Museum of the Occupation.

There was a solid mass of cars moving along the embankment at a good speed, and he had absolutely no idea how to insinuate himself into it. Two or three impatient motorists instantly settled on his tail. Not a single gap. The people behind beep-beeped to urge him on. Vadim spotted an infinitesimal break in the flow, gritted his teeth, swung the wheel and stepped on the accelerator. Andrei Vladlenovich immediately collapsed on to him with a leathery rustle. Get off me, you stinking carcass!

Vadim stuck to the extreme right lane, hunched over tight and clutching the driving wheel in slippery palms, letting everybody overtake him. He wondered what they were thinking about the gaudy sportscar crawling timidly along the kerb like a sissy schoolgirl. That the driver was more tanked up than his motor, perhaps . . . The cops would think the same, of course, and this was a serious set of wheels, so if the rich owner was pissed you could take him for a bundle . . .

Junction. Traffic lights. Brake. Chest crunching against

steering wheel. Boss butting windscreen with dull thud. Get back, you. The right indicator blinking on the wide back end of a lorry that announced that it came from Isover. What was over? Nothing yet. Should he switch his indicator on? How? Fuck only knew. Bugger it. The exit to the bridge was on the right. Vadim stuck close to the flapping awning at the back of the lorry, straining hard not to fall behind and desperately afraid of not reacting fast enough if the lorry braked. He just managed by the skin of his teeth to duplicate all its manoeuvres, so that two turns later he found himself on the bridge.

There were only two lanes here and he couldn't creep along at his old speed any longer. But then there weren't any turns. Feeling like he was dying, Vadim put his foot down in anguished abandonment, exchanging the risk of attracting attention for the near certainty of smashing headlong into a pillar or somersaulting over the kerb. The Pontiac went hurtling under a pylon, a great two-pronged fork stuck into the river. Over the bridge. The sweat was streaming down his back. Past the House of the Press. His clothes were wringing wet, any second now the dark patches would start appearing on his jacket – and that was supposed to be waterproof. The dark bulk of Zadvinie came hurtling towards him.

Suddenly from somewhere behind him, over the river, there was a loud, cosmic whistling and crackling that was everywhere at once and nowhere in particular and a gigantic, ghastly, polychromatic glow. Vadim almost cried out. Fireworks. As if it had suddenly recalled something important, the wild dance music struck up again inside Four-Eyes. It carried on playing as far as the Slokas-Kaliciem crossroads. The Isover lorry abandoned him there, turning right, while Vadim turned off on to monstrously perilous

Slokas Street, full of illogical twists and turns, treacherous crossroads and aggressive trams.

When the car smashed its way through something with a sickening, scraping crackle and its front end crunched into something else, slamming the steering-wheel into his ribcage in the time-honoured manner, and came to a halt, Vadim decided that was probably enough. He shifted the lever and straightened up. Rather, he tried to straighten up. But no way. Not a chance. He had solidified as if he were made of cement, stiffened into position: hunched over in the driving seat with his hands on the driving-wheel. For one moment he genuinely thought that he would NEVER straighten up again.

Time for a break, Mister Four-Eyes. You can get out and stretch your legs, take a leak. You don't want to? I can't hear you too well through that plastic bag. You say the weather's not turned out too well? You're right there. But I've got to get out, like it or not. Such is the karma of the subordinate. You're the boss and I'm the fool.

Outside was a dense thicket of wet bushes. The snow was pelting down in broad, damp clumps and heaping up – the same snow that had plastered over the entire bloody windscreen. In such cases the done thing is to turn on the windscreen wipers – but that was another thing Vadim didn't know how to do. Naturally, the moment he had tried fiddling with the instrument panel, he had slammed into this pine tree. It wasn't really a great disaster, except the right headlight was kaput. He couldn't see anything by the light of the other one, except for the bloody trees. But even with its nose rammed into a tree trunk, surrounded by wet willows and besmirched by meteorological excretions, the bright, tangy-fruit-coloured accessory of the open Californian highways looked no worse than the flashy-dressing son-in-law and head of REX Bank's press service in the role of a straggling bundle of second-hand rags with a glue-sniffer's bag stuck over its head.

Vadim flopped down on to the seat. At least now he could give some thought to exploring the dashboard. What was this bloody thingummy here? Fuck only knew. After n hours (in fact it was something less than forty minutes) of jolting progress through the forest of his childhood, Vadim had slipped into a state of numbed automatism, a variation on the old, familiar frozen-processor condition, only a little more active. He had bounced patiently along at about twenty kilometres an hour over the ruts in the battered earth roads, turning at right angles with strictly aimless regularity – the forest tracks here had been laid by rampaging geometricians. He had immediately become totally and absolutely lost. That is, as soon as he turned off the asphalt on to the dirt surface that receded into the tree trunks and bushes, he had ceased to understand where he was. There had been absolutely no question of locating the pit he wanted from his memories of so many years ago. Initially he had evidently been circling around close to the Lacupes cemetery – every now and then the bright spot of his headlights had thrown up a wire-mesh fence and crumbling gravestones. Then a big road (by comparison with the others, that is) had led him out to a farm and the dogs had started barking. A little while later they had started barking again – it could quite easily have been the same farm and the same dogs. And then it had started snowing.

He himself didn't know what it was he had done, but with a plastic click and a squeaky whisper the wipers begin licking rhythmically at the glass. Break-time was over. When he started reversing, Vadim was almost relieved to feel something happen that ought to have happened much, much sooner. It was really strange it hadn't happened already. The wheels began spinning idly, without gripping the filthy snowy sludge. He felt almost disappointed when the studded tyres quickly found a hold. Right, let's blast a few bushes. Smack! Straight into another tree trunk, this time with the rear end. Sorry about that, Four-Eyes, just can't seem to get the hang of your motor somehow. Hey there, bro, you've started to pong a bit. Easy now, easy, what do we want with driving into that ditch? It's not time for us to be going down the drain just yet . . . Finally the Pontiac rasped its wing against yet another pine tree (the mirror folded flat) and began swaying over the potholes in the road again, like a small drifter in a beam sea.

Bushes. Tree-trunks. Bushes, tree-trunks, bushes, tree-trunks, bushes, tree-trunks, crossroads. Left, right or straight ahead? Straight ahead. At the roadside the headlight picked out the crumpled shell of a limo, obviously burnt out back in the Palaeozoic era. Was that a hint? Why shouldn't he . . . What with? Maybe he had a spare can of petrol in here somewhere? Why would he? Toss a match in the petrol tank? But then it was only in the movies that they were inclined to explode in that fantastic fashion, with a little encouragement from the pyrotechnicians. The longer Vadim went on, the less clear it became just what he was supposed to do with *him*. Left, right or straight on? Right. You could carry on jolting around like this all night and still never find a single pond. Or even more likely, get stuck fast at some point. Just dump him? It would only take them two days at most to find the motor: this wasn't a real forest, more like a woodland park. Oh-oh, was he stuck now? No, not this time either. There probably wasn't another set of wheels like this in the whole of Riga. And what could he do with the body? Bury it? Again, what with? He certainly didn't have a spade. Just dump it? Drag it off into the bushes? Garbage, garbage. Lefristraighton? He was on the point of turning left for the sake of variety, when he turned right instead – and almost immediately the bushes and tree-trunks retreated beyond the reach of his single dipped headlight and Vadim felt, rather than saw, that he had emerged into open space. Stop.

He had to go out in the snow again. True, it wasn't falling so thickly any more. You could just about say it had stopped. The forest around him looked like randomly dumped heaps of blackness, but straight ahead the darkness was thinner and more three-dimensional, and there was an even breeze blowing out of it. A field. Open space, watery snowdrifts, impassable mud. The road ran round the edge. Hang on though, hang on. It couldn't be . . . He couldn't allow his mind to believe it – too much of a luxury for someone in his position – but he already knew. He knew that he knew this place. Remembered this field. The pit was right here. Only which side of the field was it on? No fucking problem, we could find it now. Hear that, Four-Eyes, we're going to find it, it can't get away now! Chin up, bro, we'll soon have you fixed up. The deed's as good as done.

And he really did find it, even though he had to drive almost all the way round the edge of the immense square field to do it. Twice he got stuck, once quite impossibly. Once he nearly tumbled into an open culvert. He went past a farm, provoking the usual fit of professional enthusiasm from the inevitable yapping mutts.

The pit was pretty puny. Not much of a pit at all, to be honest, not really serious. Maybe it had degenerated over the years, or maybe his memory had misled him. But it would still be three metres deep, wouldn't it? Maybe . . . in the middle . . . The sides were flat, with only one high bank. He had no choice anyway. No other choice and no more strength. It was okay for him to collapse now.

He drove round the black puddle and up on to the high bank, smashing the side of the car against a tree – really giving a go this time, so that the right rear window cracked all over – then turned the radiator towards the drop. Wouldn't it be a howl if it wasn't deep enough! But he was really only winding himself up – he wasn't bothered about anything any more. Not a single, solitary thing. In fact, if Vadim hadn't found the pit, he would have just abandoned the car on the road with the body in it. Okay then, Four-Eyes, are we off? Somehow Vadim couldn't lift his foot off the brake. Let's go! He couldn't. As if to encourage him, Four-Eyes suddenly burst into trilling song again – and then Vadim managed to overcome his foot's stubborn resistance. He released the pedal (the car started moving slowly), opened the door and got out. The boss needs you, you don't need the boss. The telephone was in high spirits, gleefully taking the piss out of someone or other.

The cancan was wild and riotous, the girls squealed and tossed up their skirts, shot their slim legs up in the air – and to this appropriately solemn funeral march the requisitely respectable, canary-yellow catafalque carried the boss Vadim didn't need to the edge of the pit, stuck its nose over and went plunging downwards with a clumsy flip of its backside and a long, loud scraping sound. Vadim strolled up to the edge. Aha. It had been bound to happen. The yellow roof was still visible above the water.

He carried on standing there (the foul muck was falling more heavily from the sky now), until the light-coloured square became substantially dimmer, darkened significantly and then disappeared altogether.

9

The spectacles.

Four-Eyes's stratospherically priced, futuristically designed Yamamoto specs. Clinging to the upper chamfer of Vadim's monitor with their chitinous little claws. Four-Eyes's specs, gazing up into his eyes with a distinct air of superior condescension, despite their inferior position, the cold-smoke-cured left lens obliquely traversed by the sly squint of a narrow, ironical crack. Four-Eyes was winking at him, hinting, sharing some secret expert knowledge extraneous to the daily activity of the press room.

Those spectacles were the first thing that Vadim saw when he entered the office and instantly he was hit by a malfunction. A sync glitch, the kind you get during a collective death-match shoot-out on the net: when the psychotic screen posts the anxiety-inducing message 'Out of sync' and the communal play-space layers off dolefully into a set of mutually incompatible, mutually incomprehensible, stuttering, stammering quasi-realities. One of the separated strata of Vadim's consciousness contained his TV alarm, set for half past seven, the sluggish stream of water running reluctantly from the tap, the cheerless sunshine-yellow of a Hungarian Icarus bus, the crumpled yawns of the bus-riding population, the repugnant wintry greyness of the windy sky, 'good morning', 'fourth stop, please' and two 'Hi's. From first thing in the morning, the repetitive inertia of this routine reality, insulated from the previous day's events by eight hours of death-like sleep, had imperiously asserted its authority. Eagerly incited and encouraged by reason's natural instinct for self-preservation, it had removed the contents of the previous evening to the realm of bad trips, nightmares with rubbery arms and legs, and other such mental aberrations. Meanwhile another, incompatible stratum of consciousness, a horror-movie caricature of a blood-and-guts thriller, oozed out through the dark, raw, abrasion on the palm of his right hand, the bruises on his chest and shoulder, the weary, creaking protest of his muscles and joints at the slightest movement, the brownish fringe on the sleeves of his jacket (it didn't wash off!) and the filthy smears of thick suburban-forest mud on his shoes: it stared wildly out of the mirror with demented eyes, deceptively dissembled and deferred to the jostling throng in the street, then took swift, devastating aim at its stunned target through a pair of Japanese lenses. Out of sync. Way out.

'Hi! Good morning . . .' Vadim approached his cubicle with maximum achievable nonchalance, switched on the computer and swept the glasses into his pocket as if by some chance afterthought. Nobody took any notice of him. 'Hi, Vadim,' Olezhek responded absentmindedly from next door, picking away at Microsoft's teeth with his mouse. But reality was fundamentally on the blink. The fear – concrete, physiological and very strong – was back again, and there was no way the mechanical automatism of some depressingly familiar file menu or the diarrhoea-dribble of some dumb fax – '. . . shoot me over those inserts again, you know, for *Career* magazine . . .' – could overcome it.

Fear took the form of a geometrical figure, a triangle with the following three vertices: a bronze dinosaur wearing a crown; a set of desk drawers protruding from under the desktop with the top drawer firmly locked for the very first time in its entire life; and the pocket of Vadim's jeans. The first two remained static, while the third moved around with him, which meant there was nowhere Vadim could go to get away from the fear. The fear also had an annexe, less physically substantial, but more spatially extensive, located a little distance away, where the stomach-celebrating samurai was preparing, as ever, to snack on his own viscera.

Within the louvre-lined entrails of the closed command module, the phone screeched for a first time and then a second. The second call was abandoned very swiftly, after just a couple of rings. Whoever it was that had tried in vain to caution and protect Andrei Valdlenovich via the hysterical howling of his mobile the day before must have realised it was too late.

'Vadik, can I borrow this?' Svetochka the copy editor quizzed him with a smile, kneading the crumpled mug in her fingers. 'What's up with you today?'

Vadim nodded half-heartedly. And hastily covered the suspiciously empty projection with a plastic stationery holder that resembled a set of inverted rocket-engine nozzles.

He tried to concentrate on the Infonet Foundation's quarterly report on the influence of global communications and multimedia on the banking business. Even before, it had been a hard struggle for the interminable figures and foreign business terminology to retain any semblance of meaning. Now they had been emptied of it completely and become entirely indistinguishable from the absurdist hieroglyphs that made up computer code. Yet more desynchronisation. Vadim himself was no longer in sync with his surroundings and the people in them. He had become incompatible with the life of the press room.

His colleagues still greeted him, still passed on ephemeral queries concerning work, the computer still obeyed his commands, the telephone still consorted with him – but that was all mere force of habit. In reality, employee Apletaev no longer belonged either to the press room or to REX. Or to the single, unified order of things universally accepted by all his law-abiding fellow citizens. He contradicted it. The glistening red map of the Antarctic, the sloshing flop and rustle of a plastic bin-liner, the wet forest undergrowth, the bright square fading away into the black water had implicitly excluded him from the universal social paradigm. He was out of it.

The monadic rank and file PR unit had mutated, like a normal cell affected by cancer. A couple of people had already tried knocking on the door of Four-Eyes's office, and someone had asked, 'Hasn't the boss been in yet today?' (Each time, Vadim's gaze had glued itself to monitor and his neck muscles had tensed up in a reflex response.) After about an hour someone had exclaimed in surprise: 'Didn't he let anyone know he wasn't coming in today?' These were all symptoms of irreversible decay – desynchronisation, degeneration, disintegration – the camouflaged source and origin of which was busily fingering his keyboard, constructing bogus texts and swooning in panic every time the door of the office opened.

The terror churning Vadim's stomach into a sick mess was highly specific – it was the terror of exposure, arrest and the zone. Not the requisite (as one might suppose) sharp pangs of conscience, and certainly not the clearly articulated self-reproach: 'Yesterday I KILLED A MAN'. Nothing of the kind. No reminiscences of Dostoevsky here. He felt rotten, really rotten – but solely and exclusively because he was afraid of being sussed.

The cleaning woman . . . The cleaning woman! How often did she clean the press room. Every day, in the morning? Once a week, on Saturday? Would the cleaning woman move the drawers? Or Murzilla? Dust the stand, or something like that? The apexes of the infernal triangle metamorphosed into insoluble problems. He couldn't scrape the pediment clean and carry out a heap of bloody paper now, right in front of everyone. And staying behind after everyone had gone was a sure way to attract suspicion . . .

Prompted by a sudden stirring in the convoluted lining of his guts, Vadim swung round, groped, picked up the first diskette that came to hand without looking. Clicked it into the PC. Went into the hard drive. Snaked his way to WORDART. Highlighted the incriminating *txt*s in yellow and transferred them to the disk. One after another in stuttering sequence the bomb-fuse files flickered out from left to right as they were moved. Vadim pulled out the floppy, tucked it into his back pocket.

About an hour later the door opened, leaving a narrow gap that was filled by the Head of Information Security, Mikhail Anatolievich Pylny – sharp, angular and hinged like a folding knife. Dragging his lace-up boots over the floor – swi-i-ish . . . swi-i-ish – he bisected the press room along a decisively direct line from the door to Four-Eyes's empty compartment, took a confident grasp of the door handle and pulled. Tried again with a puzzled air. Tugged suspiciously. Scanned the premises with the radar of outraged bewilderment.

'Andrei?' he enquired of the room in general, haughtily demanding a reply from no one in particular.

Vadim froze.

'We've been looking for him ourselves, Mikhail Antonich!' replied the room in the person of Vadim's neighbour Olezhek, who popped out from his cell like a demented genie from his bottle. 'He hasn't been in at all this morning! Here, I've had all these slogans all ready for handing . . .'

Paying no more attention to Olezhek's clumsy attempts

to screw words together into a sentence, Mikhail Anatolievich unfolded his mobile phone and irritably punched the number that must have been recorded in his memory a hundred times over (Vadim had fused with the letters on his screen, but in some strange way he registered every move that Pylny made). The Head of Information Security waited, tapping out an irksome message in Morse with one boot. Despite himself, Vadim pictured the Pontiac with its Pirelli tyres mired at a crooked angle in the garbage-littered sludge on the bottom of the pit: the door gaping open, his boss nestled against the windscreen, the skirts of his Paul Smith coat fluttering majestically, and his mobile, the swanky Siemens M35I ('Out there in Tahiti I went surfing with it and even took it down with the aqualung, check it out, like totally waterproof, yeah?') with its little green eye trembling soundlessly in the chilly gloom. A hysterical smirk began twitching at the corners of Vadim's lips. He straightened them out in fright – he'd notice! But the dominoes of uncontrollable associations were already clattering in sequence along that borderline between asinine humour and mystical terror: he saw Four-Eyes reaching out in a flurry of fine sand, taking the phone, raising it to his plastic bags, and a garland of bubbles gaily gurgling out from under the distended neck-tie . . . He shook his head to drive the vision away, tore his eyes away from the screen and tumbled straight into a deep air-pocket: Pylny was looking at him! But then, with a censorious twitch of his bony jaw that revealed the lump of the Adam's apple buried in the flabby folds of his neck, Pylny clicked his mobile shut, swi-i-ished his boots, remarked brusquely to the room in general 'If he comes, it's urgent!', slammed the door and was gone.

There were six hours left until the end of the working day.

'Fucking great bed,' security guard Gimniuk opined patronisingly, with a proprietorial slap at the soft surface of the Lithuanian couch. 'It'll suit. Comfy on that, is it?' He winked, more to himself than to Vadim, and mimed gale-force pitching and rolling with his open hand. 'Eh?' He stared, waiting. 'Hey! I asked you a question, carp!' The security guard's slovenly, doltish bass was suddenly distended with purple overtones of stormy menace that demanded immediate propitiation and mollification, or else you were for it . . . 'I ask – you answer. Straight off, sharpish, savvy? Is it comfy for shagging? Well?'

Vadim nodded.

'Can't hear you!'

'Yes.'

'Better,' Gimniuk approved tersely, settling back, placated, into his former derisive good humour. 'It'll do. When I feel like it,' – he cleared his throat suggestively – 'I'll shaft my women here. Of course, you live like a real slob, but it'll do for a screw.' He rammed his fist against the submissive edge of the mattress once again, stood up and set off round the room.

'Yeah, right, okay. Telly, video . . . Like a bit of porn, do you?' The security guard's heavy shit-crushers flattened the pile of the carpet.

Vadim observed his progress. Gimniuk apparently remained faithful to his working uniform away from work too – and Vadim realised there was nothing illogical about that, in fact he wouldn't have been able to accept Gimniuk as Gimniuk without it. It was only the absence of the truncheon that seemed somehow illogical.

Stopping by the window, the security guard devoted a moment of pensive contemplation to the fifth-floor view of prefabricated dormitory-district boxes glowing in the dark before turning back unhurriedly towards Vadim.

'Nah, carp,' Gimniuk declared with a razor-sharp squint that contrasted with the gentle, regretful tone of his voice, 'you still don't get it . . .'

'No I don't,' said Vadim.

Still squinting, the security guard nodded briefly, again more to himself than Vadim. Then he opened his eyelids wide and looked Vadim straight in the eye with that trademark sullen stare (that wall of ice behind the pupils), gave a stentorian snort, thrust out his lower lip and cautiously (still staring Vadim in the eyes) lowered a hefty gob of snot on a viscous thread of spittle, like a steeplejack on a cable. Splat. Straight on to the black top of the Philips video. Then he turned back to the window.

Vadim sank down on to the edge of the 'fucking great bed'.

'Right, you wanker, listen up.' Gimniuk swung round sharply, as if he'd just woken up, dropped himself from a height into the armchair (which croaked in fright), slithered down into a quasi-recumbent position, dangled his arms over the armrests and dumped his dirty shit-crushers on to the glass top of the automobile-wing coffee table with a merciless crash. Instead of Gimniuk's pale eyes, his tank-track soles goggled up at Vadim like a test-card pattern that has suddenly replaced the picture on the TV. 'It's like this. I'm not going to say it twice. I got you off the hook, you jerk. Voronin's not on the disk. Not on the BANK's disk,' he clarified with deliberate emphasis. 'But I copied all your stupid shite on to MY disk, get it? The whole thing, the works. Your mate Voronin entering the building . . . And going up to your floor . . . And you getting into the motor . . . and packing the stiff into it . . . You useless fucker!' For no apparent reason, he lurched forward in the armchair, popping up over the top of his titanic boots, gesticulating wildly. 'You useless fucking jerk! Driving off like that! So terrified you pissed yourself, were you? Or don't you even know how to drive? First time you'd ever seen a car, was it? You wanker!' And then, panting incredulously, he slumped back down again. 'Anyway, I stuck the whole fucking lot on a DVD and tucked it away in a nice safe place. So you wouldn't get any bright ideas into that clever-dick head of yours about fucking me over. Now,' said Gimniuk, reversing the position of his emphatically stacked boots in visual demonstration of the fundamental thesis to follow, 'I'm going to be the clever one. I'm going to tell you what to do. Get it? . . . Can't fucking well hear you!'

'I get it.'

'You sure?'

'I'm sure.'

'That's just fucking great.' The security guard took his feet down off the coffee table and sat up briskly in the armchair, nervously twisting his fingers together and immediately untwisting them again. The nostrils of his pimply nose flared and Vadim realised with a sudden shock that Sergei Gimniuk looked as if he had a bad case of the jitters.

'Now, listen,' Gimniuk continued. 'Tomorrow, at exactly nine o'clock in the evening, you'll be in the centre of town. You won't go hanging about after work with your mates until nine o'clock, you'll come here, and then go back into the centre. And don't go making yourself obvious. In the centre, at exactly nine o'clock, twenty-one hundred hours, got that? You'll go into a telephone box. And dial . . . Get a pen, sharpish, write this down! You'll dial 9534958. Got that? 9534958. Have you got it down right? Show me! That,' said Gimniuk, leaning forward slightly and shifting the coffee table with his knees, 'is the Man's mobile number . . . And you'll tell him . . . Write! You'll tell him . . .' The security guard's face set solid in an expression of obtuse concentration, as if he were standing up at the front of the class declaiming a poem learned off by heart. 'We know all about your plans . . . You writing? . . . concerning your partners from the Moscow region. If you don't want them . . . to find out all about everything . . . Got all that? . . . be ready at any moment . . . moment . . . to hand over a hundred thousand US dollars in cash . . . in hundred dollar bills. Don't try to trace this call or go to the police. If you do, then . . . Get a move on, you fucking wanker! . . . then we will immediately inform . . . your partners. Wait . . . for our next call. And be ready to carry out . . . carry . . . out . . . any instructions we give you . . . quickly and precisely . . . quickly . . . and . . . precisely. That's it. Got all that?' Gimniuk waited for a nod, then carried on gazing at Vadim's face, watching for a reaction. 'You'll tell them that, then hang up and blow, sharpish. Don't start rabbiting with them, right? Don't answer any questions. Learn off everything I just said! Learn it off and burn it. Don't just sling it, burn it. Right, you wanker . . . You got a mobile? What, no mobile? What kind of useless cunt are you? Why the fuck haven't you got a mobile? Wassup, too poor, or what? Don't pay you enough in your shagging press room, do they? Okay . . . Right. Right. Then you grab a bloody motor straight off – and bugger off home. At the double! At exactly half past . . . bugger, you won't make it . . . okay. At twenty to nine make sure you're sitting here . . .' Gimniuk prodded Vadim's grey push-button Panasonic phone, 'and waiting for my call. God help you if you're not! I'll give you a bell and tell you what to do next. And you'll do it. Without asking any questions. And don't even think about getting uppity. Don't even fucking think about saying a word to anyone!'

Gimniuk was observing Vadim with increasing scepticism now, as if he already regretted having involved a dozy pillock like him in a serious deal like this.

'I don't want you to just fucking sit there, nodding away like a wanker, I want you to cop on,' Gimniuk was calm and convincing now, like an expensive psychoanalyst. 'It's a crying fucking shame you were never in the forces. If you haven't been in the forces then you haven't got a bastard clue what life's all about. What did they teach you in those colleges of yours? Nothing but a heap of crap, smart-arse con-tricks. In the army or the navy they'd have taught you all about real bloody life, not that kind of shite. Because the first year you're in, you're a carp. And a fucking carp isn't some kind of second-grade citizen. It's nobody, nothing. Get it? NO-BO-DY. While you're a carp, you can't even think, let alone go putting one over on anyone else, you can't want anything or not want anything, you can't go getting uppity or asking questions. The only thing you know how to do is what an officer or a yearman tells you. If he fucking tells you to clear the entire parade ground of snow, then you do it, even if you shred your bastard arse into a Union Jack in the process. No one gives a toss if you want or you don't want, if you can or you can't, or what you might happen to think about it. No one. If a yearman says to you "Five jars", then you go down without being told, sharpish – and you stay there until they've lashed five jars across you . . .'

Gimniuk expounded the situation simply and clearly, with appropriate expression and even with some feeling, leaving no doubt at all that he was not just putting on a front, but really did think of himself at that moment as a mentor, teacher and guru, stern but fair, impressing the harsh, universal truths of manhood on an infantile individual snared in his own puny and premature delusions of adequacy.

'So just remember: you're not a fucking press–service desk-man any longer, not some clever fucking dick with an education. You've got no boss, no ma and pa, nobody. You're a carp. And all you've got is me. And the only thing you know how to do is what I tell you. Savvy? You? Bastard? Can't hear you!'

'I savvy.'

'Louder!'

'I savvy!'

'What fucking way is that to answer an officer?'

'Yes sir!'

Gimniuk smiled in genuine admiration of the results of his educational work. But he quickly turned more serious:

'Everything,' he continued in the same tone as before, 'that means EVERYTHING. If I tell you to give me your woman, you give her to me. You got a woman?'

'No,' Vadim lied.

'What, not even got a woman?' For some reason this particular piece of information reduced the security guard to almost hysterical rapture. His pale eyes glittered in that already familiar fashion. 'Why you witless plonker! Why, you wally, I always knew you were a plonker, but fuck me . . . No, fuck me . . . You're bloody unbelievable, you queer bastards.' Gimniuk's words vibrated and sparkled in triumph. 'You fuckers stroll past the security desk making out like you're all so . . . so fucking big time! You work in a shagging bank! Make real big bucks! Real big shots! And like I'm just some kind of shit. Like low-life scum, just the security man. That's what you all think. Like I'm some kind of saphead. You tell me "good morning" and I'm supposed to shit myself in delight, am I? That right? That right, I asked you?'

'No.'

'What no? What no?' Seemingly without even

realising it, Gimniuk had worked himself into a state of such profane exaltation that now he was lashing himself on, winding himself up with every phrase, like a biker kicking at the pedal to rev up his motorbike. He had turned bright red. 'Who are you, anyway, you bastard? What kind of man are you? You're not a fucking man at all! You're a sack of shit! Pissing fucking useless!' At this point the security guard listed over to one side, stuck his right hand behind his back, pulled out a small black pistol and started turning it over in his hands. Studiously ignoring Vadim, he drew back the breech with a slow, ostentatious movement and clicked a little lever – the safety catch, Vadim guessed – once, twice. Only then did he deign to cast an indolent glance at his companion.

'You've got to know who to show proper respect to,' Gimniuk concluded in a voice that was quite absurdly exaggerated in its swagger. Lazily he got up and sauntered around the room, holding the pistol pointing downwards with his arm held rigid slightly away from his body, as if he were about to finish off someone lying on the floor. Lazily he ran his eyes over the walls. Inevitably, his gaze latched on to the copper frame where Vadim had placed his version of the REX office supplies requisition list. Gimniuk went closer. Slowly putting the pistol back into his belt, he started reading.

Vadim got up from the couch.

'What's this fucking shite?' Gimniuk asked, swinging round aggressively towards him.

Vadim took a step forwards, threw his arm backwards and punched the security guard in the face with all his strength. Something broke in his hand.

'Aagh!' said Gimniuk, clutching at his face. He hunched over without trying to defend himself and the glance he shot up at Vadim switched in rapid succession from serious pain to inexpressible disorientation and burgeoning fear, escalating instantly into panic. Something red started dripping out from under his hands.

Vadim lashed a foot into his crotch. Missed his balls, apparently, and got him somewhere in the base of the belly, but Gimniuk doubled up obediently, maybe even exaggeratedly, and Vadim thumped him in the ear a few more times with his aching fist.

The pistol fell to the floor with a hefty clatter.

'Aghh!' Gimniuk crawled to the foot of the wall, attempting to defend himself as far as possible with his elbows and forearms. From somewhere underneath a single eye peeped out crazily.

Vadim picked up the pistol. It was rather heavy, with a warmth that felt unlike metal. His hand was hurting more than ever now, throbbing mercilessly. Gimniuk was squirming at his feet with his elbows jutting out. Vadim stood over him for a moment, then spontaneously lashed out at him like a footballer kicking the ball.

Aha, so that is the safety catch after all. Click.

'What you doing?' said the security guard, responding immediately to this last action, slithering about inside his own knot. 'What you doing?'

'Get up,' Vadim whispered, swinging the barrel in his direction.

'You . . .'

'I. Give. The. Orders. Up. Quickly. No. Talking.' The adrenalin had turned his voice to paper. The pulse in his long-suffering hand was a thunderous boom. The swollen palm clutched the pistol butt awkwardly. 'Get up.'

Gimniuk leapt up, tumbling over himself. He was still clutching his nose: it was obviously broken – the breast of his uniform jacket was generously splattered. But the only thing the security guard had eyes for now was the pistol.

'Move.' Vadim jerked the barrel towards the hallway. Gimniuk staggered backwards. He knocked over the standard lamp, recoiled, staggered back again as far as the wall and glued his back against it.

'That way.' The burnished steel cursor pointed to the doorway. 'Move.'

Gimniuk's systems seemed to have jammed solid: his back was fused to the wall, his eyes were fused to the muzzle of the pistol. Vadim waited a moment, then grabbed hold of Gimniuk's collar (designed to be inconveniently upright by the avant-garde pacifist designer Birmanis), jerked him away from the wall (the seams split) and, jamming the pistol into his ribs and using a knee to help him on his way, shoved the unresisting ex-sailor out into the hallway. After a slip on the lino, he drove him along the little corridor and dragged him into the bathroom. There he slammed him hard against the bath, smacking the solid-metal of the little handgun across his kidneys, and pressed his forehead down against the cold enamel of the bottom. The security guard stood leaning down into the bath with his legs straddled wide: his hands were braced against the cast-iron sides, his backside jutted up above the edge, unexpectedly massive and broad, broader than his shoulders. Vadim forced the barrel of the gun into the colourless, sweat-soaked naval crew cut with its fine sprinkling of dandruff.

'What's all this garbage about partners in the Moscow region?' Vadim asked hoarsely.

'Eh?'

'Who are these partners the Man has down in Moscow?' Vadim forced the barrel in harder. 'Well?'

'The Lunino mob!' Gimniuk finally copped on and began reeling off a choking recitative that resounded with a cast-iron echo. 'Bro . . . mobsters, the Lunino mob. The public prosecutors in Switzerland had their boss, Vcheras, but he got off the hook . . . Our . . . The Man . . . he . . . launders their greenbacks, through the bank. They've been working together for ages, real big-time deals! The Lunino mob's bought up half of Russia . . . They collect all their loot and bring it up here, in cash, then the Man launders it. REX is a foreign bank for them, not Russian, kind of international but handy, right next door, everyone speaks Russian, they understand . . . And Vcheras has got stuff going on in Latvia, got property up here . . . They give the loot to the Man and then he hands it back all legal, laundered squeaky clean, minus a cut, and there's no way you can fucking tell, it's all done right . . . Seven years they've been doing it . . . And then this, like . . .' He hesitated.

'Well?'

'Well, like, this time, right, it's massive bucks, millions, I don't know exactly how much, but it's really big money, strictly cash, your actual greenbacks. They're going to hand it over to the Man . . . But the Lunino mob, right, Interpol's been on their trail for ages, and up here they're in Europe, right, like away from home. And the Man knows, he's got major contacts, he's done like this deal with the fuzz, with Interpol, that he'll hand them over and spill all the dirt, like accounts, numbers, the whole works, how they launder their bucks here, and they'll grab the lot of them. Only first they're going to hand over the dosh to him, some time before New Year it's got to be. It doesn't exist, it's not in the books anywhere, it's all in cash, unofficial, no documents . . .'

'Are you jerking me about?' Vadim shifted back slightly, lifting the pistol from the back of Gimniuk's head just a little. The security guard stayed in the same position anyway. 'What sort of garbage is this?'

'Straight up . . . (spit) . . . My uncle's a consultant, he's in the know, he does all sorts of stuff with the Man, he knows the score with these big bucks, no fucking shit, they're going to have a meet, honest, and what's a hundred thousand to the Man, it's bugger-all, and he's shit-scared of the Lunino mob. If we grass him up they'll waste him straight off, for sure, they're animals, honest, they couldn't give a fuck about anything, they're Russian hoods!' Gimniuk was breathing loud and fast, constantly spitting out blood.

'Where's the disk?'

'What?'

'The DVD!' Vadim gave the retired naval backside a hefty clout with his knee.

'Here! I've got it . . . (spit) . . . In my pocket . . .'

'Which pocket?'

'In the left pocket of my jacket!'

'Take it out.' Vadim moved further back, one step away from the bath.

'Okay . . .' Twisting round without straightening up, taking care not to rise above the level he'd been set, Gimniuk tried to reach into his uniform jacket and missed. 'Straight up, it's all here!'

Vadim took the silvery disk out of Gimniuk's trembling fingers and tossed it on to the washing machine. The security guard replaced his face to the plughole, drew a breath and started spitting in readiness to talk and follow orders.

Vadim took another step back towards the wall and took aim over Gimniuk's black backside at the colourless crew-cut lolling in the bath. He couldn't grip the ribbed metal firmly enough with his shattered right hand, so he grasped the pistol with both hands. He set his forefinger on the trigger, squeezed his eyes shut and pulled.

The retort was much louder than he had expected: it

blocked his ears and filled his head with a high-pitched hum that drowned out a separate pair of clangs. Vadim opened his eyes. Security guard Gimniuk had hardly changed his position, except that his belly was bearing down against the edge of the bath with his entire weight – and his feet in the tall lace-up boots, which had been braced under half-bent legs, had now slid feebly apart on the tiled floor, shoving the woven bath mat to one side.

Vadim set his own foot between them with deliberate precision, transferred the weight of his body on to it and bent down to take a look. In the middle of the cropped back of Gimniuk's head was a small round hole. Around the head the white enamel was splattered with an asymmetrical halo in a familiar red.

Vadim carefully set the pistol down on the glass shelf above the sink (the deodorant tumbled into the sink with an empty clatter), stepped across to the toilet bowl, folded like a melting candle, and huskily puked into the porcelain funnel a clot of almost pure gastric phlegm with a faint brownish tincture of coffee.

10

Slurp-slurp. Slurp-slurp. But this was a different kind of slurping: harsh, metallic, slippery-scrapey. More like shlurk-shlurk. Shlu-urk went the flat, dull blade as it went up; shlu-urk it went as it came down, displaying its almost illegible brand: 'Stainless'. An identically repeated sound, a uniform action. A greyish-brown rod of abrasive material lay in his other hand. He would have to run the knife over it (an archaic, mediaeval process) for a lot longer yet − the blade was impossibly, obscenely blunt. Every now and then, Vadim tried the edge with his fingers, but was repeatedly convinced that this would be a very long job. So he had time to think things over and make up his mind. Think things over thoroughly. Make up his mind about everything. His hand was really hurting now. Shlu-urk-shlu-urk. Shlu-urk-shlu-urk.

The knife was a grim specimen, especially for a kitchen knife − thick plastic handle, wide blade. Only it was terribly blunt. Shlurk-shlurk. Eventually, when he cut himself for the second time, Vadim called himself to order. He'd put it off. long enough already.

The security guard's monumental backside still dominated the bathroom: despite having climbed the ranks of the navy, warrant officer Gimniuk was waiting patiently for the jars he had been prescribed. Vadim stepped closer uncertainly. Isolated now from its source, the shlurking sound lived on in his ears. How should he begin? Turn him over? What for? The arse was as good place as any. Mm-yes . . . He bent down over the security guard, pulled the jacket up on his back. Shlurk-shlurk. Subconsciously Vadim had been expecting to see a striped navy vest, but no. Instead the warrant officer wore a depressingly civilian vest next to his skin. The belt . . . The belt was the mother of all belts, you'd be totally shagged after sawing through that. Vadim put the knife on the washing machine and forced himself to put his hands in under the body's belly. After a few seconds of fumbling, the buckle clanked against the cast iron bath. He straightened up, hooked a finger under the leather strap, pulled it through the loops of Gimniuk's trousers and tossed it away. Shlurk-shlurk. The logical thing would have been to go on to unbutton the trousers and then simply take them off, but the very thought of fiddling with Gimniuk's flies, so close to his genitals, almost set him puking again.

Shlurk-shlurk. Vadim stuck the knife inside the company trousers and began ripping them apart. Just as he had feared, the strong fabric parted with difficulty. Vadim tried to stick to the middle seam. The knife fidgeted between the dead man's buttocks, and Gimniuk wiggled his backside playfully. Vadim was clearly going to end up puking one way or another.

Shlurk-shlurk.

The seam parted with a crack as far as the perineum. The taut, black arse split open defencelessly to reveal a pair of crumpled sky-blue underpants, 'family specials'. The staccato strokes of the shlurking merged into an undifferentiated whistling. The whistling gathered speed. The longer it went on, the worse it got. Unable to bring himself to touch Gimniuk's trousers with his hands, Vadim stuck the blade into his pocket, the right one first, blunt side down, and started jerking it. Then the left one. A blue pack of LM lights fell out. The midshipman's legs, pale and flaccidly plump, had a sparse covering of light hairs. The fold of skin at the inside of the knees was especially disgusting.

Damn, the boots. The tall, pseudo-military, black, lace-up shit-crushers with the ribbed tank-track soles. Keeping his eyes averted from the still life in front of his face, Vadim squatted down and, holding on to the ankle with his other hand – he had to – slipped the blade under the lace and sliced through it in several movements. Grabbed the cracked leather of the right boot with both hands, getting them covered in filthy street mud, even though it was already half-dry. His tugging on the foot set the midshipman's entire body in motion. Buggeration! The boot went flying away under the sink.

The intense, slimy stench that he had liberated expanded to fill the bathroom. The light-brown sock with pink rhomboids had come half-way off, but the shiny, stiff heel of the cotton monstrosity only reluctantly parted company with its owner's skin, crackling quietly in discontent. And even when it came away it still looked solid: a gleaming calloused roundel reiterating the curve of the yellow callous on Gimniuk's heel. But Vadim somehow managed not to puke his guts up even at the second sock.

The longer it went on, the worse it got.

Vadim stood up. The underpants. Suppressing the response of his own gut with a strenuous internal effort, he hooked the sharp edge of the knife (just think, only yesterday he'd been cutting bread with it) into the upturned lower edge of the family specials. The material parted without any resistance, the elastic stretched and snapped. And then Vadim's resolve almost snapped at the sight of that dimpled, slack, drooping expanse that was the warrant officer's arse, that bluish-white tint, contrasting even with the legs, of skin that had never seen the sun, marked here and there with the ripples of stretch marks, the stark clarity of every black speck where a hair follicle hadn't developed because of the constant friction against the chair at the security desk. He span round and collapsed over the toilet bowl. Because there'd been nothing left in his stomach for ages, the spasms were especially excruciating.

But then after that he couldn't give a damn any longer. . .

The militaristic black remnants of Birmanis's designer masterpiece, the bright scraps of underwear, the malodorous, calloused, cheesy socks, the gaping, cracked shit-crushers, the Q&Q quartz watch all went into a voluminous brown polythene bag. Vadim pulverised the DVD with a hammer in the kitchen and added it to the rags. In the sitting-room he got undressed to the waist. Rummaging in the cupboard, he found an old faded tracksuit from his college days and pulled on the sweatshirt. He glanced at his watch. 4.50.

He sat on the couch for a while, trying not to think about what lay ahead. A macabre, cryptic calm and a cynical confidence were condensing inside him. There was no more whistling in his ears. The cardboard-thin partitions of the five-storey barracks-block confirmed that life was all around him. Somewhere he could hear the violent ranting of Russian trash-pop, somewhere a clear, young woman's voice was screeching with deadly hatred over the background sound-track of a choking child's roar: 'Go to slee-eep! What did I tell you? Go to slee-eep!'

It was time. Vadim picked up his hammer. Looked at it, hefted in his hand.

He put it down and took a different one off the kitchen table. Solid metal with both ends of the head studded with blunt, four-sided points – for tenderising meat. From a drawer he drew a pair of scissors. Big sprung blades, like secateurs, with jolly, bright-green plastic handles. For cutting through chicken bones. Back to the bathroom he laid out his arsenal on the top of the washing machine, then went down on his hands and knees to examine the chipped floor tiles. Gimniuk's calloused feet dangled right in front of his nose. He shoved aside rumbling tin buckets and rusting boxes of washing powder. There! The cartridge case. The little cylinder had hidden itself in behind the loo, beside the yellow-ochre paint on its concrete base. Into the plastic bag.

Next!

In his present state and condition the warrant officer and security guard no longer personified either the vigilant maintenance of law and order or the uncompromising masculinity of the naval code. The naked Gimniuk hung over the edge of the bath, displaying a massive soft bum composed of sticks and slices of liver sausage with a matt lustre of fatty beige.

Vadim bent down and lifted up the dead man's head by the ears. There had been quite a lot of leakage, and fragments of various consistencies were scattered across the bottom of the bath. Struggling to hold the twisted head with his left hand, he pushed his fingers into the warm, thickening paste, and fumbled among the fragments, lumps and crumbs. It took him a while to find the flattened round bullet. Into the plastic bag.

Next.

Vadim grabbed hold of Gimniuk's shins with his filthy hands and, using the legs as levers, forced the stubborn, unwieldy veteran of the Arctic Sea to settle into the cast-iron tub. One of Gimniuk's arms – the left – slipped under his backside and his feet braced themselves high up against the wall. His pelvis was higher than his head and his greyish little penis tumbled sideways out of the undergrowth. His face looked as if it were covered with a cosmetic face pack. The hole in his forehead was not so neat and tidy any more, and there was something glimmering inside it. Vadim didn't look.

Next.

He had stripped Sergei Gimniuk of his military rank and dismissed him from the service. Now he had to strip him of his identity. The erasure of a personal history. But not Castaneda's way. Castaneda didn't write about this. The metal handle of the meat hammer slipped in his bloody palm and yesterday's painful abrasion was still throbbing painfully. What was the difference between an identified body and an unidentified one? He gripped the hammer with his left hand as well. The former was evidence (the dead man, Gentlemen, worked in the same bank as the tenant of one of the flats in this building. A very neat coincidence, Gentlemen). He went down on one knee beside the bath. The latter was simply a batch of decaying organic matter. Braced himself against the edge with his right hand. How did you identify a body? Took aim. Visually. From the face. Paused. From the teeth, maybe. He didn't know the state of affairs under an advanced private dental care system. But in the old Soviet detective novels they used to identify bodies from their teeth. He turned his own face away and swung the hammer down on to Gimniuk's.

The blow felt muffled, like hitting a plank wrapped in cloth. A couple of warm damp spots splashed on to Vadim's cheek. The spiked lattice pattern of the meat-hammer was imprinted on the midshipman's temple. Vadim drew the hammer back as far as possible and, without closing his eyes or turning away, merely squinting to keep out any splashes or solid fragments, lashed out hard, then lashed again, and again, and again with all the strength he could muster. Most of the nose area subsided inwards readily enough, but a solid triangle of bone remained at the bridge. He had to aim directly at it twice, and at the second blow everything located between the exit hole in the forehead and the eye-sockets caved in completely, together with the nose bone. An irregular rhomboid appeared in the upper part of the face, between the brows: at the third blow, his hammer sank halfway into it with a wet sound. Headcrusher. A very popular game. Two days running. The sign of a genuine fan.

Vadim set about extending the rhomboid. Here, under the nose, there was a system of little bones connected together at various angles to form a network of cavities. Vadim instantly reduced it to chaos. The upper lips peeled away, the teeth crumbled more easily than the jaw. When Vadim was finished with that, the entire centre of the face had been transformed into a funnel, a pit. Face off. He paused to assess the job, then added a few more blows just to make sure, without encountering any particular resistance.

The very first blow to the protruding lower jaw twisted it to one side, the second blow missed and reduced the tongue to bloody pulp. Vadim bashed the lower teeth with sharp, abrupt blows, as if he were striking the head of a nail, until eventually the jawbone, entirely twisted out of the ligaments below the ears, split in two. The forehead proved hardest of all, but it was easier to aim at. By the end, Vadim's own face was covered in blood.

He dropped the hammer, lowered his head into the sink, twisted the cold tap open and rubbed his hands together for a long time, splashing water on to his face. How else could you identify a corpse? Vadim tried the sprung scissors in a hand numbed by the cold. His hair was streaming. From the fingers, that was how. Ticklish drops trickled jerkily down across his temples. From the fingerprints. If they've been recorded anywhere . . . Vadim didn't know if they had. He picked up Gimniuk's hand, grabbed the thumb in his fingers and set the joint between the stubby blades. Squeezed the jolly, bright-green handles together. The end of the thumb, consisting almost entirely of a strong, square finger nail, fell into the bath. Vadim dropped Gimniuk's wrist and picked up the off-cut. Into the plastic bag. Two. Into the plastic bag. A standard automated process. Three. The repetition of simple actions. Four. The stumps streamed blood. Five.

Now he only had to free the left hand from under the body. But freeing it turned out not to be that simple. The jolting manipulations set the feet tracking across the tiles on the wall, one knee hammered against the cast iron. Right. We're off. One. Two . . . Four . . . That's it. Into the plastic bag. The hammer – into the plastic bag. The scissors – in there too. What was left lying in front of him was no longer Sergei Gimniuk. It was garbage that had to be disposed of.

Vadim rinsed off his hands again. Now what? The head? Back to the kitchen again. He teased a few crumpled plastic bags out of the narrow crevice behind the evenly buzzing, elderly fridge and chose the most suitable. This was getting to be something of a habit. Too small. Looked okay . . . No, a hole. A great ghastly gash. No good. Oh. That would do. No holes, more than big enough. A sweet puppy and a sweet kitten in an endearing embrace gazed at him with eyes that took up half their faces. Lovely. Parcel string. Wouldn't it break? It shouldn't.

He slipped his hand under the sticky, matted short pile of the dead man's crew-cut and pulled the little cat and dog over the remaining hemisphere of the head. The absence of a chin proved to be an unexpected inconvenience: there was no projection under which to tie a knot. But the parcel string was far more practical than the golden necktie with the scarabs. The body hadn't got smeared all that badly. It was mostly on the chest, shoulders and shoulder blades. And the bag too, of course. The little kitten and the puppy.

Vadim took the shower-head down off its crooked bracket and turned the water on full. The pressure was so high that the cross-barred exit of the drain couldn't cope and the level of dilute, frothy red began rising in the tub. The streams of water rattled against the plastic bag. In order to wash the body down thoroughly, he had to roll it over again. And once again the corpse's out-thrust legs caused Vadim serious problems. After struggling and swearing for a while, he bent both the knees and drew them in to the stomach. The blood had already dried and was hard to wash off. The stiff brush for scrubbing the bath came in handy.

Right, that'll do. The drain sucked everything in with a final grunt.

Vadim tugged off his polluted tracksuit top. Into the plastic bag. He barely managed to squeeze it in, the bag was crammed full. Changed back into civvies. 10.51. A bit too early. People could still be out and about . . . He went out of the flat. This was when the most dangerous stage began – the public one.

His floor, the fifth, was the last. On the communal landing a vertical iron stepladder led up to the square trap-door of the attic. A near-lifeless light bulb kept watch under the dusty plaster surface of the ceiling. Light, however dim, was bad. They would see him: from the street or through the spyholes in their doors. Light was number one.

Number two was the padlock with the curving metal rod that yoked together the brackets on the two halves of the trap-door. Not a very serious lock, as a matter of fact, but even so he didn't have a key for it. Saw through the rod? With a hacksaw? Too loud, too long. They'd hear, look through the spy-hole, light, they'd see. Yes, the light. The first thing of all.

Or not? No. First of all, the basement. Where was his key to the basement? Bugger it . . .

In all the time that Vadim had been renting this flat he had never used the basement and had never had any intention of using it – and he had clean forgotten where his keys to it were. Where? Where could they be, in theory? This was a real problem . . . He flung open cupboards, pulled drawers out and pushed them back in, tipped their contents on to the floor, turned the entire hallway and kitchen upside down . . . Bugger all. Twenty minutes later it turned out that the keys had been lying under his very nose the whole time.

Right . . . Torch! Torch, torch . . . Torch.

Vadim went downstairs and out into the street. It was sprinkling with rain. Not even sleet. Rain. On New Year's Eve. A colony of primitive organisms had established itself under the canopy outside the entrance: large youths with dull, slack faces toying with bottles of beer, a substandard young female with an unnatural colour to her pelt, incessantly neighing and snorting on a single note. That was a bugger too. But at least they weren't familiar faces. Or put it this way – Vadim didn't know any of them. He'd never bothered to look closely at the people who shared his entrance.

Under their indifferently hostile gaze he unlocked the basement door. The purulent electric lighting traced out concrete steps leading down into impenetrably black earthy-potato dampness. He descended, to the insistent accompaniment of the girl's buzz-saw merriment.

The torch sprang to life. Pipes of varying function, thickness and flexibility crawled around in the dust. Impure, suffocating heat blasting out from some of them and disturbing the chilly dampness. The shoddy partitions dividing up the already cramped space in an entirely random fashion displayed their apartment numbers without the slightest trace of ordinal sequence – the painted digits aspiring to individuality with squalid aplomb: the more boldly they were daubed on, the clumsier they were. Seventeen, seventeen, where could number seventeen be?

They'd been repairing flat number seventeen all summer long, a euro-standard job too. Vadim had many times observed the rubbish that was generated being despatched to the dump: the overall volume had seemed to exceed by far the volume of a standard little Soviet flat. Some things – either items that had been laid in but never used, or things that had not been entirely used up – had been taken down into the basement: rolls and sacks of some sort. He was actually counting on the sacks most of all – he remembered the huge, opaque plastic sacks in which they had brought down all their mysterious bits and pieces (more sacks, plastic again . . .) Although to say 'counting on' was probably putting it a bit too strongly. He was hoping for something or other. One of the two. Something. Or other.

There it was – cubicle seventeen. Crammed right up to the gills. The lock – nothing like the feeble item on the trap-door to the attic – was so comprehensively self-sufficient and self-important that it made the fundamentally nominal character of the planks appear perfectly natural. Breaking through a plank like that didn't even feel like a crime, it was more like charitable shock-therapy. And you might say that Vadim was already a specialist. That was also becoming something of a habit. The kind of habit that is second nature.

A sink. Metal. Rusty. Some chairs and other useless junk. Boxes. Damned if he could be bothered to figure out what was in those. And the dust, the dust . . . What's this we have here, under the oil-cloth? Window-frames. Taken out complete with the glass – did they put in plastic double-glazing

163

then? But where are the sacks? There were sacks here . . . Now you see them, now you don't. Fuck. Well?

Vadim was left loitering drearily in this graveyard of domestic consumption, swallowing dust. On this rubbish heap of history. The enveloping darkness completed the stage-setting perfectly. Perhaps now, even if he tried now to return to the world outside, he wouldn't be able to. It was over, he'd been rejected from the historical process. Discarded.

What about this? Come on, come on . . . Yes! Perfect! Even better than he'd expected. Linoleum. Tattered at the edge, but thick and hard – brilliant. Padded. A great big roll of the stuff. Taller than Vadim was, about three metres. And maybe five metres long. A room. That was right, fifteen square metres, just like his big room. You couldn't dream up anything better.

Ah bloody hell! It was a heavy bastard. Heavy wasn't the word. Unliftable. And dirty. Bug-ger-ing hell . . . Who would have thought that murder was such heavy physical labour? If he ever did get it to the fifth floor . . . Stop. The fifth floor. They'd spot him, it would be just his luck. Someone would come out . . . It wasn't that late yet. Those goblins at the entrance. Shit! A fine little scene – some geezer lugging around a roll of old linoleum at eleven o'clock in the evening. Taking it upstairs too. And what if they managed to find the body straightaway? Wrapped in this stuff . . . No, it was no good. And the light in the entrance hall. That was it. We could cut off the light. The switch was right here, on the way down into the basement. Aha! Aha . . .

He'd been expecting something of the kind from the very beginning. There was no switch. Only a crudely cemented-over hole where they'd ripped it out of the wall. Because the light in the entrance hall had been switched on an automatic switch for ages now. Progess, bugger it.

His processor was about to freeze up. A total jam. Vadim sat down beside the linoleum that he had dragged on to the icy steps. Outside the buzz-saw was working away with the same enthusiastic diligence as ever. Now there was a person in a good mood. Optimism, a cheerful, life-affirming outlook on the world . . . It looked as if the goblins had settled in for a long stay.

What was to be done? The light would be on all night long. You couldn't do anything about that. But why not? He could do something about it up on his own floor. Unscrew the bulb. The cover came off easily. So the neighbours wouldn't be able to see the most interesting part. But there was still no way you could avoid the noise. The lock on the trap-door? Break it off. With a hammer (a hammer again . . .). And about the noise. The attic ladder rattled too. Were his dear neighbours sound sleepers?

Vadim had no idea at all who lived to the right of him. Apparently nobody, at least not permanently. But to the left there was a text-book family: father-mother-son-daughter-dog. A mongrel terrier, a cross between a bulldog and a rhinoceros. He thought the dog was quiet, but . . . How would it react to a racket outside the door at night? The shot! There was no way they could have failed to hear the shot! What's all this toing and froing at such a late hour? Don't worry about it, it's only Vadim wasting a few guys, dragging the bodies around. He always does that at night. Such a nice, polite, cultured young man, always says hello . . .

He was soon chilled to the bone. Overcoming with some difficulty the resistance of the air, which had thickened incredibly, becoming substantially less transparent in the process, he got to his feet, picked up the torch and went outside to join the young folk. The scene with the glances and the delicate maidenly laughter was repeated in reverse order. When he was on the third floor, locks turned on the second, voices muttered, he heard one say 'well, cheerio!' – and a group of humanoid units went clattering down the stairs. He would have liked to believe it would be a bit quieter here by three o'clock in the morning. Or by four. At the very deadest hour of night.

That was when he would come out. Sneak out as quiet as quiet, without waking up the neighbours' dog. He'd go back to the basement. Lug the linoleum up to the fifth floor. It didn't matter that he knew he could never lug it that far, no matter how much he wanted to. It didn't matter. He'd break the lock off. It didn't matter that the blasted bulldog-rhinoceros was certain to start barking. Somehow or other he'd break it off without making a noise. He didn't know how. Then he'd lift the lino up into the attic. It didn't matter that the vertical ladder made it five times more impossible. He'd lift it anyway. And that was when the real work would begin. The most important part . . .

Vadim sat at the window of his flat, contemplating the task before him. The room on the outside was related to the original in which he sat like a bad black–and–white (or rather yellow) photocopy. For lack of anything better, the window employed this unconvincing duplicate to compensate for the total absence of any landscape view behind it. Conforming strictly to its designated function, the entire dormitory region was enveloped in deep sleep and impenetrable darkness. At regular intervals the wind lashed the fine rain noisily against the glass. The reflection of Vadim's cigarette was like the indicator light on an electrical device. Then the device was unplugged: the cigarette had burned down to his fingers. Vadim dropped the long butt on to the windowsill.

The windowsill already had a scattering of dirty butts of the same excessive length. It was just that his hands were filthy and he was holding the cigarettes in the middle to put them up to his mouth. But then his face had to be just as filthy. And his clothes were filthy too. Everything was filthy. His teeth felt gritty. Bastard basement. Bastard lino.

When Vadim had already lugged the lino (literally hauling it over the steps) up to the landing between the third and fourth floors – the sixth landing – he had suddenly remembered, entirely out of the blue, that just before Christmas his neighbours on the left had upped and gone away, complete with son, daughter and mongrel, to stay with relatives in Russia. Until the New Year. And they'd even asked Vadim to keep an eye on their flat as far as possible. Of course, this event had taken place some days ago – it had simply slipped his bruised and battered mind. But, by a process of mental aberration, Vadim's memory of the event became transformed for him into its cause: he realised that a supernatural effort not only transcends the laws of physical possibility and the limitations of logic, it actually expands them – so it was Vadim himself who, through sheer will power, had cleared the fifth floor so that he could work away in peace.

From that moment on, he had no longer doubted that he would get everything done properly. And that absolutely everything would go just right. Everything would be just fine. It was New Year, everything had to be just fine.

In memory of this achievement, Vadim reached mechanically for his looted pack of cigarettes and shook another one out on to his palm. The last one. He had inherited eight of them from Gimniuk. Or ten. He'd never really smoked a lot . . . He lit it with a match. Unlike all the others, this match didn't break. When he had first started lighting Gimniuk's fags the lingering echo of the savage effort his muscles had just undergone completely disrupted his coordination.

He had unscrewed the light bulb anyway. Breaking the lock had taken a bit longer and been a bit noisier that planned. But then things had been easier with the lino. He had passed a length of TV aerial cable through the roll (from the endless reel of the stuff borrowed from the diligent household managers in flat seventeen) and made a lead with which to drag it up the ladder to the attic. For good measure he had tossed up Rita's present, the black Lycra sheet – wide, double-bed size, just right. The draughts careering around the attic had howled gently without disturbing the putrid, dank, stagnant atmosphere; his torch had noted without enthusiasm the perennial incrustation of bird shit, probably from pigeons, and the pigeon skeletons; the rain lashing on the roof close over his head had sounded strange from the inside.

The fluffy cylinder of ash retained its form. Now the cigarette would burn his fingers again. Vadim didn't bother to wait. He stubbed it out against the window-frame and got up. 3.48. Lino and sheet were in place. Time to bring their friend to join them.

The chubby little chappy had settled down into the bath very cosily – curled up on his side. Reveille time! Unceremoniously, Vadim unceremoniously grabbed the body by its already cold ankles, turned it over and dragged it out. The plastic bag rustled in protest. Hang on, am I imagining things, or are the neck and shoulders hardly bending at all? Thinking of stiffening up, are we? Oho! And we've developed little blue patches over there. . . Gimniuk had apparently made the transition to a different state. He was no longer simply a non-functional, inoperative human being, he had been transformed into an independent and, in its own way, entirely self-sufficient thing. Existing according to its own rules and only capable of being judged by its own criteria.

The thing flopped down on to the floor in a double flop: first the backside and then the head, so to speak. It was heavy, of course, but no heavier than Four-Eyes. Most people regard the social as the absolute criterion by which to assess the comparative worth of their neighbours. Vadim pondered briefly the fallibility of this method. People as widely separated in the social hierarchy as, let's say, the head of the press service of a major bank and an absolutely insignificant doorman from the internal security service could be equated very simply: by weight. Vadim dragged the body as far as the hallway and dropped the legs.

As far as Gimniuk's weight was concerned, he would apparently now have to explore every aspect of that question in close detail. Maybe it would be worth . . . you know, in pieces? Okay, if things carried on the way they were going much longer, then the possibility was not exactly a million miles away. But for the time being we could manage without. Vadim unreeled the TV cable. What was the best way? By the legs? Yes, probably by the legs.

He lashed the corpse's ankle-joints together with a double figure of eight, adding lots-and-lots-and-lots of extra loops of cable on top. It was awkward to tie, too thick, not pliable enough. He stuck the end through and under. Right then, you fucker, bring your stuff to the door . . .

The ladder was two and a half metres. Only two and a half. A height exceeding the corpse's by less than one third . . . The chubby little chappy's back lay on the landing, his legs rested at a right angle against the ladder. The bare soles of his feet, vaguely white on the underside, glared up at Vadim in the attic with the same expression as the ribbed soles of Gimniuk's boots when they had resided on the automobile-wing coffee table. It was an insolent expression (see, I still got what I was after: look at the way you're sweating and straining over me, gasping for breath – and here I am free and fucking easy, just laid back, relaxing, get it, Carp?). All Vadim had to do now was to detach the body from the concrete. And then – two and a half metres.

Easier said than done. The smooth plastic insulation of the cable slipped through his instantly sweaty hands. Vadim tried winding it round both wrists. The first tug felt as if it had crushed every bone in his hands (his poor right hand was well and truly buggered). Frail, useless little bones, the meta-carpals. The Fathers of the Inquisition had been particularly fond, as the museum in Prague had testified, of all sorts of vices. Bastard hell, he was going to rupture himself for real . . . Handling people was heavy work.

Bracing his right knee and his left foot against the floor of the attic, throwing his body backwards, his face distorted in agony, and whinnying in torment, Vadim pulled. There was a piston moving in the opposite direction inside him, down towards the groin, proportionally increasing the pressure, increasing it until it was impossible to bear, until he was about to burst, compressing his insides, squeezing those whinnying groans out of his mouth and that sweat out of his pores, almost squeezing his guts out through his backside. The stepladder clanged nervously whenever the corpse touched it. It was the kind of thing that made you appreciate just how little metaphoric imagery there is in vulgar expressions like 'his eyes popped out of his head'. And what a genuinely fragile thing the human spine is.

Vadim managed to get up and straighten his knees. His shoes barely even gripped the floor surface. He felt that

Gimniuk could quite easily win after all and pull Vadim back down on top of him. Scre-ew, you-ou, scre-ew you-ou, you bastard, I've done you once, and I'll do you twice, and I'll do you three times if I have to. I'll do anybody and anything I like now, is that clear? He took a step backwards. And another. No, no bloody way . . . And then another.

Afterwards he laid his cheek on the sandy-grained little crumbs that covered the entire floor and listened to his own heartbeat.

After that he got up. Easy, easy . . . yes, he really had got up. Stood there. Not erect, of course, in the sense of full-length, that is – the roof was in the way! – but firmly on his feet. Relatively speaking at least. Felt for the torch. Gimniuk. The cable. The reel. Where was the sheet? The sheet. The string. Now he just had to add up the parts together to get the whole.

The sheet – spread that out. Achoo! That dust was really destroying him. Gimniuk – put him on the sheet. Like that. Now let's straighten him out . . . Wrap him up. Properly now, properly, so there won't be a single crack, so he won't stink too much. Now let's tuck in his feet . . . Oh, buggery. The cable . . . Achoo! Yes, there was the knife, he'd taken it specially for this. He wasn't going to untangle all that stuff. Everything was covered in shit. Shitty birds. The feathered tribe. Now let's wrap him up. And now let's tie him in. With the string. Once more round the head. Round the waist. Achoo! The legs, the legs . . . Aha. Good. Achoo.

A dead ringer for a stiff, no matter which way you looked at him But we could fix that. Otherwise, what had been the point of farting about with that roll for so long? Bugger, why is it so low in here? Vadim rolled out the lino. And there it was – a room. Now for the bundle . . . No more warrant officer, no more security guard, no more Sergei G, no more corpse, just a bundle. A glorious evolutionary journey. And now the concluding, final, crowning stage – the stage of the roll. Let's roll him up. Over! Over! And over again! Excellent, perfect. Well, not ideally circular in cross-section, more of an oval, but then nobody was perfect. On the other hand, THIS certainly did not arouse any associations with a human being. And now for the cable. Let's cut it again. Wrap it round in two places. Dead solid. Fine!

Due to its imperfect circularity, the crowning stage of Gimniuk's evolutionary journey did not roll perfectly either. But Vadim coped with that simply by kicking it along. He kicked the roll along the floor to the far end of the attic and shoved it into the corner.

He appraised his work. It would do. It fitted organically into the general shitty desolation of the surroundings, it wouldn't attract attention. Even if it did. Even if they took him out. Even if by that time he hadn't rotted completely. They'd never fucking identify him.

Vadim not only closed the trap-door of the attic behind him, he actually hung the lock back up. Or rather, he did a bit of stage-setting. Hooked it round the brackets somehow. It seemed to hold all right. Obviously, when they climbed up, they'd see it had been smashed. But to the casual glance everything looked normal.

Every muscle in his body throbbed and ached. His arms and legs felt like they were going to drop off at any moment. As if he'd taken on Gimniuk's obligation to decompose and fast-tracked its implementation. And his face was all black. Simply black. Not to mention his hands and his clothes. But bugger that. It wasn't blood.

It wasn't evidence. We could wash it off. Wash our face this very moment.

Yes, about the blood. There was still plenty of it – in the

bath and on the walls. On the tiles. Not a really huge amount, but . . . Fortunately that would be no sweat to wash off. He'd done right to off him in the bathroom, hadn't he?

Fifteen minutes later, at most, he had finished washing everything. The enamel was chipped beside the plughole, at the spot the bullet had hit – he would have to paint over it. Vadim hung up the shower-head and looked around critically. The little black pistol had settled in on the glass shelf under the mirror with unostentatious dignity, in the company of the shampoos and deodorants. Vadim stuffed it into his pocket with an entirely instinctive movement – he couldn't leave it lying there.

The last thing. Oh, Lord, could it really be the last? Don't relax yet, don't relax, you jerk (if he relaxed at all he would collapse instantly) . . . The plastic bag (how many plastic bags could there possibly be?) with the clothes, the fingers, the tools. What had the poor tools done wrong? Right, so was he going to carry on cutting his bread with that knife, then? For breakfast. Yes, the knife, he would have forgotten about it. Aha. Damn, it wasn't heavy enough. But it would still sink, surely? It ought to . . . But what if it didn't? What else could he stick in there?

A dumbell. Five kilos. The daily disposal of corpses would bring us closer to the desired state of the unstoppable Schwarzenegger than any morning exercise. Apletaev's body-building gym. That was it. Now just tie up the neck. With the same string. Perfect!

But in the hallway he discovered that it wasn't quite time for 'Perfect!' yet. He had forgotten about the jacket. About Gimniuk's outer clothing. A short, thick, pricey leather jacket with a sheepskin lining (in this instance the warrant officer had disappointingly betrayed naval style for air force chic – the kind of thing that World War II American bomber pilots were supposed to have worn). It wouldn't go into a plastic bag. Bugger it anyway. It would be a treat for the tramps. At least somebody would benefit from the wanker. He threw the bomber jacket across his shoulder. 4.42.

Outside, the wind mocked and jeered, hammering away with some unsecured sheet of tin. The warm, wet gusts saturated with ultra-fine droplets clogged his throat, preventing him from breathing. Vadim bent his head and shielded his face. Not a single streetlamp was lit, and scarcely a single window. The visibility was only slightly better than in the forest the day before. The dormitory district, packed solid with human beings – an immense nocturnal repository of thinking matter – appeared absolutely uninhabited. In fact, it became clear that, at this hour of the night, the city – like everything else invented and created by people for their own survival, comfort, etc. – had another side to it, visible, comprehensible and meaningful only to itself.

Gimniuk's jacket nosedived into the first rubbish container. Silent shadows flashed by in the corner of Vadim's eye. Cats? Rats? Stegocephalians? In the tight vent of the yard, compressed between the nine-storey buildings, the wind almost knocked him off his feet. The whole way – and he had to walk quite a distance, eight blocks – Vadim didn't come across a single car, not even a single taxi. Although that, of course, was good – about as good as it gets.

As Vadim rounded a bend, he graduated from 'Level 1: Dormitory District' to 'Level 2: River World'. The superfluity of pre-fab landmarks (quite useless for purposes of orientation due to the undifferentiated dullness of their crowded mass) was replaced by their total absence. Close up the darkness was frayed away almost to whiteness, but further off it was pure, unconditional, monolithic, dimensionless.

With a mere sprinkling of abstract lights, like some ancient star-studded screensaver: there was no telling how far away the lights were, so they gave no impression of the size of the darkness. Only the wind hinted at that – wide and even, no trace remaining of the convulsive claustrophobia of the narrow lanes and yards – rattling the invisible wires of high-tension power lines in the hypothetical heights.

The wide empty space that confronted Vadim – hummocky, littered with withered, fibrous grass (reeds?) – had almost been transformed into a bog by the half-melted snow. Vadim jumped, sank, squelched, floundered. His feet were instantly soaked. He stumbled over lumps of concrete, almost falling. The river declared its presence with a powerful, uniform rustling. Folding up as they ran in at a wide angle towards the shore, the waves were just barely marked by streaks of foam.

With some difficulty Vadim located a pipe. A sewage pipe, maybe, or some other kind – with a huge diameter, half-sunk into the sandy shore that went on to become the sandy riverbed, with its massive concrete segments protruding only a little above the surface of the water and running out twenty or thirty metres into the river. With some difficulty he walked out along it. He could see bugger all, and the waves that constantly broke over the segments made the curving surface slippery. With some difficulty he kept his balance as he swung the plastic bag and tossed it into the Daugava. It disappeared into subspace, lost to all five senses simultaneously.

On the way back, with four blocks to go to his house, the drizzle was upgraded to rain again.

Three blocks to go . . . Two and a half . . . He saw them from some distance away – or rather, not them, but the car: either he saw it, or he heard the muzak, the regular thumping coming from inside the open door. He only actually saw them as he walked past, right up close: four or five bulky silhouettes in shapeless jackets. The motor was garbage. The headlights weren't on.

At Vadim's approach they stopped yelling and swearing at each other and fell silent; they stayed silent while he was passing them. Then, when he had already moved on about five steps, they called after him: 'Hey, mister'. Flat, toneless, hardly even a form of address. Here we go, thought Vadim without turning round, without either reducing or increasing his speed. 'Mister!' – louder, more insistent.

At that moment the unresponsive Vadim reached an ink-black gap between blank end-walls. He heard them running up behind him and stopped after all, swung round. 'Mister . . .' – muffled now, almost matey, gasped out after the running. The first one walked up. Moved in real close (half a head taller than Vadim), the others moved up and surrounded him. Yes, four of them, big and strong. You couldn't make out their faces in the dark. 'Strike us a light, mister' – the first one smelled of cheap booze. 'Give us your wallet' a voice on the left said impatiently.

How-sick-I-am-of-the-whole-damn-lot-of-you, Vadim said to himself without the slightest emotion, sticking his hand into his pocket without any clear intent.

His right hand. Into his right pocket.

'Wassup, don't you understand, cunt?' The first one reached out his hand, either to push him or grab him by the tits or clutch at his face. Vadim took his hand out of his pocket. If there had been a wallet in his pocket, he would probably have given them the wallet. And if the safety catch of Gimniuk's pistol had been on, he would never have been able to cope with it. But after that shot into the colourless crew-cut, Vadim had forgotten all about any safety catch.

176

The flash was too bright and too close – he didn't manage to make out the face. Without even waiting for the first one to fall, Vadim stretched his arm out to the left – towards the other sound-source – and fired twice more. It was only then that the others reacted and made a dash for it. Silently, but quite incredibly quickly, in precisely opposite directions. And neither of them went to the car.

11

The improvised poster showed two classic wooden hole-in-the-ground privies, one perched on top of the other. On the door of the upper convenience, reached by a stairway with a whimsically carved balustrade, there was a plaque that said 'Management'. On the door of the one below it said 'Employees'. Vadim painstakingly smoothed out the piece of paper smeared with glue on its reverse, sticking the non-conformist flyer over the Banzai promotional poster on the door of the boss's office. He stepped back and admired the effect.

When he had turned up handsomely late at his desk today, he had found the light on in Andrei Vladlenovich's cubicle (following its sullen December habit, day had never really dawned, and as a token of mourning for the deceased Gimniuk, Riga had contrived to make itself as much as possible like his beloved Arctic-circle town of Severomorsk). 'Four-Eyes is back!' was the first thought that naturally occurred to Vadim. But that was just it, of course, he wasn't. In fact his boss's unexplained absence from the press room for the second day running had already generated a universal state of subliminal agitation. 'Pylny Himself is in there!' they whispered to Vadim in the rapturous rhythms of rumour. But a forceful official announcement, delivered in the gravelly tones of the Head of Information Security and brooking no objections, had informed the employees that Andrei Vladlenovich had gone away on planned compensatory leave for overtime and wouldn't reappear in the bank before New Year: luckily today was already 29 December, which was the last working day but one.

Vadim had laid eyes on Pylny for himself soon enough: he emerged from behind the shuttered glass partition, accompanied by Citron and his conventionally standardised PA – and immediately rested the full weight of his existentially desolate gaze on Apletaev. The sense of desolation undoubtedly derived from an awareness of the general imperfection of human nature, which was manifested most graphically in the concrete example of the antisocial and villainous actions, culpable under both civil and criminal law, of the said Apletaev – concerning which, in keeping with his position, Pylny had naturally long been in the know. Perhaps from the very beginning. Perhaps even from that very moment when the first spore of sedition had settled in the fruitful soil of the Apletaev brain.

'You're late,' Pylny asserted rather than asked.

Feeling a weakness in his knees and a sinking sensation in his stomach, Vadim leapt to his feet and began incoherently . . . But no, dammit, at this Vadim frowned, glanced up from his chair into the elongated wax-museum features and simply agreed:

'Afraid so.'

Pylny probed Apletaev with his watery weepers for as long as he thought was necessary to make clear to him the hopelessness of his situation and the punitive omnipotence of the Information Security Department, and then pronounced in the tone of a funereal 'Amen':

'Be in my office in an hour.'

Vadim, to all appearances crushed and clearly having abandoned all hope in advance, turned to look at his monitor. 'The KM regulations prohibit the use of excess payments for the settlement of customs dues,' the monitor pontificated,

'However, if the GSD has allowed it, the guidelines are as follows. Debt to the budget: D2311 K55; permission not to pay the amount due: D55 K5721; if VAT can be written off to pre-tax, then: D5701 K2311, if VAT cannot be written off to pre-tax, then: D7510 K5721 (K2390)'. The monitor was raving. It was a grave case of manic-depressive mental divergence psychosis. In defiance of the rules of the Russian language the monitor was employing words the language didn't possess and entirely random punctuational combinations to describe a hypothetical variant of the relations between conventional concepts of something that had no real existence.

If Vadim had made just a little effort and recalled a bit of the esoteric knowledge he had acquired over the previous two years or so, he could probably have deciphered the meaning of the abbreviation VAT and guessed what lay behind the mysterious letters D and K. A structured sequence of intellectual operations might even, quite possibly, have allowed him to reconstitute the message that the anonymous author at the business information agency had embedded in his missive to humankind. The problem was, Vadim knew in advance that the inner logic of this text, and all others like it, bore no relationship whatever to the logic of objective reality. The systematic peeling away of leaves from the given informational cabbage made absolutely no sense in the light of his a priori knowledge of the result, or rather, that there wouldn't be any result – no stalk. Since the file represented a fictitious schema for the relational disposition of pecuniary magnitudes and since these magnitudes did not exist anywhere in the real world in the form of tangible bundles of crisp banknotes, and since any banknote anyway was in essence only a symbolic representation of some fragment of a standard gold bar, and the value possessed by that bar was itself exclusively symbolic, it followed that all business information and all business operations were precisely analogous to the delirious ravings and gesticulations of a drooling schizoid emitting sounds and performing movements that are perfectly meaningful to him but absolutely meaningless to everyone else.

Vadim, naturally, knew all of this; he also knew that the psychological mechanisms which motivated his continued participation in the collective PR-mumble and business-drool were simply the next level of insanity, in compliance with which he engaged in decanting nothingness out of nowhere into nowhere for the sake of a conventional medium (money) which could be exchanged for a conventional absurdity (a coffee-table made from an automobile wing or, if his prospects should improve and he were to prosper in this occupation of augmenting the volume of nothingness, a Siemens M351 mobile phone, which bestowed the incomparable bliss of conversing about conventionalities and absurdities even while you were diving with an aqualung or decomposing at the bottom of some pit in a forest).

He had already known all of this, in the abstract. But this morning his cognizance of it had suddenly become acute and positively PALPABLE. As if the supply of some brain-numbing narcotic had been cut off. Actually, it was clear enough what it was. The word 'inertia' surfaced again in Vadim's mind. Despite its towering heaps of self-generated and self-perpetuating grotesqueries, the familiar, universal and exclusive socio-economic paradigm possesses (precisely by virtue of its familiarity, universality and exclusivity) an overwhelming inertial *comprehensibility*. But killing four people in two days had evidently generated a counter-impulse of equal force that had neutralised this inertia. Vadim had stopped moving along with the general flow at the general speed, and the world around him at every level, from the conscious to the instinctive and emotional, had been revealed for what it really was. Total and absolute schlock. A grotesque and ludicrous mimetic simulacrum of real life in which there was absolutely nothing worth doing, let alone being afraid of. That was how Vadim had come to enter the office today feeling so perturbed by the gaping hole where yesterday's fear had been.

In fact his temptations now amounted to an irresistible itch. He wanted to provoke this false reality that had been foisted on him for so long into revealing its falseness over and over again. And there and then, in the comprehensively transparent grid-space of the press room, laid out in accordance with the supreme principle of totalitarian-bureaucratic design, under which everyone supervises everyone else, Vadim set about transgressing the bounds of the permissible.

First he moved the set of drawers back in under the desktop. The black amoeba (with just a slight brownish tinge) only forty centimetres in diameter, which was all that Andrei Vladlenovich had bequeathed to posterity, peeped out curiously at the light. But no one paid the slightest attention.

'Here, Vadim, thanks.'

It was Svetochka the copy editor returning the crumpled Polish mug to its owner.

'What does that stuff written on it mean, by the way?'

'I've killed four people,' Vadim explained.

Svetochka composed her face into the semblance of a smile, indicating that she realised the other party was joking, but she didn't get the point. Vadim thought for a moment, pulled out one of the drawers, rummaged inside it and took out the amusing picture of the privies that he'd unearthed on the Web. He had run it out on the printer because it was so witty, but then hidden in his desk because its content was so reprehensible. He smeared the back of it with office glue from a lipstick tube and, as his colleagues watched, he slapped it over the samurai.

This did draw a reaction, and a rather rapid one. 'Are you crazy or what?' asked Olezhek, twirling his finger next to his temple in a gesture of irritation rather uncharacteristic of pederasts, and tore the pip (politically incorrect picture) off in a furious fervour, leaving behind scattered scraps of glued-on paper. Vadim realised Olezhek wasn't just poncing about, he was genuinely outraged by the stupid prank. The gay PR man was entirely under the influence of the narcotic that no longer worked on Vadim, and in his case it must have had the painkilling power of an opiate. Whenever there was an attack on the euphoric self-confidence that the hallucinatory delirium of the banking business induced in its subjects, it generated paranoia and fury.

And of course the above didn't just apply to Olezhek or just to Vadim's colleagues at the bank. The overwhelming majority of his fellow-citizens were hooked. In two years Vadim had become habituated to the rapid, nervous-stress reaction of people who learned in conversation that he worked at REX. Take Rita, for instance. She had willingly spread her slim legs for him precisely because a guy from a bank was the 'right stuff'. And it was the same idea that had propelled him to start shoving his fifteen and a half centi-metres up between those legs: a fashionable design bureau was the right stuff too. Their work-outs on the black sheet recently donated to warrant officer Gimniuk's lonely hearts club had satisfied a social need rather than a sexual one. Or rather, there was no way any longer of telling one from the other: like the way long-time heroin junkies with their dark, shrivelled little pricks are sure that shooting up is better than sex, simply because for them drugs have long ago taken the place of sex and the other joys of life, and of life itself.

When he remembered about Rita, Vadim felt ashamed. He hadn't called his girl since Christmas. And that was definitely NOT the right stuff. He roused himself, reached for the phone and dialled the mobile number of the promising layout artist.

'Hallo?' the layout artist responded efficiently and impersonally, although her display must have informed her who was calling.

'Rita?' Vadim asked the obvious with exaggerated enthusiasm.

'Oh!' Cold irony with a hint of resentment in the subtext. 'What a surprise!'

'Hi!' said Vadim, vainly attempting to banish a note of cloying affectation. 'How are you doing?'

'Thank you for asking.'

'Don't bother to mention it, Rita my love.' For some reason he lowered his voice and began speaking faster. 'Listen . . . I'll tell you why I'm calling . . . There's something I've been wanting to say to you for ages . . . But I couldn't do it . . . It's important,' he added vindictively, remembering.

The receiver maintained a haughty silence, but with an audible undertone of expectant curiosity.

Vadim paused, filled his lungs with air and yelled loud enough for the entire office to hear.

'Go fuck yourself!'

As he pushed open the tall, heavy flap of the door to the bank's main building, Vadim almost gave in to the feeling that came over him every time he entered the echoing marble expanse of the entrance hall. A feeling – without the slightest exaggeration – of solemnity and reverential awe. A feeling carefully encouraged in him, as it was in every visitor, from the moment he crossed the threshold of the Citadel (that, by the way, was what was written on the plaque outside the doors: REX – Citadel). The impudent intruder ascended the additional flight of indoor steps (marble, marble!) to the security post (a strategic-missile control bunker – a different league altogether from the modest cubicle of Gimniuk's colleagues), walked up the staircase that cunningly set the guard imperiously positioned at the top (the Custodian, Watcher etc. – also in a different league from your average Fed) in elongated perspective, with the chthonian torso tapering upwards and narrowing along the lines of the deltoid muscle concealed beneath the jacket collar towards the even sides of the isosceles triangle of chin, the cone of which, only slightly truncated by the categorical line of the lower lip, left a spot at the very pinnacle of the pyramid for the source of that derogatory, all-disparaging, all-demolishing gaze. Every subtle detail had been thought out: the gaze set at the pinnacle of the pyramid was intended to evoke subconscious associations with the famous allegorical picture on dollar banknotes, instantly directing the impudent intruder's cognitive flow into the right channel.

If the intruder was sufficiently impudent to approach the ID Control Point and insist on his right to Access and Communion, the very essence of the new arrival's personality was extracted under the watchful gaze of at least three guards (right now there were two in black civilian suits and one in black military uniform) – Your pass! Which was Verified, Clarified, Scrutinised . . .

The fact that Vadim was an employee of the same bank, only from a different building, gave him no privileges. Far from it. As a PR and advertising man, a petty functionary of the ancillary press service, he was merely a cheap conjurer clowning about in front of a bunch of simpletons from the target group with their dilettante jaws hanging open, or at best a hypnotist slipping his gullible subject into a submissive trance. Whereas here, in the occult *sanctum sanctorum*, a genuine magical mystery was worked, alchemical reactions occurred and the fundamental laws of physics were violated. This was a bank, a factory of the absurd, unparalleled anywhere in the universe. A place where they made money out of money. Where out of nothing they made even more nothing. But the kind of nothing that could be converted into an incalculable number of material objects. This incomprehensible process, the concentrated mystical essence of the entire capitalist economy, had always enthralled Vadim, enhancing the psychological impact of the long procedure of Verification, Clarification and Scrutiny (maybe they ought to weigh me on scales, like an applicant for Heaven – check my righteousness content).

But today, once again, something obscured Vadim's vision. What he saw at the top of the stairs was merely an expensively dressed, muscle-bound hoodlum, whose beady eyes, set almost invisibly between the temples and superciliary arches, expressed nothing but an innate stupidity as impervious as the already familiar narcotic stupefaction. Like the semi-transparent eyelids of birds, this film of artificial endorphins overlay the pupils of absolutely all the specimens of the Citadel's fauna that Vadim encountered along his way. The said specimens were pumped full to overflowing with the narcotic concoction, which was why they ran along the corridors (two out of three with mobile phones pressed to their ears) looking like hyperactive sleepwalkers, wearing spectacles (an extremely common detail of the look) to conceal the film over their eyes, and pressing the phone to their ear so that the random background noise pouring out of it would prevent any irritating stimulus from the outside world penetrating their happy universe of monetarist hallucination. The triumph of pseudo-life in the main building became all the more obvious the more agitated its subjects' frenzy became, and the more brightly their inspired faces reflected the glow of the non-existent mega-benefits towards which they were ostensibly dashing headlong.

The most interesting thing, thought Vadim, squeezing into the lift (the girl on his left had just finished talking to her mobile phone, and the young guy on the right had just begun), is who the hell suddenly needed to get such a huge amount of biomass hooked on phoney stimulation and make it expend all its natural vitality working up a sweat over doing damn-all? Why were they drawing off the excess energy of the species of Homo sapiens so assiduously and earthing it into the humus of money and flashy window-dressing? What eschatological millstones were being turned by these junior managers, senior brokers, black traders, distribution agents, dealers, legal consultants, press-attachés, personal assistants and exclusive distributors with the soles of their shoes scuffing the wall-to-wall carpeting of their offices and their fingers caressing the buttons of their IBM keyboards?

One of the three mirror-walls menaced him with a sullen, unshaven misanthropic monster in an old leather jacket (he hadn't managed to get the blood off the Chinese jacket after all). His right pocket had a slight bulge in it. The Doppelgänger's on the warpath, Vadim thought with a sudden warm, friendly feeling and gave the swine a wink. People around him looked askance.

The third floor, on to which the lift voided Vadim, contrasted with all the others. It was the bosses' floor, where Citron and Pylny had their lairs, together with the rest of the large-bore managerial vermin. Here the pace, the decibel levels and the expressions were different. The local corridor fauna was less varied and less active: the sluggish, silent species endemic here seemed to have collapsed in on themselves entirely. Distinctive sexual characteristics were only possessed by representatives of the indefinite female category traditionally referred to as 'models' (models of what? – that was what Vadim had always wanted to pin down), as ubiquitous in a milieu of this kind as cockroaches in a communal kitchen, which was why they seemed like a species of small domestic parasite (not in the sense of their size, which as a rule was fairly large, but in the sense of their general existential insignificance) or rather, in this case, office parasite (although they must have possessed a nominal business function as secretaries of some kind or other).

Abandoning his scuffed leather jacket at the threshold of Pylny's office, Vadim experienced a strange feeling of reluctance. Of course: it didn't relate to the jacket, but to the contents of its right pocket. In the infinitesimal time period that Vadim had been carrying Gimniuk's pistol around with him, he had managed to establish a mysterious telepathic rapport with it. Or maybe it was the other way round and the pistol was feeling out its new owner: it needed the symbiosis (which, if you thought about it, was already in effect). Vadim had never been one to suffer (at least not since he attained the age of responsibility) from the infantile intellectual's typical platonic attachment to weapons. He had done his poring over the relevant reference texts in his childhood, at the same age as he sweated over selected articles from the Concise Medical Encyclopedia. But now that he was the owner of a pistol (plain and unattractive specimen though it was), i.e. of a device designed exclusively for the extermination of one's neighbours, he had discovered that, little by little, it was taking control of him. The sensation of being armed somehow resonated very precisely with the persistent, slightly feverish state of agitation induced in Vadim by his contempt for the shamefully spurious professional reality around him. It somehow seemed to feed that agitation.

'Sit down,' said Pylny in a voice filled with weariness, almost disgust.

Vadim thought there must have been a time when the Head of Information Security had begun his interrogations of the petty dissident types entrusted to his tender care in the same way: giving the detainee the impression even before the conversation began that the patient and essentially benevolent investigator was taking a lot of trouble over him, and he was just being obstinate, the way he had been for God knows how long without ever getting anywhere. Joining in the game despite himself, the 'detainee' timidly seated himself on the edge of a chair, guessing that he was supposed to be feeling nervous. Pylny maintained an unjustifiably long pause, intermittently burying his long nose in the print-outs lying in front of him on his desk (a piece of furniture as dark, massive and uncompromising as a gravestone – nothing like the eye-catching design, say, of Four Eyes's ground-hugging model), or fixing his client with expressionless eyes the colour of swamp weed.

The process dragged on, and for want of anything better to do Vadim began staring out of the window. The menu on offer out there was none too varied either: an unfamiliar foreshortened view of their own nondescript building and the blank wall beside it, photocopied on to a scrap of hopeless December sky. In total contrast the interrogation room was filled with intense light and heavy, subtropical heat.

'Everything that is about to be said in this office . . .'

Vadim started, not immediately realising where the rasping phonemes were coming from.

'. . . must remain inside it,' Pylny concluded in a coarse bureaucratic tone, without any emphasis.

'Naturally,' Vadim agreed hastily and readied himself for dialogue. However, instead of a hail of questions, what came next was pause number two.

'How can you explain the fact that, instead of an efficiency rating of 63.2, the draft balances for advertising have 59.6?' This second utterance from the Head of InfSec took Vadim unawares just as he had been all set to endure another Great Silence.

'Er-er . . . mm–mm,' he struggled vainly to figure out what the question was all about. 'You see. Mikhail Anatolich. This is a very involved, ambivalent . . .'

'Did you draw up the New Year address?' Pylny interrupted without letting him finish.

'Eh? . . . Yes, Mikhail Anatolich. On the personal, so to speak, instructions . . .'

Pylny twisted the neck of his thick Mont Blanc pen and nodded reproachfully, as if to say, 'Right, sweetheart, we've got your number.'

'It received a high evaluation,' said Vadim, in a formulation that surprised even him.

'And what were you doing in the press room on 27 December this year from 18.10 hours until 19.35?'

Pylny raised his eyes from his Mont Blanc to Vadim's face and Vadim realised that this was the real question. It was like boxing. Two feints and the third blow's the knock-out.

'I was analysing an Infonet Fund report on the influence of global communications and multi-media on the banking sector.' He blurted out what he'd prepared in advance in a single breath.

'And what did Voronin say when he discovered you in the press room?' Pylny threw in immediately without pausing for a second.

Did he know? Or was he just winding Vadim up? I've got to answer. Answer . . .

'Voronin?' Vadim repeated in unnaturally natural amazement. He had no choice in any case but to stick to the incomplete version of events he'd started with the deceased Gimniuk. Apart from that, he recalled very clearly the precept of one of the patriarchs of the Lubyanka: 'Never admit anything! Even if the husband catches you by the prick while you're screwing his wife, deny everything. Your prick'll shrink in fright and you'll escape.'

'Why, did Andrei Vladlenovich actually . . . did he come into the press room? On the twenty. . . er. . . the day before yesterday? No, no . . .' Vadim held up his hands and spread his fingers, decisively dismissing, sweeping aside the very possibility of such a thing. 'Voronin didn't come in . . . well, not while I was there. Definitely.'

'Why are you trying to mislead me?' Pylny tapped his Mont Blanc on the edge of his monstrosity of a desk in regret and condemnation, combined in proportions that were hard to determine.

'Perhaps it was while I was out?' Vadim suggested timidly, switching automatically into dodge mode. 'I went out to the toilet, you see, perhaps we missed each other, didn't notice each other somehow,' he rattled on, performing the truncated gestures required by the situation and even seeming to apologise with the way he twisted his torso. And the quicker he rattled on, and the more fragmented his efforts to cover up and wriggle his way out of it became, the more comical the whole business began to seem. He realised perfectly well that, as the character he was playing and even as himself, he ought to be feeling afraid, but all he felt was a merriment that sparkled like champagne.

'It is in your interest to be as frank with me as possible,' said Pylny, finally shifting into the language of the investigator.

'Yes, yes, naturally. . .'

'Remember. When and under what circumstances during the period in question did you see Vitaly Mansky from the IT department?'

That one really caught Vadim on the hop. Vitalik. . . He'd forgotten about Vitalik. Vadim strained his memory and recalled Vitalik winding a scarf round his neck. Vadim was coming back from the loo – Four-Eyes was in the press room. It looked as though the PR boss and the IT minion must have run into each other on the stairs.

He'd slipped up there. To be quite honest, he'd blown it. Vadim's story obviously didn't add up. He had to edit his statement urgently, only he couldn't see how. So he began frowning anxiously, imitating an attack of Alzheimer's:

'Vitalik? But surely . . . On the twenty-seventh . . . No, no, I remember. Yes, Vitalik . . . But wasn't he . . . I thought . . . As far as I can remember . . . It wasn't the day before yesterday after all . . . I must be mistaken . . .'

'You are mistaken,' Pylny stated categorically, 'or else you are deliberately lying.'

How do you like that! So the old goon could add two and two together. The question was, how long could he keep it up? Vadim began feeling genuinely curious. Right then, let's try to shake you up a bit:

'Ah yes, of course!' Fortunately the fit of amnesia had passed. 'Now I remember! The twenty-seventh! Yes, yes!'

'What do you remember?' Pylny fastened his eyes on

Vadim with the determination of an encephalitic tic. 'Give me a concrete, precise, clear reply!'

'Vitalik!' exclaimed Vadim, beaming in joy and relief at being able to offer the investigator a little satisfaction. 'I remember Vitalik! He *was* there! On the stairs, I can just see him now, with a fluffy scarf.' He pointed at his throat like an alcoholic looking for a drinking partner and traced out an imaginary noose with a speedy finger. 'He was winding it round his neck!'

'What did he say to you? Tell me!'

'He said . . .' Vadim froze. 'He . . . he said . . . Ah! What he said to me was "Cheers!"'

From craning forwards in anticipation Pylny slumped back against his chair and his knotty fingers came down in a sonorous chord on the desktop.

'Apletaev,' he said in a distinctly threatening tone, 'don't you come the joker with me.'

Vadim contorted his entire body into an allegory of perplexed willingness to offer every possible assistance, and woe at his own lamentably paltry ability.

'You,' Pylny insisted, trying to consolidate progress achieved. 'Saw. Voronin.'

'No, no, no. You must have misunderstood what I said! It was Vitalik! Yes, I did see Vitalik, and it was on the twenty-seventh! But not Voronin . . .' Vadim said mournfully, lowering his gaze. 'I'm sorry . . . I really am . . . That's the way it was . . . I don't know why . . . I didn't meet him.'

Mikhail Anatolich gave a tap of his Mont Blanc and they continued in the same vein. Pylny came on heavy. Vadim goggled at him with his honest eyes and stuck bluntly to his story. Eventually the InfSec chief got up out of his armchair and measured out the floor of the office from one corner to the other. Then he loosened the knot of his tie in exasperation.

'It's like a sauna in here,' he growled to himself. He tapped out a three-digit internal number on the telephone. 'Call Margulis . . . Why is my air conditioner still running hot? A whole week now! It's like an oven in here. Do I have to bring you up here under armed escort? . . . Yes! And make it tomorrow! Or even today!' He slammed down the receiver, carried on grunting for a while, then opened the tall Jugendstil window. A cold Baltic draught suddenly blew through the subtropics.

Pylny returned to his desk and started rustling through his papers in a highly disgruntled manner.

'You have an ongoing relationship with Rita Daugaviete from the Kliava & Co. design bureau?' he asked suddenly, swooping in from an unexpected angle.

'I used to,' Vadim replied laconically, not in the least outraged by such a crude intrusion into his private life.

'How's that? Why?'

'You see, Mikhail Anatolich . . .' Vadim paused modestly for a moment. 'You know . . . Only just today, to be precise . . .' – he glanced at his watch – 'fifty . . . no, I beg your pardon, fifty-one minutes ago, I told the afore-mentioned Rita Daugaviete of Kliava & Co. to go fuck herself.'

Pylny blinked. There was something here he couldn't get his head round. The situation had spilled out of the standard frame and his reaction was to deal with it in the way that cost least effort: he ignored it.

'So,' he said. 'How often do you see Mr Chernosvin?'

'Who?' Vadim asked in entirely genuine surprise.

'I see.' Pylny scribbled on the rustling sheets of paper with his Mont Blanc, jotting things down and weighing things up. 'Right, I see . . .'

Pylny's sullen questions were tossed out without any

apparent correlation or system, yet with the stoicism of a clairvoyant playing battleships. With ostentatiously indifferent consistency he landed shell after shell right beside the walls of the stubbornly silent submarine of his opponent's self-control. Then, when that opponent finally broke down and sobbed and exposed his own submarine – Here! Take it! I surrender! – Pylny would shake his head in sadly sarcastic amazement: why, you crazy freak, did you think you could hide THAT from us? Did you think we wouldn't find out? What unforgivable, absurd naïvety! Every step you take, every single one . . . But then he would allow sarcasm to give way to the sympathy of the experienced padre who has spied out a wandering soul that is perhaps still not completely lost to repentance and say: here's a pen and a piece of paper, write it all down, a full and frank confession mitigates the seriousness of the offence . . .

But you don't know a damn thing, you wrinkled old buzzard, thought Vadim as he mechanically parried Pylny's attacks. You don't even have a clue. And you obscure the issue and play the omniscient secret policeman precisely because you DON'T. You don't even know what has happened to Voronin. He disappeared. Didn't warn anyone. His family's probably worried. His father-in-law probably is too, eh? 'Who's that little son-in-law of mine been shooting his mouth off to? Has he taken my wedding present and scooted off back to his whores in Tahiti?' I'd love to take you by the collar, you haemorrhoidal old fart, and just lay things out the way they really are. And then watch your blank old face . . .

'So you claim,' Pylny ploughed on tirelessly, 'that you handed in the key at the security post to security guard Fyodor Podlesny? Are you sure you remember that? How certain are you?'

'More or less.'

'What does that mean?'

'It means exactly what it means. No more and no less.'

'Listen here, Apletaev . . .'

'Mikhail Anatolievich . . .' Vadim had begun feeling extremely uncomfortable in the regulation pose, with only half his arse on the seat, his back straight, his body inclined towards the investigator and his neck extended ingratiatingly. He seated himself more comfortably, lounging back. 'Have you got anything to smoke? To smoke . . .' He waved two fingers in front of his mouth to make his question clear.

'What?' Again Pylny couldn't get his head round what was happening. His bony jaw even dropped open slightly, as if his processor had frozen – and it took a lot less for that to happen to Pylny than to Vadim.

Basically the behaviour of the haemorrhoidal InfSec boss was governed by an obscenely primitive programme. Pylny could only function within the limits of a set situation and role: the big boss, the fiscal authority, the hand of chastisement.

I've had enough of this sodding game, Vadim thought, beginning to feel irritated himself now. Everything always seems to turn out the same way – they're always trying to screw me. What makes me the natural victim? Let's try playing my way now. Just for a change. At least that'll be more honest, right?

'Mikhail Anatolievich,' he continued hastily, forestalling a further series of irritating sallies, 'that's enough. No more. Now I understand the whole picture. That is, I understand that YOU don't understand a thing. You're clueless. As our mutual dear departed friend, Sergei Gimniuk, used to say, you don't cut it. You can't hack it. And you probably can't suck it either.' He rested the calf of one leg across the knee of the other, observing with satisfaction the now completely and absolutely frozen state, which could only be rectified at best by rebooting and at worst by total reformatting. 'And since it seems to me that neither of us is enjoying our little conversation too much and, if it drags on like this we're liable to end up beating each other black and blue, I suppose I'll have to enlighten you.'

Pylny emitted a grating interjection similar to the helpless moan produced by a frozen PC when you press any key on the board. Vadim took no notice.

'Okay. Andrei Vladlenovich Voronin, head of the press service by profession and shithead by vocation, whose fate is evidently what interests you most of all – he's bought it, snuffed it, popped his clogs. That very evening, the twenty-seventh. Of course he was in the frigging press room, that's obvious. You're right about that. And I did see him. I knocked him down. Then finished him off. Like a pig. Smashed his skull in. With that fucking statue. Crunch! And I hid the body. In a stinking pit in the forest . . .'

The appearance of inanimacy adopted by Pylny – and which actually suited him remarkably well – proved deceptive: he made a sudden rapid movement of the hand towards the telephone. But Vadim – ah, the swift reactions of youth! – leaned across the desk and got there ahead of him. He grabbed the receiver, then seized the Japanese button box, tore it off its cable and flung it to the far end of the office, where it jingle-jangled in its death agony. Vadim stood up and stretched. He stuck his hands in his pockets and started walking round the room exactly the same way Pylny had been doing a little while earlier.

'Only that's still not the whole story. Because it was no slip when I referred to that thick bastard Gimniuk, the beloved nephew of our own beloved boss's special consultant, as departed. I blew him away too. With his own pistol. In the back of the head. Brains spattered everywhere. Then I smashed his ugly mug in with a hammer! A hammer! Made a real mess of my bath, he did, the bloody sailor. Why are you looking so peculiar all of a sudden Mikhail Antolievich? Hell-o-o! Pylny! Can you hear me? Excellent. Then carry on listening. That's still not the whole story. Before he messed up my bathroom, Gimniuk told me an amusing little tale he had heard from his very own uncle. About our beloved boss and his friends from Russia. From Moscow, to be precise. From a suburb of Moscow, to be even more precise. A certain Lunino. Perhaps you know it?'

Vadim walked round the desk and stopped in front of Pylny, who stared up opthalmopathologically with bulging eyes and slowly rolled backwards in his armchair.

'Dearie, dearie me,' said Vadim, wagging his finger menacingly at Pylny, who leapt up, stumbled and staggered backwards. 'That's really not right now, is it? And such a respectable bank too, the very biggest in the Baltic! Such a huge reputation! All those posh pretensions! And those connections! And doing things like that! Laundering money for gangsters! Who could ever have thought it?'

Vadim continued advancing on Pylny until he had crowded him up against the window. The head of InfSec felt his shoulder-blades bump against the half-open frame and stopped moving. He couldn't go any further.

'Well, Pylny,' said Vadim, morosely summing up the situation, 'Still not a sound? Nothing to say?'

Pylny opened his mouth to reveal a set of nicotine-yellow teeth, then closed it.

'That's a pity . . .'

The Head of Information Security's shoulders were sprinkled with flakes of dandruff. Behind his back the bank's building site stretched out in an untidy sprawl.

'Just a moment,' said Vadim, suddenly remembering. 'What's Mr Chernosvin got to do with all this? Well?'

Pointless.

'All right,' Vadim summed up. 'Okay. So you've got me shafted . . .'

Pylny began a gesture of protest, but before he could complete it, Vadim grabbed hold of his tweed collar with his left hand, siezed his trouser belt with his right and, without any real effort (the old dodderer was incredibly light, like a mummy!), lifted the secret policeman off the floor and tossed him through the window. Pylny's elbows smashed against the window-frame, his shiny boots flashed through the air and he disappeared from view, still without saying a word. Vadim waited a moment for an impressive impact, a succulent smack. But what he actually heard sounded rather vague and unconvincing. Vadim glanced out of the window.

Mikhail Anatolievich Pylny had fallen on to a vertical steel reinforcement rod that had pierced right through his body and now protruded slightly from his chest. He was half-lying, half-hanging on the rod with his arms and legs flung out like an athlete in a textbook illustration of 'the principle of the golden section' – as if he were supporting an invisible hoop with his hands and feet. His head had fallen back so that his face was hidden.

12

Shelves filled with bottles rose all the way up to the ceiling. The select, elite booze had been removed from the common plebs of the world of alcohol and placed on a separate display stand with feature-flattering lighting. Each nobly-born bottle stood in splendid isolation, like a Stradivarius violin. And the most elite, the most nobly-born of all, were set behind the gothic-arched glass doors of their own autonomous little cupboards. As if they were those drums which, according to the New Russian apocrypha, that same Stradivarius had made, not for the average slobs, like his violins, but for the genuine likely lads. It was the drums that Vadim was interested in. Such was the requirement of the moment.

Upon leaving the Citadel, he had been convinced that the feeling he had had the previous night was not mistaken: that logic and probability really were flexible and malleable, effectively tractable for a transcendently dominant will. According to all logic and probability, with all those countless plain-clothed and uniformed guards milling around, he ought to have been nicked there and then. Especially since Pylny's extravagant dive had not passed unnoticed, and seemed, on the contrary, to have produced a great impression, thus causing those guardians of the law to cast off their indifference and immobility in an amusingly startled fashion and begin convulsively bustling about and dashing around. On this occasion, however, Vadim had been ignored. Ignored so absolutely, indeed, that the suspicion had even entered his mind that perhaps an object which had deleted itself from pseudo-life ceased to be noticed by its subjects. Or simply ceased to exist for them?

But then why did that dick of a cut-price security guard (a sale special, designed for shops and other public places) keep glancing at him with that air of disdainful suspicion masquerading as spurious interest? Maybe he couldn't quite square Vadim's pitiful leather jacket with the price tags behind the gothic glass?

Okay guys, now let's watch your processors freeze up . . .

Lagavulin. Islay Single Malt Scotch Whisky. At least that had a ring to it. Sort of substantial. Kind of impressive. And the figures looked good too. Age: 16 years. Price: 26 lats and 40 centimes. Vadim was no expert on 'coloured vodka', all those flashy, gourmet-style cognacs and whiskies – no true connoisseur – but he had heard that 'single malt' was supposed to be high-class. In fact what attracted him above all was the coincidence, which could surely not be devoid of mysterious significance, that the bottle of dark glass with the inconspicuous, aristocratic label and a name that sounded peculiarly felicitous to the Russian ear, cost approximately the same amount as was presently lying in Vadim's wallet. He began double-checking his cash resources. Yep, twenty-five, twenty-six lats. Small change. Thirty, thirty-five – ha! That would be a hoot . . . Thirty-six, seven, eight (eight!), nine . . . No, he was one centime short. Would you believe it – one single sorry centime!

He began groping around in the pockets of his leather jacket, which had already developed holes in places, and accumulated a deposit of dubiously indeterminate debris. When the pistol got in his way, he pulled it out without thinking about it and caught a glimpse of momentary turmoil somewhere in the margins of his peripheral vision: the cut-price security guard struggling to assimilate Gimniuk's shooter. Vadim gave him a smile of encouragement. Wassup, you suspicious-minded git? Why so nervous all of a sudden, you wanker? Think positive! Everything's cool, you jerk. I must have a permit if I'm so casual about it, right? Never mind the fact that I haven't really got any permit, that I couldn't give a toss for all their frigging permits. Fortunately, you don't know anything about that. Fortunately for you, that is, of course . . .

He put the pistol away . . . Lucre, filthy lucre . . . Maybe he'd missed some? Bugger all here. Ah, but what was this? One centime. Turned completely black. The only way you could determine the denomination was from the minuscule diameter.

Exactly one centime. Definitely a sign from on high.

And now, mesdames et messieurs, attention s'il vous plaît! Voilà! With a single subtle gesture and a brief exchange of words the disreputable-looking visitor, who had barged into this expensive shop to indulge his idle imagination in a fruitless session of consumerist onanism, was transformed into a valued client. The guard rapidly adjusted his stance from the standard 'What do you want?' to 'What would you like?' The girl behind the counter beamed so intensely that there could be no doubt about it – she had fallen hopelessly in love at first glance. This was it, genuine passion, true romance! The impression of real, live money negated absolutely the impression made by the things that symbolised it, like a guy's threads or the expression on his face. In relation to real loot, these things were mere second-order abstractions.

True, money was also an abstraction and a symbol – but of such a promiscuously dissipated kind that it wasn't really very clear what it symbolised. It appeared to be the surrogate of a certain value, for which the service personnel here were presently exchanging the surrogate of their politeness. And the reason for all of this was a third surrogate. The surrogate of palatal pleasure.

Vadim indulged in the surrogate nature of his purchase just as soon as he had pushed through the glass door of the shop – which swished open with a vigilant valediction from its little jingle-bells – hooking a fang into the paper snugly encasing the narrow neck, ripping it off, tugging out the cork and taking a swig straight from the bottle. He spat. The high-class scotch possessed a quite distinct and familiar reek of burnt rubber. No doubt about it – burnt rubber insulation, the kind of stink you sometimes got in a tram . . . It was absolute, unconditional shit, but neither the producer nor the consumer were in the least bit concerned about the shitty nature of the product. In this case, as in every other, the whole deal came down to nothing more than a mutually advantageous rip-off.

He had just begun pondering on this insight when the whisky exploded under his palate like a home-made bomb produced by technically competent urban guerrillas – a dastardly device stuffed with sharp metal scrap – and the precisely directed blast wave struck upwards, bypassing the nasal cavity, imperiously sweeping aside its accumulation of unnecessary olfactory clutter, targeting the brain directly, and every sharp-pointed scraplet skewered its own specific cell of the cortex at a furious impact velocity. No, Lagavulin didn't reek of rubber and it wasn't shit. If he was really honest about it, it wasn't even booze. To call it a beverage would be wrong: far from slipping down the gullet into the stomach, the liquid ceased its physical existence right there on the tongue, from where it made its direct assault, not even on the brain, but on CONSCIOUSNESS, in an endless sequence of purely ethereal emanations: acute astringency, velvety consistency, stratified fragrance, the dark languor of oak timber insufflated with the open expanses of heather moors, the soughing breath of weathered chalk cliffs, the damp, chilly tang of sea salt. And the difference in taste between Islay Single Malt and the pitiful local vodka with the misleading name of Moskovskaya far transcended the difference between them in price.

But it was a different matter, of course (lashed on by the winds of the Arctic Sea, Vadim's thoughts had accelerated to an impressive rate of knots) that some whisky cost twenty-six lats, but there was also some whisky that cost two hundred and twenty-six. And whisky that cost two thousand. Maybe even twenty-two thousand. There was no way anyone was going to convince him that whisky that cost two hundred lats TASTED ten times BETTER than the one he was barbarously swigging from the bottle just at that moment. Oh no, bro, that was just an absolutely unadulterated rip-off. Blatant delusions of grandeur. 'I've got a tie just like that, only it cost ten thousand.' Beyond a certain limit (which was easy enough to detect – if only you wanted to), money ceased to be the equivalent of anything at all and started reproducing itself by means of those who earned it and spent it. Beyond that limiting point man, the crown of creation and evolution, became a simple reproductive organ, the palpable prick (cunt) of that abstract entity, the money supply.

Vadim applied himself assiduously to the Lagavulin, paying no attention, as a matter of principle, to the presence or absence of vehicular transport, and crossing the street on a red light. Go on, sound your horns, you lousy freaks . . .

There was a certain set of formulae by means of which those thinking (as it seemed to them) financial genitalia talked themselves into believing that they experienced a certain existential malaise in the performance of this reproductive function of theirs and suffered chronic frustration on that account. Vadim too – until just recently. For instance: 'You need money so you don't have to think about it'. Or: 'Money brings freedom'. But both of these were absolute crap. The only freedom that money could bring was the freedom from thinking about yourself in the process of its self-reproduction.

A poor man who was obliged constantly to think about money because he didn't have enough to feed and clothe himself did at least preserve in his own mind the connection between the symbol and what it symbolised. But a man who had reached the level of material prosperity at which thinking no longer operated with the symbol of the object, but with the symbol of the symbol, was drawn into the process of propagating the void, quite regardless of his own will, or his own NEED. When you bought, let's say, a second-hand motor, you could still be concerned about the speed and convenience of your own displacement in space. But when you exchanged a swanky BMW for an even more swanky Merc, you were already acting solely and exclusively in the interests of the burgeoning void. Congratulations, buddy – you've finally made it into the category of prats! And the amplitude of your swank is directly proportional to the intensity of your prathood.

It was a Munchausen ladder, attached to nothing, built on top of itself, the route taken to the full moon of the annual Forbes 'Top two hundred' – that planetary register of the richest and the most super-powerful – by all those overfed, shortwinded industrial magnates scrabbling upwards over each other, those silicon-valley-computerised billgateses in the round old-age-pensioner specs, those stars, starlets and superstars (breed champions from the livestock complexes of Warner Bros. and the hydroponic glasshouses of EMI), those sabre-toothed Russian oligarchs and oil-gulf Arab sheikhs, those top whores whose body parts were parcelled out in the insurance companies' files like joints of meat in a butcher's shop, those subtle soroses of stocks-and-shares speculation, the whole lingamic-vaginal sack of shit . . .

With the refreshing delight of discovery, Vadim realised that he was drunk. Well-soaked but not yet totally soused. The vivid manifestations of circumambient schlock were beginning to provoke a keenly felt sympathetic response with their very hideousness: it was fun to hate them. Shiny-glittery little Chrissy-tree santas. Li-i-ittle people . . . Vadim walked through the city centre enveloped in the sparkling energy field generated by an excellent mood and whisky fumes, elbowing his way through the festive throng (festive again – just what was it that they kept celebrating all the time?). He was sterile in the midst of the pandemic, uninfected by a single pecuniary bacillus, without a single centime in his wallet. He didn't have a job. He didn't even have the right to be free – not after five murders! But he still had a few millilitres of the necessary in his hand and prosperity in his pocket.

With neither a purpose nor, accordingly, any specific direction, in mind, Vadim either stopped dead for no particular reason in the middle of the crowded pavements, provoking miniature swirls in the current, or began moving perpendicularly to the general pedestrian motion, with people either running into him or flowing round him. The people looked at him – especially when he raised the fancy, dark-throated bottle to his lips. But actually only very occasionally: the little people had no time for him. Or for each other. The little people had no time in general. But they did have plenty of DIRECTION: oh, one thing they certainly had was a goal in life, and to judge from their faces – no less confident, businesslike and aggressively determined than the faces in those citadel corridors – this had to be some goal! The mother of all goals! Each one of them had a goal, and because each and every one of them paid no attention to the others, it followed that it was precisely his or her goal, and only his or her goal, rather than the goals of all the others, that was genuinely important. Not just kind of important, but important in all absolutely ferocious-fuck-you-formidable seriousness. The paradox was that absolutely everybody was wearing that same expression. Vadim had been wrong to slander his colleagues at the bank: pseudo-life also continued outside the walls of REX. Of course it did.

He kept getting a wild urge to stand in some particularly awkward spot, take out his pistol, shoot in the air and howl at the top of his voice, 'Hey! You jerks! Do you see me? I've topped five guys!' simply in order to disrupt this incomprehensible single-mindness, in order to throw their implacable course-recorders offline, if only briefly, to watch their gazes turn from inwards to outwards and focus on him . . . He was almost on the point of doing this, when he suddenly realised what was really going on. Where they were all running to. Or rather, what they were running AWAY from.

Somewhere deep inside themselves, every one of these running people carried a gram of antimatter. Their constant movement, never ceasing for an instant, turned a small internal dynamo. A generator maintaining a magnetic trap that prevented the antimatter from coming into contact with matter and detonating in mutual annihilation. And the people were so busy, so obsessed and so nervous, because they realised intuitively the danger of even the very briefest of halts.

Vadim walked through the eternally piss-soaked under-pass with the eternally crimson confession 'We [heart]

Antonio Banderas' on the faded tiles of the walls, and came out on to the embankment. A strong wind had driven all the pedestrians away from here and strangely rearranged the river, replacing its agitated waves with a dappled marking of time, ruling off the surface into strips with longitudinal ribands of foam. The raw, dank gusts blew straight through him, but the Lagavulin, combusting cleanly and completely inside, neutralised the chill, leaving no dross or soot. A river tug chugged past, looking like an armoured personnel carrier half-buried in the water. A bearded hippyoid in a gaping orange oilskin jacket was smoking on the deck.

Maybe I've already detonated my antimatter? Broken off my run, stopped, and – ba-boom! A crater in the road, blinking lights, ambulance men. And everything that's been happening to me these last two days, all the butchering and clearing and headcrushing is no more than a single second of expanded ante- . . . or post- . . . mortem hallucination. Like in *An Incident at Owl Creek Bridge*.

Vadim lowered himself on to a lattice-backed metal seat with a view of the uninterruptedly grey left bank, which was actually interrupted by a single oppositionally minded five-storey yellow structure. In doing so, he became aware of an angular discomfort in the back pocket of his jeans. The disk. He'd forgotten all about it. The final refuge of the useless jerk-off non-conformism born in the Pentium's hard drive.

Outmoded and irrelevant. Setting his scotch down on the paving slabs, Vadim reluctantly stood up, strolled across to the cast-iron railings and tossed the little plastic square into the water. Tossing things into the water was another new habit he'd acquired recently. Drowning the evidence. He walked back, sat down, took a swig. Even closed his eyes in pleasure.

In fact, to be perfectly precise, he hadn't really stepped

on the brakes. On the contrary, what he'd actually done was break loose from his prescribed niche, and now he was careering recklessly through space, generating massive gravitational disturbance, threatening catastrophic collision with the law-abiding heavenly bodies revolving around their own axes and dutifully tracing out their cautious orbits in the plane of the ecliptic . . . No, not that either. A bullet. He'd been fired, shot like a projectile, there was no way he could diverge from his trajectory now. Whatever it might impact on . . . A wall. Someone's head. A target.

Bugger that, bugger that! Gulp.

'Well now, and just what are we up to here?'

Uh-oh. Here we go. Back to the issue of money and extortion. What was that thought about new habits and traditions . . .

There were two cops. Identically indolent, identically distended in their winter uniforms, identically – professionally – impudent. Except that one of them was like one and half of the other. The small one had a pointy, loathsome little weasel face; the big one had the standard, broad, bloated, red, cash-hungry kisser.

'We're drinking,' said Vadim, explaining the obvious. 'That is, I'm drinking.'

In the singular.

Plain as pigshit. Municipal cops. A quite remarkable category of law-enforcement officers, rivalled only by the highway patrol, for whom extortion with menaces was their fundamental and most important function.

'Lookee here, he's pissed already,' the weasel-faced pig informed his portly partner with malicious glee. Without answering him, without even looking at Vadim, but gazing into empty space with phlegmatic melancholy, the other pig slowly, very slowly pulled his notebook out of his pocket.

Vadim said nothing, waiting to see what would happen.

'Are you aware,' the portly partner enquired wearily of the general surroundings (Vadim was immediately reminded of the deceased Pylny – what impressive unity of style across the security organs!), speaking with distinctly strait-laced fastidiousness, but also an a priori implacability that excluded any suspicion of the slightest possibility of leniency 'that the consumption of strong drink in public places is prohibited?'

'I'm not bothering anybody, am I?' Vadim enquired ingratiatingly in reply. 'Not creating a disturbance? Insulting religious sentiment?'

'For the consumption!' – the weaseloid's malicious glee had dilated into something more like malevolent rapture or exultation – 'Of strong alcoholic drink! In public places! A fine!'

'Wassat you're drinking?' The portly partner peered at Vadim.

Vadim turned the Lagavulin label to face the municipals. As he expected, their processors froze. Now it was Vadim's turn to feel malicious glee.

'Oh, whisky,' the weaseloid exclaimed somewhat uncertainly, then immediately reverted to exultation. 'Strong drink! A fine!'

'I haven't got any money,' Vadim confessed perfectly honestly. 'Not a centime.'

'But you have money for whisky?' (Vadim was struck by the distinct note of class animus just below the surface in the weasel's voice.)'Try looking a bit harder!'

Vadim smiled a wry smile and shook his head.

'We'll have to take you down to the station,' said the portly partner, closing off the road to salvation with a small amount of philosophical regret that the specimen before him had fouled up his last chance so foolishly and ineptly, but mostly with implacability (after all, it was the specimen's own fault, and although vengeance might be terrible, it was just). 'Follow us.'

But Vadim didn't budge.

It was the same old familiar story. Of course, the bit about the station was a load of bollocks. They didn't want to take Vadim down to any station, or waste time sweating over any reports either. What they wanted was a banal bribe. An ordinary, common or garden five-lat note slipped into their greasy palms. Vadin marvelled at the incredibly natural manner in which dutiful adherence to professional principle – it wasn't faked, after all, it was genuine! – was combined in these two with such a practical and entirely understandable compulsion to rip off at least a few lats – any amount was welcome – from everybody they came across. All the armour-plated dignity of representatives of authority and people with power combined with the manners of Bolderaya's juvenile nocturnal yobs.

'Why all the rush to get down to the station?'

'We'll write up a report. The fine's twenty-five lats,' said the weasel, drawing out the words so that they sounded like a ritual chant.

No, they didn't just want to squeeze a bribe out of him. They wanted Vadim to abase himself as well, to offer them it. After all, they weren't just any old hoodlum riff-raff. They were Authority.

'Let's take a walk!' said the portly partner, moving in close with unambiguous aggression – the direct approach at last – and Vadim spotted that familiar wall of ice behind the pupils of his eyes.

'Na-ah,' he said and took a gulp from the illegal bottle, 'I'm not going anywhere.'

'Wassat?' the squealing, yobbish notes in the weasel's voice were camouflaged no longer. 'Then pay the fine!' He moved in close too. Now both cops were looming darkly over Vadim.

Right then. That was clear enough.

'The fine?' he echoed, glancing from the weasel to the wild boar and suddenly failing to register any difference between them. 'Aha.' He put his hand in his pocket. 'Jussasec.'

The weasel's reaction to the pistol was not quicker, perhaps, but it was certainly livelier: he leaped back an entire metre. His swinish, snarling half-smile widened a little bit – and then froze like that, transformed into a grimace. The bullet caught him in the belly, and he staggered forwards, stooping over lower and lower all the time, eventually enacting the logical conclusion to this sequence of movements by gently lying down flat on his face on the pavement. His legs, surprisingly long and thin in their blue uniform trousers, bent and straightened out several times independently of each other, out of sync.

Vadim shot the other one in the face, firing twice into the wall of ice. The red face instantly jerked back, splitting open from the inside to expel an even redder redness. The portly policeman spread his arms slightly as if bewildered, span round with his knees collapsing as he went, and slumped noisily to the ground.

The echo was deafening – but it was immediately lost in the windy expanse. The spent shell-cases jangled vestigially. Vadim looked round. There was no one running towards him, or away from him, no sirens howling, no swat team hurtling down the road. He shrugged, picked up the bottle with his free hand and, stepping over the outstretched legs of the filth, set off along the embankment, sipping as he went.

The pistol (more evidence to be drowned) described a steep arc terminating in an unintelligible gurgle. Vadim appraised the level of liquid in the bottle. There was still more than half left. Fucking great!

13

Stalin. Hitler. Pol Pot. 53. 45. 98. Years of death. A good number.

But the fact that it was Citron's personal mobile number, for his cronies – did that mean anything from the viewpoint of the pseudo-science of numerology? Indubitably. In numerology absolutely everything had some kind of meaning. Vadim crumpled up the already creased piece of paper on which were written the idiotic instructions dictated by Gimniuk, and, above them, the significant number. Not seeing a rubbish bin anywhere nearby, he simply dropped it on the parquet flooring.

The 'yes' came immediately, after the very first ring.

'Edward Valerievich?' Vadim asked, just to be certain, although of course he had instantly recognised the physiologically erect baritone.

'Yes,' – after the very slightest of hesitations: Citron had not identified his caller from the voice.

'This is Vadim Apletaev.' Vadim exchanged malevolently gleeful grins with his doppelgänger, who had appeared full-length in the mirror on the opposite wall of the club's lobby. 'I work in your press service . . . used to work.'

Another hesitation, twice as long. Citron was remembering. He remembered. Calculated. Very quickly, actually. The result of his calculations was obviously not very easy to digest, but he betrayed no emotion whatever.

'I'm listening.' Calm anticipation. Appropriate self-control for a capitalist shark. Fish-like.

'You see, Edward Valerievich, I know what a hilarious

214

stunt you're planning to pull with the Lunino mob. I was thinking maybe I should tell them about it?'

Citron said nothing.

'I'm in the club entrance at the moment. If you're not in a hurry to get yourself steam-rollered into the road somewhere, make sure I can get inside. And listen to what you can do for me. I'll wait for five minutes.'

Vadim and the doppelgänger both hung up their phones. The reptilian face in the mirror hadn't changed. Vadim wouldn't have asked for a light from someone like that in the street. He'd acquired a bit of an edge in the last few days, this doppelgänger, looked a bit sharper and more mature somehow, although he hadn't shaved once . . .

'Wassup, bro?' Vadim greeted him spitefully. 'After all, money's only shit, isn't it?'

'Money,' said his confidant, not reacting to the base taunt, 'is simply nothing. You're the one who turns into shit the moment loot becomes your final goal in one sense or another. But as a means . . . All's fair – in war at least.'

'A means . . . Next you'll be telling me that loot brings freedom.'

'No, but freedom brings loot,' said the doppelgänger. Jutting out his stubbly jaw in jaunty insolence, he swung away and swaggered towards the blank metal door of one of Riga's most swanky, elitist night-clubs. Leaving Vadim no choice but to follow.

Citron was in no hurry to get steam-rollered into the road: the security guard (naturally, the standard model, with an expensive suit that made him look like one of the Citadel crew, but a coating of dubious, entertainment-sector gloss reminiscent of a maître-d'hôtel) was actually rabbitting on his mobile just at the moment Vadim went in. On seeing Vadim enter, he said something affirmative into the phone, hurriedly switched off, scanned Vadim hastily with hyperbolical professional perspicacity and nodded: okay, come on, follow me.

The Banzai complex possessed a multitude of large halls, small halls, dance floors and cosy corners, but the guard led him through into the restaurant. Vadim had never thought of himself as any great specialist in oriental exotica, but even he twigged that the decorators of the Banzai must have reckoned their generous clients were total noodles. The sliding paper screens painted in flagrantly muted watercolour, the bamboo curtains, the tatami mats that clients traipsed straight across in their outdoor shoes, the comprachico bonsai trees in thick-walled pots, the waitresses gift-wrapped in kimonos! Against one wall of the restaurant a figure dressed in armour glowed with a dull gleam, illuminated by delicate rays of light converging from the ceiling of unpainted wooden boards set directly on to concrete. Vadim took a close look as he walked past: it was training armour, for kendo practice. A fencing mask, a light cuirass. But the single-edged katana sword in the hand, or rather, in the glove, was the genuine article. And there were plenty of tanto-daggers, surikens, triple-bladed sai daggers and other armourer's junk scattered profusely across the walls.

The guard led Vadim to the far corner of the dining hall. The screens dividing up the internal space had mostly been closed. But the last cubicle (beside a door that was entirely European and yet despite that – or perhaps precisely because of it – had been duplicated by an emphatically oriental-dragonish bamboo curtain) was not observing the general rule of privacy. Glancing inside in an automatic reflex response, Vadim discovered with a mildly surprising feeling of satisfaction that Citron's whore was sitting there. Dressed in a carmine evening dress, Lada was meditating absently on a little umbrella protruding from a cyclindrical layered cocktail.

The vapid expression on her averted cover-girl face was parodied on the rough-hewn features of the quite incredibly lanky bodyguard sitting to one side of her. From under the tiny knife in his knobbly fingers flowed a serpentine teletype tape of bright orange peel. Vadim gestured to the whore in boorishly-affable greeting, but the gesture went unnoticed, crashing into the screen that was slammed shut with a quiet squeal by bodyguard number two, who had appeared from the side.

Behind the door and the bamboo curtain, two flights of steps led downwards. On the final step a bodyguard moved aside to let Vadim past. Well then, thought Vadim (as he strove to overcome the resistance of a door stamped with a complex seal that read: 'VIP Zone'), he would use Citron's loot to set up . . . a nice little setup. A classy restaurant. He would call it, let's say 'Chez Gimniuk'. It would be up in an attic. A genuine penthouse place. The waitresses . . . no, waiters (the deceased warrant officer was an uncompromising man's man) would wear loincloths of padded linoleum. And all the food would be served in linoleum too. Baked. They bake in clay, don't they? And instead of cutlery – a tenderising hammer and secateurs.

In the VIP Zone the oriental element had contracted to indecent prints that looked like paper cut-outs, and been distinguished from the rest of the complex by plump, leathery comfort. At the focal point of leathery plumpness, performing the same function as the immobile kendo practitioner who had somehow acquired a samurai sword upstairs – i.e. providing a vanishing point for the spatial composition – stood yet another black-suited guard (there were so many of them that Vadim was beginning to think he was going cross-eyed). The guard towered up behind an expensive armchair, in which, in contrasting mode – calm and collected, leaning forward towards a low, almost empty table – sat Edward Valerievich himself. His light jacket was a genuine joy to behold – a general's uniform. These two constituted the entire population of the hall – but no: a second guard stepped out from behind Vadim, closed the door peremptorily and performed a rapid body search of the ex-REX employee. He then nodded to the boss.

Citron watched his former hireling approach without adjusting his pose. His right hand (no less soft than his armchair) was clutching (no less courteously and tenaciously than the latter clutched himself) a tulip-shaped brandy glass (also resembling E.V. in its roundness). The glass was clutched in a sophisticated fashion, with the palm warming the brown liquid from below, swirling it with insouciant mechanical regularity. The patterned rhomboid of the bottle from which the liquid had evidently come – bearing no label, since it clearly considered it unnecessary to introduce itself to the simple layman – was located on the table, in the left-hand corner and was nearly full. In addition to the bottle, there was also a vast triangular napkin and on it, looking as if it had been manufactured specially for some specific surgical procedure, a zealously glinting young torturer's set. For a lobster or something of the sort, Vadim assumed. Except that there was no lobster.

Escorted on his way to the table by three pairs of eyes, but seeing only one, for the first time that day Vadim felt what an extreme surfer probably feels at those least sweet of moments when the wildly rushing, foaming crest of a wave beneath his feet is suddenly replaced by emptiness. Gestured at by Citron to take a seat, he sank down helplessly into this vacuum, but the awaiting armchair seemed to have no intention of intervening to prevent contact between his backside and the floor.

Eventually it did intervene – but only derisively late, when his knees had already risen to the ludicrous level of his chest. Energised by his anger and irritation, Vadim regrouped, assumed the same pose as E.V. and stared resolutely into Citron's unchangingly, unpleasantly impassive eyes. Edward Valerievich set his glass down on the tabletop without bothering to take a sip.

'I'm listening,' he said coolly, exactly as he had on the phone.

Vadim grinned, baring his teeth.

'A lemon.'

Something Vadim couldn't identify flitted across those steady eyes.

'Excuse me, Vadim,' – not a single facial muscle twitched, but Edward Valerievich's tone was substantially warmer, almost compassionate, like a doctor speaking to a patient – 'have you lost your fucking marbles?'

Vadim smirked even more hideously:

'A lemon. Citron. A million bucks. In cash. Immediately. Or I tell the Lunino mob everything.'

Edward Valerievich pursed his lips slightly and lowered his eyes to his brandy glass. Then he looked up, not at the blackmailer, but at the bodyguard who was watching the door, and gestured gently in Vadim's direction with his balding head and his left hand simultaneously.

Vadim had no time to analyse the sequence of premonitory thoughts that swept through his mind, each one lousier than the one before: a relentless force swept him off the armchair (like a mighty ocean breaker tossing the extreme surfer aside) and threw him down on all fours. Instantly – Vadim never even felt the blow – he lost all feeling in the lower half of his body. This was not right at all. Vadim struggled to regain control over his limbs, but he couldn't. He was left in a strained half-sitting, half-lying position on the floor, trying not to gasp at the liquefying pain.

'. . . out the back way, we don't want him getting noticed around here.'

Citron had apparently been giving instructions for some time already, and clearly not to Vadim. 'Yes, and take a car from Alik, don't touch any of ours.'

'You're making a big mistake.' Vadim squeezed the words out, as if he were mouthing a line prompted by someone else (and a mediocre talent at that).

Pushing himself up on to his elbows, he could see one of the table's massive legs directly in front of him and another, in reduced perspective, further away, and behind that Citron's suede moccasin convulsively stubbing its nose into the floor, as if E.V. were crushing a cigarette butt or learning to tap dance.

Across the kidneys, the fucking kidneys. The bastard hit me across the kidneys . . .

'Don't,' said the invisible Citron, halting the creeping advance on Vadim of the invisible guard. The assured intonation was alarmingly out of tune with the fidgeting moccasin. 'You're going to shake it all out of him: who from, who for . . . And about all this shit we've had going down these last few days – I reckon it's all part of the same thing. Absolutely everything, you understand me? And quickly. Damn . . . There's only fifteen minutes to go . . . Okay, you shake it out of him, then you ring me straight away. Or maybe not . . . No, ring me immediately. But don't do anything with him until I tell you to. Is that clear? Get a move on, time . . .'

The oblique response to Citron's words was a tug that jerked Vadim upwards and set him on legs that had just begun taking orders again – but apparently not from their owner, only from the force that had dealt with their owner in such a brusque and proprietorial fashion. Then something hard slammed into his belly – a small rock . . . aargh! . . . sharp intake of breath – but clearly this was just a nudge, not intended to lay him out, merely to liven him up. It did liven him up: after this easily understood prod of encouragement, his eager-to-please legs staggered off with remarkable alacrity towards the exit where the guard, solicitously holding Vadim up by the collar, reached out to open the door. Before he could do so, it suddenly anticipated his action by bounding towards his hand of its own accord, very nearly smashing into Vadim's nose.

At first Vadim was sure it was stress that was making his brain produce endless reproductions of black and white security guards. His visual analysis mechanism was spinning completely out of control: the open doorway was swamped by a crowd of these unwieldy men with cheerless, dead-pan faces, all dressed well but with monotonous uniformity. But the bilateral bafflement that instantly set in on both sides of the doorway suggested that, if he was seeing things, he wasn't the only one.

The first to react was Vadim's escort: yielding in the face of superior numbers, he switched into reverse, moving back towards the wall, easily repositioning his charge at the same time. Following a momentary pause, the visitors moved forward, instantly filling the small room – one, two, three, four . . . a lot. In fact, not every one of them was actually wearing a suit: a couple of them were draped in long, loose leather coats and one of them staggered in with a black bag on his right shoulder of monstrous proportions.

Five of them.

As, dumbfounded, Vadim mechanically tracked the saturation of the VIP Zone by these athletic figures, he momentarily caught the expression on Citron's face – and realised that, of everyone, Citron was the most surprised by what was happening. But his expression of surprise instantly disappeared, replaced by the preceding poker face.

After a little irresolute dallying the new arrivals arranged themselves, as follows: three, including the one with the bag, facing Citron's table; two facing the sculptural composition 'Removal of the Body of the Marbleless Employee Apletaev'. The heavy cool that had been the welded outer armour of Citron's heavies for so long was melting away to reveal leaden-footed bewilderment. Something here was not going right, definitely not according to plan.

Yet another pause, an annoying, uncooked lump in the porridge.

One of the threesome arranged before Citron, their backs to Vadim, stood out from the rest. In size and appearance he was hardly any different from the others, except for his age (past the big four-oh, as compared with an average age of thirty or thereabouts, and his figure was a bit fuller), but from his suit, which was light, like Citron's, even Vadim could guess he was a general. Another general. The meeting on the Elbe.

'Good evening, Edward,' the newly arrived foreign commander said in a dull and deliberately colourless voice, as if he had a gumboil that made it hard to speak. 'Is everything in order?'

'Good evening, Grigory,' said Citron, supplementing his evenly measured professional cordiality with a note of evenly measured surprise. 'You're early.'

'You got some kind of problem with that?' The visitor was either less refined by nature, or he'd had some reason to be displeased beforehand.

'No problem at all, on my side,' E.V. replied uncon-tentiously.

They said nothing for a while, peering at each other with a subtext. As if imitating them, Vadim's jailer and the two heavies facing him exchanged prolonged glances.

'Okay,' Grigory conceded, then immediately, without turning round, jerked his head in the direction of Vadim and the bodyguard. (Well, what do you know, he'd noticed them!) 'What about that?'

'That,' Citron responded instantaneously – just a tiny little bit too instantaneously – 'is my business. Take him away.' The last phrase was addressed over the heads of the visitors to Vadim's escort.

'Nah, hang on there,' Grigory blurted out gruffly, 'There are questions.'

'Grigory,' Edward Valerievich insisted with increasingly emphatic cordiality, 'there aren't any questions.'

Meanwhile Vadim's captor had been given a specific order, finding himself the only one in this universal state of suspended animation who had been furnished with an algorithm specifying action, he began lugging Vadim towards the exit.

'Stop!'

Instantly changing his tone, Grigory finally swung round towards them. 'Hey, you!'

Seeing that Citron's heavy had already taken hold of the door handle, the general somehow seemed to hint at taking a step in his direction, but no more than that; the hint was converted into action by one of the hoods who stepped towards Vadim and his escort and blocked their way. Without letting go of him Vadim's escort whisked him to one side, then froze, nose to nose with the other hood.

The *mise-en-scène* had changed: the focal point of the composition was now the three figures by the door.

'Grigory!' said a hint of bluff distinctly audible in the imperious, categorical tone. 'I don't get it!'

'No, I'm the one who doesn't get it!' Of course, Grigory had picked up on the bluff: and in addition he had superior numbers on his side. 'I get the impression that you . . .'

He never finished what he was saying. The situation, which seemed to have shifted unambiguously to his advantage, now changed yet again. The door beside which the log-jam had formed slammed hard into the shoulder of the Grigorian heavy, he leapt back and stuck his right hand into his jacket. This last gesture instantly triggered a chain reaction: all the extras taking part in the performance did the same, including the two new ones who had squeezed in through the crack of the open door. Vadim recognised one of them as the lanky guy who had been peeling an orange beside Lada in the restaurant.

Now it was four Grigorians to four Citronians.

Not a trace remained of the performers' bogus laid-back cool. That initial 'something' that wasn't right had escalated and now hung poised, just waiting for a push.

It came.

As always, from the least likely direction: from the one performer who had so far played the most passive role of all.

Since the blow to his kidneys, Vadim had been in a fragile state of suspended will – as if he had assigned control of his body to his jailer, and no longer needed to do anything for himself. But now even his jailer had withdrawn into frozen inaction and Vadim's ownerless body, totally out of the blue, entirely disregarding his reason, fired off a convulsive motor impulse: it gave the bodyguard a smart kick in the shin, tore itself free of his weakened grip and slipped backwards along the wall. The bodyguard was a professional, and so the skittish employee Apletaev's rash outburst ended where it was bound to end – on the floor. But, when Vadim came clattering down on to his elbow for the second time, he immediately howled out, catastrophically disrupting the tense silence:

'He's going to grass you up to Interpol! Then he can keep the loot!'

While these words were being uttered the following occurred: Vadim's bodyguard turned towards him placed a restraining hand on his shoulder, the Grigorian heavy next to him turned back again – and there was a pistol in his hand. There was just enough time for Vadim to notice that this pistol was beautiful and resembled the deceased Gimniuk's black shooter about as much as a borzoi hound resembles a mongrel mutt.

The exposure of the Russian pedigree rod (a quite inexcusably brazen gesture, as if the bodyguard had taken his dick out in respectable company) and the sight of its lustrous length and angularity, detonated the situation irreversibly and it exploded into ubiquitous, universal motion. The air was suddenly thick with metal – full of countless pistols, shotguns (apparently) and things that looked like submachine guns. Shooters of every sort appeared from every side in confused disorder and were jammed into every single character on the stage.

Apart from Vadim.

'If he's not talking bollocks,' (the most terrible thing about Grigory's intonation was the total absence of any intonation) 'I'll bump you off myself, Edward. Personally.'

'Is that a threat, Grigory?' The calculatedly dispassionate delivery of the phrases they exchanged was the necessary concomitant of their ready-made, almost childish simplicity. 'You have to answer for words like that.'

'I'll answer for them,' said Grigory, reciting the next line from the textbook. He nodded at Vadim. 'But first he can answer. Go on.' The last phrase was addressed directly to the ill-starred employee Apletaev.

'You're making a mistake, Grigory.' Despite the ritual nature of the phrase, somehow it was quite clear that Citron was not investing any meaning in it. 'We need to sort things out calmly. Calmly, you understand me?'

From down on the floor Vadim couldn't see his former boss, but from the way everybody's eyes swung away from Citron's table towards the gun-toting bodyguard, and then from the abrupt twitch of that bodyguard's face, Vadim was able to reconstitute the sign (gesture?) transmitted to the guard by Citron. In obedience to this sign, the bodyguard's pistol skipped from his opposite number towards Vadim – and immediately flew into the air as the bodyguard staggered back against the wall, leaning down as he went, as if suddenly overcome by an irresistible urge to straighten his trouser leg or unlace his shoe, and only then . . .

Volumetric expansion, multiplanar detonation, unabating annihilation. The sound was so loud the accommodation couldn't accommodate it. Hot, heavy, dense, ceaseless, unbearable. Legs, legs, legs. The whole world had been crammed absurdly full with legs. Vadim dragged himself under the table. Clung on tight. Something jingle-jangled down on him.

Close close close close close close. Scattering and rolling. Heavy impact. Shuddering collision. Disintegration. A chaotic negative: several photos combined in a single frame. The darkness slowly reshuffling itself. Slowly, endlessly.

His eyelids began to hurt. He unclenched his eyes.

Shock protection. The soles were practically up against his nose. Probably about size 48. In the middle of each one a round plastic inset with the words *Shock Protection*. And a telephone, a mobile: Vadim had never seen one as small and elegant as that before. Paradoxically the telephone was mid call, its little green screen glowing independently. That was how he'd summoned them, Lada's guards. Simply dialled under the table and let them listen. Listen. Listen! The silence couldn't believe its own ears.

Vadim closed his eyes again just in case. The blood rustled melancholically in his ears, like communal water in the pipes. There was an indefinable but insistent smell.

Strong.

Not very soon and not very friskily he crawled to the edge of the table and peeped out from under it with half an eye.

Scattered all around in abundance. Motionless. Absolutely. Limbs. Unsorted, in a heap. Pushing aside the trouser-legs and the attached boots, Vadim extricated his head and shoulders. His gaze was met by a broad, young face with a peevish and dissatisfied expression. Then he realised the face was not examining him but the floorboards. Vadim dragged his body further, somehow managing to free it altogether. He pulled out his hand: there were several small, irregular glass granules clinging to the palm. Something slippery, dark, familiar that stained very badly.

He got up – and barely managed to stay on his feet. His foot skidded. A shell-case. There were huge numbers of the damn things. His head was spinning as if he were seriously drunk. A helicopter. Vadim supported himself against the table. It was messy. Lying on the table, his bulky limbs flung out in wild abandon, was a warrior in a leather coat, a Grigorian, his head resting in a scattering of broken glass. The tablecloth was stained all over and it smelled – sharply and repulsively – of what it was stained with. Including the cognac.

They were all lying there. A large number of voluminous, heavy objects that only a moment ago had been living creatures now clogged the room with cropped heads, backsides, shoulders, legs, coat-flaps, watches, fingers, splatters, streaks, smells. The word 'room' was purely nominal: strictly speaking, there was nothing much left of the room. Not even the walls: the pale-yellow plaster had been hideously pitted with countless notches and holes; several of the prints had disappeared, several others had lost their glass and acquired ragged tears. The leather of the disembowelled armchairs was hanging off in tatters, displaying their stuffing. And everywhere – or was it some kind of glitch? – there was fluff. Weird, inexplicable fluff.

Vadim undocked himself from the table, stepped over an outflung arm.

The lean, mean stock of a brown, shiny, pump-action shot-gun clattered under his foot. He kicked it, walked on, stumbled. The bag.

The massively long and thick bag dragged in by the visitors. Vadim was about to step over it too, but he stopped.

Squatted down. Reached out. Without really under-standing what he was doing or why. He didn't understand anything at all.

The cheap zip rustled as he slid it open with the little brass tag. Delicately, with the tips of his filthy fingers – throw the hair back off the face – Vadim pulled open the bag. Identical briquettes of grey-green paper, cancelled out with white stripes. The white stripes were what the taut bundles were fastened with so very precisely (on account of their multiplicity). Vadim separated one from the brickwork, inwardly prepared for it to prove impossible, for the money to turn out to be a monolithic, plastic block. Bugger it. It was possible. He tore off the white stripe. Flicked through the deck of dollars with a crackling rustle. Put the money back, back where it came from.

It was pointless even trying to guess how much of it there was. Vadim's mind was simply not capable of dealing with money in this form and this quantity. Money, loot, lolly. What was it but a handful of change, a slim wad in your wallet, a credit card, a string of zeros in the press-release you were writing . . . an abstraction? A stack of paper bricks half a metre by half a metre by two metres, enclosed in a synthetic fabric bag that could barely contain them – that wasn't money. Fuck only knew what it was. Delirium, oxymoron. It was totally substantial and three-dimensional, an absolutely, unconditionally material abstraction.

A black hole. A super-dense star, a region of appallingly huge gravitation. Magnetised utterly and completely, Vadim's gaze and his thoughts went tumbling down into that hole. There's no telling how long he might have sat there in that stupor if not for the sound behind him.

Vadim turned round, the joints of his legs cracking as he straightened them, and observed spellbound as a tousled and tangled, but apparently entirely unharmed Edward Valerievich clambered out from behind the shredded back of the chair in which he had been sitting the whole time. Citron, Vadim's former boss, his fat face set in a mask of irrational resolve. Meeting a barrier of flesh as he attempted to skirt the table, Citron scrambled on to the tabletop with surprising agility and advanced across the tablecloth, kicking the recumbent body in the head as he stormed the barricade to throw himself at Vadim.

Vadim automatically drew the fabulous, fairy-tale bag towards him, but Citron latched on to it from the other end and tugged furiously. Then, seeing that Vadim would not let go, he pushed his adversary in the chest with dismaying strength. Vadim lost his footing, falling over on to an anonymous body, and E.V. seized the loot, shoved it behind him and bent down towards something on the floor.

Vadim didn't catch on until it was already too late and Citron was holding the pump-action shot-gun in his hands. Vadim leapt up and grabbed the gun by the barrel, but he couldn't tear it out of Citron's grasp – the bastard was just as strong as he was. They struggled for the gun, panting in furious concentration. Vadim saw his boss, who had hold of the stock, paddling the trigger ineffectively – evidently the breech was not cocked. Finally Citron let go of the gun and moved in close, trying to stick a fist in Vadim's face and a knee in his crotch.

He missed both targets, but the manic, thrusting energy of the ferociously snorting, short-arsed Capitalist over-whelmed his opponent's resistance. Citron pressed Vadim hard, hammering away unceasingly, aiming either for his solar plexus or his nose. It was a while before Vadim was able to make any reply, and when he did, he too missed, landing a blow off-target against his opponent's plump chest. Edward Valerievich grabbed hold of Vadim's wrist, the slim wrist of a hereditary intellectual, with the mighty mitt of a master of life: they struggled again in a clumsy frenzy, grunting and straining, swaying, trampling the corpses – and eventually, of course, they fell over. Citron fell awkwardly, with his ribs across the edge of the tabletop. Vadim broke free and made a dash to escape, but the preternaturally tenacious E.V. held him back by his jacket, leapt on him and threw him down on the table. In his left hand there was something glittering and gleaming, a small two-pronged fork from the recently noted set of lobster accessories – and Citron intended, no matter what the cost, to thrust the said fork into his ex-subordinate.

Yes, this was no Pylny. The head of the major Baltic bank had oodles and fucking oodles of vitality, and to spare;

Vadim squirmed about on the table, panting and straining under the substantial weight of the big bank boss, unable to do anything about the situation. Citron pressed down, sweaty and hoarse, breathing right into his face – fuck you, you fucking bastard, you and your fork!

It was not hatred, no, it was revulsion, physical revulsion for the man wriggling around on top of him, stinking of bodily secretions, that helped Vadim. He tensed up his entire body, like a single muscle, thrust his legs up suddenly and managed to catch Citron between the legs with his hip.

Floundering. Rotation. Another fall. They tumbled on to the floor – but this time Vadim was on top. Vadim clamped both of his hands round the hand his boss was using to clutch the fork. Paying no attention to the banker's other three thrashing limbs, the recent petty clerk gave a guttural whisper and pressed down with every last ounce of himself – with all his mass (whatever it was) and with all his youth, masculinity and hairy Pleistocene atavisms, which were apparently still intact. Citron gave a panic-stricken gurgle, releasing a couple of bubbles through his tight-clamped lips, and the twin prongs plunged down towards the heaving swell of Edward Valerievich's neck, crimson above the shoreline of its sweat-soaked white collar.

Citron's left fist smacked resoundingly against Vadim's ear, but Vadim was already unstoppable. A blind and remorseless mechanism was working inside him. He pressed, pressed, pressed, absolutely intent, groaning and growling on a single note, pressed, pre-e-e-e-essed! . . . and the points moved lower, lower, lower, lower, lower, gently now, gently now, what's the problem, bro, gently, gently, that's it, relax, calm down, stop that, what's the problem, what's wrong, what's wrong, quiet, quiet, right, that's it, it's all over, over, over, over . . .

A final twitch.

An empty gap.

A moment's silence.

Right.

The bag.

As he was reaching for the hold-all, Vadim discovered that for some reason he had picked up the shot-gun. He tried to stuff it into the bundle, but it wouldn't fit. He unfastened the zip all the way, shoved the gun firmly down into the money, and pulled the tag towards him. It wouldn't close.

Then something clicked. Vadim began lumbering across the devastated VIP Zone, picking them up and gathering them together in his arms, sometimes dropping them: pistols, nickel-plated and burnished, short and long, the separate oblique rectangle of a cartridge clip, a faceted, dark-green grenade, an automatic-pistol with a stubby barrel and a long, protruding magazine, another grenade, another pistol, another magazine. He stuffed them into the bag, tucking them in round the edges, hammering them into the dense bank notes. He almost managed to get it shut – only the stock of the pump-action shotgun was left protruding.

Vadim took hold of the bulging bundle's handles. It was as much as he could do to separate it from the floor. He gasped. Dropped it. Saw Grigory.

Or rather, he identified the body lying face-down from the colour of the suit. There was a handle peeping out from his trouser belt: it had to be an old habit from the times when underarm holsters were only ever seen in contraband videos. Vadim relocated the revolver – chubby-cheeked cylinder, snub-nosed little barrel – behind his own belt. Then he returned to the problem of his oxymoronic booty. Hunching over, he just managed to hoist it up on to his back. He set off, staggering, towards the exit. Just try getting out through the doorway with a great hulking brute like that – shee-it!

The little basement had justified its grandiloquent name: the VIP Zone's massive doors and special ceiling (designed to guarantee sound-proof confidentiality) had done their job: upstairs Vadim discovered a scene of entirely undisturbed digestive tranquillity. One of the gift-wrapped waitresses staggered back, aghast at the eruption into the prestigious dining spot of this blood-spattered, ragged desperado crushed beneath his wholesale market-trader's baggage. The waitress was removing an empty cocktail glass with a little folded umbrella from the private compartment nearest to the stair-case. As before, the fusuma screen was open, and there behind it, as before, was the young woman Lada – with her expression frozen to her face, as before.

Vadim barged in, dumped his heavy load on the tatami matting, and dumped himself on the chair opposite Lada.

'Hi!'

'Hi.' Lada demonstrated no vasomotor response of either surprise or recognition. But even so, after a pause of approximately ten seconds, running her glance idly round the hall, the young woman enquired incuriously:

'You with Citron?'

'More like from Citron,' said Vadim, surveying the empty table in disappointment. So that was the way it had all been set up. A serious meet under the cover of a social occasion. The club, the dames. All stage-scenery.

'Where is everybody?' the scenery asked with a feeble wave of her hand, no doubt meaning her bodyguards.

'They're all dead,' Vadim happily informed her.

Lada finally looked directly at him.

'And Citron?'

'Him too. By my own fair hand,' said Vadim with a carefree wink.

'Yeah?' She used the tone of voice normally employed in response to an unimportant but pleasant surprise. 'You did right too. I've been wanting to myself, only there was always something . . . How did you do it?'

'With a fork.'

'Class,' she said with a dreamy smile.

Two club security guards sprinted past them towards the VIP-basement, not looking around them.

'Let's go,' said Vadim.

Lada looked him over appraisingly. She tugged on the lobe of one ear with her mirror-bright nails.

'Okay.'

She smiled at him. She'd flicked her 'on' switch, Vadim realised, half-stunned. So that's what it looked like. For hours she idled away the time in standby mode, then with a single, ultra-brief effort of the facial muscles, she reanimated herself. Vadim felt like his knees were giving way and his insides were turning to syrup.

'Where to?' she asked.

'Your place.'

Lada tossed her head, stood up gracefully and went out first.

As he passed the armoured model equipped for kendo practice, Vadim lifted the sword out of its hands and added it to his arsenal by simply threading it between the handles of the bag.

Greenbacks. Bucks. Spondulicks. Dollars. Entire, untampered-with, paper-bound packs, and stray hundred-dollar, five-hundred-dollar, one-thousand-dollar, five-thousand-dollar, ten-thousand-dollar banknotes, scattered unevenly, in heaps, in piles, in a solid layer and in autonomous isolation on the oiled amber floorboards, on the hard, square rush mats and the soft oval rugs, on the narrow shelves for cosmetics protruding from the wall, on the low triangular table squatting on bamboo legs, on the flat-screen, environmentally friendly Bang and Olufsen television, on the protruding hood of the electric fire, under Lada's suntanned shoulder-blades, stuck to Lada's suntanned shoulder-blades. All over the room. Patches, fields, smears of green mould – a vision of the earth from space.

Vadim paused for an instant at the edge of the trap-door, choking on the gaping emptiness. Then he squeezed his eyes tight shut and, baring his teeth, went hurtling down headlong with a lost cry that he didn't recognise as his own. Down he tumbled, pulled by the stupefying weight of an uncredibly expanded, swollen part of himself, grabbed by the crude Newtonian 9.81 metres per second, driven and squeezed into the narrow, mucilaginous, swee-eet (oh the horror of the *salto mortale*) swee-eet soft fleshy softness, on down, deeper into the very heart of Lada, into the lovingly, densely packed contents of the pelvis minor.

Everything at once. Everything blown to hell. Totally unrecognisable. A new environment. Nothing to grab hold of, to lean on, everything topsy-turvy, spatial orientation lost. In order to have at least something to hold on to, he grabbed her mane, the hair of that species as rare as the magical unicorn. He rode her.

Then out of nowhere, as instantly and pitilessly as the terror, came the joy, the bliss, the ecstasy! Unseen currents seized him, lifted him, tossed him upwards . . . Immense, powerful hands. Swaying, rocking, pumping, that's it, that's it, that's . . . yes, yes yes, more, more, more, yes, yes, come on, come on, yes, yes, bitch, bitch, yes, yes, ah you animal, ah you whore, whore! More! He had parted company with the earth, moving faster and faster, he had to jump off this disembodied lift, God only knew where, right now, come on

– hup! – he leapt off, slithered out of Lada's convulsive twitching, grabbed her dangling breasts and turned over her slim, light body – scattering the rectangles of paper across the smooth boards with the slippery, gleaming hips, the smooth backside. Firm heels thrust against his shoulders; he ran his fingers over the tensed calf, thigh, buttock muscles, here! She thrust forward. Fuck me! Come on! His prick, bustling like a badger, darted into the musky oven-burrow – snarling and snorting, choking in bestial abandon.

Free fall. Sky-diving. Like the senses of a dying man, all three dimensions failed: he was in a boundless gaseous state, where there was no more top, no bottom, no right, or left front or back. Then he entered the fourth dimension where there was nowhere to fall because there was no time and nothing ended.

On her belly. On her back. And finally on top. Lada slipped herself on to him, now, now!

Throwing herself back, she forced him in, squeezing her knees together painfully under Vadim's lower ribs, and started moving like a piston, slamming her backside down rhythmically, grabbing and tugging at Vadim's swollen warhead with her gathered vaginal throat. Vadim reached out squeezed the swinging mammaries, almost expecting them to honk – but Lada only squealed, waving her head around lunatic-fashion. Her mouth slid over shockingly to one side, her damp, dark hair stuck to her wet face.

You can't drown in air. You dive. Float. Somersault. Vertical, Horizontal. The adrenalin-endorphin-testerone splashing around inside you. Bubbling . . . Foaming . . .

He closed his eyes and saw that the surface of the land was very close now. Earth. Soil. Solid ground. He could already make out the irregularities in the terrain, the bared teeth of the cliffs, the rocks that he would go hurtling into at any moment, crushed, shattered, splashed, smeared. The air was forcing his jaws apart, thrusting itself into his mouth, choking him, blocking his breathing, sealing up his ears. The brown eroded surface of Eden. At max velocity. Ten, nine, eight short counter-thrusts of the hips, five! two! zero! Pull the ring on the cord.

Lada's sensitive ring narrowed still further, moving downwards along his entire length, fiercely, firmly, from the head to the balls, yes, yes – and then back again with terrible strength, yes! – the shot, the ejaculation of the long, silky clot, ten kilograms of compressed fabric unfolding in a single intense clap. Triumphant self-abandon, a spasm of generosity. There! Take it, inside, for free. His personal gene fund, biological concentrate – the molecular threads tighten, the DNA spiral springs back . . .

He opened his eyes. Above him the white heavenly dome adorned with the black-and-yellow yin-yang lamp was swaying, drifting. Vadim hung suspended, free and unfree, utterly weightless. Slamming shut her collapsible structure with a single shudder along her entire axis, Lada subsided on to him with a long, expiring gasp. She brushed her ticklish hair across him, licked his shoulder. Then she detached herself, rolled over on to her back, into the money, and laughed.

Vadim came down to earth a couple of minutes later, landing squarely on his two feet. The paper notes clung to his bare soles. When he finally got his bearings, he still felt weightless. The weightlessness was localised along the contours of his body – devastated, drained, squeezed dry. Totally dry. That was it. Dry.

'Have you got anything to drink?' he asked.

'In the fridge. Bring me some too.'

Rustling his feet through the dollars, Vadim strolled into

the kitchen, opened the door of the epic refrigerator and stuck his head in. He staggered back.

Taking up the entire volume of the lower chamber with its fluffy, pneumatic torso, it's head squashed against the freezer above, squeezing a heap of displaced shelves against the wall with its swallow-like wings, mincing and clattering its sharp-clawed, webbed feet across a jumbled heap of jars, boxes and packages, goggling crazily at Vadim with its flat little eyes, standing almost a metre and a half tall, was a white-paunched, yellow-necked emperor penguin. The penguin indignantly opened its flat-sided beak, fluffed up its feathers and squawked in outrage.

14

Ah, but spitting lilac shit like that – no, gents, that's just not on. Round here, for doing that sort of thing, you get wasted – get it? – wasted. Take *that*, and take *that* too, and *that*, you lousy bastard . . . Bloody hell, the brainshaver doesn't affect you! That means you haven't got any blasted brains, so you're resistant to infrasound, you bas-tard! Bugger this. Now you've really pissed me off, you and your fucking shit, you bloody bog-monster. Holy shit, whoah, hang on, let's nip round the corner, put in a few medical repairs, catch a bit of a breather. And the pits is we haven't got a single sodding cartridge. A nice little secret cache, that's what we need, a cache . . . A cache. Hah!

An LSD-gun. Not exactly a mega-monster-zapper, of course, but not bad. Right, come on, come on. Come here, now we're really going to zap your insides, give you the screaming black willies, screw you, for good and for keeps . . . Hah! Got it. Wassup bro, don't like that? Not feeling so great now, eh? Feeling real bad all of a sudden. Life's tough for everyone nowadays. Surely no one told you life would be a fairy-tale. Hoopah. Finita. Why you scumbag, even your blood's poisonous. You can't even snuff it like a decent bastard . . .

How many? Forty-seven. Well, you're not going to get to the next level with a score like that. And I don't reckon there are any first aid kits around here either. I need a first aid kit. Well, you can't have a first aid kit, bugger you.

Now, that's an idea.

Whose arse shall I stick my firecracker up? Yours. Ooh,

you nifty bastard. See that somersault, and that one, and then that one up the wall like that, now take that! It's all over? Yeah, take a look, all over. So what was it we were afraid of? Exit. No bloody problem . . .

Leaning back in his chair, Vadim triumphantly surveyed Sarah Taft in a haute-couture combat jumpsuit and the luminescent title of the game's next level. But he felt like he'd had enough. Quit. Even more than that: he was sick of it. Do you really want to quit? Yes, I do, I do. Y. You were right, doppelgänger, you reptile.

The previous night the reptile had finally lost all sense of decency, decided to ignore the restrictions of the mirror-frame, and made a full frontal appearance in Vadim's dream. That is, first he'd been preceded by a whole gang of unmistakable mega-whores of various tribes and races who had smashed their way in, at least half a dozen of them. Not one of them wearing anything except their pubic hair, and not even all of them had that. Then, following this freaky avant-garde, the doppelgänger himself had grooved in – fully clothed, but in absolutely outrageous style: white tails with camouflage trousers. His stubble was already at the week-old stage – evidently time flowed differently in looking-glass land. The doppelgänger had a huge, stretchy black bag dangling heavily over his shoulder, just like the one Vadim had purloined from the Banzai. On seeing his reptilian face, all the whores had nimbly arranged their bodies into a strange acrobatic figure resembling a divan – on which the doppel-gänger had proceeded to sprawl in the most loutish possible manner. He had immediately extracted from somewhere a bottle of 16-year-old Lagavulin and then another vessel – a perfect double of the nameless cognac bottle that had been a casualty of the shoot-out. They were followed by a one-litre beer mug. The doppelgänger filled it up to the top – with equal parts from both bottles – took a good long swig, burped in satisfaction and only then turned his gaze to Vadim.

'This is better than pseudo-life,' the reptile declared with conviction.

'But you see, the whole trick here,' Vadim told him thoughtfully, 'is that everything's really far more simple than it seems. More simple and more stupid. More depressing. All that garbage that they spend their time on,' – he put on a fearsomely preoccupied face and mimed talking on a mobile phone – 'there's no one forcing them to do it, no one provoking them or urging them on. The worst thing about it all is that there is absolutely no rational force behind the transformation of people into smug, self-satisfied devices (who was it that defined contemporary Homo as "self-satisfied man" – Ortega y-Gasset?) for the manufacture of emptiness. Not even any slightly individualised force. Nothing but a law of nature. Like universal gravitation. Or rather, in this particular case, the irreversible increase in entropy.

'Nature in general and the biosphere in particular strive to maintain equilibrium,' – he swayed his open hands in front of his face, presumably in imitation of a pair of scales – 'a balance . . . But man, well, you know, he's superfluous to requirements. A beast that's escaped from the global biological community – he just had to go and build himself civilisation. He has this neat little thing called reason – maybe you've heard about it. And one way or another, with the help of this little item, he's managed to reach a stage at which the satisfaction of the simple, basic needs of life – like not actually dying of hunger – requires very little effort. Take a wolf in order not to peg out during the winter, he really has to stretch himself to the limit physically, there's never any let-up. But even the most pitiful tramp out on the street only has to dig around in a rubbish bin to collect a few bottles, and drop into the premises of the Order of Malta for a free bowl of soup – and he can survive. It's a God-awful kind of life, but your actual wild animals could never even dream of anything like it. Result? Man has this huge mass of physical and emotional energy that never gets used in the process of his survival.

'So, using the same old tin can,' – Vadim tapped on his own to illustrate the point – 'he invents himself some entirely abstract goals just to keep his brains, hands and nerves occupied. The basic picture's clear enough (more of the same old natural needs): fill your belly, copulate, be the leader of the pack (that is), fill your belly fuller and copulate more often and more exquisitely than all the rest). There is no way we can get away from our biological basis. But the more simply the primary needs are met as civilisation advances, the further the artificial needs move away from them. Until the connection is completely lost. Why in hell's name, my dear fellow, do you need a machine for slicing a lemon? Just how hard is it to cut it with a knife? And what about that Mercedes you sweated so much blood to buy – can you eat it? Derive unparalleled pleasure from shagging it up the exhaust? I'm sorry, you see, but reason is irrational (from the point of view of natural harmony). So the goals it invents are the same. Irrational.

'In some ways the social sphere is an extension of the biosphere. Nature maintains the balance through the Rexes and the Mercs. All our yuppie wheeler-dealers are no better than lemmings. Only, instead of drowning themselves in the sea, they make a career, earn money and buy things. If all this scummy lowlife were suddenly to start doing something that made sense, just think what an anti-entropic surge that would create! Disorder and confusion. So having exited from the biological community, your sapiens is booted, so to speak, into the social sphere. At the new level a fundamentally cadaverous system is created, of which the sole and exclusive function is to deprive human activity of meaning. And this system is actually created by man himself . . .'

'A sort of homeostatic universe, right?' the perspicacious doppelgänger chortled, propping his elbow on the smooth bolster of someone's bum. 'The universe maintains its structure . . . We've read something about that somewhere, of course.'

Vadim gave him a reproachful smile, as if to say: Who could ever have doubted it? And continued.

'. . . But reason is incorrigibly expansionist. It's always pushing in some direction or other. That's its essential nature: to push things forward, pile things up, augment, accumulate, intensify. And so civilisation never stands still, it gets more and more complex and its entropy is quite deplorably reduced. Additional lightning-conductors have to be created to earth the energy of humanity. So now they've invented virtual reality. What a massive energy surplus *that* diverted into the swamp! It's just a load of hooey when they tell you the Internet and all that stuff will accelerate the development of civilisation. Like hell. That's not what it was invented for. It's exactly the opposite. It's there to keep technological civilisation self-contained and short-circuited. To stop it breaking out. To prevent someone suddenly remembering about our abandoned expansion into space and using computers for that? Get it?

'In fact the putrefied sublimational essence of the Net is best demonstrated by the Net itself. What makes up the overwhelming – overwhelming! – majority of information posted and circulating on the Net? Porn. Naked bums and tits,' (the reptile slapped his 'furniture' in agreement) 'by the bale, the tonne, the gigabyte. Seventy per cent of total traffic. And of the other thirty per cent, twenty per cent is just plain

NONSENSE. Nonsensical forums. Ludicrous chat rooms. Texts that are a total waste of space. A meaningless mish-mash of weak-witted wordage. Just think about it: for centuries now, ever since humanity invented scientific and technical progress for itself, since about the time of the Renaissance, it's been scrabbling, clawing, clambering its way towards this Internet. And there it is, the crown of evolution, the first global, instant, free, uncensored means of com-munication in the history of Homo sapiens, an inexhaustible reservoir of knowledge, a planetary nervous system . . . A portrait, cast from our own selves, so to speak. A generalised portrait. And what face do we see in it? The face of a mentally retarded, juvenile sex maniac. A lewd idiot. Congratulations! Humanity, my friend, I'm proud of you!

'Okay. To take an example dear to my heart – Headcrusher and similar computer games. Here you have the direct earthing, the virtualisation of the young male's instincts, destructive and otherwise – an active support for the traditional social lightning conductor, so that our young male won't start actualising his destructive potential right here in the social sphere . . .'

'Well, I don't know how you do things there in the mirror,' said the doppelgänger, interrupting Vadim in an unbelievably rude manner, 'but speaking for myself, I prefer to take out my monsters in real life.' And in confirmation of this assertion, he shook the bag, which gave out an uncom-fortable, multiply metallic clatter.

'Hang about,' Vadim queried, 'just who's in the mirror here?'

'Well not me, that's for sure,' the reptile snorted self-confidently.

This was such barefaced effrontery that Vadim had woken up. But now, as he tried to pass the time while he waited for Vitek in the same way that he had been passing the time in this little bar for the last few years, he felt an unexpected weariness and disgust. He fished the golden-brown stick of a Captain Blake out of the soft pack and took a drag, watching a small but recognisable Bill Gates with a Carlson propeller on his back dashing about the black screen from one Microsoft 'window' derisively equipped with a handle that wouldn't open it to another, unable to clamber into any of them. Vitek occasionally designed his own screensavers, to keep his hand in. He had emigrated to the catering trade from programming. But he still had plenty of close contacts in the latter area, including some rather special ones.

'Rejoice, you have good news. He says maybe by tomorrow.'

Vitek had come up to Vadim from behind, moving incredibly quietly for a man of his large dimensions.

'The passports and the diplomatic baggage. Give.' Vitek held out an imperatively demanding paw and Vadim promptly placed the entire pack of Captain Blakes in it. Vitek tipped out about two thirds.

'How much?' Vadim clicked Lada's Dupont lighter in front of Vitek's fat chipmunk cheeks and observed the way Vitek instantly sucked in half of the strong, pipe-tobacco-filled cigarette.

'Double.'

'Okay,' Vadim agreed without a moment's hesitation.

'Quarterly,' said Vitek, squinting attentively.

'Okay,' Vadim repeated, figuring that the best-case scenario gave them a chance of seeing in the New Year in the plane.

'Yeah, and they need three photos each of you and your girl. And quickly. You never used to smoke.'

'I started,' Vadim said with a shrug.

Vitek drowned his finished Captain in the glass he'd brought over with him. The butt hissed and choked.

'Shit vodka,' Vitek declared. 'It doesn't light . . .' He took a gulp of the shit vodka, deftly avoiding the butt with his lips. 'What did you do, rob the bank or something?'

'Aha.'

Vadim picked up the massive, stretchy black bag (it gave out a multiply metallic clatter), shook Vitek's massive mitt and, under his respectful gaze, clambered up the steps out of the basement. He turned away from the bitter blast of the icy wind, wrapped his coat tighter around himself, winced, shuddered and pulled his head into his shoulders. But even as he turned away, and wrapped himself tighter, and shuddered, and slipped on the smooth, polished humps of ice into which successive thaws and frosts had transformed the seasonal meteorological garbage that poured and sprinkled down incessantly from above, to be subjected to stubborn, dejected kneading by the soles of countless shoes, Vadim was filled, contrary to his usual habit, with a ferocious joy.

It was almost unbearably pleasurable to know that he no longer belonged either to these godforsaken latitudes, or to this grey, listless, faded country, or to this grey city that had pissed him off so completely, or to this foul, freezing grey slush, this filthy muck. I've only two more days left to watch all this, you tossers, two more days – and then I'm leaving, going as far away as it's fucking possible to get from this lousy place. I'm going away and I'm never, you hear me, NEVER coming back. I'm not yours any longer, and I'm not the same as you. I refuse to stay up here in the northern frosts, with you grey-faced cattle, with your boring, repulsive, dismal faces, your self-satisfied obsessions, your senseless singleminded-ness. You shitty-arsed lemmings, with your hustling-bustling greed! Fuck the damn lot of you! Stay here and chase after your pitiful money and rotten rip-off swank, get frozen and soaked, fall, break your bones, crack your skulls open, die in agony, I don't give a shit . . .

He strolled on as far as the corner of Brivibas and Elizabetes – that inflatable King Kong, the five-metre tall Santa Claus, scowled moronically, showing off those no doubt super-sharp teeth each the size of a Soviet spade as he continued to point out the road to Pskov with his mitten.

His electric eyes glittered in ghastly triumph.

Vadim stopped. He crossed over to the King-Kong side of Brivibas Street, on to the little island which until August '91 had been occupied by the cast-iron figure of the leader of the international proletariat. The bulge of the scarlet rubber backside was right there in front of his eyes. At least half of the figure consisted of that backside. There were several enigmatic metal boxes lying at the feet of the massive monster – evidently they somehow maintained the required degree of distension (something like compressors?).

Vadim swung the bag round from his back to his chest and slid the zip a quarter of the way open. Stuck his hand in without looking. Found the handle of something and pulled it out. Grigory's gleaming, snub-nosed little revolver scowled up at him from his palm.

Vadim turned the tidy mechanism over in his hand as he figured out what was what. Then he cocked the hammer with his thumb and, without aiming, fired straight ahead six times, until the cylinder was empty. The 'bulldog' six-shooter had an even lighter recoil than Gimniuk's pistol, but it made one hell of a bang. Only after the rumbling in his ears had settled did he hear the distressed carbide hiss of the air escaping from the punctured backside. Vadim tossed the revolver over his shoulder and stood there for a moment, making sure that the grand New Year arse really was losing its taut, impudent elasticity and vivacious convexity and developing cellulite creases. An agitated crowd was gathering rapidly in the margins of his field of vision. Vadim zipped up his bundle, slung it on to his back, swung round and set off obliquely across the park.

'And this is my pride and joy! You might call it the pearl of my collection.'

The leisurely hand of the arch-magus and seventh-generation healer, Great Master of Sorcery, corresponding member of the Academy of Astral Energy Protection, certified Doctor of Psychic Fathoming, Archpriest of the Church of Unified Energies (the titles jostled for space on the face of his business card) indicated two little black beans that looked like plasticine models of a lapdog's turds.

Vadim and his guide had already passed, freezing in momentary respect at each item: a massive bent, knobbly prick (a south Peruvian Indian pipe for burning ecstasy-inducing incense), a bunch of rather smaller wrinkled, purplish phalluses (dried mushrooms from the Yucatan peninsula that granted the power to see the spirits of the upper and lower worlds), a cracked leather pancake with little jester's bells (a shaman's tambourine), a little monster of rags and clay stuck through with crooked knitting needles (Haitian voodoo doll), an irregular and outrageously rusty sedge leaf with a short stem bound round with colourful thread (a Bora–Bora tribe ritual knife).

Vadim was expected to demonstrate the respectful curiosity of the simple layman and he was perfectly happy to demonstrate it.

'In the jungles of Central Africa . . .' (The certified arch-magus was portly, stout, even obese; despite their large

248

calibre, the massive, inscrutable spectacles in ostentatiously expensive horn frames were completely lost among the fleshy rotundities of the pleasant, chubby face.) 'In the impenetrable jungles of Central Africa there lives a tribe which even now, just imagine, is still ruled by a council of twelve sorcerers. The most terrible punishment known there is not death – since that is the exclusive prerogative of the will of God. But the sorcerers can put a criminal to the test. This they do by offering him a choice between two of these apparently identical pills. One of them is completely harmless, but the other contains a deadly poison that slowly paralyses respiration and decomposes the lungs. For about an hour and a half the criminal writhes in agony, breathing out bloody foam and gradually going insane, indeed quite often he fails to hold out to the end and simply dies from the shock!'

As he delved deeper into the details of the implementation of the supreme measure, the archpriest began to shed his stately imperturbability, growing ever more agitated, making smaller and more animated gestures. Vadim listened to him, nodding and understanding less and less what the hell he was doing in this place. The urge had been virtually subconscious: in the vestibule of the business centre rented out as separate offices (the photographic studio that Vadim required was located on the ground floor), he had spotted a familiar logo – a cross inscribed in a mandala on a Star of David – and simply followed instructions on the sign. He had been almost delighted when in the modernist-bureaucratic style reception area for 'offices 214–216' he discovered the sombre buffalo in a suit. Naturally, the buffalo had been disinclined to admit this dubious visitor into the CHURCH OF UNIFIED ENERGIES. However, a hundred-dollar portrait of Benjamin Franklin had proved adequately convincing.

'Right, you know everything,' said Vadim, interrupting

a sweeping gesture illustrative of certain excruciating details of the death of the luckless African tribesman in mid-phrase and mid-phase. 'Tell me this. If you shove a penguin, about so big, an emperor penguin, into a fridge, what'll happen to it?'

The astral energy protector paused in motionless silence, acquiring the maximum possible similarity to the aforesaid penguin.

'Okay, okay, then.' Without being invited, Vadim made himself comfortable in one of the two armchairs in the immense, dimly lit office (the bag clanged to the floor at his feet) and jabbed his finger at the other chair in invitation. 'Screw the penguin. Why don't you just tell me about my own future instead, eh?'

'Ah, so you require a prognosticatory consultation?' The seventh-generation healer sat down facing him, relieved.

'Something of the sort.'

'But are you aware of my rates? I have a reliable, patented . . .'

Without saying anything Vadim tugged the first crumpled bill that his hand encountered out of his pocket. It turned out to be a five-hundred, a collector's item, or so Vadim had heard, a rare bill with Mr William McKinley on it. He had expected another dumb penguin show, but on the contrary his reliable, patented host deftly picked up old Bill without the slightest hesitation and stowed him in his wallet of genuine human skin.

'Well then . . .' The arch-magus stretched his hands out with the fingers spread wide, as if he were intending to warm them at a fireplace, and began kneading, palpating, squeezing, pinching and tapping Vadim's invisible astral outline. This continued for quite a long time.

'In your future,' the archpriest began in a sepulchral

voice, after he had kneaded and palpated his fill, 'I see a great deal more good than negative. Your life will acquire greater stability and regularity in all areas. Tranquillity. Confidence. Rootedness. I would say HARMONY. This will be facilitated by the constantly increasing profitability of your business.' (The certified one enunciated the final word in a special tone of cautious triumph.) 'Which business, already successful at the present time, will in both the near and also the distant future display a tendency towards smooth but stable growth . . .'

Vadim leaned across the runic table and plucked the inscrutable spectacles off the distinguished nose of the Great Master. The master's little eyes proved to be unexpectedly dim and shifty – perfectly piggy, in fact.

'Okay then,' said Vadim, disappointed. He replaced the spectacles, admired them for a moment and explained. 'That way's better.'

'What on earth do you think . . .' The outraged magus's right hand darted under the table top and began jerking about, as if its owner were feverishly working a telegraph key. 'I . . . Why . . .'

Vadim sighed and bent down to the bag. The buffalo from reception stepped into the room at just the same time as the bundle yielded up yet another catch: a long burnished pistol.

'Death,' Vadim quoted, 'is the exclusive prerogative of the will of God.'

He lowered the barrel of the gun and kicked the runic table – the lapdog's turds rolled dangerously close to the edge:

'Choose. Come on, get a move on, arch-penis.'

The arch-penis, it should be said, demonstrated amazing self-control. He carefully avoided looking in the direction of the door and remained calm. Having clarified what was required of him, he entrusted himself to the supreme will without any hesitation. Carefully picked up the closest plasticine turd and popped it into his sensuous mouth.

Vadim and he waited to see what would happen. Nothing happened.

'Are you satisfied now?' the archpriest enquired in the voice of a professional negotiator remonstrating with a terrorist maniac who has hung himself all over with dynamite and taken over a nursery school.

'By no means,' Vadim replied in elevated style. 'Eat the other one.'

'But, you must admit, that's not . . .' The penis's finest gentlemanly feelings seemed to have been wounded, but he didn't really appear frightened.

'Eat it, I said!'

'But . . .'

'What did I say?' Vadim raised his rod again. 'Get it down you.'

The penis was an extremely courageous man. He therefore unconditionally preferred an agonising death lasting an hour and a half in a puddle of bloody foam and scraps of his own hacked-up lungs to an easy instantaneous death from a bullet in the forehead. No doubt the gods were duly impressed and rewarded this valiant deed as it deserved. The second little turd did no more harm than the first.

'Mm . . .' said Vadim, perplexedly scratching the bridge of his nose with the barrel of his gun. 'If it doesn't work, then it doesn't. The supreme will and all that . . .' He thought for a moment and then pointed the pistol at the doctor of psychic fathoming's head. 'But in addition to the supreme will there is also arbitrary individual caprice!'

Who was it that said that in heaven they have a climate and in hell they have a society? There it was written in black on white: the Society Islands. French possessions in Oceania. With a heavenly climate. But then heaven was in the next world too . . .

Vadim slammed the atlas shut and added it to the Russian-French phrase book that was already settling into the pocket of his leather coat (the copper centime of change went into his jeans, to join the tangled bundle of one-hundred-bucks and fifty-bucks notes). The shop door clanged as it let him out. The festive intonation had already a New Year lilt. Even when he got outside the jangling still didn't stop: the ubiquitous ringing of jingle-bells continued, taken up and amplified by the trams that were crammed to bursting-point at rush hour on the final working day, the Christmas-tree baubles and all sorts of tinsel frippery in the warm shop windows, the orange light bulbs drooping sloppily in the naked crowns on the garlands that were gradually lighting up. The capital city, having stumbled through yet another shitty day in customary fashion, was crumbling ingloriously into the blind, chilly twilight.

The wing of the hard-working Zhiguli nestling at the lowly kerbside of life and Krishian Baron Street had got covered in filth during the recent thaw and someone had traced out on the black surface: 'This isn't dirt, it's sweat!' Walking was only possible by taking shorter and shorter steps, on rigid legs with feet held slightly apart – this black ice was serious stuff. Everyone else was also hobbling along in the same penguinesque fashion, and the vehicles, wary of trauma, were moving at a similar speed. It suddenly dawned on Vadim that the entire city was creeping across the icy crust with all of its one and a half million lower extremities and all of its countless tyres, struggling hopelessly to put on the brakes, to stifle the annual burst of speed, to grind to a halt before it reached that something absolutely inscrutable and incomprehensible which lay at a distance of only thirty-something hours, and towards which it was drifting fatally closer every second, before it reached that vast terrifying abyss of the unknown – and at the same time, realising already that it wouldn't be able to stop, that just a tiny little bit further and it would go flying straight into that gaping maw, it was smiling to keep up its courage, trying to cheer itself up with that ceaseless background jingling of bells, winking electrically at itself as if to say: up there ahead things will be much better, I see in your future more good than . . . But even as it sought to deceive itself in exactly the same style and manner as the recently deceased certified arch-penis, exactly like the latter it knew perfectly well that this was all a sham, that there was only one future tense – the future indefinite: and that the indefinite was always terrifying.

Vadim also realised that he had been too hasty in detaching himself from the city, that as long as he was here – physically, bodily – he was subject in the same way as everyone else to the general suicidal movement, that his only chance was to leap off at the last moment: but whether he would, whether he could, whether he'd be in time – that was all still highly problematical. Meanwhile inside him the timer was already ticking away, counting down the seconds . . .

He waited for a bulky Hoetika garbage truck to pass and crossed Blauman Street. The programme board of the Daile cinema displayed the sulky, green, squeezed-lime countenance of the Grinch who Stole Christmas. In the window of a music shop Britney Spears leered disapprovingly at Jennifer Lopez. Two young bohemians tumbled out of the bohemian café Oasis, bantering loudly in Latvian and chortling merrily. Vadim thought the one on the right, wearing a reddish, waisted, sheepskin jacket looked familiar. Olezhek, the youthful PR talent, his colleague of yesterday. Nu tad baigi forshi, ha–ha, lieliski, protams! . . . said the youthful talent.

ELIMINATE? YES.

'Oleg,' Vadim called. Louder: 'Oleg!'

The queer stopped and glanced round, still smiling, looking for whoever had called his name. Saw Vadim approaching. The smile deteriorated into an irritated grimace of hypocritical amiability.

Vadim ran through his usual routine on the move: he swung the bundle round, unfastened the zip, stuck his hand in. This time his fingers encountered something strange, a grooved object with a round cross-section. He pulled it out: the long, slightly curving black handle and small guard of the samurai sword he had taken from the kendoist at the Banzai . . . Vadim shrugged the bag off his shoulder, exposing the narrow, metre-long blade, hefted the sword in his hand, waved it in front of him. In the light of the streetlamps a wavy pattern slid along the length of the oiled blade. Vadim took a firm grasp of the comfortable hilt with both hands.

Grinning in a highly uncertain manner, Olezhek took a step backwards. His companion, whose face had also frozen in immobility, started in a different direction. The crowd skirted round them, not hesitating yet, but already paying attention. Vadim stepped towards Olezhek, raised the katana above his head and brought it down perpendicularly on his ex-colleague's shoulder.

The gay PR man half-squatted down, gave a brief yelp, swung round and set off down the street with extreme alacrity. Pushing aside the passers-by, Vadim darted after him. He managed to reach Olezhek's back with a stroke of the sword and the sheepskin coat split open, exposing bluish-grey clumps of woolly fleece – but the poncy pederast only legged it even faster. People scattered to get out of their way. The third blow caught the queer on the back of the head – and then he collapsed instantly, without a sound, face-down. But he immediately started crawling, squirming and protecting himself with his arm, so that Vadim's further blows landed all over the place, copiously splattering everything around him with bright red. Someone gasped, shrieked and squealed – and as if he had taken the hint the prostrate pervert finally began squealing in despair: so loudly and piercingly, in fact, that in order to put an end to the repulsive sound as quickly as possible, Vadim kicked the PR ponce over on to his back, took aim and slashed at his face with all his strength, as if he were chopping firewood. The blood spilled across the light, powdery snow on the ice-bound asphalt in a fat, elongated tongue, the blade bit deep into the skull and stuck. Vadim left it there, went back and picked up his ever-lighter bag.

The human factor enclosed him in an agitated, fluid circle – at every movement Vadim made the gapers, gawkers and gogglers, flowed back to what they estimated was a safe distance.

Now there was squealing in several different places at once – though only out on the periphery, behind the people's backs. But it was unceasing now. The words 'killed' and 'police' were mentioned. So there was an unhealthy undercurrent of feeling developing . . . Why, you bastards. Vadim turned off on to Lachepleche Street. The observers and commentators trickled round the corner after him, pointing and calling for help.

Then a new crowd came flooding out of a gateway, cutting across his route – the film had just finished in the Daile cinema. Vadim squirmed his way in, excuse me, melted in, pardon, and under cover of this assembly (which, fortunately, was not focused on his performance, but Jim Carrey's) he slipped through into the yard of the cinema. On the right, by a brick wall with a gnawed upper edge, an embryonic rubbish tip had established itself – a gutted fire-fighting equipment cupboard with wire-mesh doors, a domestic Christmas tree retired before its time with a lacquered wooden coat-hanger dangling on a crumbling branch, a soot-stained snowdrift of plywood, roofing slates, soaking paper. The weather-beaten attic-storey of a little wooden house peered sleepily over the chipped and battered section of wall. Vadim tried the cupboard – it held. He hoisted up his bundle, jerked himself up and dragged himself on to the sheet-metal slope of the little house's roof. Then he set off, swaying, along the rattling slope . . . A little yard. He threw the bag ahead of him. It made a loud clatter, but there was no one to be alarmed, the rubbish skips couldn't care less. Vadim jumped down himself, walked through another gateway and found himself on Blauman Street.

He walked at a leisurely stroll now, as far as Terbetas Street, then down along it, past the Cabinet of Ministers, as far as the Vernissage Club – the extremely vulgar little building was being positively promoted by floodlights in various colours – past the main university building, through the little square by the Municipal Canal, towards the Laima clock. In the middle of the cult square, that unfailingly popular point of assignation with its constant quorum of devotees, he remembered about the TV camera connected up to the Net. So now Vadim Apletaev, wanted man, multiply reproduced by the number of threads in the World Wide Web, must be strolling through the Internet portal in on-line mode in full view of the entire world . . .

At that moment, with a metallic drone like a thumbnail

scraping along a thick guitar string, the clock's two-metre-tall flasks of semi-transparent, one-inch thick, quartz glass set in oxidised copper frames began moving, and swapped places: now the blue one was on the top and the red one was on the bottom. The tiny one-centime pieces, discrete quanta of hour-glass time, rushed towards the narrow throat. The heavy hand trembled on the patterned metallic dial and shifted on to the Roman numeral six – eighteen hundred hours. Meanwhile the timer inside Vadim was already hurrying on:

32.00.00 . . . 31.59.59 . . . 31.59.58 . . .

15

Well, well. He'd become Alekss Aliohins. Agent of the Satversme State Security Service. Our sure hope and certain support. Bulwark of law and order. And legality too, naturally. The sword and shield of the Second Republic. Mister counter-intelligence agent. How very appropriate.

Having leafed through the passports Vadim twisted the covers this way and that, peering hypercritically at the seals, which he actually knew absolutely damn all about anyway. The thick envelope – two blue civil passports, two IDs for defenders of the constitution, accompanying documents for diplomatic baggage – had been ferried round to the agreed tavern by a diminutive, absolutely ordinary-looking chick: short bleached hair, duck nose, fringed jeans, MD-player earpiece stuck in her ear. She had come alone and left alone, but while she was checking with practised rapidity through the contents of the envelope that Vadim handed her, he had spotted the ends of her metacarpals, transformed into shock-proof hammer-heads. What use would a hacker have for armour-plated knuckles? Or a cracker – whatever the right name for them was . . .

Can we get across the border with these? No problem, you won't get your fingers burned with these, they're in the police computer, and in the department of state information. Better than the genuine article. But I wouldn't advise you to try coming back with them. You know, just in case. But I'm not planning on coming back . . .

And then there was his faithful partner Inesse Auzinya, female agent of the Satversme State Security Service. Vadim chortled and raised his eyes at the synchronised squeaking of two wooden chairs (light old Soviet-regime dacha-standard) being drawn up to the unoccupied, conceptually battered table behind him. Vadim's foot had raked the black bag under his table closer, but a single rapid glance at his new self-appointed neighbours had been enough to make it clear that they could not possibly have anything to do with the structures of power – official, semi-official or unofficial.

Vadim looked around. During the afternoons the stylish rock and roll bar No one Writes to the Colonel was as good as empty; apart from the black-sweater-clad barman, there were only the two cruddy individuals behind him, one of them lecturing the other. Behind the round parapet of the bar the barman was practising that most ancient art of all barmen: taking down an almost empty one-litre bottle of vodka from a shelf that looked like a helicopter rotor blade, he twirled it in his fingers, tossed it up in the air, caught it by the neck. Caught it three times out of four. But then, it was thick glass.

11.14.32 . . . 11.14.31 . . .

There were two men in front of him.

To look at, the first one was a typical snot-nosed punk, very young, healthy, sullen, pumped-up, short-cropped. Except that the features of the inexpressive face weren't insolent and bloated, like those of the classic district goblins at a local rumble, but more concentrated and compressed, as if their owner was in danger of shitting himself at any moment. The second one was a complete contrast: short, narrow-shouldered, as old as Vadim himself. The fine, cultured features and the long kid-leather coat suggested strongly that he was gay. But if he was a queer, which he very well could be, he was latent, suppressed. Totally crushed and flattened, in fact . . . Vadim understood what these two were all about almost immediately. As soon, in fact, as he saw the red T-shirt under the goblin's unbuttoned jacket: the white circle on the chest, the black hammer and sickle in the circle, *à la* swastika on a Third Reich banner, the inscription running above it – 'Slash them and nail them'.

Vadim was facing a pair of rare and rather exotic creatures: marginal political radicals. The Che Guevaras of our own little sandpit.

'Gentlemen,' Vadim remarked ungraciously. 'I did not invite you to sit down.'

The one with the narrow kid-leather shoulders calmly set down on the table an elderly Eriksson mobile with a yellow panel.

'You've got the Lunino loot,' he said casually, but the well-trained public speaker's voice made its point anyway, resonating on the stressed syllables. 'You're going to hand it over to us. Right now. You're going to take us to where you left it and hand it all over, all present and accounted for. Or else,' – he nodded at the mobile – 'I'll phone the police. Right now.'

Interesting . . . I wonder if it was Vitek's friends themselves who sold me out to you? And why you? Or did you just pick something up from a casual acquaintance at some gathering, put two and two together, follow things through?

Meanwhile, the voice behind his right shoulder was saying: '*But if you want to do serious business, yeah? You understand you have to know just what you're getting into. Serious business, not some useless crap or other, like ripping off a pocketful of greenstuff and blowing it on the whores in a couple of clubs, but real, genuine business . . .*'

The two men stared fixedly into Vadim's face – the younger one like a soldier looking at a louse, the older one like an infantry general looking at a nit. He had known these pocket-size Che Guevaras from various factions and combat groups ever since his days as a columnist. He had never been very fond of them. He had even devoted several trenchant analytical columns to their activities. The radicalism and aggression of these guevaras was not derived from mindless, feral xenophobia or upstart protozoic mediocrity, like that of your typical post-modern extreme lefties or extreme righties. All those were simple and . . . in fact they were absolutely *In*comprehensible, and it wasn't even worth trying to rationalise their incomprehensibility, it was just something to be eradicated with no particular feelings – for strictly sanitary, hygienic like. Like shooting mad dogs. Exterminating rats. Delousing.

The kid-leather Che's brothers-in-arms were far from being that simple, but they were far more comprehensible. In fact they were almost his own colleagues, very nearly his intellectual brothers. They too were far from stupid or untalented and by no means indifferent, but actually ambitious, damn it. They too refused to be satisfied with pseudo-life, the idiotic cultivation of pecuniary fat cells. Their synthetic Nietzschean-Bakuninesque ideology was eclectic in the extreme and didn't give a toss for any kind of logic or ethics: it was governed exclusively by aesthetic and emotional feeling, creatively contrived and efficiently structured. Of course it was – it had been invented by clever boys from good families, swots from the top of the class, the select minority. Vadim himself had even pinned one of the little posters produced by the radicals to the door of the editorial office as a provocative joke: a special services Ninja in a black mask, pistol muzzle pointed directly at the viewer, scarlet lettering at the top: DEMOCRACY IS A DISEASE! And below it the confident assertion: HERE'S THE DOCTOR. But as this ideology's advertising slogans grew more garish and its designer posters and fascinating web-site packaging became slicker, its lack of seriousness and authenticity became all the more obvious and its inner, stinking subliminal nature all the more clear.

These boys were far from being bombers, fanatics and zealots, tin heroes with neither fear nor reproach. The sharply worded slogans, the uncompromising demands, the declarative contempt for intellectual weakness, the combatant, bronze-torch-lit Aryanism, the great-power pride and chauvinism were a means for sublimating their own puniness and spinelessness, their fatal tendency to that self-same accursed intellectual weakness of reflection, their own inferiority complex as a national minority in a minor nation. Their banal fear in the face of the big, bad predatory world with its big teeth. Their phobias and complexes. Reduced to a ferocious frenzy by their fear of petty hooliganism, these boys had demonstratively and publicly declared themselves petty hooligans. And that was precisely why they had been hated by the columnist Apletaev with a particularly caustic hatred – the hatred that is reserved not for enemies, but for traitors.

'Guys . . .' Vadim lowered his gaze to his hands. No matter how much he shook them, the spots of rust were still there from that blasted crowbar. 'You're on the left, right? You ought to . . . mmm . . . despise money. It ought to make you sick just to hold it in your hands. Humiliating filth, know what I mean.'

'Nobody asked you,' the narrow-shouldered one snapped back, picking up the Eriksson in a slim-fingered hand with a fine sprinkling of freckles. 'Hand over the loot, or I make that call.'

A loudspeaker perched between two back-lit ventilation grilles disturbed the air under the ceiling with a circular Marilyn Manson lyric – something about revolution. An old woman completely used up by life hobbled across to the bar's line of fortifications and deftly laid out a series of yellow, crumpled pieces of paper in front of the barman in a mysterious game of patience. Without looking at them, the barman tipped some coins into the old woman's cupped hand. Behind his shoulder the idiot was still going hard at it:

'. . . and you've got to say to yourself: I can do that, I will do that, I'm not just some useless jerk, you know? And then you absolutely have to get it done, and chuck everything else, you understand, everything, absolutely everything, you're not bothered about anything else, apart from the goal, you understand, then everyone will say: yes, he's a real man . . .'

'Guys,' said Vadim, frankly playing the fool. 'Why are you being like this? I'm basically one of your own. I topped a bourgeois and few mobsters. I hate them as much as you do.'

'All of you,' the kid–leather one rapped, almost as if he were speaking at a meeting now, 'are the same kind of shit. Every one. That banker of yours, and your mobsters, and you too. And if one scumbag offs another, it just means there'll be less work left for us to do later.'

'. . . money, you know, it's nothing money. You've got to understand that. It's the most important thing you've got to understand. That's all. It's just money . . .'

'Let me tell you a little true story.' Vadim picked up a bottle of Tabasco sauce from the table and twirled it in his hands. 'One night kendo master Miyamoto Musasi was walking through the forest near the town of Edo. Suddenly the legendary virtuoso of the sword . . .' Vadim dripped some sauce on to the back of his hand and licked it off – tears immediately sprang to the corners of his eyes, it was so unbelievably hot – '. . . felt that the harmony of the world behind his back had been irreparably disrupted. He pulled out his trusty family sword . . .' – Vadim wiped away the tears that

264

had formed and cautiously set the Tabasco back in its place – '. . . and struck out backwards twice. When he turned round, there lying on the ground were two bandits with knives in their hands, both sliced in half by the "hawk's wing" stroke.'

'What are you going on about?' the slashing and nailing goblin asked.

'What I'm on about,' said Vadim, leaning forward, propping his shoulders against the edge of the table and looking up at the gentlemen radicals from below, 'is that it makes no difference if the particular tosser concerned is a banker or some bandit. The main point is that he's a tosser. But tossers come in different shapes and sizes. Not necessarily rich. Take your kind of tosser, for instance . . .'

'. . . *but we'll never, ever earn a lot of money!*'

The kid-leather Che had been watching Vadim closely. Now he finally noticed Vadim's fiddling under the table – and automatically bent down to look.

Vadim's pump-action shot-gun fired with awesome power. The soft, round, massively heavy twelve-calibre bullet, 18.2 millimetres long, slammed straight into the bastard's forehead with awesome power. The bastard's head burst like a rotten water-melon. Crimson blood and yellowish lumps of grey matter from the dim-witted brains sprayed out in a fan, splattering half of the tavern. With awesome power the body overturned the table, somersaulted over its own head and slammed its legs against the floor. Vadim leapt to his feet. The second bastard leapt up and began feverishly tugging something out of his pocket. Vadim looked straight into the bastard's vicious, little, slow-witted eyes and jerked the breech of his pump-action shot-gun, shooting him neatly in the forehead. The bastard gave a fearsomely loud inhuman howl and his entire body smacked against the wall with awesome power. The bastard collapsed at Vadim's feet.

11.04.01 . . . 11.04.00 . . .

The lamp above the table – a cone of sheet metal on a long, striped flex that looked like it had come from an antediluvian iron – swayed like something out of a complicated art-movie, a single moving element inserted into a still frame, emphasising in shifting light and shade the general absolute lack of movement (even the swirling blue-grey shroud of tobacco smoke above the next table seemed to be frozen). Maybe the background would have been in black and white, making the swaying to and fro of the yellowish spot of light across the table-top even more effective. It would have been a good way to end the film.

11.03.57 . . .

The film wasn't over yet. Vadim bent down to the bag and hooked it up with his left hand. Then he set the shot-gun on his shoulder and walked to the exit. On the little metallic bridge (looking pretty much like the ramp for a cargo plane) over the crevasse dug through the floor to reveal the infernally illuminated innards of the basement, he remembered something. Went back. The guys at the next table still hadn't got around to moving, although the swirling tobacco clouds had drifted a little closer to the ceiling.

The one who'd been doing the lecturing – he looked like a street-wise Winnie-the-Pooh – was still holding his half-emptied beer mug suspended in the air. The skin that had gathered into folds above the motionless eyes was stirring in a vague, autonomous motion. His listener was sitting with his back to Vadim, the naked back of his head pulled down into his shoulders. Vadim released his grip on the handles of the bundle, adjusted his grasp on the shot-gun and pulled back the breech (the ejected shell-case emitted an audio signal from an adjacent reality).

'By the way,' – the long snout of the shot-gun took aim at the twitching skin of its own accord – '. . . money is just a load of garbage.'

I could have done without the politics, Vadim thought in annoyance as he wallowed in haste through the unsightly, slum-town mishmash of that less decorative part of the Old City (daubed in paint on an eyeless, peeling façade: 'Delighted to see the Reichstag in ruins!') which was being driven back in planned stages by euro-standard upgrades to the underbelly of the city: the railway station, the bus station, the Central Market. Things had seemed to be proceeding correctly and logically but, as always happens in politics, due to certain subtle nuances of context, certain external circumstances beyond one's control, they had acquired an undesirable taint, an ambiguous smell. Things were not so good. Not so very elegant . . . But if that was the way things had turned out – he came out at the fork in the tramlines in front of the market with all its kiosks, benches, parking-spaces, telephone booths – then things ought somehow to be . . . balanced out.

10.54.08

'Prime Minister's chancellery,' responded the well trained duty-voice on the state phone line.

'Hello. I wish to pass on some extremely important information to Mister Sandis Stelle. It's a highly confidential matter.' Vadim couldn't help laughing, but he managed to put his hand over the mouthpiece in time. 'It concerns yesterday's mass murder in the Banzai club. I know what happened, who set up the massacre. I was an eye witness. I am willing to give you . . . Are you listening to me?'

'I am listening very carefully.'

'I am willing to give you the details and talk about the

causes. I know the system used for laundering Russian criminal money through a major Latvian commercial bank. I am willing to provide material evidence. I have in my possession a very large sum, a huge sum in dollars, that was due to be laundered. But I need certain guarantees.'

'I am listening,' the voice repeated.

'I wish to speak to Mister Stelle in person, today and in a secluded place. I need your answer within the next half hour. Goodbye.'

.10.12.02

Vadim bit off a fragment from the toasted border of his multi-deck hot sandwich, chewed it and washed it down with Guarana soda. The motorcycle he was eyeing was tribal, more like an expressionist rendition of a pedigree corrida bull by Picasso than anything else: big, rotund and wide-chested, red and white, with the horns of the handlebars curving out from behind the pear-shaped front face of the streamlined cowling. A highroad and ringroad Kawasaki. It would do. He'd driven a moped in his childhood days, hadn't he, a shagged-out blue Delta?

He crumpled up the greasy napkin and tossed it away, drank up his energiser. Walking up to the bike, he took a good close look at the cyclopean eye of its speedometer, sunk deep into the instrument panel. Oho. 300 km/h.

'Do you like the bike?' Ah, there was the owner: ginger hair, two metres tall, big wide smile, red overalls, white helmet under his arm. English speaking.

'Give me the keys,' said Vadim.

'Sorry?' The smile widened even further. So we don't understand Russian, you tightwad foreigner?

'Ze kee,' Vadim said in English, rubbing his thumb against his forefinger in an international gesture. 'Ze keeses, anderstend?'

'What key?' Vadim wondered if there were any physical limits to the breadth of a smile.

'Ze baik's kee.' Vadim showed the foreign tightwad the first gun handle that he could locate. Repeated his demand syllable by syllable: 'Ai. Nid. Ze. Kee.'

. . . 06.03.45 . . . 06.03.44 . . .

The Mezhapark. A mansion not far from Kishezers. A high stone wall. Sheer metal gates. A discreet copper plaque. SIA Intergarantija. Beside it a closed embrasure.

In the distance, a sports motorbike approaching along the narrow asphalted lane. The rider is not visible: in the twilight only the dipped beam of the headlight and the reflecting cowling can be seen. The roaring gets louder. The motorbike drives up and turns sharply, braking to a halt on the little private square. Now the driver's figure is visible from the back in silhouette, outlined by the lamp above the gates – without a helmet, with a shapeless bag across his shoulder.

Fade in. The embrasure opens.

06.02.59 . . .

The brightly lit, semi-circular porch of the mansion. The rider, a man of about thirty in a scruffy leather jacket, accompanied by a broad-shouldered young guy in a dark weatherproof jacket, climbing up the steps with the bag. The young guy – obviously a security guard – presses the button of the intercom.

SECURITY GUARD 1: Caspar, our visitor is here.

VOICE FROM INTERCOM: I'm letting him in.

A click. The door swings inwards a centimetre.

06.02.48 . . .

The hallway on the second floor of the mansion. The ambience of a hunting lodge, or rather, a lodge for fishing and sailing. A cold fireplace in the corner. On a shelf – a sextant. Higher up – the discreet eye of a video-camera. On the next wall – a glass-fronted frame, the kind in which they usually put collections of exotic butterflies, but this one holds various kinds of sailors' knots. Opposite that – a stuffed swordfish. Globes, astrolabes, a model sailing-ship, another marine animal – a sea-urchin, looking like a very large chestnut. Another two broad-shouldered security guards in double-breasted jackets.

SECURITY GUARD 2: Labkavar. Mister Stelle is expecting you.

His partner raises the probe of a portable metal detector.

SECURITY GUARD 3: I'm sorry, but we'll have to check you out.

The visitor nods.

SECURITY GUARD 2 (gesturing): Put your bag over here, please.

The visitor places the bundle on the little table without any objections. The security guard with the metal detector runs the device over the bag. The metal detector jangles repulsively.

SECURITY GUARD 3 (with caution verging on hostility): What have you got in there?

VADIM (smiling and approaching the bag): You know, nothing special, I brought it to show you, take a look for yourself . . .

He tugs the zip open. And takes out the automatic pistol.

06.02.39 . . .

The porch. The security guard in the weatherproof jacket is smoking. The sound of hasty, stuttering bursts of gunfire from inside the house. The security guard tosses away his cigarette, flings the door open and disappears into the house. For five seconds there is silence, nothing but the door closing with a slow creaking of hinges. Then there is another brief burst of gunfire.

06.01.31 . . .

The study of the mansion's owner. Sitting at an antique-looking desk with two columns of drawers, afraid to move a muscle, is a thickset, middle-aged gentleman of somewhat uncouth appearance, dressed in extremely expensive clothes. The visitor in the leather jacket is striding to and fro in front of the desk, brandishing the automatic pistol. Suddenly he breaks off and bends down. He takes a massive two-handed saw out of his bag. The saw's plastic handles are a poisonous orange colour. At the sight of the saw, the thickset gentleman twitches in his armchair, but manages to control himself. The visitor unceremoniously sweeps the papers, the telephone, the inkstand, the clock, the ornamental trinkets and the carafe off the desktop. Throws down the saw in front of the gentleman.

VADIM: Saw.

MR STELLE: What?

VADIM: Saw.

MR STELLE: How?

VADIM: Any way you like. (Assumes a picturesque pose, with the hand holding the automatic pistol extended.) 'If you happen to have earned a hundred lats, don't drink them away, but buy something useful, a saw for instance!' (Lowers his arm.) I've earned a hundred lats. And I've bought you something, a saw for instance. Saw.

MR STELLE: What . . . What should I saw?

VADIM (looking round the study): Er . . . Saw this desk of yours. (Seeing the gentleman is hesitating, he encourages him by slamming a foot against the column of the desk.) Well! Well! Don't you understand me?

The gentleman licks his lips and grasps the orange handle clumsily. The visitor nods benevolently. The gentleman positions himself to attack the edge furthest away from him and tries to saw. The teeth of the saw immediately get stuck in the tough timber, the gentleman tugs at the saw, rocks it, trying to loosen it – the wide blade jangles indignantly.

VADIM (menacingly): Too hard for you?

Without answering, the gentleman puffs and tugs, shudders, flushes and sweats.

VADIM (raising the barrel of the pistol): I asked you a question. Too hard for you is it?

MR STELLE (exhausted): Yes . . . too hard.

VADIM (spreading his arms in genuine amazement): Then what the fuck were you spouting on about?

05.59.35 . . .

The gentleman is sitting, tied to the back of the armchair with the flex of the telephone. His eyes are totally blank. It is clear that his grasp of what is happening is already weak. The visitor has arranged himself in a free and easy pose on the desk in front of the gentleman, dangling the dirty toe of one shoe. The double-handed joiner's tool is sticking up beside him from behind the desktop.

VADIM (continuing to oratorise from the desk): . . . If you're a failure, a loser, if you are, to put it bluntly (he inclines his body towards the tied-up gentleman in a mock bow) a waste of space – then you've only yourself to blame! Your prosperity is your own problem and nobody else's (he jumps down from off the desk), and you have to deal with it! I'm not going to do it for you! (In visual corroboration of his words, he shakes his head.) Do you feel like shit? Uncomfortable? Afraid? Then it's your own fault! And what sort of man does that make you?

The gentleman gives a low, heart-rending moan. The needles of the sea-urchin are protruding from his mouth.

VADIM (listening closely, looking closely, even inclining his head – and finally straightening up again with a boundlessly Jesuitical expression): That doesn't bother me!

Once again the visitor takes hold of the sagging, seemingly empty bag. Slips his hand in up to the elbow. Feels around for something. Pulls out his trophy. Inspects it. It is a ribbed, dark-green pineapple. The visitor seems to have forgotten about the gentleman. The ananas (Russian), pineapple (Anglo-American), shao-liu-dan (Chinese) has completely absorbed his attention. Eventually he slips his finger into the ring of the pin and moves right up close to the gentleman, with the grenade dangling on his index finger.

VADIM (speaking into Mr Stelle's ear in an intimate, confidential whisper – with the grenade dangling right in front of the gentleman's eyes): Nobody . . . do you hear . . . no-bo-dy . . . is going to help you . . .

So saying, the visitor pulls away the trouser belt under the gentleman's flabby little belly with one hand, raises the grenade to his own mouth with the other, tugs out the pin with his teeth – and drops the pineapple into the gentleman's trousers.

05.59.25 . . .

The hallway on the second floor. Viewed from above, from the ceiling. Jutting into the field of vision from the left are the motionless legs of one security guard and from the right, the sideways-twisted head of the other. Suddenly the top of the door of the study swings into the field of vision as it opens. The visitor emerges from it very quickly, crosses the hallway, disappears from sight. The study door slams shut. Then it almost immediately flies back out, accompanied by a single loud boom, and remains hanging there by its lower hinge. Chips of wood and various indeterminate bits and pieces are swept out into the hallway. And then, launched practically from the precise point of observation, the pressurised jets of the sprinkler system spurt out in a dense

garland, criss-crossing the entire frame. A siren starts to howl.
. . . 04.13.06 . . . 04.13.05 . . . 65 km/h . . . 70 km/h . . .

Hey hey hey . . . Here I go now . . . Here I go into new days . . .

Down Export Road, along the concrete wall of the port, across the cobblestones, reading them like a Braille alphabet, overtaking the trams with their glowing insides, past the one-time Orthodox seminary transformed into the Anatomicum, past the who-gives-a-shit corpses and the scrupulous scalpels, past the little freaks who choked on formaldehyde, across the bridge, over the metropolitan canal, along the concrete wall, past the speed boats and yachts stored in a watery appendix to the port, past the yellow-and-green Viada filling station, past the red Viking Line ferry with its tight perforation of portholes, past the tall building of the defunct Soviet export/import agency Agroprom, along the wall covered in aniline graffiti, past IT COULD HAVE BEEN WORSE – THEY COULD HAVE CUT YOUR PRICK OFF AND THROWN IT OUT OF THE CAR (they hadn't fitted the 'R' in completely), a forest of reinforcement rods, under the Vantov Bridge . . . I'm pain, I'm hope, I'm suffering . . . Yeah hey hey hey yeah yeah . . . here I go into new days . . . past Riga castle, aka the Presidential Palace, past the medieval masonry and the modern-day politics, past the state banner and the pre-election issues, past the tax rates and party-building, along the embankment, past the Anglican church built out of ballast brick, along the opposite bank, past the dead water, past the streaks of rust on the funnels, along the embankment, past the floating restaurant Mississippi at its winter mooring, past . . . Hey hey hey . . . Ain't no mercy . . . Ain't no mercy there for me . . . I'm pain, I'm hope, I'm suffering . . . the Technical University, under the Kamenny Bridge, towards the traffic light, red, prop his foot against the asphalt, exhaust fumes reddened by brake lights, the little silvery pump of the diskman found in the saddlebag of the Kawasaki pounding into his ears the heavy-rock contents of the disk inserted by the owner, yellow, green, go . . . Do you bury me when I'm gone . . . Do you teach me while I'm here . . . to the left, across the tramlines, back past the residence of the Order of Malta, to the right, past the cast-iron-black Red riflemen, past the lumpy pencil-case of the Museum of the Occupation, on to Grenetsieka Street, under the orange boom, ignoring the indifferent traffic cops – and into the national sanctuary of the historical centre . . .

04.10.38 . . . 04.10.37 . . . 30 km/h . . . 25 km/h . . .

Under the transparent wall of the two-storey restaurant Amsterdam an exaggerated Lincoln Navigator jeep with preterhuman engine tuning was idly rustling its engine – one of those roadsters which, in their country of origin, are driven about by young girl students from rich families to demonstrate their superior swank, but which are driven, east of the former Berlin wall, by sturdy, strapping mobsters of varying degrees of legality, due to their nouveau-riche ignorance. Cigarette smoke seeped out like frosty breath through the narrow opening above the driver's window.

Just as soon as I belong . . . Then it's time I disappear . . . HA!

Without stopping, Vadim braked, bit out the pin of the final grenade with a practised movement – and rolled it off his palm in through the gap. Go.

Hey hey hey . . . And I went . . . And I went on down that road . . . 04.10.34 . . . 04.10.33 . . . 25 km/h . . . 35 km/h . . . 40 km/h . . .

Past the large-format display windows of the Centrs department store (paper tickets with percentage-proof reductions in the empty crotches of naked dummies), on to promenading Valnya Street, through the flavoursome evening crowd, past the Riga hotel, left again, on to Kalkya Street, between Unibanka (granite façade) and Hansabanka (marble façade), with the plastic MacDonald's behind him . . .

I'm pain, I'm hope, I'm suffering . . . Hey hey hey . . . Yeah . . . And I went on down that road . . .

Immediately after the smart Pepsi-Forum, Vadim brought his Kawasaki to a halt. On his left he now had a view into a glimmering, deep, bluish aquarium: behind the thick glass of the fashionable Nostalgia café, in that transparent, otherworldly medium, wealthy young people – likely young lads and lasses – were dragging out their ichthyological existences: cold-blooded, empty-eyed, incomprehensible.

Do you bury me when I'm gone . . .

Vadim stood in the middle of the street, encircled by its neurotic merriment, and watched. Thick glass. Insuperable, the barrier that he had never overcome. A different world. An alien world. Thick glass.

Do you teach me while I'm here . . .

The ichthyological girl sitting at the nearest table raised her head. Indifferently observed the strange dude on the motorbike unhurriedly extracting an automatic pistol from his saddle-bag and a magazine from his jacket pocket. Inserting the latter into the handle of the former.

Just as soon as I belong . . .

Following the girl's gaze, her ichthyological boy also looked at Vadim.

Then it's time I disappear . . .

The glass collapsed, came away in a single sheet of irregular pieces that instantly lost their transparency. The long burst of fire swung the weapon about; the barrel wagged this way and that – then the magazine was empty. The automatic pistol went flying on to the road. Go!

04.09.45 . . . 04.09.44 . . . 20 km/h . . . 35 km/h . . . 60 km/h . . .

Do you bury me when I'm gone . . .

04.02.36 . . . 04.02.23 . . . 98 km/h . . . 100 km/h . . .

Do you teach me while I'm here . . .

03.59.13 . . . 03.59.07 . . . 70 km/h . . . 55 km/h . . .

Just as soon as I belong . . .

03.59.05 . . . 03.59.03 . . . 32 km/h . . . 0 km/h

He abandoned the Kawasaki in the far corner of the rubbish tip at the back of the service garage under the Kantsiemsky flyover. Crossed the railway line on foot at Zasulauks station, wandered aimlessly for a while between the cheap private sector houses lurking in the bare little gardens.

Then it's time . . .

He found the stop and began waiting for the number 22 bus to the airport.

I disappear . . .

DIS-A-PPEAR HUH!!!

16

Eight and a half hours earlier . . .

The worst, the most shameful thing about it was that nasty little vibration in his semi-disembodied legs – there was just no way Vadim could control it. He even felt as though he was perfectly calm (well, relatively speaking, of course, but his head was amazingly clear, I'm tougher than I thought) but he just couldn't do anything about his damn leg muscles. He really wanted to sit down – but it wasn't happening, he was locked solid. HE had tied Vadim's hands behind his back using Vadim's belt. Made Vadim take it off and then twisted it tight so deftly and cruelly that Vadim had instantly lost all movement and sensation in his hands. And now Vadim was standing with his spine and the back of his head pressed against the wooden post in idiotic, self-parodying St. Sebastian stance, breathing the smell of the metabolic waste left by local tramps, feeling his left temple swelling up and trying to get at least some kind of handle on the situation. So far unsuccessfully.

There was pain, there was humiliation, fear – of course there was – but the bottom line was still that rubbery, elastic incomprehension. Because, by default, none of what was happening could be happening.

'. . . Boden . . .' After shaking its contents out on to the floorboards, HE twirled the briefcase in his hands. 'Boden-what?'

'Bodenschatz.'

Conically converging, rough, dirty walls – that was the

roof. A little window and below it a little snowdrift. In addition to the urine and shit – less sharp, but more basic – the stifling, mouldy-timber smell of floors rotting for centuries. The attic of a warehouse. From the umpteenth century. A tramps' den condemned to reincarnation as a penthouse.

'Fucking incredible,' HE said, flicking his nail against the clasp of the briefcase. 'So how much does a thing like that cost?'

'Ninety-eight.'

'Lats?'

'Yes.'

'A ton, then. A hundred lats. So you spent a hundred lats on bodenschatz. On a bloody briefcase.'

Vadim said nothing.

'You, bodenschatz!' HE tossed the briefcase into the far corner of the attic; a broken roofing-slate clattered. 'Is that the way it was, I asked you?'

'What do you want?' Vadim tried to talk in short but complete phrases, in a neutral tone of voice.

'Me? What do I want . . .' HE shuffled the scattered papers with his foot, kicked the diary. Sighed. 'I want to understand. I've been trying for a long time, but I still haven't got anywhere. Maybe you can explain to me. What does a man have in mind . . . A young man . . .' HE prodded the mobile phone with the toe of his shoe. 'How old are you?'

'Twenty-six.'

'A young man of twenty-six.' HE dragged the mobile across the floor with his foot. 'Who's out on the morning of the thirty-first of December . . . on a holiday . . . Walking fast. Looking real determined. In this coat here. In this suit. With this bastard briefcase in his hands. Bodenschatz. So where were you going?'

279

'I was going to work.'

'Ah, fuck off!' For a moment HE stopped demonstrating the basic control skills of football with the mobile phone. 'On the thirty-first!'

'I have urgent work to do.'

'Urgent work. And what is it you do?'

'I'm a shipping broker.'

'Oh!' HE actually seemed pleased at that. 'And what does that look like?'

'What does what look like?'

'Well, what does your work consist of?'

'I freight ships.' Vadim shifted his weight slightly, attempting to reduce the pain in his forearms: the wooden edges of the square post were biting in unbearably now.

'Na-na! You explain concretely,' HE said, bristling up, suddenly aroused – but not aggressively, more excited – making small gestures with his hands. 'What do you do? What exactly does your activity consist of? Well, what does it look like, your WORK? Words, words – manager, broker, freighter, frigger. Sure, it all sounds real beautiful but WHAT DOES IT ACTUALLY MEAN? In practice?'

'I find the owner of a cargo. Who needs to get it to a certain place or places by a certain time. I find a carrier. A ship-owner, if it's a sea delivery. Maybe a haulage company, if it has to go by truck. I help them make a deal . . .'

'Wait. What does that mean – I find? I go running round town asking everyone I come across "Do you happen to need a cargo delivered?"'

'I phone them.'

'You phone them . . . And so?'

'Well, in principle – that's it. I phone. I find out. I persuade. I make terms. I fax a draft contract . . .'

'So that means you just sit there on the phone all day

long, if I understand you right? You sit there all day in the office with the phone in your ear — and you just keep phoning . . . From morning till night, right?'

'Yes.'

'And that goes on one day, two days, a week, a month . . . How long have you been doing this?'

'More than two years.'

'So tell me — do you enjoy it? This kind of work?'

'Yes.' Vadim felt a twinge of wholesome rage. 'I enjoy it.'

'So what is it you enjoy? Poking at buttons all day long?'

'Listen,' Vadim said, blithely discarding every fundamental of psychological diplomacy in one fell swoop. 'Just what is it you want, eh?'

'I want to have a talk. Don't get so nervous. What're you frightened of?' The excited interrogator reached inside his belt. 'Is this what's making you nervous?' He pulled out a pistol. 'Okay. Why don't I just put it away.' He tossed the shooter into his huge bag. 'Right. That's gone now, it doesn't exist. I just want to have a normal sort of conversation. Clear things up. So what is it you enjoy about your job?'

'I enjoy,' said Vadim, suddenly sensing quite clearly that he was seizing the initiative, 'fulfilling my responsibilities well.'

'And do you fulfil them well?'

'Yes, I do. Better than anyone else in the firm.'

'And you're proud of that?'

'I have a right to be. I'm a professional.' The dishevelled psycho listened intently. He looked less like a psycho. 'I know how to do my job. I can be relied on. I never let my boss or my clients down. Is that a bad thing?'

'No. I reckon that's probably a good thing . . .' The

psycho rubbed his stubble, looking genuinely perplexed. 'But don't you ever get the idea that it's all just bullshit anyway? Getting paid for knowing how to talk on the phone?'

'I don't get paid for knowing how to talk on the phone. I'm an intermediary. A link. Absolutely essential. Without me this business is impossible.'

'Business?'

'Do you eat bananas?'

'Sometimes . . .'

'Well, they were brought on a ship that I freighted. You understand? When it comes down to it I don't rip anyone off, either directly or indirectly. I'm not a swindler. Or a parasite. I have an honest job and I do it honestly. What else are you interested in?'

Now it was Vadim who was pressuring his captor.

'Hmm . . .' HE started pushing the phone around with his shoe again. Drove it into a heap of trash and something gave out an iron clang. 'Goal . . . What interests me, for instance, is this: Do you always go to work in a suit? And wearing a tie?'

'Why?'

'Do they make you wear it, or is it your own choice?' Now his interlocutor had began rolling that clanging object round the floor. Vadim couldn't see what it was.

'Yes, it's a requirement where I work.'

'And a demand like that doesn't get up your nose?'

'No. It doesn't get up your nose, does it, that hospital orderlies walk around in white coats? Or building workers wear overalls? It's just the clothes for the job.'

'The clothes for the job . . . So did the firm pay to have this made for you?'

'No.'

'That means,' – with a visible effort and a clanging, grating sound, HE traced out a semi-circle on the floorboards with his foot – 'you laid out for it yourself?'

'Yes.'

'And how much did your suit cost?'

'Why,' – Vadim's spite was suddenly aroused – 'do you want one like it?'

'What I want,' – the other man turned completely away from Vadim, engrossed in his metallic trundling – 'is for you to tell me what you spend your money on.'

'Shall I give you a full answer?'

'No, no need. I want to know what's most important to you. You know, your goal. What you earn your money talking on the telephone for. Do you spend it on drink? Do you buy clothes? Or are you saving up for an expensive car? Have you got a car?'

'No.'

'But you're planning to buy one.'

'I suppose so.'

'And what kind are you planning to get?'

'I don't know yet. It depends on the situation.'

'Well, a second-hand one or a new one at least?'

'Second-hand. Probably. Untie my hands, eh? I can't talk to you like this. It hurts like hell.'

HE swung round.

'You won't do a runner?'

'How can I, when you've got a piece in your bag . . .'

'You definitely won't do a runner?'

'No I won't.'

'Okay then.' The psycho who might not be a psycho went up to Vadim, walked behind him, tugged a bit and laughed: 'No fucking way of untying you here.'

'I've got a knife.'

'Oho,' HE said, delighted. 'A knife? An actual blade?'

'A penknife.'

'Where?'

'In my trousers, in the pocket. No, the right one.'

HE tugged at the little chain connecting the loop on Vadim's trousers with the pocket knife. Jerked it, tore it off. Stepped back behind the pillar. 'A knife like this is only good for picking your teeth.'

Vadim felt that his hands were free. The first thing he did was sit down, dumping his backside straight on to the polluted floor. He slumped back against the post and began rubbing his dead wrists.

His liberator creaked the floorboards nearby. Vadim glanced at him sideways. HE was thoughtfully extracting from the red plastic body all the little blades, tweezers, files, corkscrews, awls, and bottle-openers that fitted into it in that mysterious fashion.

'So what kind of second-hand motor do you want?'

'I don't know. Maybe a BMW.'

'The bandit's battle wagon? Fancy something flash?'

'What's flash about it?' Vadim's wrists had begun to throb painfully. 'Spare parts for second-hand beamers are cheap and there's no problem getting hold of them. And they don't break down very often.'

'Okay then. But a motor's not the most important thing for you. What is the most important thing?'

As his wrists thawed out, Vadim tried not to screw his face up from the agonising pain that was especially bad under his nails.

'Perhaps that's none of your business?'

'I decide what's my business.' HE looked admiringly at the unravelled Swiss army knife that now looked like a small boiled crustacean and flung it down hard on to the floor beside Vadim. It ricocheted off to one side, one of its limbs clattering off in the opposite direction. 'Let's not make me get the shooter out, okay?'

'Okay, okay,' said Vadim, tensing up – his hands were pulsating regularly now, getting back into a normal circulatory rhythm. He figured things out: the bag with the gun – about five metres, but the psycho was walking backwards and forwards between it and Vadim. NO, not now. 'I . . .' – he paused – 'I'm going to get married.'

'Yeah?' HE stopped. HE must have been looking at Vadim now, but Vadim sat there with his gaze fixed on the floor. 'Seriously?'

'Believe it or not.' Vadim clenched his fists and opened them again several times.

'And who to?'

'To my girl.'

'Right then, come on.' The psycho squatted down in front of Vadim, but Vadim still didn't look at him. 'Tell me about your girl.'

Vadim raised his eyes quickly – and met HIS eyes.

'Fuck off, will you?'

The psycho smiled a razor-sharp smile that contrasted with his soft, regretful voice:

'Nah, bodenschatz. You still don't get it.' He flung out his right hand in a precise movement. Picked something up off the floor. Stood up, adjusting his grip. It was the lump of metal he'd been kicking with his foot – a massive one-and-a-half-metre-long crowbar with an even coating of rust. He aimed the splayed, flattened, sharp end at Vadim.

Vadim would probably have been up for a fight, he was even ready to take on the pistol, but no way was he ready for the sheer filthy, crude, lumpish materiality of this massive brute of a weapon.

'Let's get on with our talk,' the psycho said with a blissful smile. 'What's this girl of yours like?'

'What interests you about her?' Maintaining contact with the post, Vadim straightened up in several stages.

'Well, what's her name, for a start.'

'Lena.'

I'll kill you, thought Vadim. I'll kill you, you son of a bitch.

'How old is she?'

'Twenty-two?'

'Is she working, studying?'

'Yes.'

'Yes what? Hey! Hello!'

'Why are you doing this?'

'I told you: I want to understand. How you homunculi live, you bastard, what for.' The fuckhead swung the rhomboid head of the crowbar. 'What you think, what you feel . . . Do you love her? Hello!'

'Yes.'

'Been seeing each other for long?'

'A year and a half.'

'How did you get to know each other?'

'The usual way.' Vadim gritted his teeth. 'Nothing out of the ordinary. She's . . . a friend of my sister. Studying in the same year.'

'Where's she studying? What's she going to be?'

'A psychologist.'

'What year's she in?'

'Fourth.'

'Does she earn a bit on the side?'

'Yes.'

'Where?'

'In a rehabilitation centre.'

'Treating junkies?'

'Something of the sort.'

'What does she look like?'

'Listen . . .'

'Yeah?'

'Why . . .'

'You. Boden-fuckoden.' The crowbar smashed into the boards a couple of centimetres away from Vadim's foot. 'Didn't you get the question?'

'I got it.'

I'll kill you.

'Well?'

'What?'

'Is she beautiful, your . . . Lena?'

'Yes.'

'Well, a bit more specific. Height?'

'Short.'

'Hair?'

'Chestnut . . . Light-chestnut.'

'Her eyes? Her eyes?'

'Grey.'

'There, you see. Probably really is beautiful. What does she call you?'

'Vadik.'

'Have you proposed yet, Vadik?'

'No.'

'But you're going to?'

'Yes.'

'Soon?'

'Yes.'

'Where?'

'At my place?'

'Wouldn't be planning to propose while you're on the job, would you?'

'Go fuck yourself.'

'Don't get so nervous.' HE set the crowbar across his shoulder. 'Right, so you'll propose to her. She'll accept. She will accept, won't she? Otherwise . . . So you'll get married. So you'll have a kid. Won't you? You will. And not just one. Okay. Then what?'

'That's it.'

'That's it?'

'What else do you want?'

'Me. This conversation's not about what *I* want . . .'

'What. Do. You. Want. From. Me?'

'I told you that. To understand.'

'So what is there you still don't understand?'

'I reckon I understand pretty much everything.'

'What is it about me that you dislike so much?'

'What makes you think I dislike you?' Supporting the crowbar with his left hand, the psycho mechanically rubbed his right palm on his jeans without looking at Vadim. 'I like you just fine.' HE looked at his hand, took hold of the rusty iron bar with it again and starting wiping the other one. 'That's the worst thing about it, I do like you.'

'Listen, dude. What have I ever done to you? We've got no reason to fall out. Why don't I just walk out of here right now, okay? It's at least a minute and a half to the nearest phone. There's no way the fuzz will get here in less than five minutes. You'll get clear away no matter what. Okay?'

While HE wasn't looking . . . Smack him in the face with the right. Knock him down. He had to knock him down. And then – the bag.

HE didn't even bother to look at Vadim. Even as he grasped the crowbar in both hands, even as he took a short

288

swing. That was the way he struck too. Hard, without taking aim, he jabbed the flat, sharp end into Vadim's belly, into the soft flesh. Vadim was amazed that anything could hurt so much. But even more terrible than the pain in the torn muscles of his abdomen and stomach was the feeling of the unconditionally lethal irreversibility of what was happening – because to the very end Vadim had still not believed in its reality. He lost his legs, he fell flat on his face, blinded, feeling stuff pouring out of him unstoppably – out of the wound, out of his slack bladder. And then HE hit Vadim twice: on the neck and the back of the head.

17

She counted the cartridges again, went into the room and killed everyone who was in there. After that she only had one clip left. There weren't any other doors in the room; only a pair of wide armoured gates with a magnetic lock. She didn't have a key. She had to go back out into the corridor. She had to walk carefully here, taking care where she put her feet: the floorboards groaned, creaked, sagged, threatened to collapse. Filtering in through cracks and holes in the walls, the ribbons of sunlight swayed like waterweed or drying sheets – and their touch on her face was just as damp. She crept as far as the corner, stood there for a moment, raised the barrel with the swelling of its silencer, listened to the dust-fall of the unholy silence.

No-thing.

She slidy-slipped round the corner, leapt up, squeezing the trigger as she went – and immediately took a gooey stinking gobbet of lilac shit full in the face. And another, and another – pinning her back against the plaster on the wall. The shit oozed through the pores of her Kevlar bullet-proof vest with a sucking sound, instantly melting her clothes, eating through her skin and muscles, breaking into her chest cavity, encasing her heart in hardening wax.

She went into the room and killed everyone who was in there. After that she had only one clip left. There weren't any other doors in the room; only a pair of wide armoured gates with a magnetic lock. She didn't have a key. She had to go back out into the corridor. She had no other choice. Ignoring the give-away creaking, she made a dash for the corner, changing her machine-gun for a brain-shaver as she went, and projecting out ahead of her a deceptive clone – her fingers getting tangled in the keys as she entered the code on the panel of the modulator. She squatted down, clicking the tumblers; the first, second, third infrasound generators twirled round in the sawn-off end of the truncated casing. *She* – the other one – was just the same, no difference, only without any bullet-proof vest, without any 'mimicrodon' emulator-overalls, without any jet pack, without the membrane of a pellicular gas-filter clinging to her face like a fruit mask, without any autonomous orientation block, without a single one of the thirteen kinds of weapons; naked, slim-boned, narrow-hipped, the nucleus of every one of her cells, every short-trimmed nail exposed and vulnerable. She stepped out from behind the corner with implacable resignation and set off provocatively, acting a part, towards IT. A faultlessly proportioned female face with golden irises, half-closed, ultra-thin, trembling eyelids, the bow of the upper lip above the rounded fullness of the lower one – and now they part dreamily, deliberately, pucker up – and a gooey, stinking gobbet of lilac shit pins her back against the plaster on the wall . . .

Pushing off with both legs, shooting herself upwards on a long burst from the jet-pack, she – herself – flew over the head of the clone in its death agony, covered in creeping lilac grease, planted her feet against the plaster on the wall and leapt back like a somersaulting firecracker, spraying infra-sound. As she bounced back a gooey, stinking gobbet of lilac shit caught her in mid-air, pinned her back and started eating its way in – allowing her time to take a good look at the complex wriggling of ITs infinite number of multi-jointed limbs, its smooth, impenetrable metallic chitinous plates, the multicoloured wires exposed in the sliding channels that opened up between them, sparkling with damaged insulation, and the flaccid blood-vessels oozing viscous, poisonous pus which was working its way into the pores of her Kevlar bullet-proof vest with a sucking sound, instantly melting her clothes, eating through her skin and muscles, breaking into her chest cavity, encasing her heart in hardening wax.

She went into the room and killed everyone who was in there. After that she had only one clip left. There weren't any other doors in the room; only a pair of wide armoured gates with a magnetic lock. She didn't have a key. She had to go back out into the corridor. She had no other choice. Ignoring the give-away creaking, she made a dash for the corner, checking her handgun – everything except the brain-shaver had been used up, wasted, flattened – clicking the tumblers in advance.

'Ze brein-sheiver dazn't vork heya. Facking beast has no brein at oll. You need to tern back, yeah? Jast a leettle . . . bifo ze corner.

'Okei, rait heya. Zere is a seecret areya in ze vall, you press zee, how you coll it . . . ze breeck end get LSD-gan.'

Not exactly a mega-monster-zapper, of course, but not bad. Right, come on, come on. Come here, now we're really going to zap your insides, give you the screaming black willies, screw you, for good and for keeps . . . Hah! Got it.

'End nau you yooz ze . . .' Vadim paused, trying to find the right word in English. Failing to find it, he twisted his finger in the air and put in a substitute, accompanying the gesture with industrial growling for added clarity: 'Ze skrr-oo-draiver.'

'What?'

'Ze skroo . . . Namber fo. Yes. Yes . . . Kill ze fucking asshol . . . Be kerful, ze blad is . . . Oho, not bad. You got it. Press ze button.'

'Thanks. Seems like you're an advanced headcrusher.'

'Eh-eh . . . ve try our best.'

While she stood back and triumphantly surveyed the luminescent title of the next level, Vadim leaned his elbows on the top of the control panel with a sensation that was becoming familiar. It was like a double shot of class liquor – watching Sarah Taft playing at Sarah Taft. Or rather watching Smilla Pavovich. The rising Hollywood superstar of Ukrainian-Yugoslavian extraction. Right here in the empty Riga airport. With just two hours left until New Year.

Actually, there was no bloody way he would ever have ID'd her: she didn't have that tousled hair in radically spectral tones, or any of the obvious identifying features of the species *superstar vulgaris* that he would have subconsciously anticipated. There was just this chick with a perfectly standard teenager-type appearance standing at the simulator-stimulator – short-cropped hair, skinny jeans, shapeless bright-coloured sweater – tugging on the joystick, her entire body subliminally echoing the pirouettes of the virtual acrobat.

It wasn't even she who had caught Vadim's attention, it was what was parked at the table beside her. Vadim had once read a substantial screed about the bodyguard trade in one of the glossy magazines. The well-informed author, a competent specialist, had claimed that the fashion for pumped-up gigantopithecuses was ancient history: the top professionals now were cultured gentlemen of pleasant appearance, or – even better – elegant ladies, with the total overall business-image. Apparently the genuinely modern bodyguard mix was education, IQ, quick reactions, intuition, the ability to foresee, calculate probabilities and ward off any situation potentially dangerous for the client.

In that case the items parked at the next table were not

genuinely modern bodyguards, or even any kind of body-guards. They hadn't exactly been designed for calculating probabilities. The mere fact that it was possible for such objects actually to exist in nature at all, coupled with their location in immediate proximity to the client, excluded a priori the slightest possibility that anyone might entertain even the faintest shadow of a thought concerning the feasibility of either direct or indirect participation in the creation of a potentially dangerous situation. Sitting there, calmly maintaining their vital functions at the end table of the absolutely deserted little airport café with a view of the airfield, were two exponentially awesome, infinitely intimidating monsters of mind-blowingly humungous proportions. One of them was a blacker-than-black dude with a shaved head. The other was a traditional Europeanoid of a general blondish hue, but they were both over two metres tall and weighed more than a centner and a half. Standing on the table in front of them was 1 (in words in brackets: <u>one</u>) tiny green can of Sprite.

Apart from this demoralising pair, the only other person in the café had been the crop-headed shrimp at the games console. Vadim had thought he saw something familiar in the rapid-change fire-fight on the screen. He had moved closer to take a look, and the huge black dude had moved out conscientiously from behind the table and stood there with his chin hanging over Vadim's head. Vadim's body had even sounded the panic signal as its physiological imagination conjured up in concrete detail the fatal consequences if the bodyguard were to fall on him. 'When they extricated V. Apletaev from beneath the black man, he was as flat as his own jokes in better times.'

. . . 'Thanks for the tips,' said Smilla Pavovich affably in slightly accented, but perfectly correct Russian. 'By the way, I don't give autographs.'

'Any problem?' asked a rumbling from on high.

'It's okay, Tony.' Smilla hesitated, wondering whether she should storm the next level or retire from the game.

'All these computer games are really just a load of crap,' Vadim told her disdainfully. 'And Headcrusher's a load of crap too. And your film will be a total load of crap. You should never have signed that contract.'

The superstar swung round and now looked at Vadim with direct personal interest. She twitched the crested head of the joystick at the Quit icon.

What the guy coming towards them resembled most of all was a young university professor of the humanities. Pale and thin, with strands of black hair too sparse for his age lying very close to his long skull, wearing sloppy khaki trousers and a sweatshirt with a hood over a sweatshirt without a hood. Spectacles with narrow lenses. And hassled out of his head. He came speeding up, flung a smooth curve round the body-guards without reducing his speed or reacting in any way to Vadim and began dumping sloppy heaps of incomprehensible American English on the table that Vadim and Smilla were sitting at. The hassle-head's long finger lashed out neurotically at the small display of a Newton electronic notebook. Smilla replied in equally nervous and incomprehensible fashion. They snarled at each other for about a minute, at the end of which the hassle-head sped away, abandoning Newton on the field of battle. Smilla, now just as hassled as he was, immediately gulped down half her glass of orange juice in irritation.

'Cool!' said Smilla, smacking the glass down resound-ingly on to the tabletop. 'Seems like I'll be seeing in the New Year in this fuckin' snack bar . . . What's that garbage you're smoking?' She waved the smoke away from her face sullenly.

Vadim gallantly stubbed Captain Blake out in a saucer.

'Listen,' he said, taking a gulp of hot Irish coffee. 'How come you ended up here anyway?'

'Fuckin' promotion. Fuckin' tour. Fuckin' Europe,' she said, not looking at Vadim. 'Fuckin' Russia. Fuckin' Cohen.' The last phrase was uttered with especial emphatic abhorrence, and Vadim assumed it referred to the gentleman recently departed. 'Fuckin' party. How d'you say it in Russian? Twisted my arm, right?' Vadim nodded. 'I didn't want to. He twisted my arm. Publicity, important people. Fuckin' bizz.' She pulled the Newton over towards her and began prodding at the screen with her finger. 'Fuckin' Mikhalkov – who's he? The Oblomov Club. Fuckin' Russian New Year, fuckin' caviar. Fuck this fucking fatherland of the ancestors! Fuckin' weather,' she explained looking up from the little screen. There's a blizzard at Sheremetievo. That arsehole Cohen was afraid to land, the cocksucker. So we landed at the first port we could find. And look, here it is!' – she spread her arms, as if she were making a formal presentation of the depressing fuckin' snackbar to someone – 'New Year Russian-style.'

They said nothing for a moment.

'And anyway,' – after failing to get anything out of the Newton, Smilla shoved the notebook aside – 'Now the entire timetable falls apart.'

'Timetable?'

'Moscow on the first. London on the second,' Smilla listed off the dates with the efficient monotony of a personal organiser. 'Interview. The BBC. Los Angeles on the fourth. Negotiations with the producer. Contract bonuses. Sydney on the twelfth. Andre's playing there.'

'Andre?'

'My boyfriend,' – judging from her tone of voice, gentle

Smilla would have gladly drowned her boyfriend in the latrine – 'Tennis. Ranked number five. From the twenty-fifth onwards, shooting. And I've still got to learn kung-fu . . . Cohen hired some Chinese guy. Mister Liu? Mister Shu? He's a tenth dan,' she added, noticing Vadim chuckling.

'What the hell do you need it all for?' Vadim asked, tipping his cup and admiring the golden sand of the coffee grounds.

'All what?'

'All this pseudo-life.' (Smilla gave him a puzzled look.) 'Bullshit. Garbage. You're not short of dough, are you? So why do you knock yourself out with this shit? Traipsing all over the world. Acting in idiotic films. Stupid jerks hassling you all the time. Don't tell me you enjoy it!'

'It's my job.' The puzzlement in her eyes had acquired a different quality now: she couldn't figure out what was the right line of behaviour here.

'You've got a shitty deal,' Vadim said with a shrug.

'I've got a shitty deal?' The superstarlet was stung now: her dark eyebrows shot upwards (her eyes really were almost unreal). 'YOU have the nerve to tell ME that I've got a shitty deal!'

'Sure I do,' Vadim confirmed calmly. 'I have a great time. I do whatever I want. But it seems to me like you don't even know what you want. You waste your time on this total garbage that's no good for anything – apart from the money that's reproduced at your expense. I wouldn't change places with you.'

Smilla Pavovich couldn't think what to say to that.

'Okay, it's your business,' said Vadim, looking at his watch: it was time to go and meet Lada. 'No skin off my nose.' He stood up. 'Cheers. Happy New Year.'

★

Now it was all over. Farewell to arms. Vadim locked himself in with the latch. Carefully lifted the porcelain lid off the tank, carefully balanced it on the edge of the toilet bowl. Turned his last, still unused, weapon over in his hands – the nickel-plated one that would look good in a movie. It was over. Now it really was all over.

The 'diplomatic baggage' – two high-volume, heavy-weight bags (how had Lada managed to shift them? But then, that kind of load was no strain) had bypassed all the X-ray checks and been despatched to the luggage section. Apart from the Lunino inheritance, they hadn't taken a single thing with them. Boarding had been announced. Lada was waiting at the turnstiles. He put the pistol in the water. Set the lid of the tank back in place. The Singapore flight. Departure 23.10. Two changes. At Singapore they would change for Sydney. Then it was a direct flight. And hello Gauguin.

He undid the lock and stepped out, automatically moving aside for some guy who apparently needed to get into Vadim's cubicle in a hurry, even though the toilets were absolutely empty (if you didn't count that other cunt standing over at the sink) . . . Vadim still hadn't really absorbed this strange circumstance when he received a sharp blow to the solar plexus and promptly stopped breathing. His assailant then hooked an elbow round his neck and yanked him back into the cubicle. Vadim felt himself swirled through the air and then, as if it were a door on hinges suddenly shoved open, the white, almost clean, formica partition came swinging at him from the side and smashed into his face. It instantly turned black, bounced away and hung there swaying crookedly up above him – now it was the toilet ceiling.

The ceiling was blurred and hazy – the tears were gushing from his eyes. His nasal cavity was swamped, flooded. Thick, salty, warm, acrid snot streamed out on to his face, accumulating in his throat. Vadim gulped spasmodically, and spasms of nausea rose up from lower down in response. His entire head had become a reservoir of pain. It was wedged into the narrow gap between the partition and the toilet bowl, one cheek pressed against the cold porcelain. A dark figure loomed up out of the haze and a quite different pain came from a quite different point of his body, a hundred times more vicious, cancelling out absolutely everything except itself. He had been kicked in the balls. Vadim writhed, pulling up his legs with a wet, snivelling snort, slipping over on to his side, curling up round the toilet bowl. His assailant lashed him across the backside. The door slammed.

He felt like someone had stabbed the screw from a mincer up into his crotch and twisted it a couple of times. His entire body was reduced to bloody mince. Pressing his forehead against the porcelain, Vadim tried to spit, but he couldn't spit out all the blood. Something solid came out with the liquid. A tooth? A tooth. His tongue felt out the breach in his upper jaw.

'Where's the money, wanker?'

He didn't understand.

'Where's the money?' Someone kicked him again, not hard, not trying to cause him pain this time, just getting his attention.

'What?'

Someone turned him over on his back again. By the arm. Vadim saw the man leaning down over him.

'Where's our money, you lousy queer?' The man was losing patience. 'Well?'

'In the baggage . . . Two suitcases . . .'

'What suitcases?'

'Br . . . brown. With seals. Diplomatic baggage.'

'The flight? The flight, you bastard!'

'Singapore . . . It's leaving now.'

The interrogator straightened up and darted out of the cubicle. 'I'll go to the baggage hall, you finish him off, then follow me!' He flung the words out without stopping. Another man appeared in the doorway, probably the one who had been standing by the sink. Casually closed the door. Glanced at Vadim with no expression at all, took a pistol out of the front of his jacket.

After zigzagging and ricocheting all over Riga, Vadim's trajectory had carried him into the airport, then crashed into the toilet wall, terminating abruptly on the piss-covered tiles of the floor. Now it really was all over . . .

'I said right from the start we should be casing the airport,' the second man mumbled to himself in melancholy satisfaction as he screwed the smooth cylinder of the silencer on to the barrel. 'Running around the place like crazy mutts.' He shook his head. 'Near as dammit missed the fucker . . .'

The man looked at Vadim with the same expressionless expression and lowered the gun into his face.

'A bad head gives the legs no rest,' he said in didactic tone.

The diameter of the muzzle was about a centimetre less than the diameter of the silencer.

18

PLEASE WASH MY HAIR. PLEASE SHAVE ME. READY (NOT READY). WHAT IS THE WORLD RECORD FOR MEN (WOMEN) IN THIS EVENT? QUEL EST LE RECORD DU MONDE CHEZ LES HOMMES (LES FEMMES) DANS CE SPORT? THAT HURTS. C'EST DOULOUREUX. PLEASE PAINT IT WITH LIGHT (DARK) LACQUER. YOU HAVE GONE PAST YOUR STOP. VOUS AVEZ DÉPASSÉ VOTRE ARRÊT. YOU NEED TO BE HOSPITALISED. WHAT CROPS DO YOU GROW? QUELS CULTURES CULTIVEZ-VOUS? WHAT COLOUR IS YOUR UMBRELLA (RAINCOAT)? WE WOULD LIKE TO LOOK ROUND A DAIRY FARM (POULTRY FARM, PIG FARM). OPEN YOUR MOUTH, SHOW ME YOUR TONGUE. OUVREZ LA BOUCHE, TIREZ LA LANGUE.

Smilla turned towards me, sticking out an unexpectedly long tongue that almost touched the tip of her nose.

'Gracias . . . I mean merci,' I said and turned over the page of my phrase book.

NOW THEN AT THIS MOMENT LONG AGO RECENTLY. IN WHAT YEAR DID IT HAPPEN? I ARRIVED IN GOOD TIME. I WAS LATE. WE ARRIVED TOO EARLY TOO LATE A SECOND A MINUTE AN HOUR HALF AN HOUR A DAY A WEEK A MONTH A YEAR A CENTURY A MORNING AN AFTERNOON MIDDAY MIDNIGHT. YOU MUST NOT EAT. YOUR GUM IS SWOLLEN. J'AI UNE GENCIVE ENFLÉE. SPIT OUT.

I really did feel like spitting all the time. I couldn't stop my tongue from probing at the fresh stump on the site of my left upper incisor. Even though it got scratched, it refused to desist. And so the saliva kept building up in my mouth. The alcohol stung the split gum, *une gencive* – so I had smoked almost a full pack in half an hour trying to dry it out (naturally, we were flying in the smoking salon). But then Smilla had been doing her best to help me.

. . . 'Give me a cigarette,' she said, continuing to look at the man on the floor. She snapped the fingers of her free left hand. 'Have you got any left?'

I automatically reached for my pocket. The pistol got in my way – a long barrel, with a silencer. I looked around for a place to park it. Stuck it into the urinal. She tossed her weapon on to the tiles with a carefree clatter, fished a tubular Captain Blake out of the proffered pack, I clicked, she dragged. Blew the smoke out at the ceiling, looked up at me, but down at me at the same time (from under half-closed eyelids):

'So where are you flying to?'

'To Tahiti . . .' I answered, trying to moderate my lisp. I tentatively touched my swelling nose. B–bugger . . .

'It's warmer there than in Moscow,' Smilla declared thoughtfully, heating up the tip of her cigarette with a decisive drag. 'I'm in that boat,' she chuckled. 'Or rather, in that plane. Let's fly. Only you get a wash first.'

While she and I were trying to obtain a ticket on a flight already announced for boarding, energetically flourishing her American passport and creating a disgraceful scandal, promising to pay any amount of bucks, hastily attempting to convince the stupid woman behind the counter that yes, there was absolutely no luggage whatever, I was sweating a bit, wondering how she and Lada would get along. But they got along just fine. I was even rather amazed by it: they just sat there chatting away quite simply, jumping unthinkingly back and forth from rooskey to anglo.

The window was a black, lifeless screen. By way of compensation we had a flat TV above our heads showing some emteevee or other. A plane really is like teleporting after all. Get in at one point on the planet. Get out at another. A universal pap-diet of Euro-pop, an ergonomic armchair, standard buckshee booze from standardised stewardesses.

The television interrupted the latest in the series of spice girls and began counting down the final seconds before the final news broadcast of the year. Even the time up here was as abstract as it could possibly be. We were seeing in the New Year according to Greenwich. 00.10.22 . . . 00.10.21 . . .

The New Year asteroid had crashed into Earth half a day earlier at a longitude somewhere in the region of New Zealand, and the tidal wave was engulfing the time zones one by one, translating Present Continuous into Past Perfect: nullifying it. Countdown to zero.

. . . The double zero of a pistol barrel with a silencer: one zero inside another. I squeezed my eyes shut. A shot. The complex sound sequence of an avalanche happening close by: a heavy rustling, a rasping of metal on ceramic, the plastic slapping of the snagged toilet-seat. She had flung open the door and shot him in the side of the head at point-blank range. He had had just enough time to turn his head, but there simply wasn't enough space to realign his hand . . . I struggled to my feet, picked up the pistol with the silencer. The second guy, meaning the first, must have heard the shot. But it seems like he only remembered he didn't have a piece after he smashed his way into the toilet. And saw two muzzles trained on him

. . . 'I know it's noisy, that's because I'm on a plane . . .

What shagging payments? Have they fucking flipped, or what? Loan? It's a load of shit, not a loan, they can stick it up their backsides. Eh? He's going after us? No chance . . .'

In an hour and a half of flying the despicable specimen in the next row had really pissed me off. Constantly lecturing, straightening guys out and goal-orientating them into his pot-bellied little satellite Globalstar with its protruding little aerial. And what's more his face was definitely one I'd seen before somewhere; and what's more, his wide-shouldered young secretary was casing the cabin from the next chair in a fashion so familiar it gave me the creeps.

'. . . Get all our assets out of there and ring Edwin immediately. Let him liquidate the lot. Yes, and no arguments. Why the fuck would I want a spiel with him about anything? Who's he anyway?'

'Lada,' I said, leaning across Smilla, 'that freak with the mobile, the one just across the aisle – isn't that Chernosvin? From CerveLatBank?'

'That's him, darling. Chairman of the board. Citron's chief consultant. I thought straight away, fancy us flying with people like that . . .'

Just fancy.

'. . . yes to Singapore. Aha. He-he. Aha, urgently. Before the funeral . . .' Mr Chernosvin snorted once again. 'They were the ones who did him and . . . Why, the bastard. That fat jerk – why did he have to turn so ratty?' I began listening more closely. 'That's right and then . . . You have to know the right way to deal with people like that. These are really serious people. No! You don't say . . . Now they'll come to me. No! That fat arsehole set them up . . . See! Sure, it all goes through us now. This is very serious business. Exclusively through us. Sure, well here I am in the plane, who are you trying to teach?'

304

So it all goes through you, does it? Exclusively through you?

On the TV they were shuffling through all the New Years that had already happened: fireworks, dancing, champagne, masquerades, snowdrifts, palm-trees, smoke bombs, delirious drunken dames, Melbourne, Jakarta, Tokyo, Manila, Vladivostok, Shanghai, Delhi, Hong Kong, Wellington, Moscow.

Chernosvin put his mobile away, glanced at the screen, checked his watch, leaned over towards the secretary.

'They won't give me any,' the secretary replied uncertainly. 'You go and ask.'

The secretary got up and moved forward along the aisle.

'Only it has to be out of the fridge,' Chernosvin called out after him.

I squinted at the girls. Smilla was acting crazy, pulling a loony face. Lada was splitting her sides laughing, her face in her hands.

With his beige-jacketed back turned towards the corridor, Chernosvin rummaged around in something, then stuck whatever he was looking for down into his side pocket. Getting up, he set off down the aisle towards the tail of the plane.

'I'll just be a moment,' I told the girls.

. . . Toilet occupied. Behind the door the airborne sewerage system cleared its throat. Now he'd open the door. I moved closer. Waited for a few seconds. Nothing happened. Another twenty seconds. What was he doing in there? I rapped urgently on the door with my knuckles:

'This is the second pilot! Open up, please! We have an emergency on board!'

'What is this?' The body inside stirred in dissatisfaction.

'An emergency! Open up please!'

As soon as the lock clattered, I leaned my shoulder hard against the door, shoving the occupant back into his little cell. He sat down on the toilet bowl and I hit him at the base of the neck with the rigid knuckles of my right hand. He wheezed and his head slumped back against the wall. I clicked the lock. Toilet occupied.

Chernosvin's jacket was hanging on the hook and the left sleeve of his shirt was rolled up. Lying on the edge of the metallic sink was a white disposable syringe. Tinkling gently in the hollow of the soap-dish was an empty glass ampoule. INSULIN. So that was it . . .

I took the syringe and half-emptied it into the sink. Pulled the piston back up. Two cc's of air. Picking up the pale, skinny arm – the branching blood vessels were not hard to make out in the hollow of the inner elbow – I took aim and jabbed in the needle. Air embolism. I wiped the syringe down with toilet paper, put it into Chernosvin's dangling hand, closed the soft fingers. The syringe fell out. The bubble of air makes its way through the vein to the heart and the heart stops. I went out, closed the door.

The secretary hadn't got back yet.

'Right then, ladies, make room.' I sat down in the middle seat.

'Where did you get to?' asked Lada, flicking a super-thin Vogue into the ashtray. 'One minute left till New Year. They'll be handing out the champers any moment now.'

Down at the end of the aisle the stewardess was taking long glasses out of her trolley. The secretary squeezed past her with an inaudible apology, holding a dark bottle beaded with condensation, its narrow throat wrapped in foil. Looked around, trying to find his boss.

On the box the festive church bells, sleigh-bells and

jingle-bells launched into their elated clamour. 00.00.02 . . .
00.00.01 . . . Zero-zero zero-zero zero-zero.

I hugged both of them and kissed them by turns:

'By the way, where's the champagne?'

www.randomhouse.co.uk/vintage